SECRET UNDERT
The Seventh Buryin' Bar

"The story's resolution is satisfying on many levels. de Castrique draws the reader into his protagonist's world with consummate grace."

—*Publishers Weekly*

"Buryin' Barry" unearths a corrupt plot in his sleepy North Carolina town....The hero's easy charm in his seventh case makes the reader feel like a longtime Gainesboro resident and a sleuthing sidekick."

—*Kirkus Reviews*

RISKY UNDERTAKING
The Sixth Buryin' Barry Mystery

"De Castrique's latest mystery continues the irreverent wit and independent spirit that has marked the series thus far. The focus on the beautiful setting of western North Carolina and its Cherokee traditions is well crafted. ...This is a complex and well-executed police procedural as well."

—Library Journal

"De Castrique's engaging sixth mystery featuring funeral director and deputy sheriff Barry Clayton...offers insights into the political, economic, and cultural ramifications of Indian casinos, along with a large cast of believable characters with a wide emotional range."

—Publishers Weekly

FATAL UNDERTAKING
The Fifth Buryin' Barry Mystery

"…de Castrique gives readers a tantalizing mystery full of humor and eccentric characters, along with a nice dollop of current social issues."

—Booklist

"De Castrique writes complicated mysteries that lead his sleuth on journeys of self-discovery while unwrapping the motivations behind murder. Here the focus is on how greed warps the human spirit. De Castrique's unassuming but commanding prose style is comparable to James Lee Burke and Margaret Maron."

—Library Journal (starred review)

FINAL UNDERTAKING
The Fourth Buryin' Barry Mystery

FOOLISH UNDERTAKING
The Third Buryin' Barry Mystery

"As important and as impressive as the author's narrative skills are the subtle ways he captures the geography—both physical and human—of a unique part of the American South."

—Dick Adler, *The Chicago Tribune*

"De Castrique returns with his third adventure featuring undertaker Barry Clayton. When his father was stricken with Alzheimer's, Barry left a police career in Charlotte to return to his tiny Appalachian hometown of Gainesboro, North Carolina, to help run the family funeral business. Barry's loving, respectful relationships with his parents and uncle are part of what makes him such a compelling protagonist: family loyalty is the driving force in his life. In this adventure, Barry is preparing for the funeral of Vietnamese Y'Grok Eban. Y'Grok was part of the Montagnards, a fiercely loyal resistance group who helped save the lives of countless Americans during the Vietnam War—including that of Gainesboro sheriff Tommy Lee Wadkins. When someone attacks Barry and steals Y'Grok's body, the likable undertaker has more than embarrassment to worry about.... Another stellar entry in an outstanding series that deserves wider recognition: the family focus and rural North Carolina setting make it a natural for Margaret Maron fans."

—*Booklist* (starred review)

"...a fabulous thriller that grips the audience from the moment the corpse is purloined and never slows down..."

—*bookcrossing.com*

GRAVE UNDERTAKING
The Second Buryin' Barry Mystery

"It's not every day that the second entry in a series trumps the debut—but de Castrique accomplishes just that with this follow-up to *Dangerous Undertaking*....The plot is nicely layered with suspense...but what really stands out about this series is de Castrique's rich yet respectful portrait of life in the Appalachians...a first-rate installment in an excellent series."

—Booklist

"Realistic and sensitively drawn characters, including Barry's Alzheimer's-afflicted father, together with a neat plot that builds to a powerful ending...lift this poignant novel…"

—Publishers Weekly

DANGEROUS UNDERTAKING
The First Buryin' Barry Mystery

"I really enjoyed this book. Mark de Castrique writes with an authentic insider's voice. He clearly knows and loves these mountains and he respects the people who live there."

—Margaret Maron

"Adept at both the grizzly and the graceful, de Castrique has produced a marvelous mystery you won't want to put down."

—*Publishers Weekly*

Secret
Undertaking

Books by Mark de Castrique

The Buryin' Barry Series
Dangerous Undertaking
Grave Undertaking
Foolish Undertaking
Final Undertaking
Fatal Undertaking
Risky Undertaking
Secret Undertaking

The Sam Blackman Mysteries
Blackman's Coffin
The Fitzgerald Ruse
The Sandburg Connection
A Murder in Passing
A Specter of Justice
Hidden Scars

Other Novels
The 13th Target
Double Cross of Time
The Singularity Race

Young Adult Novels
A Conspiracy of Genes
Death on a Southern Breeze

Secret Undertaking

A Buryin' Barry Mystery

Mark de Castrique

Poisoned Pen Press

Poisoned Pen Press

Copyright © 2018 by Mark de Castrique

First Edition 2018

10 9 8 7 6 5 4 3 2 1

Library of Congress Control Number: 2018935809

ISBN: 9781464210358   Hardcover
ISBN: 9781464210372   Trade Paperback
ISBN: 9781464210389   Ebook

Poisoned Pen Press
4014 N. Goldwater Blvd., #201
Scottsdale, AZ 85251
www.poisonedpenpress.com
info@poisonedpenpress.com

Printed in the United States of America

For Linda

Chapter One

"I want you to put me in jail." Archie Donovan, Junior, sported a wide smile as he made the request.

I stared at him in disbelief. "What?"

The two of us sat in the back booth of the Cardinal Café where Archie had urgently summoned me for a mid-morning cup of coffee. He'd walked from his insurance office and I'd strolled the few blocks from our funeral home, wondering with each step, what harebrained scheme he would propose. It looked like I wasn't going to be disappointed.

"Yes, Barry. You're a deputy sheriff."

"Part-time."

"Well, it's still official when you're on-duty."

"I'm not now."

Archie shook his head. "I don't want you to arrest me now. It will be at the parade."

I slid farther back in the booth, glancing around to see if anyone was overhearing our ridiculous conversation.

"Archie, you want to give me more background before I say no?"

Archie and I had known each other since grade school and in those years we'd been as compatible as oil and water. In junior high, Archie had dubbed me "Buryin' Barry" because my family lived in Gainesboro's one and only funeral home. The name had stuck through high school, and even today a former classmate might rib me in public. In short, Archie could push all my buttons without even trying. Now that we were both in our mid-thirties, I'd come to realize he wasn't mean, he was just tone deaf to the impact of what he said. That never stopped him from talking.

He leaned across the table. "Now, you support the Boys Club and Girls Club of Gainesboro, right?"

"Yes." I recognized his strategy of getting me to start saying yes before the poisoned-pill question was sprung.

"And you agree that they help mold young lives so the kids don't wind up in your jail?"

"Of course. Just get to the point."

"I want to raise money to help them. Through the Jaycees float in the Apple Festival Parade."

"By being arrested?"

Archie's eyes gleamed. "By being bailed out. Everyone thinks it's a great idea."

I restrained myself from asking who everyone might be.

Archie took a sip of coffee and then pushed the cup aside. "All right. Let me start over. I'm chairman of the Jaycees charity committee that's responsible for raising money. You know, like the annual haunted house."

"Bad example," I said. One year, at Archie's insistence, I'd lent the Jaycees a casket for the Halloween fundraiser, only to have a man murdered in it.

He shrugged. "Well, then not like it. Everything will be out in the open. The float will feature kids from the Boys and Girls Clubs and I'll be on it, standing in a mock jail, wearing one of those old-timey striped prison suits. The lettering on the float will say 'Free Archie and help our kids.'" He spread his hands as if the beauty of his proposal was now self-evident.

"I get it. People raise your bail for charity. How much?"

"Ten thousand dollars."

I whistled softly. "I don't know, Archie. That's a lot of money. How long can you stay on the float?"

"Just for the parade. Then I'll go to your jail. I'll post pictures on Facebook. I bet Melissa Bigham and the *Vista* will want to follow my progress. Every morning the paper could run an update." His eyes brightened even more. "Maybe list donors and corporate sponsors. How much will the funeral home kick in? It's great publicity."

I signaled time-out. "None of this is my call. You can do what you want with your float, but the jail's another matter. Tommy Lee has say over that, not me."

"But the sheriff listens to you. And he's always doing outreach programs. It's a win-win, a no-brainer."

Both expressions grated on my ears. "Win-win" reduced everything to a game, and "no-brainer" meant some decision was being made by someone without a brain. I took the easiest exit I could find.

"All right. I'll ask Tommy Lee, but no promises." I made a show of looking at my watch. "Sorry. I've got to go. Appointment at eleven."

Archie's smile vanished. "Someone die?"

"No."

The smile returned. "Good. I was afraid it was one of my policyholders. When they die, they stop paying their premiums."

I wondered how much money could be raised to keep Archie in jail.

As I neared the funeral home, I spotted a silver Mercedes parked in one of the handicapped spaces near the ramp to the front door. My eleven o'clock appointment had arrived early. Normally, this wouldn't have been a problem because my partner, Fletcher Shaw, would have covered for me. But young Fletcher had taken the week after July Fourth for a vacation in the Bahamas with his girlfriend. He'd confided that he hoped to bring her back as his fiancée.

I quickened my stride and looped around the lot to come in through the back porch of the old antebellum home. Mom stood at a counter in the kitchen, wearing an apron over one of her Sunday dresses, arranging an assortment of cookies on a china plate. A tray with service for coffee was on the kitchen table.

"There you are," Mom said breathlessly. "Mrs. Sinclair showed up thirty minutes early. I was still in my housecoat."

My mother lived upstairs, where she and my father had raised me, their only child. After Dad died, I tried to convince Mom to move to a retirement community but she would hear nothing of it.

She set the cookies on the table with the coffee. "Fortunately, Wayne was still here and took her into the parlor."

Her brother, my Uncle Wayne, had moved upstairs a few months ago after selling his home in the county. If anything offered the possibility of encouraging Mom to join a retirement community, it was being under the same roof as Uncle Wayne. Although they loved each other dearly, they clashed over everything from politics to which blossoms made the best funeral arrangements. Mom was short, round, and cheery. Wayne was tall, slim, and skeptical. He was mid-seventies; she mid-sixties and forever the little sister. The only thing they shared in common was a headful of curly, cotton-white hair. And the belief that I was the smartest son/nephew in the world.

"Is he still with her?"

Mom rolled her eyes. "If he hasn't run her off." She lifted the coffee tray. "Bring the cookies and we'll see."

I followed her out of the kitchen and down the hall to the parlor. Before we were halfway there, I could hear Uncle Wayne speaking at the decibel level common to those who are hard of hearing.

"It's a crime, I tell you. I just don't want you shocked when you hear how much."

I tensed. Uncle Wayne must have jumped to providing cost information, something that was supposed to be left to Fletcher or me. My uncle quoted prices from memory—from 1975. And he apologized for them. I wondered how much damage I'd have to undo and whether Mom's homemade cookies would make our guest more amenable to whatever adjustments would be necessary.

"Barry's here," Mom called, as she crossed the threshold. "And I brought coffee." She set the tray on the table in front of our guest who sat on the sofa. Uncle Wayne was in a wingback chair angled across from her.

Mrs. Sinclair looked grateful for the interruption. She wore a gray skirt and a white blouse with a small rounded collar. The top two buttons were unfastened to reveal a pearl pendant hanging from a delicate gold chain. She started to rise, but I shifted the cookies to my left hand and offered my right.

"Please don't get up, Mrs. Sinclair."

"Janet, please." She stood anyway.

Her grip was firm.

"And thank you for the coffee. Black will be fine."

I set the cookies on the table and stepped back so Mom could pour.

"We were just getting started," Uncle Wayne said. "I was telling her how outrageous it is what the newspapers charge for an obituary. I mean when someone leaves this Earth, that's a news event. The family shouldn't be expected to pay for it any more than a sports team should pay to post the score of a game."

Janet Sinclair looked bewildered by the comparison, and I worried if she envisioned her loved one sandwiched between a stock car race and the local shuffleboard tournament.

"Wayne, can you help me in the kitchen a moment?" My mother wrapped her demand in the veneer of a question, but even Wayne understood he had no other option.

"Certainly, Connie." He stood and gave a slight bow to our

guest. "A pleasure to make your acquaintance. Barry will take good care of you."

I remained standing until they left and then took the chair my uncle had vacated. Janet Sinclair took a sip of coffee and I took the chance to examine her more closely.

She appeared to be in her mid to late forties. Her pale skin had a hint of blush on her cheeks. Her black hair was cut short and a stark contrast to bright blue eyes. Those eyes were free of crow's-feet. If she'd had cosmetic surgery, it was excellent. The only discernible indications of age were lines along her neck where the skin wasn't as tight.

Unlike so many bereaved who came to our funeral home, Janet Sinclair gave no sign she'd been crying—no running mascara, no tissues clenched in tight fists. All she'd said when she'd spoken with my mother earlier was could we meet at eleven. Her early arrival suggested an urgency that hadn't come through her initial request.

"I'm sorry to show up a half hour before our appointment," she said. "I was to meet our insurance agent, but he'd evidently been called out of the office."

Archie, I thought. He'd been so excited about his parade appearance that he'd skipped out on a client.

"That's all right. Any questions about what my uncle might have told you?"

She smiled. "No. He was waiting for you. He was lamenting the cost of obituaries because I asked if you handled them."

I made a mental note to tell my mother that Uncle Wayne hadn't strayed off the reservation after all.

"Yes, we can coordinate that for you. Has there been a death? I'm sorry but I don't know the circumstances of your visit."

"I guess you could call this fact-finding. I'd like to make preliminary arrangements for my husband and me."

I eyed her more closely. She looked healthy. Perhaps her husband was gravely ill and she wanted to make suitable plans for both of them.

"Why don't you describe what you and your husband think you would like? Then I'll know what suggestions might be appropriate."

She nodded. "Is our conversation privileged?"

"Privileged?"

"Like with a lawyer or a priest."

In my years in the funeral business, no one had ever asked me that question. My father had told me he had met a few terminally ill husbands who wanted to keep their conditions from their wives as long as possible, but Dad told them he'd never lie if asked directly.

"There's not legal protection," I said, "but we do adhere to a strict level of confidentiality. If for some reason I had to appear in court under oath, I would have to reveal the substance of our conversation."

She pursed her lips, not happy with my answer.

"That will be the same for any licensed funeral director," I added. "But we don't gossip. As long as you're not requesting anything illegal."

She arched an eyebrow. "Illegal? Like what?"

"Well, like a burial on land not approved for cemetery use. One man loved to hike and wanted to be interred at an overlook in Pisgah Forest. Sprinkling ashes is one thing but a grave and headstone is something else."

"Nothing like that," Janet Sinclair said. "But we will be going back north to a cemetery outside of Paterson, New Jersey."

"If you'll give me the name of a local funeral home you'd like to use, we'll be happy to coordinate."

"No."

Her emphatic tone surprised me.

"Well, we can step out of the picture and you can deal directly with the Paterson funeral home for transportation."

"No, just you. I can give you the name of the cemetery so that you can contact them directly."

I sat quietly for a moment, trying to figure out why she'd avoid a local funeral home in New Jersey. And why she wanted this conversation to be privileged.

She sensed my reluctance. "My husband, Robert, wants us to be buried with his parents, but there's a family rift. We own our plots outright so there's no legal issue." She gave a humorless laugh. "His siblings never visit the graves, so they may never even know we're there."

"Okay. I understand." I told her that, but I'd never known a family feud to be so vehement that it extended beyond death.

"Wonderful, Mr. Clayton. It will be a comfort to my husband."

"How's his health?" I asked. "Was your visit today prompted by a medical condition?"

"No." She hesitated, weighing a decision whether to say more. "I was reviewing our life insurance and that just got me thinking. If you would go ahead and give me an estimate, I'd appreciate it. I'll give you the address of the cemetery, but please don't contact them yet. Put in what you think will cover everything. For both of us."

"But I don't know what they'll charge for opening a grave."

She tapped her foot nervously on the carpet. "Then make a general inquiry. Tell them you have clients thinking about burials there, but that you're going to be handling everything. When the time comes, either my husband or I will give you full instructions." She paused as her voice choked. "Or if both of us were to die in a car or plane crash, our attorney will send the information."

"All right."

She relaxed. "And then would half up front be sufficient?"

I smiled. "That's not necessary. We don't encourage prepayment plans. I recommend you set the money aside in your own account. Let's hope it will be there a long time."

Her eyes teared. "I wouldn't count on it, Mr. Clayton."

Chapter Two

The Paterson cemetery bore the bucolic name of Forest Glen. My knowledge of New Jersey conjured up "Turnpike Glen" as probably being more appropriate. I found the number online and called. The phone rang and rang. I was surprised that no answering machine picked up, especially if the office staff was at lunch. After what must have been twenty rings, I lowered the receiver toward the cradle. A voice sounded just in time for me to snatch the phone to my ear.

"Hello? Hello?" a woman repeated.

"Yes. This is Barry Clayton with Clayton and Clayton Funeral Directors in Gainesboro, North Carolina."

"Give me your number. I'll call you back this afternoon. Things are crazy at the moment."

Having no other choice, I did as she asked. Business in New Jersey must be good. Cemeteries weren't known for crazy times.

I drew up an estimate of our charges including transportation, an overnight in the city, and embalming. Cremation would have eliminated all these costs but Mrs. Sinclair had said neither she nor her husband wanted that option. I would have expected that response to come from our local mountain people who weren't big on turning their loved ones into ashes, but, as Northerners, the Sinclairs could have preferred the growing trend for cremation.

When I'd estimated a cost for every item except for Forest

Glen's charges, I closed the computer file and turned my attention to my first problem of the morning—Archie.

Although his plan for raising funds for the Boys and Girls Clubs was admirable, Archie had a talent for snatching defeat from the jaws of victory. His exploits were well known to Tommy Lee, and I felt confident the sheriff would nip this jail-bail escapade in the bud. I dialed his direct line.

"Sheriff Wadkins' office."

I recognized the voice of Marge Colbert, Tommy Lee's administrative assistant.

"It's Barry. Is the High Sheriff of Laurel County in?"

"Early lunch. I expect him back in about twenty minutes. Can I give him a message?"

A message describing Archie's idea wasn't one I wanted floating around the department.

"Twenty minutes, you say? I'll come in if his calendar is clear."

"It's a slow day in paradise," Marge said. "But I thought you were off-duty this week?"

"It's a slow day here at the gateway to paradise. See you in a few. You know you can't get along without me."

Marge laughed and hung up.

I grabbed a quick lunch with Mom and Uncle Wayne at the kitchen table. My favorite. A peanut butter and jelly sandwich. I'd probably had ten thousand so far.

"So, did you get Mrs. Sinclair straightened out?" Uncle Wayne asked.

"More or less. They want to be buried back in New Jersey, but they want us to handle everything up to the cemetery there."

My uncle set down his glass of milk and cocked his head. "No local funeral home?"

"No. Maybe she thinks we'll be cheaper even with traveling to New Jersey."

"Could be. God only knows how much them big city funeral homes charge. A thousand dollars for saying, 'Sorry for your loss.'"

I laughed. "Maybe. I've got a call into the cemetery. So, if someone phones with a New Jersey accent, get the charge for opening and closing a grave."

"The husband must be sick," Uncle Wayne said. "The wife's too young to be finishing up naturally."

"They may just want to have their affairs in order," Mom said.

"Of course she could be one of them trophy wives," Uncle Wayne said. "And the old man's friends are dropping like flies. He probably doesn't even know she was here."

"Maybe he just doesn't want to talk about it," I countered.

Uncle Wayne took a deep drink of milk that left a white mustache. He licked it clean and then clicked his tongue. "Well, we all have to talk about it someday, don't we? Sooner or later, everybody in Gainesboro comes through our doors."

I swallowed the last of my sandwich, chasing away thoughts of the day I'd have to face the death of my uncle or mom.

The temperature for this second week in July threatened to top eighty-five with high humidity—a heat wave for our mountain town. I decided my earlier walk to meet Archie was enough outdoor exercise so I drove my jeep to the Sheriff's Department behind the Laurel County Courthouse.

When I entered the bullpen of cubicles, I heard the click of keyboards, but didn't bother to see which of my fellow deputies were in. I went straight to Tommy Lee's office and knocked on the jamb of his open door.

He wheeled around from his computer screen and gave me a wide grin, a grin that wasn't impaired by the scar running from underneath the black patch on his left eye and across his cheek to his jawline. The disfigurement was a permanent display of his courage in Vietnam when he'd led his platoon through a firefight despite a shrapnel wound that took the eye and part of his face.

"What the hell are you doing here?"

I slid into the chair opposite him. "Nice to see you too."

"So…what? Things too quiet at the funeral home?"

"With Uncle Wayne living there now?"

Tommy Lee laughed. "I get it. Feel free to hide here all you want, but I don't have the money to pay you for more than your part-time hours."

"I'm not here to go on-duty. I'm here to discuss a problem. Archie's got a proposal."

Tommy Lee let out a long groan and shook his head. "What is it this time?"

I told him Archie's idea, expecting the groans to continue. To my dismay, I could see Tommy Lee giving the fundraising gimmick serious consideration.

"I'm just telling you because I promised Archie I would," I said in desperation. "I didn't think you'd want to turn the jail into a circus."

"Both my kids grew up in the Boys and Girls Clubs. I coached the softball teams."

Tommy Lee's son and daughter were now grown, but the nostalgia in his voice was unmistakable.

The sheriff rubbed his chin. "And I've got some additional funding for our Junior Deputy program in the elementary schools this fall. The parade could be a good kickoff. Maybe we partner with the Jaycees on the float."

The annual Apple Festival Parade was held every Labor Day weekend, right when school was getting underway. Had I crossed into an alternate universe where Tommy Lee thought Archie had a good idea? The prospect was unnerving.

"What about me arresting him?"

Tommy Lee gave a hearty laugh. "Hasn't that always been your dream?" He leaned back in his chair. "There is one thing that bothers me."

"What's that?"

"That the department doesn't have representation on the float." His grin turned wicked. "You know, an officer."

"The sheriff would be good."

"Oh, I always drive my patrol car as the lead vehicle. It's tradition. But, you, as the arresting deputy. Well, it's perfect. Archie in the mock jail cell, you standing outside holding a big key. We'll be the most memorable float in the parade."

"What about Archie coming here while the money's being raised?"

Tommy Lee shrugged. "We usually have a vacant cell. You don't have to stay with him. And there's the ten thousand-dollar bail. Archie might be here a while."

"He might," I agreed, and told myself I'd be doing it for the kids.

"So, tell Archie I approve on the condition that the Jaycees also include the Sheriff's Department in the float's signage."

"I can't believe you're making me do this."

He threw up his hands. "Hey, I'm not making you do anything. I'll be happy to tell the Boys and Girls Clubs you refused to help."

I shook my head. "Then how would you like me to wave? Like the Queen or the Pope?"

"Your choice. Now, I'm not such a hard ass, am I?"

"No. Just an ass."

Tommy Lee laughed and shooed me out of his office.

When I returned to the funeral home, Uncle Wayne met me in the hall.

"That lady called from the New Jersey cemetery."

"Could you understand her?"

"She spoke pretty good for a Yankee, but I don't know if she understood me."

"What do you mean?"

"I said we were asking for the cost to open and close a grave for the Sinclairs."

I realized with concern I'd neglected to tell Uncle Wayne that Mrs. Sinclair had asked not to be identified. That we simply wanted a quote.

"What did she say?"

"That her computer files showed no Sinclair plots. I thought maybe the name was pronounced differently in New Jersey. So, I tried Signcloor, Sinclayire, and every other way I could say those letters."

"That's strange. Mrs. Sinclair was very specific that it was her husband's family plot. Must be some computer glitch. Did you get a general price?"

My uncle folded his arms and leaned against the wall, self-satisfaction visible on his face. "Yep. Put the figures in the estimate myself."

"Thank you. But that wasn't necessary."

Uncle Wayne smiled like he used the computer every day. I'd have to check the form to make sure he didn't blow out any other data.

"And the lady asked me to give you her apologies for being so short with you when you called. They had a big graveside service going on and somebody fell out of a tree."

"A tree?"

"That's what she said. Guess they do things different in New Jersey."

I thanked my uncle again for getting the information, reviewed the estimate pleased to see he hadn't sabotaged any of the calculation formulas, printed the itemized figures, and dropped them in the mail to Mrs. Sinclair. I debated whether to inform her of the cemetery's mix-up with her husband's family, but to do so would have revealed my uncle had specified the name. Since there was no immediate need for a grave opening, I let the matter go. We could deal with it if and when the time came.

That night my wife, Susan, and I sat on the back deck of our cabin, enjoying a bottle of Chablis and sharing the stories of our day. Susan, a general surgeon with the O'Malley Clinic, had kept her last name, Miller. She'd performed appendectomy and gall bladder operations that morning, strictly routine and, in my mind, not as deserving of sympathetic comment as my Archie predicament. She was on-call so I'd stepped up to drink most of the wine. I'd just finished telling her about Uncle Wayne and Mrs. Sinclair when her cell phone rang.

"Ten o'clock. This can't be good." She answered it as she stood and walked back inside.

Five minutes later, she emerged in a change of clothes and with her chestnut hair gathered in a bun ready for her scrubs.

"Patient in the ER with a broken leg. Save my wine. I hope to be back by midnight." She eyed the bottle that was two-thirds empty. "And save some for yourself if you want to join me in a nightcap." She bent over and kissed me.

"Good luck. I'd say 'break a leg' but that would be in bad taste."

She laughed. "Taste never stopped you before."

I nursed my wine and listened to the crickets.

I awoke to our yellow lab Democrat barking a greeting. Then I heard the refrigerator door open and shut. Susan stepped onto the deck, Democrat at her heels and her unfinished wine in her hand.

"That was interesting." She slid into the chair beside me.

"Interesting case?"

"The man fell off his stepladder painting his ceiling. A simple, not a compound, fracture. So I was overkill. But, from the swelling and discoloration, it was obvious he'd delayed coming to the hospital for several hours. One of those macho-types who probably thought a shot of bourbon and an hour's rest would do the trick."

"Sounds like me. A real man's man."

"A man's man is a valet, and you whine about a hangnail."

"Well, they are annoying. So, was his tough-guy attitude what made the case interesting?"

"No. His name. Robert Sinclair."

I sat up straighter. "Really? Small world."

"Small town," Susan said. "With small-town coincidences."

Tommy Lee's voice rang in my head. "Never trust a coincidence."

Chapter Three

The summer season proved to be a boon to the Gainesboro economy. Low gas prices and high temperatures sent tourists into the mountains by the thousands. Summer residents complained the influx meant heavier traffic and fewer parking places, an ironic lament because the permanent locals had been saying the same thing about those same summer residents for years.

I was busy on both fronts—the funeral home and my deputy duties. The return of the snowbirds from Florida shifted our senior demographics upward and spiked funerals to at least one a week. An increase in population also meant an increase in traffic accidents and petty crime that stretched Tommy Lee's department to where my hours bordered on full-time responsibilities. My partner, Fletcher Shaw, had indeed returned from the Bahamas with a fiancée and was caught up in wedding plans. Still, being busy made the weeks fly by for both of us, and soon we were facing the reality of the Labor Day Apple Festival.

During the week leading up to the parade, decorations were hung from streetlamps. At the north and south ends of town, banners proclaiming "The 75th Annual Apple Festival" were strung over Main Street. The shops offered festival specials, and every sort of apple product, from cider to pies to dried carvings of animals, were for sale.

With all the hubbub, Archie grew more fixated on his pending role. He called me at least once a day with concerns ranging from whether he needed a PA system on the float to whether the Sheriff's Department had any chains left from the chain gang days. I could hardly wait to lock him in a cell.

Parade day dawned clear and cool. The temperature was predicted to rise, but the low humidity promised a hint of the approaching autumn. The organizational site for gathering marching bands, convertibles bearing local dignitaries, and floats was the Gainesboro High School parking lot and athletic field at the north end of town. Each unit had been assigned a number, and volunteers guided bands and vehicles into their proper positions. I saw Mayor Sammy Whitlock arguing with a parade official that his Mustang convertible should be right behind Tommy Lee's patrol car. His Honor, looking like a bowling bowl wrapped in a seersucker suit, was hopping up and down proclaiming he was the leader of the town and should therefore be the leader of the parade. Mayor Whitlock would be the kind of leader to take the whole parade down a dead-end street. The poor official, seeing me in uniform, waved me to come over. I mouthed "off-duty" and for the first time felt glad to be on a float rather than in the thick of traffic and crowd control.

I saw Tommy Lee standing by his car, talking to our Grand Marshall, North Carolina Commissioner of Agriculture Graham James. Mayor Whitlock, as usual, had tried to get Angelina Jolie, but her manager had again sent her regrets. We all suspected Whitlock just liked getting letters that he thought had been personally dictated by Angelina.

The parade participants had been cordoned off into designated areas: floats in one section of the parking lot, cars in another, and the marching bands on the grassy edge of the football field. The air was filled with the sound of brass instruments tuning and snare drums rolling in short bursts. Schools from Laurel and surrounding counties eyed one another suspiciously because the judging stand would name one of them Best of Parade, or as we locals called it, "Pick of the Crop."

The parade would undergo final formation as it began its route. It would be like shuffling three decks of cards together, each merging into its proper slot. The float for the Jaycees and Sheriff's Department was last. Archie took that as a compliment, like Santa Claus coming at the end of the Christmas Parade. Anything that followed would be anticlimactic.

I found him already on the float. He wore a black-and-white-striped prison uniform he'd ordered from an online costume store and he had loosely wrapped an iron chain around his ankles. I was supposed to handcuff him when the parade got underway.

He sat on a stool inside a fake jail cell constructed of cardboard tubing spray-painted black.

Surrounding the float were kids ages eight to fourteen who had been selected to ride. Adults tried to herd them into organized groups according to whether they wore a Girls Club or Boys Club tee-shirt.

The sides of the float were decorated in red and white crepe paper with gold letters spelling Gainesboro Jaycees and Laurel County Sheriff's Department.

I had to admit the whole design was impressive and if Archie raised the ten thousand dollars, I'd do the unthinkable—congratulate him on a good idea.

A small stepladder had been set up at the rear and I climbed it to join Archie.

"Oh, good, you wore your gun." He stood and pumped my hand like I was a dry well.

"Always, when I'm arresting a dangerous criminal."

He laughed and spread his arms. "What do you think?"

"Looks good." I saw bowls of wrapped candy sitting on the cell's floor. "You throwing that to the crowd?"

"Yeah." He bent down and retrieved one of the small packets. "Apple-flavored taffy. Try one."

I took the candy and read Donovan Insurance and Investments: Don't delay—Call today! "You couldn't get these with your picture?"

His expression grew serious. "I wanted to, but Gloria said I'd wind up in trash cans up and down Main Street. Not a good advertising environment."

Gloria was Archie's wife and always exhibited good judgment. But she'd married Archie. Ah, there was no explanation for the affairs of the heart.

"And I've been working on a routine with the kids," he added.

"What's that?"

"You have to wait and see."

We heard clicks of a camera shutter and turned to see Melissa Bigham of the *Gainesboro Vista* firing off a series of shots.

"Wait, Melissa," Archie shouted. "Get one of Barry putting the cuffs on me."

Melissa was the star reporter and photographer for our local paper. Only a few years younger than me, she'd received offers from much larger markets, but her love of the mountains trumped big-city bylines and bigger salaries. Her short blond hair, small stature, and cute looks caused politicians and corporate executives to underestimate her. They did so at their own peril.

Melissa lowered her camera. "All right, but then I've got to split. Mayor Whitlock is going to blow a gasket if I don't take a picture of him with the Commissioner of Agriculture."

I snapped one of the metal cuffs on Archie's wrist and then held the other poised above his free hand. The camera whirred.

"Got it." Melissa turned to go and then stopped. "Archie, how much money have you raised in advance?"

"Five hundred dollars. Only nine thousand, five hundred more to go."

Melissa winked at me. "So, you're confident you'll be out by Christmas?"

"Oh, with the friends I've got in this town, I'll be out by this time tomorrow."

I wondered if Tommy Lee would allow a Christmas tree in a jail cell.

Thirty minutes later, the parade got underway. As the last float, we were thirty minutes after that. The day had warmed, the children grew cranky and Archie and I were sweating through our clothes. But, a rousing cheer erupted when the tractor pulled us forward, and as we turned onto Main Street, Archie yelled, "Okay, kids, just like we practiced."

The left side of the float shouted, "Free!" The right side followed with "Archie!" The chant continued unabated. It was going to be a long parade route.

Archie turned to me and grinned. "Great, huh?"

"Yeah. Just great."

My prisoner bent to one of the candy bowls. "Barry, I can't throw the taffy in these handcuffs."

"You should have thought of that."

He lifted the bowl with his bound hands. "I'll hold and you toss. We can't disappoint the spectators."

So, I lobbed candy while "Free Archie" rang around me. We had traveled only three or four blocks when the float halted.

"What's the problem?" Archie asked.

"Maybe a band is performing at the judges' viewing stand."

"You think every band will do that?"

I shrugged. "They're not supposed to stop for more than a minute or two, but some of these band directors love to showcase their performance."

If a band was showing off, it was certainly taking its time. Ten minutes passed. The kids stopped chanting; I stopped throwing candy. Then I heard the wail of several sirens coming down Church Street, the road parallel to Main. I looked beyond the float in front of us and saw Deputy Reece Hutchins running between the parade and the spectators. Reece wasn't in the best of shape, and his red face told me he was winded.

"Something's wrong," I told Archie. I hurried to the front of the float and jumped to the tongue connecting it to the tractor. A second jump landed me on the pavement as Reece arrived.

"Barry," he gasped, "someone attacked the Commissioner of Agriculture." He gulped for air. "At Fourth and Main. Tommy Lee sent me—"

I bolted before Reece finished the sentence. As I ran down the street, I heard people call my name and ask what was happening. I ignored them because I had no idea. Who would want to attack the Commissioner of Agriculture? Why?

I neared the intersection and saw where police cars and an ambulance had arrived by the cross street. An EMT tended to Commissioner James, who had slipped off the back of the convertible and sat half in and half out of the rear seat. Tommy Lee stood with another EMT by the curb. The crowd had been pushed back. Two men lay on the pavement, one facedown and the other face-up. The man face-up was covered in blood. The man face-up was Uncle Wayne.

Chapter Four

Tommy Lee intercepted me as I ran toward my uncle. "He's alive, Barry." He glanced at the commissioner being treated in the convertible. "Wayne's the medics' priority. He's going to the hospital first and a second ambulance is en route for Commissioner James. He has a minor shoulder wound."

I pushed by the sheriff. "I need to see him."

My uncle's eyes were closed, but I saw his chest rise and fall with ragged breaths. His white shirt was soaked with blood, but I didn't see the source of the bleeding. I recognized the EMT. He was adjusting an inflatable neck brace. He must have determined there was some potential head or neck injury that required stabilization before Uncle Wayne could be moved.

"Is he conscious, Jake?" I asked.

The man looked up and shook his head. "But his pulse is strong. That's a good sign, Barry."

The rattle of a wheeled gurney signaled a third medic had arrived. I turned to see Lila Black, another EMT I knew, lowering the transport device till it was only six inches above the pavement.

"All right," Jake said. "Barry, if you and the sheriff want to help, let's keep him as level as possible. We'll lift on the count of three."

Jake took position at my uncle's head, Lila at his feet, and Tommy Lee and I on either side. Wayne groaned as we slid him onto the gurney.

"You want to ride?" Jake asked me.

"If there's room. I don't want to hamper whatever you need to do."

"Fortunately, we're only going a few blocks."

"Okay, then."

They ratcheted the gurney up to waist-height and I followed as they rolled Uncle Wayne to the rear of the ambulance.

"Barry! Barry!" Archie came running up, his hands still cuffed in front of him. His face drained of color when he saw Wayne. "Is he—?"

"He's unconscious. I'm going with him."

"Do you want me to get your mom?"

Archie's clear thinking surprised me.

"Yes. Try not to alarm her." I unlocked the handcuffs. "Just tell her Wayne's been hurt and that I asked you to bring her to the hospital. Tell her we don't know any more than that, because we don't." I climbed into the ambulance and Jake joined me. The doors shut and the siren wailed as the vehicle shot forward, a parade of one.

Jake and I sat on jump seats on either side of the gurney. I studied Uncle Wayne but saw no signs of additional bleeding. The medics must have staunched the flow. I remembered the third person, lying facedown near my uncle. No EMT tended to him. The deputy part of my brain told me he was dead. I wondered who he was and what had happened.

"Sounds like your uncle's a hero," Jake said.

"What?"

"I heard some of the people in the crowd talking to the sheriff. Toby McKay evidently charged the front of Commissioner James' car, firing a pistol. One bullet struck James' shoulder. Your uncle jumped from the curb and grabbed the gun. He and McKay struggled for it. It went off."

"Where was my uncle hit?"

"He wasn't." Jake waved his hand over Uncle Wayne's blood-soaked shirt. "The bullet must have hit McKay's aorta. This is his blood. Witnesses said they both fell and your uncle's head hit the pavement. I don't know if he has a fractured skull, a concussion, or both. That's why he's our priority."

Less than five minutes later, we pulled up to the door of the Emergency Room. A trauma team was there to meet us. The gurney was unloaded and whisked away. I suddenly stood alone on the sidewalk. My phone vibrated and I saw a text message from my wife:

Got the call. On my way to the hospital.

At first I wasn't sure who had called her. Then I remembered she was on-call for the clinic. She was coming to operate on either the commissioner or my uncle.

Now there was nothing for me to do but settle into the waiting room and trust the medical team to do their best. And hope God wasn't ready to face Uncle Wayne.

Ten minutes later, Commissioner Graham James was brought by a second ambulance. Mayor Whitlock waddled alongside the gurney, moaning like he was the one who had been shot. A security guard stopped him as James continued down a corridor. Whitlock looked bewildered, uncertain what to do next. He didn't see me, but looked back through the sliding glass doors of the Emergency Room entrance. He grabbed the lapels of his seersucker suit and tried to pull the coat flat across the curve of his torso. He stepped forward, wringing his hands in a great show of consternation.

Melissa Bigham hurried up to him. I watched their animated conversation and was tempted to join them, but I couldn't endure the mayor's histrionics. After a few minutes, Melissa turned away and went to the admissions desk. The mayor took a deep breath and left.

Melissa asked the woman at the desk a few questions. The woman pointed at me, evidently telling her I'd arrived with the EMTs. Melissa spun around, gave a slow shake of her head, and walked over to me. I stood. She kept walking, opening her arms to give me a comforting hug.

"I'm so sorry, Barry. Any update?"

"Not so far. He wasn't shot. It's a head injury from falling." I gestured for her to sit and then took the chair beside her. "But I don't know what happened, other than somebody named Toby McKay attacked the commissioner."

Melissa eyed the waiting room. The only other occupants were a Hispanic family consisting of a young mother, an older woman I assumed was the grandmother, and a toddler cradled in the mother's lap. The child looked like he was running a fever.

Melissa leaned closer and spoke in a whisper. "I interviewed several people who were right there when it happened. McKay jumped from the curb about twenty yards in front of the commissioner's convertible. He shouted as he ran. Most people heard, 'You ruint me, you son of a bitch. You ruint me.' Then he fired a shot. While everyone else stood paralyzed with fear, your uncle ran out and intercepted him. During the struggle, the gun went off and your uncle fell backwards. Both men lay in the street and neither moved. Tommy Lee was only one car ahead and was the first authority on the scene. He called it in immediately."

"What do you know about Toby McKay?"

"Not much," she said. "He has a small apple orchard east of town. He lost most of his crop last year from the codling moth outbreak. He'd tried to save money by cutting back on pesticides and it backfired."

"Why would he blame Commissioner James for that?"

Melissa shrugged. "I don't know. Yet." She stood. "As soon as I write what happened, I'll focus on why. I hope you hear good news on your uncle. It sounds like he was a real hero." She paused and her eyes moistened. "And that's the way I'll tell it."

She'd been gone only a few minutes when Archie and Mom arrived. Mom started crying when she saw me. Archie looked scared, all of his usual confidence and cockiness submerged by genuine concern.

Mom and I hugged and I tucked her cheek against my shoulder. "He wasn't shot. He fell and hit his head. The medic said his pulse was strong." In three sentences, I'd shared all that I knew.

"Can we see him?"

"Not yet. They don't know the extent of his injuries. Susan's on her way."

I felt Mom relax at the assurance that her daughter-in-law would be here.

"What can I do?" Archie asked.

Mom broke away. "Thank you, Archie. I appreciate your bringing me. I'll be fine now."

Archie looked at me. "Barry. Anything? Should I stand guard at the funeral home?"

I had to smile at the offer, as if our business was vulnerable like an unlocked bank vault. Then I thought again. There had been instances of funeral home thefts of embalming fluid that kids used to soak cigarettes or marijuana and create a cheap drug with a high like PCP. And then there was the matter of Toby McKay's body. Most likely it would go to the hospital for autopsy, but at some point we might become involved. How awkward was that? Taking care of the funeral for the man my uncle killed. Somehow, I didn't think that would fly for either party.

"Mom, did you lock up?"

"Yes. And turned on the answering service."

The service would forward calls to my cell phone.

"Then, we should be covered, Archie."

He spread his hands. "So, I should just turn myself in at the jail?"

For a second, I didn't understand his question. Then I remembered the float, the Boys and Girls Clubs, and the fundraiser Archie had worked so hard to put together.

"If you want, but I'm sure there will be no problem if you want to wait a day or two before being locked up."

"No. I said I'd go to jail after the parade. I'm going to keep my word. I don't want to disappoint the kids on the float. They've already had one disappointment today."

Archie took my mother's hand. "And your brother's going to be all right, Mrs. Clayton. I just know it."

As he disappeared through the sliding doors, Mom whispered, "He's always been an odd one, hasn't he?"

"He's always been Archie."

We had just sat down when Susan came from the inner corridor, wearing scrubs with the surgical mask dangling from her neck. Her face was grave. So grave that a chill ran through me. I didn't want to hear what she was about to say.

"We're moving him to Mission," she said.

Mission was the hospital in Asheville, a much larger facility with many more resources.

"You're not going to operate on him?" Mom asked.

"Connie, we need to keep him in an induced coma. He has a severe concussion and the most imminent danger is swelling of the brain. Mission has the latest equipment and a medical team that handles this kind of situation more frequently. Fortunately, skull damage is minor, but we've got to get through the next twenty-four hours."

"Will you go with him?" Mom asked.

"No. I'm about to go into the O.R. with the commissioner. But Wayne will be in good hands. You and Barry should go on to Asheville."

Mom nodded. I realized we had a problem.

"My car's at the high school and Archie brought Mom."

"You've got the key to mine on your ring. Take it. I'll get a lift to yours and then come to Mission. Keep me posted. I'll check my phone when I can." She gave Mom a hug, held it, and then broke away to hurry to her patient.

Mom sniffled and blinked back tears. She managed a wan smile. "Barry, you married over your head."

When we arrived at Mission, Uncle Wayne had already been admitted into the Intensive Care Unit. Since the procedure involved keeping him in an induced coma, visiting was discouraged. A nurse suggested I leave a contact number so we could be reached in case there was any change. She said they were monitoring cranial pressure, and although the readings were high, the measurements didn't seem to be increasing. She expected the doctor would keep him in that state till at least early evening. We would have plenty of time to return before he regained consciousness.

Mom thanked the nurse and turned to me. "Since we're here, why don't we sit a few minutes? I feel better knowing he's just down the hall."

The special family area for the ICU wasn't crowded. On the Saturday of Labor Day weekend, most activity occurred at the regular ER. That parade of admittees represented barbecues gone awry, hotdogs lodged in throats, and broken arms and ankles resulting from roughhousing in the backyard or climbing a treacherous mountain rockface. The holiday fracas, as Susan called it, was the reason both she and her colleague, Dr. O'Malley, had been on-call at our local hospital. But most of these injuries didn't rise to the level of intensive care, and so Mom and I sat in a corner of an empty room where we could talk undisturbed.

"I don't like him being in a coma." Mom wrung her hands in her lap.

"It's the best approach if there's brain swelling. Susan wouldn't have said otherwise."

"But your uncle's old. What if the coma does something to his cognitive abilities? I've heard general anesthesia is to be avoided for that reason. It can trigger dementia."

I didn't know to what extent such a cause and effect had been proven, but I knew perfectly well what drove her fear. My father had developed early-onset Alzheimer's, and Mom, Uncle Wayne, and I had watched a vibrant, intelligent, and young man lose his personality right before our eyes and finally die unable to recognize any of us. His illness had brought me home from a career in law enforcement and tied me to the town I'd been determined to leave.

But that tragedy had created relationships that I now cherished. My marriage, my partnership in the funeral home with Fletcher Shaw, and the opportunity to fulfill part of my dream by being Tommy Lee's part-time deputy and frequent lead investigator. Good things could grow from tragedy. But at that moment, my uncle's recovery was all that mattered.

My cell rang. I recognized the number of Tommy Lee's mobile.

"Mom, I'm going to step out in the hall and take this."

I walked toward an exit sign for a stairwell. "This is Barry."

"How's your uncle?" Tommy Lee asked.

"Mom and I are with him at Mission. They're keeping him in a coma and monitoring his cranial pressure. The doctors are cautiously optimistic. Thanks for checking."

"Call me if there's any news. Wayne's one of a kind. We need to hold onto him as long as we can."

"I will. Anything more about why Toby McKay did what he did? Melissa Bigham said it might relate to last year's crop failure."

"That's tied in but we believe what drove him over the edge was this year's."

"His crop failed again?"

"It grew too well. Toby used old batches of lead arsenate, a pesticide that's been banned for years. He sprayed so frequently the chemicals infused through the skin and into the apple itself. The USDA and NC Department of Agriculture ordered the entire crop destroyed."

"What about crop insurance?"

"I doubt if he had any. Probably couldn't afford it. He and his family were on food stamps. And no insurance is going to pay a claim that was caused by illegal activity."

The words Melissa said that Toby shouted, "You ruint me," became clear in their context. "So, Commissioner James symbolized the forces against him."

"Yep. That's probably part of it."

He let the sentence hang out there.

"Part of what?" I asked.

"You didn't ask me how I knew he was on food stamps."

"I assumed someone saw him using them."

"Actually, they don't use stamps any more. I found his EBT card."

"What's that?"

"Electronic Benefit Transfer. The state government issues it and money is deposited each month for approved food items. The merchant is paid by swiping the card. At least that's the way it's supposed to work."

I could tell by the tone in Tommy Lee's voice that the card was more than an indication of Toby McKay's poverty.

"Where'd you find it?"

"In Rufus Taylor's wallet."

"Rufus who owns the convenience store out on 64?"

"Yep. Taylor's Short Stop. Some kids found his body behind the counter about forty-five minutes after your uncle saved Commissioner James."

"You out there now?"

"Yep. When your uncle's out of danger, I could use your help, Barry. The SBI will be all over the commissioner's shooting, but Rufus was one of our own and I'm not going to let the state boys run over us. It's our case and I want you on it."

Chapter Five

I tried to get Mom to go home or at least spend the night with Susan and me. She was adamant about remaining.

"What if he wakes up and we aren't here?" That question met every proposal I suggested and it was all I could do to get her to the restroom by agreeing to enter if something happened.

Fortunately, I was discharged from that responsibility when Susan arrived around six that evening.

She reported Commissioner James had sailed through his shoulder surgery and would be released in a few days. He'd asked about the man who had stopped his assailant, and when a recovery room nurse informed him that his surgeon was the man's niece-in-law, James had insisted upon speaking to Susan.

She delivered his gratitude to Mom with the promise that the commissioner would come to see Wayne before returning to Raleigh.

The three of us spent a restless night in uncomfortable chairs only to greet the dawn with no change in my uncle's condition.

Mom awoke with a start when a ray of sunshine pierced through the blinds and struck her eyes. She blinked and looked around the room. "What about Democrat?" In all the craziness of the day before, she'd forgotten about our dog.

"Fletcher heard what happened," I said. "He went up to the house and gave him food and water. Freddy's on alert if we need him."

Freddy Mott worked part-time when the workload grew too heavy.

Susan stretched in her chair. "Would anyone like coffee? I'll be happy to make a run to the cafeteria."

Mom shook her head, but I stood. "Yes, but I'll get it. I need to stretch my legs."

Before Susan could object, I ducked into the hall. I wondered if there had been any overnight developments in the Rufus Taylor murder, and I was anxious to talk to Tommy Lee. But, it was only six-thirty, and yesterday had to be as exhausting for him as it was for me. I decided I'd wait another hour before trying to reach him.

At six-thirty on Sunday morning, the hospital corridors were practically deserted. The only patrons in the cafeteria were staff who were coming on or off a shift change. I got two cups of black coffee and headed back to the intensive care floor. My phone vibrated on my belt, signaling a text message, but with each hand wrapped around a hot cup, I could only quicken my step. I assumed the message was from Susan and there had been a development.

When I entered the waiting room, I knew what the text had said. Tommy Lee sat on the other side of Mom with his broad, rough hand atop hers. He looked like he'd spent the night in the room with us. A dark crescent hung beneath his good eye and a matching portion appeared from underneath his patch. Gray stubble coated his unshaven cheeks. His wrinkled uniform spoke to hours on-duty and perhaps a few winks of sleep in his office.

"Good morning, Barry." His gravelly voice rumbled hoarser than usual.

"Thanks for coming." I nodded, handed Susan a coffee and offered the second one to him.

He waved it away. "No, I'm caffeined to the gills. Another cup and I'll be bouncing off the walls. I just came by to say Patsy and I are very upset about what happened and praying for your uncle's recovery. And to tell you the department has been flooded with calls of concern from hundreds of people. Wayne's action was so selfless and brave, and it was witnessed by so many that he's become a hometown hero." A smile crept through the serious cast of his lips. "P.J. said Wayne will never have to pay for another haircut."

Pete Peterson, Junior, aka P.J., owned Mr. P's barbershop, the business started by his father and, for over seventy-five years, the gathering place for men's gossip on Main Street. My uncle would treasure free haircuts more than a Congressional Medal of Honor.

"That's very sweet," my mother said. "And I know you must be exhausted. Why don't you go home, Tommy Lee? Barry will let you know if there's any change."

The sheriff took a deep breath and nodded slowly. "I think that's a good idea." He stood. "If there's anything you need, Connie, don't hesitate to ask."

"We won't. Give Patsy my love."

Tommy Lee looked at me. "Walk to the elevator?"

"Sure." I followed him into the hall.

Instead of heading for the elevators, the sheriff turned toward the stairwell where I had taken his call the day before. He moved through the door and onto the landing. Then he listened for footsteps.

His voice dropped to a whisper. "We arrested Sonny last night."

"Who?"

"Sonny McKay. Toby's twenty-five-year-old son."

"I never knew either one of them."

"Well, they kept to themselves out in the county."

"Did Sonny kill Rufus Taylor?"

"Maybe. But we arrested him at the hospital where he showed up drunk and belligerent. He demanded to see Commissioner James. He said he needed to tell him why his father did what he did."

"What was the reason?"

"He said he'd only talk to James. Wakefield and Hutchins brought him in and booked him on a drunk-and-disorderly charge. We're letting him sober up in a cell, and then maybe he'll be more cooperative."

"Any forensics on Rufus?"

A door squealed open on the landing above us. Tommy Lee held up a finger and said nothing. The footsteps went up.

"We're running prints and ballistics," Tommy Lee said. "We might find it's the same gun Toby used."

"Could Rufus have been undiscovered that long?"

"Depends on how busy the store was. The kids who found the body rode their bikes and saw only Rufus' pickup. They went straight to the candy section. It took them a while to decide what they wanted. Then they started searching for Rufus so they could pay. They thought he was in the bathroom. One of them peered behind the counter and had the presence of mind to use the store phone to dial 911. Given a slow day with most of Rufus' local customers in town for the parade, he might not have had any business for a while."

"Enough time for Toby McKay to shoot him and be in position on the curb of Main Street?"

"I'd say unlikely, except for that EBT card."

"Maybe Toby left it last time he was in. It was a coincidence." I quickly added, "But never trust a coincidence."

Tommy Lee chuckled. "Maybe you'll make a decent investigator yet." He clapped me on the shoulder. "I don't mean to burden you with a case. Not while we're all worried about your uncle. I just thought you'd be interested."

He left down the stairwell.

When I returned to the waiting room, I found Mom and Susan speaking with a man in a white coat whom I assumed to be a doctor. Susan introduced me to Charles DeMint, the physician in charge of Uncle Wayne's treatment.

"I was just telling your wife and mother that Wayne's cranial pressure is decreasing. We feel we can safely bring him out of the coma. Once he's out, we'll run a battery of tests, and we'll especially want to make sure there's no subdural hematoma."

The smile on Mom's face faded at the sound of the ominous words.

"Can you explain that?" I asked.

"It's not bleeding in the brain, but bleeding outside within the tissues protecting the brain's surface. The fall could have torn blood vessels there. At first, minor bleeding might not be noticeable or cause any symptoms, but as the blood collects it puts pressure on the brain. Was Wayne on blood thinners?"

"No," Mom said. "He prided himself on not being on any medication."

Dr. DeMint nodded. "When he regains consciousness, we'll run our tests, including another CT scan." He left us with the assurance that in a few minutes a nurse would allow us to visit.

And she did. We entered a glass-walled room and found my uncle lying on his back with so many tubes and wires attached that he looked like a collapsed marionette. His breathing was more regular than when he'd been sprawled on Main Street.

Mom hurried to the bedside and rested her hand on his shoulder. "Oh, Wayne," she whispered. "Don't you leave me."

We stood in silence for a few minutes, silence except for the staccato beeps of monitoring equipment.

Then Mom looked back at me. "I'll be fine, Barry. It's clear to me that Tommy Lee needs you."

Susan gave my hand a squeeze. "I'll stay with her. We'll keep you posted."

I was torn. At the moment, all we were doing was staring at an unconscious man in a hospital bed. But, we were doing it as a family.

"Your uncle acted to save a man's life," Mom said. "Don't you think he would want you to do the same?"

I wondered if Mom had somehow learned of Rufus Taylor's death, or was it simply her intuition, which never ceased to amaze me? She must have picked up some visual cue between Tommy Lee and me.

Whatever the impetus, her words rang true. Uncle Wayne wouldn't want me standing over him while a potential killer could still be at large. At this point, there was only circumstantial evidence linking Toby McKay to Rufus' death. And the timeline for driving from the small convenience store in the county to the parade on Main Street was very tight. How feasible was it that Toby could have made that trip in time? I was also curious about what Toby's son, Sonny, knew about his father's rampage. I wanted first crack at interrogating him once he sobered up.

Tommy Lee brought Sonny McKay into an interview room. A rank, sour odor preceded him. His head was down and the front of his tee-shirt was stained with vomit. He wore dirty cargo pants cuffed over heavy black work boots. His sandy hair lay askew and when he finally looked up, his dark eyes were bleary and bloodshot. His right cheek sported a blue bruise he must have suffered during his intoxicated melee.

Sonny was a good head taller than me, with a build the mountaineers would call high-pocket scrawny. I noticed Tommy Lee hadn't cuffed him, but I saw Deputy Reece Hutchins positioned just outside the interview room door. Tommy Lee pulled it closed behind him. Sonny and I didn't say hello or shake hands. It wasn't that kind of encounter.

Tommy Lee gestured for him to sit on the far side of the table and then he and I took chairs opposite. The sheriff set a Tascam digital audio recorder on the table, started it, and gave the date, time, and names of persons present.

"Sonny, do you know why you're here?" Tommy Lee asked.

The man nodded.

"You'll need to speak up," the sheriff instructed.

"Cause I got drunk and disorderly." He spoke the words like a penitent five-year-old.

"Yes. And you were trying to force your way in to see Commissioner James."

"I wanted to tell him my daddy didn't know what he was doing. That I was sorry."

"Why did your daddy try to shoot James?"

Sonny gnawed on his lower lip for a few seconds. "Because he said our apples weren't no good. We couldn't even sell them for juice."

"And you didn't feel that way about the commissioner?"

"I was upset, but I'd told daddy we shouldn't use them old chemicals. He should have used his money to buy the legal stuff."

"Why didn't he?"

Sonny shrugged. "He said he couldn't borrow any more money."

"He borrowed money? Where was he getting it?"

Sonny shifted uncomfortably in the metal chair.

"Where was he getting his money?" Tommy Lee persisted. "I know he was on food stamps and last year's crop failed as well."

Sonny dropped his gaze to the recorder. "I don't know. He wouldn't tell me."

"He was getting money from Rufus Taylor, wasn't he?"

The man's head snapped up and his eyes widened. "No. Not from Rufus." He emphasized the word *from*, which sounded odd to my ear.

"Who then?" Tommy Lee demanded.

"I tell you, I don't know."

"If it wasn't Rufus, then why did your daddy kill him? Why did Rufus have your daddy's food stamp card in his wallet?"

Sonny froze, and what had been exasperation transformed into fear.

"You found it in his wallet?" he whispered.

"Yes. Why was it there?"

The man squeezed his lips together like a vice.

"Why was it there, Sonny?"

He refused to say a word. Tommy Lee looked at me. My turn.

"Sonny, when did you last see your daddy yesterday?"

"About nine. Saturday mornings I always drop by and Momma fixes pancakes."

"So, you don't live with your parents?"

"No. I've got a trailer on the other side of the orchard."

"And is that your full-time job? Working in the orchard?"

"No. I work at Harold Carson's Auto Repair. I like fixing motorcycles the best."

"Did you have any idea your daddy was planning to attack Commissioner James?"

"No. First it came up was when Momma mentioned the parade and that James would be in it."

"And what did your daddy say?"

"Nothing. He just slammed down his fork and got up from the table. He left and we heard his truck start. He never said where he was going."

"Did you try to go after him?"

"After him where? Like I said, I didn't know where he was going."

"Did you have any reason to believe he might have gone to Rufus Taylor's store?"

"No."

I leaned forward across the table and gave him a hard stare. "Then how do you think your daddy's EBT card wound up in Rufus Taylor's wallet?"

Again, fear registered across Sonny's face. "I don't know. Rufus must have stoled it."

"When did you leave your momma?"

"About an hour later. I ate up the pancakes and then hung

around expecting Daddy to return. Momma said he was just upset about everything and was probably driving around to cool off."

"Where did you go after that?"

"I walked back to my place. I worked on my Triumph and then Momma came with the news."

"That's a motorcycle, not a car?" I asked.

"That's right. I had parts spread all over the driveway. We took off for the hospital in my truck." He faltered, his voice choking. "I had to identify Daddy's body. I didn't want Momma to have to do that."

"How did your mother learn what happened?"

"My Aunt Nelda called her. Nelda Overton. That's Momma's sister. She met us at the hospital."

"And then you left them," I stated.

He nodded. "I went to Shuman's Road House. Had a couple of beers and a few shots to calm my nerves."

"Then you came back for your mother?"

He nodded again.

"Speak up," Tommy Lee said.

"Yes. I reckon so. I don't remember too much."

"And you also tried to see Commissioner James," I said.

Sonny looked at the sheriff. "I wanted him to know it wasn't Daddy's fault."

"Whose fault was it?"

He said nothing.

"Was it Rufus Taylor's?" I pressed.

Sonny dropped his chin to his vomit-stained shirt and refused to look at us. A knock sounded on the door.

"Come in," Tommy Lee said gruffly.

Reece entered carrying a few sheets of paper. "Preliminary forensics on Rufus." He turned to me. "Archie's asking to see you."

Tommy Lee flipped quickly through the pages. "Reece, take Sonny back to his cell."

When Reece and his prisoner had left, Tommy Lee handed me one of the sheets. Rufus had been shot once in the chest and once in the head. The recovered slugs were twenty-two caliber.

"But Toby McKay used a thirty-eight," I said.

"That's right. Time for me to get a search warrant from Judge Wood. We'll need to go through the houses of both Toby and Sonny. Might have been a squirrel rifle, might have been a pistol. And I want you to visit the crime scene with me. Are you good with that?"

"Unless something changes with Uncle Wayne."

Tommy Lee nodded. "Of course. Now, while I ring the judge, you talk to Archie. Then we'll take separate cars in case you have to peel off."

Archie was sitting on the cot in his cell. His laptop was open beside him. On the floor was a takeout bag from the Cardinal Café. The door was unlocked. For a prisoner, he seemed to have plenty of comforts. From his worried look, I knew something was bothering him.

"How are the donations going?"

He closed the laptop and stood. "Not so good," he whispered. "I think the shooting yesterday overshadowed the publicity. So, I'm writing all my clients, reminding them where I am. Sort of a blog. I call it *Letters from a Gainesboro Jail*."

I couldn't stifle a laugh. "Archie, you're not Martin Luther King, Junior."

He held a finger to his lips. "Not so loud. I know. But I'm imprisoned for my cause."

"Is that why you wanted to see me?"

He stepped closer and jerked his head toward the near wall. "No," he whispered. "It's the man in the next cell. The deputies call him Sonny."

"Yeah. What about him?"

"Well, he kept me up last night with his moaning. And then he got sick. I heard him puking so I asked if he was all right."

"What did he say?"

"That he was a dead man. They killed Rufus and he would be next."

I felt a tingle in my neck at the possibility that Archie could have learned something significant.

"Did he say who they were?"

"No. He said he didn't know. But Rufus had known. He was part of them. And now with what his daddy had done, they'd be coming after him. I figured the daddy had to be Toby McKay."

"What did you say?"

"I told him I could help him. That I knew people."

"What people?"

"Well, you. But I didn't use your name. I didn't even say they were police. Just that I had influence and could provide protection."

"Archie, you're an insurance salesman. You're not Eliot Ness."

Again, Archie's finger went to his lips. "He'll hear you. I didn't give him my real name."

"What name did you give him?"

Archie reddened. "The first one that popped into my mind. Brad Pitt."

"And he bought that?"

"I told him I wasn't the movie star."

"You actually think he needed clarification?"

"He didn't see me. At least not till Reece came and took him out a little while ago."

"He say anything?"

"No. He just smiled and mouthed, 'Hi, Brad.'"

"And you've never seen him before?"

"Nope. Not before last night. He wasn't exactly a prospect." Archie grinned. "Want me to pump him for information? I told him I was in for robbery. I think he was impressed."

I wanted to scream, "You're not Brad Pitt, you're Archie Donovan, Junior," loud enough for Sonny to hear and end this ridiculous charade. But, at least Sonny had talked to him, whereas Tommy Lee and I had gotten the silent treatment.

"Don't engage him anymore," I said. "At least until I talk to Tommy Lee. Sonny will probably be cut loose pretty soon anyway."

"Okay. One question."

"What?"

"Can I still be Brad Pitt?"

Chapter Six

"Brad Pitt? He told Sonny he was Brad Pitt?" Tommy Lee stared at me with incredulity.

We were waiting in his office for the search warrants to be delivered.

"Not *the* Brad Pitt. And Sonny told him more than he told us."

"Only because he was drunk." The sheriff got up from his desk and walked to his Mr. Coffee machine to refill yet another cup.

"Sonny said he was a marked man," I said. "That they would get him like they did Rufus. Archie offered him protection."

Tommy Lee choked in mid-swallow. "Jesus, have we ever seen any sign that Archie has a brain?"

"No. And yet his whole concocted story is so ludicrous it could pass for the truth. I mean what undercover agent would call himself Brad Pitt?"

"And Sonny bought it?"

"Archie says Sonny said, 'Hi, Brad' as Reece escorted him to our interview."

Tommy Lee paced behind his desk for a few seconds before collapsing into his chair. "This goes against my better judgment, but if Archie can find something out, then I guess we'd better back him up. How did you leave it?"

"I told him not to engage in any more conversations, but he could keep his Brad Pitt name."

Tommy Lee swiveled his chair and stared out the window behind his desk. "Just when I think this job can't get any weirder." He sighed and spun back around. He pressed the intercom button on his phone. "Marge, what deputies are here?"

"Just Reece and Steve."

"Tell them I need to see them in my office. You might as well join them."

In only a few minutes, Deputies Reece Hutchins and Steve Wakefield came in. Reece eyed me suspiciously, as if I were somehow aligning myself with the sheriff against him. Wakefield, the older of the two, seemed unperturbed by being called to the office. He'd been summoned thousands of times. Marge Colbert slid in between the two men, her expression one of curiosity. She'd picked up that something was astir by the tone of Tommy Lee's voice.

Tommy Lee and I stood.

"What I'm about to tell you is going to sound crazy," Tommy Lee began. "I'll get the craziest part out of the way first. As long as Sonny McKay is here, we're to call Archie Brad Pitt."

The three couldn't have looked more bewildered than if Tommy Lee had announced he was from Jupiter. Wakefield was the first to recover. "Is it a breach of procedure to ask for his autograph?"

"Yes. He's not that Brad Pitt." Tommy Lee filled them in on Archie's overnight conversation and the potential to gather more information.

Marge shifted uncomfortably. "How long are you planning to hold Sonny?" she asked. "He's an only son and his father just died. His mother must need emotional support."

Marge's concern squelched our brief levity. We had no evidence to hold Sonny on a murder charge, and now that he'd sobered up, he should be allowed bail. Archie, on the other hand, could be looking at a life sentence if he didn't start getting some donations.

"A fair point," Tommy Lee said. "Thank you, Marge. We'll keep him till mid-afternoon. We'll charge him with a misdemeanor and release him on his own recognizance. In the meantime, we'll stay clear of the cells other than normal rounds. Be sure and let dispatch know, as well as any other officers who might come in, that Archie is now Brad Pitt."

"Sonny doesn't know me," Wakefield said. "Can I be George Clooney?"

"No. And none of this is funny. Remember Barry's uncle is lying in a coma as a result of yesterday's confrontation and Rufus Taylor's dead."

"Sorry," Wakefield muttered.

"You can bring Archie to Interview Room 2. Call him Brad. Say the sheriff wants to question him. Marge, you and Reece should be ready to intercept anyone coming in and give a heads-up."

A few minutes later, Tommy Lee and I entered the interview room to find Archie grinning with a smile so broad that the Cheshire Cat would have been envious. The sheriff dismissed Deputy Wakefield and motioned for Archie to sit at the table. Tommy Lee and I took chairs opposite him.

"So, I understand you have an alias, Archie," Tommy Lee said.

"It was spur of the moment. To be honest, I didn't want a violent man knowing my name."

"But he did say Rufus was killed by some unnamed group."

"Yes, a group that he was part of."

"That Sonny was part of?"

Archie shook his head. "That Rufus was part of. Sonny didn't make any claim except that they would be after him next."

"Did you ask him who these people were?"

"Yes. He wouldn't say."

Tommy Lee turned to me. "What do you think?"

"I think Sonny's scared. He certainly came across that way when we interviewed him."

"You offered him protection?" Tommy Lee asked Archie.

The insurance-agent-turned-jailhouse-snitch squirmed. "I was just trying to calm him down. I was worried. I heard him throwing up. Anyway, he didn't take it."

"I want you to ask him again," Tommy Lee said.

"Why would he take it now?"

"He was drunk as a skunk when we brought him in. Was he still drunk when you talked to him in the middle of the night?"

"I couldn't see him, but he was slurring his words."

"Good. Then I want you to play it this way. Tell him I pressed you to give up anything he might have told you. That I offered to recommend leniency to the D.A. on your robbery charge. A murder conviction is a much bigger fish than a robbery."

"But he didn't tell me anything," Archie said.

The sheriff held up a finger. "Point one, he doesn't know that or can't be sure. His memory of last night is fuzzy at best." He raised a second finger. "Point two, you don't have to give him any information. Say you know he didn't kill Rufus but he told you about his father's involvement in the food stamp scam and the people running it. You're willing to give him an insurance policy."

Archie's mouth opened. "You want me to sell him an insurance policy?"

"In a manner of speaking. Say you can get the names to your lawyer who will keep the information confidential unless something happens to him or you. Then they'll be released to the police. Assure him these people wouldn't dare touch him then."

Archie looked at me and then back to Tommy Lee. "What food stamp scam?"

I didn't know what the sheriff was talking about either.

Tommy Lee's one eye narrowed as he studied Archie. "Can you keep a secret?"

Archie looked indignant. "Of course I can."

"No, don't give me such a flip answer. Can you keep a secret that could have deadly consequences?"

Archie paled. "What kind of consequences?"

"Well, for starters, Rufus is dead. It wasn't a hold-up and he was shot with a twenty-two. That smacks of a professional with a suppressed semi-automatic. Sonny could very well be in danger. He won't cooperate with me but he might latch onto you."

Archie licked his dry lips. "I can't protect him against an assassin."

"I'm not asking you to. We'll handle that. You just tell him that he talked about the food stamp fraud. Then you get the names and you're out of it. Your conversation with Sonny is not to be shared unless we're in court. The secret is we found Toby McKay's Electronic Benefit Transfer card in Rufus' wallet. It replaced physical food stamps and it's used like a credit card. My guess is Rufus had loaned Toby money and demanded the card as collateral. Each month when the account was replenished, he processed fake purchases through his store. And if he used Toby's card that way, he could have been running the fraud with others and splitting the cash."

"And Toby didn't kill him?"

Tommy Lee shrugged. "Maybe. Maybe Toby went for Commissioner James and Sonny went for Rufus. But unless we find that one of them owned a twenty-two with a ballistics match, then my money's on something wider and more sinister. So, we'll keep your identity a secret and you keep the secret that you ever spoke with Sonny."

Archie's hands started shaking. "Can I have protection too?"

Tommy Lee shot me a glance telling me he wasn't going to like where this conversation was going. "Why?" he asked.

"Because I kind of posted on Facebook that my cellmate was the son of the man who shot Commissioner James."

"And Brad Pitt?"

Archie shook his head emphatically. "No. I didn't say anything about that."

"Then when you get back to your cell, you post an admittance that Sonny wasn't actually your cellmate but rather was at the other end of the corridor. Can you do that?"

"Yes, sir."

"And then let Reece take the computer and mobile phone out of your cell. Sonny will probably be released before you and he'll pass your cell door. Did he see that stuff when he was out earlier?"

"No. Everything was under my cot."

"All right. Then you can leave them there." Tommy Lee stood. "Are we clear on what you're supposed to do?"

Archie and I both rose.

"Yes, sir," Archie said. "Tell him he talked last night and offer him protection."

"Good. We're going to cut him loose mid-afternoon. Then you go back to your Facebook posting like none of this happened. Do me and you both a favor. Raise the money and get the hell out of my jail."

Armed with our search warrants, Tommy Lee and I first caravanned to Toby McKay's house. Sonny had said his mother Pauline McKay had been with her sister Nelda Overton, but we didn't know whether Mrs. McKay had stayed at her sister's or returned to her own home.

The orchard bordered Highway 64 and the farmhouse was on the backside. A dirt road long in need of fresh gravel looped around the apple trees. I followed Tommy Lee in my jeep, staying back far enough to avoid the dust cloud stirred by his patrol car.

The road ended at a patch of sparse grass and weeds that passed for the front yard of a small farmhouse. The siding was clapboard with peeling, faded white paint. A wooden porch tilted toward concrete steps without a banister. But my attention focused on two dark blue sedans parked on either side of the steps. The whiff of government suddenly filled the air.

Tommy Lee pulled in back of the first and signaled for me to park behind the second. We effectively pinned both cars against the porch. I got out and waited as the sheriff came over to me.

"Well, we don't have to worry about getting in," he said.

"Who do you think is here?"

Tommy Lee walked between the two sedans. "State boys. Probably Sid Ferguson, the special agent in charge of this region. Since Graham James is an elected official, the SBI's got to pee its scent on the case. Ferguson's putting in his face time so he can issue a firsthand report."

"Do we have a jurisdictional problem?"

Tommy Lee grinned. "Let's see whether or not Ferguson greets us with open arms."

As we stepped up on the porch, a white man in a dark suit came out the front door. His gray hair and lined face pegged him somewhere north of fifty. He opened his arms wide, but raised them palm out as double stop signs.

"Whoa, Sheriff. Mrs. McKay isn't here. You'll have to wait outside while we execute our search warrant."

"Good to see you, too, Sid." Tommy Lee retrieved his folded warrants from his chest pocket and held the one for Toby McKay's home in front of the other man. "I'm not here to see Mrs. McKay. I'm here with my own warrant."

Ferguson shook his head. "We've got this one. You can go back to DUIs and escorting funerals."

Tommy Lee kept his cool and I could see the SBI agent had expected a different reaction to his barb.

"And what one would that be?" Tommy Lee asked.

Ferguson looked at me as if to say *Is this guy kidding?* "McKay's attack on the commissioner."

"Different case. But you can play nice and I won't go back to Judge Wood to report that you impeded a murder investigation. Last I heard Commissioner James was alive and recovering nicely while the perpetrator was dead in the morgue."

The SBI agent's eyes widened. "Murder? That convenience store shooting? It's tied to this?"

"Circumstantially. That's why my deputy and I are coming inside. Unless you'd prefer you and I arrest each other."

Ferguson scowled, but said nothing. He withdrew into the house and we followed.

The living room was sparsely furnished with an old floral sofa, two rockers, and a small flat-screen TV and over-the-air antenna sitting on what looked like a bedside nightstand. Two agents wearing latex gloves were pulling the cushions off the sofa and running their hands into the crevice between the base and back. They both looked up, clearly annoyed by our presence.

Ferguson cleared his throat. "Our esteemed colleagues from the Laurel County Sheriff's Department are working a potentially overlapping case. They have a proper search warrant." He turned to Tommy Lee. "But, Sheriff, I suggest instead of our stepping over each other, you and your deputy monitor our search and then you're free to conduct your own."

"All right," Tommy Lee said.

"What are you specifically looking for?" one of the agents asked.

"Evidence that Toby didn't operate alone."

"That's our task too," the agent replied. "Anything that might show a conspiracy."

"And firearms," Tommy Lee added. "A twenty-two would be nice, preferably semi-automatic."

"Really?" Ferguson asked. "That's an odd caliber for a mountaineer unless it's a rifle."

"Our victim took two shots, close range. One to the body, one to the head. Nothing was stolen."

The three agents looked at each other, all drawing the same conclusion.

"You think it's a hit?" Ferguson asked.

"The possibility's crossed my mind. But I don't think the trigger man was Toby."

"Then what ties Toby to the crime?"

"I'll have to get back to you on that. We're just starting and I'm trying to work the case in between the DUIs and funeral escorts."

Ferguson's jaw tightened. "If the convenience store was a hit and you can tie it to the man who tried to assassinate James, then I'm very interested."

"Well, then why don't we share some information and avoid a pissing contest? You first."

Ferguson took a deep breath. He didn't like being mocked in front of his agents. "All right. What do you want to know?"

"Have you run financials on Toby yet?"

"No. We will, but it's Sunday and because of Labor Day, we don't have access till Tuesday."

"Okay. Can I have your word I'll see them when you see them?"

"Yes. Now what's the link?"

"The victim, Rufus Taylor, had Toby McKay's EBT card in his wallet. I need to find out if there's an innocent explanation or if Rufus was cashing it out. The financials could help explain that."

"You talked to FNS?" Ferguson asked.

I knew FNS stood for the USDA's Food and Nutrition Services. They had their own set of investigators charged with rooting out fraud in the food stamp program, whose official name, SNAP, stood for Supplemental Nutrition Assistance Program.

"Like you said, it's Sunday," Tommy Lee answered. "And I'm not ready for another level of law enforcement to complicate life. Are you ready to have them in your lap as well?"

Ferguson shook his head. "I've got a full plate." He smiled with what appeared to be genuine amusement. "And I don't have to do funerals." He turned to his agents. "Back to it, gentlemen. Find the sheriff his weapon and we'll close two cases in one day."

My cell signaled an incoming text. I snatched the phone from my belt.

Uncle Wayne regained consciousness

wrote Susan.

Has no memory of the shooting.

I handed the cell to Tommy Lee.

He read the message. "Go," he said.

"What's up?" Ferguson asked me.

"My uncle was in a coma. He's come out."

"I'm happy for your family," he said, with all the enthusiasm of anticipating a trip to the dentist.

Tommy Lee put his hand on my shoulder. "His uncle is the man who stopped Toby McKay and the reason you're not dealing with a murder case."

Ferguson reddened. "Then I'm really happy. He was a brave man and the entire state owes him a debt of gratitude."

I smiled to show no hard feelings. "He's been promised free haircuts for life."

The agents laughed.

"I'd take a bullet for that," Ferguson said. "Tell him the SBI sends wishes for a speedy recovery." He shifted his gaze to Tommy Lee. "And we'll have total cooperation on the investigation from our end."

"Same here," Tommy Lee replied. "I need to cover a few things with Barry. I'll walk him to his car."

I stepped out on the porch with the sheriff behind me.

"Let's take a quick look around back," he said.

He took the lead. We passed a rusted oil tank that fueled the furnace and a water hose stretched from a faucet to a chicken coop.

"What are we looking for?"

"We're not looking, we're foraging. I want to assess the McKays' food supply."

An outbuilding sheltered an old tractor hooked to a trailer loaded with ladders. More than a hundred empty bushel baskets stood stacked against the back interior wall of the shed. Between that building and the orchard lay a vegetable garden that had yet to exhaust its produce for the season. Late corn, beans, and tomatoes were closest to us. The furrowed patch must have been at least half an acre.

Tommy Lee took makeshift concrete-block steps up to a back porch door. He found it unlocked and we entered. The porch was fitted with a large work sink, wooden counters, and pegboards holding large cooking instruments. The space stretched across the back of the house. Part of the wall was covered with shelves of empty mason jars and cardboard shoeboxes. The only interior door went directly to the kitchen.

Tommy Lee opened one of the boxes and found it filled with jar lids. "This is where Mrs. McKay does her canning. Let's check the other side."

We continued our loop around the house and saw double doors closed over a slanted concrete wall on the far side. Tommy Lee lifted one of the doors to reveal steps descending under the house to the cellar.

He raised the second door and let it drop on the dirt. "Let's check it out."

The air temperature dropped ten to fifteen degrees. The cellar floor was packed earth. The house floor above was no more than six feet over us, and Tommy Lee had to stoop. He found a bare light bulb hanging from a cord and pulled the chain switch. The first thing we noticed was an oil furnace tucked up against the wall closest to the outside tank. The other walls were actually shelves rising from the floor to overhead crossbeams. They, too, held mason jars but these were sealed and filled with vegetables. Other shelves held cans of store-bought items like Vienna sausages and Spam.

"Good little food stock," Tommy Lee said. "Productive garden, chickens for eggs and meat, venison in and probably out of season, and maybe mountain trout if he's got a stream on his acreage."

"What's he need with food stamps?"

"The one green he can't grow in his garden—cash. He's got the low income to qualify, especially with two crop failures, but food's not the problem. I believe he used the card fraudulently to get cash. Without cash, how's he pay his taxes, vehicle insurance, heating oil? All those things that even a rudimentary lifestyle requires in the modern world."

"And Rufus was his money supply?"

"What's the old phrase? Follow the money? Go check on your uncle, and then be ready to start down that trail."

Chapter Seven

I found Mom and Susan standing on either side of Uncle Wayne's bed. Mom held a cup and straw as my uncle took a few sips of water.

He motioned for Mom to move the drink away from his face and gave me a weak smile. "Throat's raw," he whispered.

Monitors and IVs were still hooked to him and a white bandage encircled his head like a fallen halo.

"Then don't talk," I replied.

"Need to. Alone." He looked first at Susan and then my mother.

"Connie, why don't we run down to the cafeteria?" Susan said. "We need to eat something."

Mom nodded at Susan's suggestion and handed me the water. "Don't let him talk too much."

When they'd left, I pulled a chair bedside. "Now, don't push yourself. Whatever you have to say can be said slowly. Okay?"

"Hmm," he grunted. "Two words. What happened?"

"Do you remember anything?"

"Just waiting at P.J.'s for the parade to start. I remember seeing the sheriff's car."

Uncle Wayne had probably been hanging out with some of his barbershop buddies.

"And Susan and Mom didn't tell you anything?"

"That I stopped some man trying to shoot the commissioner." He paused for a couple of breaths. "And he died. But they sugar-coated everything."

Mom wouldn't have wanted to go into details about Toby McKay, and Susan was probably reluctant to upset either of them.

"I want to know," Uncle Wayne insisted.

So, I gave a summary of what I saw and what I knew, including the murder of Rufus Taylor, but omitting the discovery of Toby McKay's EBT card.

A few tears trickled from the corners of my uncle's eyes. "You're telling me I killed a man?"

"No. A gun went off. McKay's more likely to have pulled the trigger than you. He'd already wounded the commissioner and a second shot at closer range could have been fatal. Witnesses say you definitely saved a life. That's what you need to focus on."

"I can't remember any of it."

"That's normal. You've suffered a head trauma. You very well might not remember this conversation, and we might have to have it again. But, both the commissioner and the State Bureau of Investigation have expressed their gratitude. I'm proud of you."

He bit his lower lip and raised an arm to brush away more tears. Wires and IV tubes blocked his motion. I found a box of tissues and wiped his cheeks.

He took a deep breath and eyed the cup of water. I held the straw to his lips and he sipped a few swallows.

"What about McKay?"

"He died at the scene. There was nothing anybody could do."

"I mean about his body. Did we get the business?"

He asked the question without any trace of irony. Like we were serving any other client.

"I think the body's still in the morgue. And the family might want to go elsewhere, given the circumstances."

"But we're the best in western North Carolina. I won't be there. Fletcher and Freddy can handle it without you or me going near the family. I won't have the man I killed getting second-rate service somewhere else."

I smiled. His logic was vintage Uncle Wayne, and I felt a great relief that his unique brain seemed to be undamaged.

Shortly after Mom and Susan returned, Dr. DeMint entered. My uncle had fallen asleep and the doctor gave a brief report that they would keep him another night in ICU and if all went well, move him to a regular room tomorrow. But he cautioned us that Uncle Wayne's age might mean a slower recovery and he wanted to make sure his balance, walking, and other functions of normal daily living were thoroughly evaluated by physical therapists. In short, he recommended my uncle remain at Mission for at least four or five days to be on the safe side.

When DeMint left, Susan said, "Don't worry, Connie. Barry and I will work out how to get you here and back each day."

"No. You've got your patients and Barry needs to help Tommy Lee. I'm going to call Hilda Atwood. She's an old friend, a widow like me, and she's always asking me to stay with her. Her house is less than two miles away. I'm sure she'll be glad to help."

Susan and I agreed that Mom's plan made sense, and Susan volunteered to take her back to the funeral home to pack. I said I'd stay with Uncle Wayne, but Mom insisted that if there was anything I could be doing to help Tommy Lee, then I should make that my priority.

I phoned Tommy Lee as I drove away from the hospital. A little over two hours had elapsed since I'd left him with Sid Ferguson and his agents, and I wondered if I could catch up with him at Sonny's trailer.

"How's your uncle?" were his first words.

"The doctors are encouraged. My uncle's upset that McKay's dead and he's trying to come to grips with actions he can't remember. But, there's nothing more for me to do, so I'm headed back. Where are you?"

"Just leaving Sonny's."

"Any luck?"

"Toby had a twelve-gauge, an old thirty-aught-six, and a twenty-two bolt action—the standard mountaineer arsenal of a rabbit and bird gun, a deer rifle, and a squirrel and varmint rifle. Sonny had a sixteen-gauge shotgun and a pump twenty-two. Ferguson took both twenty-twos and I'm sending him the slugs from Rufus' body."

"He took them or you gave them to him?"

"I gave them. He can run the ballistics faster than I can. And we found motorcycle engine parts spread out where Sonny said he'd been working on a bike."

"What's your gut tell you?"

"That there'll be no match from ballistics. Rufus wasn't killed by the McKays, but he might have been killed because of them."

"Is Sonny still in jail?"

"Yes, but I'm going to release him."

"Would you hold off till I get there?"

There was a pause. "Why? You want to re-interview him?"

"Just have a little conversation."

"One on one?"

"If you're okay with it?"

"Knock yourself out. We'll be waiting."

This time I retrieved Sonny myself, being sure to pause at Archie's cell on the way.

"Pitt, I'll be back for you later. Think about what we told you."

Archie gave me the okay sign and slid his laptop under the bunk. "Go to hell," he said in the gruffest voice he could muster.

I moved on to Sonny. He sat on his bed, his head in his hands. "Come along, McKay. Just a few more questions."

He didn't bother to look up. "I ain't got nothin' to say."

"Then you can listen to me. Let's go. The sooner we start, the sooner we're done."

Sonny got to his feet. I unlocked the cell and escorted him to the same interview room. He took his seat at the table.

"Where's the sheriff?"

"He's deciding what to do with you." I slid into the chair opposite him. "We want to cut you a break."

"How's that?"

"Tell us what you know about your daddy's EBT card. Why did Rufus Taylor have it? Who's been using it for cash?"

Sonny pushed back his chair. "Look, I don't know nothin' about that. If I did, I'd tell you. My daddy must have left it on the counter or something."

"And that's the truth?"

"Yep. Maybe Rufus was stealing cards. Maybe that's why he got shot."

"Okay. We'll leave it there for now."

Sonny visibly relaxed. "So, when can I get out? I need to check on Momma. And we have a burial to tend to."

"What can you tell me about Pitt?"

"Who?"

"The movie star next to you. Brad Pitt."

"He ain't that Brad Pitt."

"So, you've been talking to him?"

Sonny shook his head. "Nothin', man. He was worried about me when I got sick last night. More concern than I got from anybody here."

"He talk about why he was in?"

Sonny looked wary. "Don't you know?"

"I want to know what he told you."

"Some kind of robbery. I didn't ask and he didn't say any more."

"Nothing about the others in his gang?"

"He has a gang?"

"Oh, yeah. Brad's quite the wheeler-dealer, and he's got a slick lawyer. He'll be out soon. My advice is stay clear of him."

Sonny spread his hands. "Hey, he asked if I was okay. That's it."

I stood. "All right. One last thing. Your father's body should be ready for release tomorrow. You and your mother need to notify the morgue who's taking receipt."

"You mean like a funeral home?"

"Yeah. Clayton and Clayton's the only one in this county, but there are others nearby."

He looked embarrassed. "They all cost about the same?"

"The local one will be least expensive."

"Your name's Clayton?"

I smiled. "That's right. But ask for Fletcher Shaw. He'll take good care of you."

I walked Sonny back to his cell and then found Tommy Lee in his office. He looked up from a series of color photographs on his desk. "How'd it go?"

I shrugged. "He's still denying any ties between his father and Rufus. So I tried to reinforce Archie's persona as a tough guy, but that's a hard sell."

Tommy Lee sighed. "Well, bring him back to Interview Two. I'll take one more crack and then cut him loose."

"Will you have someone on him? He seems genuinely scared."

"I don't have the manpower for 24/7. Not and devote attention to Rufus' murder." He lifted one of the photographs. "These are from the crime scene. Nothing to go on. Not even signs of a struggle."

"Maybe he knew his attacker."

"Can't rule it out. Too bad Rufus had no CCTV footage."

I thought about our one piece of connecting evidence. "Can we get a list of all the EBT cards Rufus ran in the last month? If it's a scam like you theorize, we ought to find a pattern."

"Already made the request through Ferguson. But don't expect any response till after Labor Day." He rose from his desk. "Pull Archie into Interview One before I get Sonny. Keep him in there till Sonny leaves."

I didn't move.

"What?" Tommy Lee snapped.

"I don't like Sonny going out uncovered."

"I didn't say he'd be uncovered. I just can't have surveillance around the clock. I've got a GPS tracker on his pickup and plan two-shift coverage. Once he beds down for the night, we'll pull back. That's the best I can do."

I found Archie so engrossed in his laptop screen that he didn't hear me approach his cell.

"Okay, Pitt. We're going to go through it all again and then again until you loosen those tight lips." I knew my dialogue sounded straight out of a Grade B movie, but Sonny wasn't exactly a sophisticated film critic.

Archie jumped and snapped the laptop shut. "You're wasting your breath. I've got nothing to say."

At least he didn't address me as "copper." I unlocked the door and he slid the computer under his bunk.

As soon as we were in the interview room. Archie clapped his hands and actually jumped in the air.

"I did it! I raised the bail." He sat on the edge of the table and dangled his feet in the air. "A certified check is coming Tuesday as soon as the banks open."

"A single check?"

"Yep. The whole ten thousand."

"That's great. Congratulations. So, how much is the total, counting the original five hundred and whatever else you raised?"

"Oh, that five hundred was seed money. I said that to get the ball rolling. Now I don't need to give it."

I started to argue that a pledge was a pledge, but realized it was Archie. As he'd said in the cell, I'd be wasting my breath.

"Who made the contribution?"

He gave me a sly wink. "One of my loyal clients who wishes to remain anonymous. The person said my *Letters from a Gainesboro Jail* were very moving. So, I'm free to go as soon as we wrap this business with Sonny."

"Did he tell you anything?"

"No, but he wants to."

I suspected Archie's fantasy of a secret undertaking with Sonny was leading him to an exaggerated assessment of their relationship. "How do you know that?"

Archie hopped off the table. "Because he asked me to come see him when I made bail. He gave me directions. A trailer on the north side of their orchard."

"Why wouldn't he talk now?"

"He said the walls have ears. He thinks our cells are bugged."

Archie's explanation sounded plausible, but the prospect of an outside meeting changed the whole dynamics of his ruse.

"I don't want you to take it any further."

"Ah, come on, Barry," he whined. "He's ready to talk. Isn't that what you wanted?"

"Yes, within the safety of our jail, not in a trailer on the side of a mountain where I can't give you protection."

Archie threw up his hands. "But aren't you giving him protection?"

"That's different. And it's not as complete as I'd like because we don't want him to know he's being monitored."

Archie stepped closer. "I can do this, Barry. You put a wire on me, I go in, I get the names, and I'm out. Why are you against that?"

"Because you're not law enforcement, you're a private citizen. You're not talking through a cell wall, you're face-to-face with someone who might think he's told you more than he did. I mean you pushed him into that belief. He might not see you as protection. He could see you as a loose end."

That possibility gave Archie pause, and I pushed on. "Remember, we haven't totally ruled him out as a suspect in Rufus Taylor's murder. He only has his mother for an alibi."

"Then why is he scared of these other people? He brought them up, I didn't. He was drunk and unlikely to be lying. He has names and I can get them for you. At least ask Tommy Lee."

I couldn't refuse that request, although I wasn't certain what the sheriff's answer would be.

"Why are you so hell-bent on doing this, Archie?"

"Because I like your uncle. And I think he's in the hospital because of something Sonny McKay knows. And I want someone to pay. Don't you?"

We met fifteen minutes later in Tommy Lee's office. Sonny had left for the hospital to get his pickup, the one Tommy Lee had gotten a court order to tag with a GPS tracker he'd borrowed from the SBI.

The sheriff listened stone-faced to Archie's pitch. I argued the points about Sonny still being a suspect and the lack of protection we could provide a private citizen who was basically acting as an extension of the Sheriff's Department.

When we'd both made our case, Tommy Lee leaned back in his desk chair accompanied by the squeal of its worn springs. "Archie, I share Barry's concerns for your safety, and for enlisting the aid of someone who is not a trained officer of the law. I would feel much better if we could completely rule out Sonny as Rufus Taylor's killer. But, we don't have to make a yes or no decision today."

"What do you mean?" I asked.

"Sonny is going to be tied up with his father's funeral arrangements. At least for the next day or two. He thinks his jail friend Brad Pitt has to make bail, so a delay in Pitt's visit to his trailer is perfectly logical. In the meantime, we need to determine with more certainty that Sonny isn't a killer. Then, I think we'll give Archie his shot."

"All right," I conceded.

Tommy Lee snapped his chair forward and gave Archie a hard stare. "But till then you stay out of sight and away from that section of the county. Sonny's going to be coming in and out of town and I don't want him running into you in the Cardinal Café."

Archie grinned. "Home and office, sir. Just my home and office."

Chapter Eight

I spent most of Labor Day Monday at the hospital where Uncle Wayne continued to improve. He mostly slept, but by evening his appetite returned and we spent dinner watching a rerun of the old *Andy Griffith Show*.

Fletcher called during *Wheel of Fortune* to say the Gainesboro hospital was releasing Toby McKay's body the next morning and that Sonny and his mother were coming to the funeral home at ten.

"Handle it however you want," I said. "I'll stay clear. Just be warned that we're probably going to be paid in vegetables."

"I'll see if I can negotiate for a pie."

"Make sure it isn't made with their apples."

"Oh, right," he said. "And if payment's a problem, I'll avoid as many hard costs as I can. I'll keep you posted." He paused, and I was ready to hang up. "Oh, one more thing. We're also getting Rufus Taylor's body. We'll have some logistical juggling to do."

"I can help with Rufus," I said. "Have you heard from his next of kin?"

"A son came in from Winston-Salem. I met him this afternoon. I understand Rufus was divorced and the ex is out west somewhere. The son wants a short service in our chapel on Wednesday morning. Burial's up at Twin Creeks Baptist Church. That's also where McKay will be buried."

"Okay. Try to push any service for McKay till Thursday. Do you know where the son's staying?"

"He said he's at his father's house. It's about a quarter mile from the store. His name's Roger Taylor. Nice guy. About thirty. He's pretty shaken by the murder."

After we hung up, I wondered if anyone had interviewed Roger Taylor about his father. That could be an important piece of our investigation. And I thought about another potential hole in our case. I'd neglected to ask Tommy Lee if he'd interviewed Sonny's mother. Between dealing with Uncle Wayne's injuries and Archie's self-initiated undercover work, I hadn't inquired about the status of Mrs. McKay. If the family had a need for food stamps, she should be as aware of the existence of the EBT card as anyone. I left Mom and my uncle to step into the hospital stairwell to phone Tommy Lee in relative privacy.

"Can you talk?" I asked.

"Yep. It's just Patsy and me grilling burgers and trying to cram the holiday weekend into two hours. Everything all right?"

"Yes. I'm with Mom and Uncle Wayne. He's making good progress."

"Give them both my best."

"Thanks. Listen, I spoke to Fletcher who said we're receiving Toby McKay's body tomorrow. Sonny and his mother are coming for a consultation at ten."

"Well, since you'll want to stay clear, you can work with me. I want to talk to Sonny's boss, Harold Carson, at the auto repair garage. And I'm pushing Agent Ferguson to get the ballistics on those twenty-two rifles our search turned up. The sooner we clear Sonny, the sooner Archie can make his play."

"Have you interviewed Mrs. McKay?"

"Not yet. Ferguson spoke with her this morning regarding the attack on Commissioner James. He sent me his notes. She claims to be completely unaware of any sign that Toby was about to go off the deep end. I was holding back talking to her until we learn more about how the EBT card was being used. I want a little more background, in case the tone of the interview shifts to an interrogation."

Tommy Lee believed in being prepared and it was always good to have the subject of an interview think you don't know as much as you do.

"Fletcher tells me Rufus Taylor's son is in town," I said. "They'll have a service on Wednesday."

"Yes. He's coming to the department tomorrow morning at nine."

"Then I'll be there. Enjoy your burgers."

He laughed. "I'll try. Although Patsy's limiting me to a single beer. One more thing. Have you talked to Archie?"

My stomach tightened at the thought that Archie could have already created some problem with our plan. "No. Is something wrong?"

"You could say that. As far as I know, he hasn't done anything stupid in the last twenty-four hours. Are you keeping close tabs on him?"

"No."

"Maybe you should check in with him. Let him know when Sonny and his mother are coming."

"All right. I'll be glad when he's out of the mix."

"Well, I'm counting on you to keep him corralled until then."

I knew he wasn't joking. "Thanks. You really know how to ruin a holiday."

I phoned Archie's cell. It rang about five times before he picked up.

"Hi, Barry," he whispered. "I'm with some clients. Can I call you back?"

"No need. Just wanted you to know Sonny will be coming to the funeral home in the morning."

"Okay. I'll keep to the office." His voice seemed strained.

"Everything okay?" I asked.

"Yes. We'll talk later." He hung up.

The night of Labor Day and Archie's with clients, not friends? I wondered what could be so urgent.

On Tuesday morning, Roger Taylor arrived at the Sheriff's Department twenty minutes early. Tommy Lee and I were meeting in his office and had the crime scene photos of Roger's murdered father spread across the desk.

Tommy Lee instructed his administrative assistant, Marge, to escort Mr. Taylor to one of the interview rooms, bring him a cup of coffee, and assure him that Tommy Lee and I would join him in a few minutes.

Tommy Lee gathered up the photos. "So, you can see there's nothing out of the ordinary in these pictures. No items knocked askew, no jimmying of the cash register. Rufus just seems to have fallen backwards behind the counter from the impact of the slugs, although a twenty-two wouldn't pack the wallop of a larger caliber."

"Do you know when the last purchase was rung up on the register?"

"Ten twenty-five. About twenty minutes before the boys found the body."

"And Toby McKay was shot around ten," I said. "So someone could have learned of Toby's shooting and had approximately forty-five minutes to get to the convenience store."

"That's assuming there's a connection between the two deaths."

"I thought the EBT card was that connection."

"As an item, it connects to Toby, but what's its relationship to Rufus? That's what I mean by connection. And how do the card and the murder connect? That's what I hope we can learn or at least uncover from Roger Taylor." He gestured toward the door. "Go ahead. Take the lead."

Roger Taylor was sipping coffee when we entered the room and introduced ourselves. As a break from procedure, Tommy Lee sat at the table beside him and I took the chair opposite.

Taylor had a long face with pocked acne scars, sallow skin, and thin, straw-colored hair. If he was thirty, it was a hard thirty.

"Thank you for coming in," I said.

Before I could utter another syllable, he said, "I was working Saturday morning. You can check with my boss man. Stokes Equipment Rental. I took a backhoe to a jobsite near the Virginia line." His voice carried a smoker's rasp.

"Okay. But you aren't a suspect, sir."

He laughed. "Like hell, I ain't. I know you boys always go for the family first. And my father and I weren't always on the best of terms. Not since my mama split from him."

"How long ago was that?"

"About fifteen years. When I was fifteen. That's how I wound up in Winston. Her people were from there."

"When was the last time you saw your father?" I asked.

"July Fourth. Brought my girlfriend up and we stayed at the Motel 6. She went shopping and I ran by the store to say hello. We'd gotten along a little better since I've been out on my own. He gave me a six-pack of Colt 45."

"Do you know why anyone would want to kill him?"

"Robbery, I guess. Ain't that what happened?"

"We don't believe so. Nothing was taken."

Roger Taylor looked stunned. "Somebody just shot him?"

"No," I said. "Somebody shot him for a reason. So, let me repeat the question. Who would want to kill your father?"

"I don't know. He kept to himself. The store was earning enough to live on. His partner was happy."

I looked at Tommy Lee. He arched an eyebrow.

"Partner?" I asked.

"Yes. He had a partner. He told me about a year ago someone was interested in buying in."

"Who was the partner?"

"He didn't say. Just that he'd now get his stock for a lower cost. Like the partner had better contacts or could buy in bigger volume."

"Did this partner work at the store?"

Roger Taylor shook his head. "Nah. He was behind the scenes."

"What's going to happen to the store now?" I asked.

"What do you mean?"

"Did your father have a will? Is his share of the store going to the partner for some agreed price?"

Taylor rubbed his palm across his thin lips. I could see the question threw him.

"I hadn't thought that far. Everything should come to me, shouldn't it? Then I'll work out some kind of deal because I ain't coming back here to spend my days sitting behind the counter of Taylor's Short Stop. And I sure as hell ain't gonna sit there and get shot."

I nodded to Tommy Lee to take the lead.

"No, we wouldn't want that to happen," Tommy Lee insisted. "Maybe you should figure out who's your father's lawyer. Did he have one for the divorce?"

Taylor shrugged. "I guess so. My mother would know. Would he be the one to help me?"

"I'd start there," Tommy Lee advised. "He might have drawn up a will for your father. Or the business arrangement for the business partnership. We'd like to know the name of the partner so we can talk to him. Maybe they had a common enemy."

"Okay. I'll try to find out today. I've got to get this wrapped up pretty quickly and get back to my job."

Tommy Lee patted Roger Taylor's shoulder. "We'll help any way we can. Maybe we can track down some of that information for you."

"Thanks."

Tommy Lee stood and asked another question before Taylor could rise.

"Did your father ever mention how much business he got through food stamps?"

"Food stamps?"

"Yeah, although he might have called them EBTs or Electronic Benefit Transfer cards."

"No. He just said more people were coming into the store. Do you think a poor person killed him? Took food rather than cash?"

"Not at all," Tommy Lee said. "It's just like with credit card receipts, we'd have an idea of who was shopping at the store. Somebody might have seen something. Poor people have eyes. There's no reason to think they'd have it in for your father."

Taylor nodded. "He'd let people run up a bill. That's why he and my mother often argued over money. That and he was bad to drink. You know what I mean?"

"We do," Tommy Lee said. "And he deserves justice. So, as you learn where things stand with his affairs, let us know. No piece of information is too trivial. Understand?"

Taylor stood and shook the sheriff's hand. "Yes, sir. Thank you." He turned to me. "You own the funeral home, right? Will you also be handling my father's burial?"

"Fletcher will. The man you spoke with. I'm spending as much time on this investigation as I can."

He started to say something, but his eyes teared. He nodded and left the room.

"What do you think?" I asked Tommy Lee.

"I think we need the name of Rufus' partner. That's our lead."

Harold Carson's Auto Repair was one-tenth garage and nine-tenths junkyard. Old cars and pieces of cars lay strewn on a hillside behind a three-bay metal building. An invasion of kudzu had launched an assault from the upper edge of the field, its vines and broad green leaves swallowing up everything in its path.

The current workload of pickups, SUVs, and sedans sat on an apron of scraggy lawn between the blue gravel lot and coarse pasture grass. Two men were bent over a fender and under the hood of a black El Camino pickup with flame decals burning down the side. All we could see of the mechanics were their rear ends.

"The big butt on the left is Harold," Tommy Lee said, as he swung his patrol car in a wide arc across the lot.

"Why have I been spending all my time on facial recognition techniques?"

He parked and opened his door. "Come on, smart ass. You can show off your interviewing skills."

The two men had turned from the engine at the sound of crunching gravel. Harold stood a roly-poly five-six and his colleague must have been a lean six-five.

Harold wiped his hands on a greasy rag as he walked toward us. The second man remained by the pickup as if we were there to repossess it.

"Howdy, Sheriff. What brings you boys out here?" He shook our hands. "Car trouble?"

"No. We're looking for Sonny. Just a few routine questions after what happened Saturday."

Harold shook his neckless head slowly and somberly. "Terrible thing. Don't know what got ahold of poor Toby's thinking. I heard he was distraught about his crop and the pesticide poisoning, but to do what he did. Guess you never know what will cause a man to break."

"Who told you he was distraught?" Tommy Lee asked.

"Sonny was worried. He asked me for some advance on his wages to help the family out. Said his dad had some unexpected bills."

"Did you give him the money?"

Harold snorted and his belly jiggled behind his bib overhauls. "Look at this place. I ain't exactly rolling in cash. To fix cars these days you need a damn computer. Don't know how much longer I can keep it together myself. It's just down to Charlie," he jerked his head toward the man by the truck, "Sonny, and me. But to answer your question, Sonny ain't here. I gave him a couple days off to take care of family business."

Harold didn't mention Sonny's stint over the weekend in our jail. It was a good bet the man hadn't been following Archie's Facebook page.

"You might check on him at home," Harold suggested.

"We were up there," I said, letting him think it was today. "We saw motorcycle parts out on the drive but not Sonny."

Harold's eyes went wide. "His Triumph Rocket?"

"Yes."

The mechanic turned to the other man. "Charlie, you ever known Sonny to leave parts to his bike outside?"

"Nah. Not Sonny. If he could marry that thing, he would."

The statement reinforced Sonny's claim that he'd left with his mother as soon as she brought him the news of his father's death.

I looked at one and then the other. "And neither of you know if Sonny was able to get money to help his father?"

"Nah. I would've helped him if I could," Harold said. "But times is tough all over."

I studied the renovated El Camino. "Looks like you got one good client, unless you've fixed that up on spec."

Again, Harold shook his head. "Would you believe that job's for Rufus Taylor? Fixing it up for his son as a surprise."

"Are you now stuck for a lot of money?"

"Nope. Rufus had been wanting to restore it for about five years, and finally saved up the cash money to do it. We were just doing some fine-tuning. All he owed was a few bucks for points and plugs. Hell, might just give the boy the damn thing. Kind of sad to have it on the lot now. If you see him, tell the boy to come pick it up as soon as he can. I ain't superstitious or nothing, but first Toby and then Rufus. They say troubles come in threes."

"When did Rufus give you the go ahead?" I asked.

"About three months ago. He said business was picking up at the store." Harold smiled. "Everybody knows there's no better place to put your money than a truck."

I doubted there were many financial advisors who adhered to that investment philosophy, but I wasn't about to argue with a man armed with wrenches. "I'll remember that. Thanks."

As we pulled out of the lot, Tommy Lee said, "That came with a bonus. The info on Rufus Taylor's prosperity."

"Yes. We got validation of Sonny's alibi and Roger Taylor's comments that his father's business was helped by a new partner. Where to now?"

"Let's go back to the office. I want to see if we've received a ballistics report and make sure the request for EBT card transactions is being expedited."

We'd driven about a mile when my cell phone buzzed. The call was from Fletcher.

"Barry. You haven't heard anything from Sonny McKay, have you?"

"No. I thought he had a meeting with you at ten."

"He did. Mrs. McKay is here with her sister and she was expecting to meet Sonny. He was going to take her home after our consultation. She's been calling his cell but he doesn't answer."

I felt my stomach knot and checked the phone for the time. Ten forty-five. "I'm with Tommy Lee. Maybe he knows something. I'll call you right back."

"What's up?" the sheriff asked.

"Sonny didn't show at the funeral home. He was supposed to meet his mother there."

Tommy Lee's face darkened. "Let's stay off the two-way. You got Reece's number on your phone? He's supposed to be watching Sonny's trailer."

"Yes." I scrolled to the number. Reece answered immediately. "Is this Barry?"

"Yes. Where are you?"

"On a side road where I can watch Sonny's driveway. He hasn't left yet."

I relayed the info to Tommy Lee and put the phone on speaker.

"Go to the trailer and check on him," Tommy Lee ordered. "Don't say you've been watching him, but that his mother had called us looking for him."

"Got it. Then what?"

"If he's okay, ask him to call his mom and then you return to your surveillance position. Give me a report back by Barry's phone as soon as you can."

The sheriff turned onto a secondary road that took us away from town and in the direction of Sonny's trailer. "I got a bad feeling," was all he said.

Less than ten minutes later, my cell rang. I connected to Reece, leaving the phone on speaker.

"Barry?" The tremor in his voice was audible.

"We're here."

"He's dead, Barry. Dead in his bed. Looks like someone shot him in the head while he slept. His head...his head's still on the pillow."

Chapter Nine

Sheriff Tommy Lee Wadkins' expression couldn't have been harder than if his face were chiseled in granite. His lone eye swept the sparse furnishings of Sonny McKay's bedroom in the rear of the single-wide trailer. The space contained a beat-up dresser, a TV tray converted to a nightstand, and a bed with Sonny's body lying prone atop wrinkled sheets.

His head rested on the pillow and faced the far wall. He wore a dingy white tee-shirt and light blue boxers. Aside from the entry wound in his temple, he could have been asleep. What little blood had flowed had been mostly absorbed by the pillow. I guessed he'd died instantly.

"Any sign of a gun?" the sheriff asked.

"No," Reece Hutchins said. "And I've never heard of anyone shooting themselves while lying belly-down."

"Then I'm going to request a mobile crime lab from Buncombe County. I want every bit of DNA, even if it's from a damn cockroach." Tommy Lee shook his head in disgust. "And I want a toxicology workup on his blood."

I understood he reacted to more than just the murder scene. His two-shift surveillance of Sonny had left the man exposed overnight, and he now second-guessed how seriously he should have taken Sonny's fears.

"Nothing more we can do here till the forensics team arrives." He signaled us to leave.

We passed a small eating area adjacent to the kitchen. An empty bottle of Rebel Yell whiskey sat on the table. A plastic drinking glass lay overturned beside it.

"Was the trailer door open?" I asked Reece.

"Well, the door was closed but it wasn't locked. Looks like someone popped it with a screwdriver."

The three of us stepped outside and examined the doorframe where something had been wedged to bend the metal enough to pry free the short bolt. Fresh scratches showed the damage was recent.

"What time did you get in position?" Tommy Lee asked Reece.

"Six o'clock. Wakefield left at midnight."

"So, a six-hour window. You didn't see any cars come out after you arrived?"

"No," Reece insisted. "And I stayed awake. There's an empty coffee thermos in the car to prove it."

"There's certainly no sign Sonny put up a fight," I said. "If the blood work confirms it, then Sonny must have been in a near stupor, flopped on his bed, and didn't hear his killer break in."

"How would they know Sonny wasn't standing guard?" Reece asked. "Sonny could have been ready to shoot them at first entry."

"Good question." I looked to Tommy Lee for his ideas.

"They could have known his habits," the sheriff said. "They were desperate enough to get to him that they took a chance. They might have been watching the house and saw Wakefield leave."

"It's possible," I said. "But easier to drop him with a rifle shot when he came out of the trailer this morning."

"What's your idea?" Tommy Lee asked. "Because my guess is the M.E. is going to put the murder shortly after midnight, based on body temp. Of course that's just my opinion, based on a skin touch."

"I'm not saying they didn't know his habits or that they weren't desperate to silence him. But, if Sonny knew them or they clearly appeared to pose no threat, then they could have approached the trailer with confidence. But Sonny was passed out and unable to open the door. When they got no response, they improvised."

"And just happened to bring a screwdriver," Reece said skeptically.

I shrugged. "I'm just floating ideas."

Tommy Lee looked at Sonny's pickup truck. Reece and I followed him over to the bed. A tool chest stood open against the back of the cab.

"Seem odd to you a mechanic would leave his tools exposed all night?" Tommy Lee asked.

"Want me to print them?" Reece asked.

"Yes. Though if whatever they used to force the door is in the tool kit, we'll know it because it'll be the only one wiped clean of fingerprints. Reece, I want you to take charge of the scene."

Reece's chest expanded, threatening to launch a few buttons into the air. "Yes, sir."

Tommy Lee looked back at the trailer. "So, I'll call in the mobile lab, M.E., and cover Ferguson and the SBI, although I guarantee they'll want to stay clear till we've got a parade lined up tying this murder to the commissioner's shooting. Then they'll jump in front to lead it. If they do come here, tell them everything has to run through me."

"You got it," Reece said.

When we were in the patrol car, Tommy Lee pulled out his cell. "I still want to keep this off the scanners." He called Carol, the dispatcher, and ran down the checklist of everything he wanted at Sonny's trailer. He also asked her to have his assistant Marge prepare a request for a search warrant for Rufus Taylor's house.

When he'd finished, I asked, "Where are we going?"

Instead of answering, he gave me an order. "Find out if Mrs. McKay is still with Fletcher. If so, tell him to keep her there till we arrive."

"Are you going to interview her?"

He gave me a sharp look. "I'm going to tell her that her son's been murdered. Then I'm going to do what I should have done right after Toby died—press her for answers, answers that might have saved her son's life if I hadn't been giving her grieving room. That mistake's on me, and I won't make it again."

"And Rufus Taylor's search warrant?"

"I want it in my hip pocket in case Rufus' son turns out not to be as cooperative as he appeared. We'll see him after Mrs. McKay."

I caught Fletcher just as he was preparing to walk Mrs. McKay and her sister to their car. Tommy Lee turned on the flashers and siren and we sped back to town.

Fletcher met us in the kitchen. "I've got Mrs. McKay and her sister in the parlor," he whispered. "They're confused as to why they have to see you, and I couldn't give them much of an explanation."

"Sonny McKay's been murdered," Tommy Lee said. "I have to break the news. Then Barry and I need to ask Mrs. McKay a few questions. I'd like to do that without involving her sister."

Fletcher's face paled. "Murdered? Where? When?"

I ignored his questions. "Is my mother here?"

"She's upstairs."

"Tell her what's happened and ask her to come down. She'll brew fresh coffee and can talk to the sister in the kitchen."

"What do you want me to do?"

"Whatever my mother asks you. Otherwise, hang close to the kitchen and be on standby."

"Let's do this," Tommy Lee said. "We'll give Mrs. McKay a few minutes with her sister before we split them up."

Fletcher went up the back stairs and I led Tommy Lee to the front parlor. Mrs. McKay sat on the sofa and her sister was on the edge of the wingback chair beside her. Mrs. McKay wore a shapeless black dress. Her sister's dress was rust brown and obviously more expensive.

Mrs. McKay rose, her face shifting to a scowl when she saw

Tommy Lee enter behind me. "What's so important? Don't you know we've got things to do?"

I stepped aside and let Tommy Lee take the lead.

"Mrs. McKay," he said softly, "please sit down. I'm afraid I've got bad news."

The woman's indignation evaporated and she looked at her sister. The other woman took her by the forearm and guided her to her seat.

Mrs. McKay started shaking her head back and forth. "I don't want to hear it. I don't want to hear it."

Tommy Lee let her continue this mantra until she stopped and looked up at us with frightened eyes.

Rather than tower over her, Tommy Lee crouched in front of her. "I'm very sorry to tell you that your son has been shot and killed. We found him in his bed and the door of his trailer had been forced open."

Her thin shoulders hunched, and then shook with silent sobs. Her sister moved from the chair and joined her on the sofa. Mrs. McKay turned her tear-streaked face away from all of us.

"I told him no good would come of it. I told him, but he wouldn't listen."

"You told who?" Tommy Lee gently prodded.

She turned back to the sheriff. "Did he suffer? Did they make him suffer?"

"No, ma'am. As best I can tell, he died in his sleep."

She leaned forward. "I've got to see him. I've got to see my boy."

She attempted to rise, but the sheriff was too close.

"You will," Tommy Lee said, "but right now we're trying to find his murderer. Sonny's trailer is a crime scene and we're required to perform an autopsy. Mrs. McKay, I'm being very honest with you. I know something is wrong in my county. Three men have died, two of them your loved ones. I also know Sonny was frightened of someone. He wouldn't talk to me, but he did share information with a fellow prisoner the night he was in our jail and he promised to provide more. And if they came after Sonny for what he knew, they may come after you."

"Sonny wasn't to blame," she whispered. "It was all Toby's idea."

Tommy Lee looked at Mrs. McKay's sister. "Mrs. Overton?"

"Yes?"

"I need you to wait in the kitchen with Barry's partner. It's important that I have a talk with your sister, and some of the information might need to remain confidential."

"Does she need a lawyer?"

"Not if she wants to move this whole process along so we can release Sonny to the funeral home as soon as possible."

"You go, Nelda," Mrs. McKay said. "I'll be all right."

I stepped over to help Nelda Overton from the sofa. The woman reached in her small clutch purse and handed her sister a lace handkerchief. "Take as long as you need, Pauline. Today, my time is your time."

I led the woman back to the kitchen where both Mom and Fletcher waited with a fresh pot of coffee. When I returned to the parlor, Tommy Lee sat on the sofa beside Pauline McKay. She dabbed at her eyes with the handkerchief, but seemed to be more composed.

Tommy Lee gave me a nod indicating I should take the rocking chair a little farther from the sofa than the nearer chairs. Evidently, he didn't want Mrs. McKay to feel hemmed in. She gave me a quick glance and then focused on the sheriff.

"I don't know who they are," she softly said. "I swear I'd tell you. I want them to pay."

Tommy Lee studied the woman for a few seconds. I didn't break the silence, knowing my role for the moment was to listen.

"I'm not saying you know who they are," Tommy Lee said. "However, I know you knew Rufus Taylor and I believe you know why he had your husband's EBT card."

Pauline McKay took a deep breath and her frail body trembled with an involuntary shiver. "Rufus demanded it. He didn't want us taking it to the other stores."

"Why would you do what he demands?"

"We've been hard up for cash money, Sheriff. That's no secret since we lost our crop last year. It hurt Toby's pride to have to borrow money, and he couldn't get none from any banks. My husband had been an apple grower all his life. I tended the vegetable garden and the preserving and canning. We bothered no one and no one bothered us. Then when the crop failed, we had bills to pay. Toby started buying stuff we needed through Rufus on credit."

"Credit's different than cash in hand," Tommy Lee said. "When did the arrangement change?"

Pauline McKay's eyes sharpened as she realized the sheriff was putting pieces together before she presented them. "When Rufus said he couldn't give any more credit without a plan to pay it back, Toby said he'd be good for every nickel when this year's crop came in. He already had the old pesticide and he'd only need some money to pay the migrants when picking season came. Then we had a surprise inspection by one of the wholesale buyers and they told the state Toby'd used the stuff with lead in it. We didn't think it would hurt nobody."

Tommy Lee nodded. "So, Rufus Taylor offered you a way out of your financial jam?"

The handkerchief went back to her eyes and she sniffled. "Rufus told Toby we could apply for food stamps. He had friends who would take care of the rest. Otherwise, his only choice was to put a lien on our land. Take us to court and force us to sell off property and equipment to pay our debts."

"Sounds like Toby's anger would have been toward Rufus and not Commissioner James."

Pauline tensed. She looked over at me. "Toby weren't scared of Commissioner James."

I didn't understand. "He was scared of Rufus Taylor?"

She shook her head. "Rufus weren't nothing but a yes man. He admitted as much to Toby. The EBT was a cash machine. There were convenience stores we were supposed to use. Like Rufus, they'd run up charges each month for food we didn't get and food they didn't sell. Couple a hundred dollars' worth. Rufus said it was reducing our debt, a debt that had been passed along to the people in cahoots with him."

Suddenly, Sonny's emphasis on the word "from" in his denial that his father was getting money from Rufus made sense. His father was getting money *through* Rufus.

Pauline McKay continued. "Rufus said someday, when we were paid up, they'd split the cash with us. Rufus told my husband he'd better go along because the people behind him wouldn't take no for an answer. Otherwise they'd come after him. Rufus said they'd hurt people. Even me. Even Sonny."

She stopped. The room fell silent, each of us thinking about how the warning had come to pass.

"That doesn't explain why Rufus had Toby's card," Tommy Lee said.

"Because a month ago Rufus decided he would be the one to control how and where the card was used. I guess he wanted more money running through his store. Maybe he was taking something off the top."

"All for a couple hundred dollars a month? That's seems like a small amount of money to be threatening people."

"We weren't the only ones falling on hard times. There's a lot of folks on food stamps who have money problems. You get ten families, and you might have two or three thousand dollars a month. You times that across other stores and other mountain counties, then what kind of money are you talking about, Sheriff?"

"Maybe enough to kill a man."

"Enough to kill my Sonny." She gave a humorless laugh.

"Rufus told Toby the debt would be paid off faster if Sonny got his own EBT card. But Sonny made too much money at the auto repair shop. Rufus said Sonny should ask to be paid for some of his hours in unreported cash so he could qualify. It would also save Harold Carson from paying as much for worker's comp and Social Security. When Rufus suggested it, Sonny said he weren't no welfare cheat. That really hurt Toby. Cut me, too, 'cause he was so much as calling us welfare cheats."

"When did you have this conversation?" Tommy Lee asked.

"Two, maybe three weeks ago. Then it come up again Saturday morning."

Tommy Lee looked at me. Sonny McKay had made no mention of it during any of our interviews.

"That's when he came over for pancakes?" Tommy Lee asked.

"Yes. I mentioned the parade and that the agriculture commissioner was in it. Sonny said the commissioner's the one who should be on food stamps and not us. Sonny said it was a disgrace. That's when Toby shoved the table against Sonny's chest, got up, and yelled, 'goddammit, I'm not taking any more shit off you. You'll see I ain't afraid for me. Not for me. You'll see.'"

"What did you think he meant at the time?" Tommy Lee asked.

Pauline McKay wiped the handkerchief across her wrinkled cheek. "That he was going to confront Rufus. But I was wrong. He went for the commissioner. I guess he wasn't afraid there'd be any danger to me or Sonny. But he was wrong."

Tommy Lee shifted on the sofa and for the first time flipped open his notepad. "Did Rufus ever tell Toby the names of the people he was working with?"

"If so, he didn't tell me."

"Could Toby have told Sonny?"

"I don't know. I think he tried to explain the bind we were in and that Rufus was only a small part of the problem."

"So, Sonny understood that there were people who posed a threat to you and your husband?"

"Probably. Toby wanted him to understand why we'd been forced into doing what we'd done."

Tommy Lee looked at me. Her statement fit with the fear Sonny had exhibited. And Sonny must have had additional information his mother didn't know, if he'd been willing to talk to Archie, aka Brad Pitt, about getting protection. The murder of Rufus Taylor would have confirmed for Sonny what his father had said about dangerous people. Maybe his drunken efforts to see Commissioner of Agriculture Graham James had been an attempt to tell James what Sonny later thought better of after he sobered up. Given the events, I understood how Archie's proposal for protection sounded enticing. Had Sonny's information died with him, or had he prepared some document for when Archie came to see him? Sonny's trailer deserved another search.

"Mrs. McKay," I said, "we appreciate your help at this most difficult time. Your husband and your son both deserve justice for what happened to them. We believe Sonny wanted to share information that he either got from his father or from Rufus. Do you know if Sonny had a spot where he put special papers or documents? Sort of a hiding place?"

"What kind of papers?"

"Oh, maybe a car title, warranty documents, or any special keepsakes?"

"No. The trailer's in Toby's name. Sonny's got the truck, so there's a title to that somewhere. Of course, his Triumph motor-cycle. There'd be a title and registration for it as well. But I have no idea where they'd be."

"If you think of something, no matter how trivial, please let us know." I didn't have any other questions.

Tommy Lee closed his notepad without having scribbled so much as a letter. "Mrs. McKay, you've been staying with your sister, right?"

"That's right. But I'm fixing to go home today."

"I advise against that, ma'am. The person or the people who

did this to your son are running scared. Whether Sonny knew anything or not, they didn't take any chances. They very well could believe you pose a threat to them. Do you think it's possible to stay with your sister a few days longer?"

"But she lives over in Canton. She can't be carrying me back and forth. Somebody's got to feed the chickens and check on the house."

"We'll do that," Tommy Lee assured her. "It's clear to me your husband was worried about your safety. He took a desperate and foolish action, but despite his mental state at the time, he knew Rufus was involved with ruthless people. If he were here, what would he want you to do?"

Pauline sniffled and took a hard swallow. "Go with Nelda. But I've got a funeral..." she faltered a second..."two funerals to tend to." She turned to me. "Both my men. Gone in a weekend. Leaving me with two funerals." She kneaded the lace handkerchief into a ball. "I know this sounds bad, but is there a discount?"

Chapter Ten

Tommy Lee and I stood in the funeral home's parking lot and watched Pauline McKay and her sister leave for Canton. The sheriff had promised that a deputy would check her house, feed the chickens daily, and if she needed to return for clothes or personal items before the funerals, he would provide an armed escort. Given the horrific circumstances that had turned her life upside down, Fletcher and I agreed to delay any service for the father and son until the following week.

When the car had disappeared down Main Street, Tommy Lee asked, "What do you think?"

"I think she told us what she knows. Toby got caught up in some criminal enterprise that he couldn't control. The loss of this year's crop was only going to push him deeper into their clutches. He was afraid to take them on and lashed out at Commissioner James."

"My hound dog could have come to that conclusion, Sherlock. But why was Toby afraid? Because Rufus told him his debt had been taken over by some bad people? Like a resold mortgage?"

"Well, something must have spooked him. And then there's Rufus taking possession of Toby's EBT card. Was that Rufus' initiative or the people behind him?" I thought about the few times I'd crossed paths with the store owner. "Frankly, I don't think Rufus had the brains to organize the kind of operation Pauline McKay described."

"And he might not have had the brains to leave well enough alone."

"You mean if he was skimming?"

"Or too loose with his new-found income. The restoration of the El Camino advertised that Rufus had suddenly been flush to pay for the work in cash."

"Do you think Rufus pushing for Sonny to get an EBT card was part of a plan to branch out on his own?"

Tommy Lee scowled at me. "Now how am I supposed to know that? The man's dead and not talking." He gestured to the funeral home. "How many dead people in there have told you their plans?"

"It's just that I'm continually amazed at your deductive abilities."

The sheriff laughed. "Sorry. I forget how impressive I can be to those less skilled. So, maybe Rufus was skimming or setting up his own thing. But I don't believe that's the motive for his murder. It had to be tied to Toby's actions at the parade. Otherwise, it's an incredible coincidence." Tommy Lee started for his patrol car. "Let's get the search warrant for Rufus' house. Maybe we'll find he has something to say, after all."

It was a little after two in the afternoon when we turned into Rufus Taylor's driveway. The house appeared to have been a small cottage that over the years had been built out haphazardly with additional rooms. The structure held the architectural integrity of a preschooler's Lego creation.

A van with a Winston-Salem Motors bumper decal indicated Roger Taylor was here. Tommy Lee gave a sharp rap on a warped screen door. Its torn mesh allowed easy entrance for any insect smaller than a robin. The pine inner door displayed a network of knots and cracks rivaling the most intricate spider web. Tommy Lee opened the screen door and knocked harder on the wooden one.

"I ain't in there." The voice preceded Roger Taylor's appearance around the far corner of the house. He wore a stretched tee-shirt with the faded words "Coon Dog Day 2017" stamped across the chest. The event occurred annually in nearby Saluda. His brown cotton twill work pants were fastened at the waist by a large safety pin and the extra leg length was rolled up to his ankles. The wardrobe told me Roger had run through whatever he might have quickly packed in Winston-Salem and now was making do with what he could wear of his father's thinner, taller sizes.

He halted, surprise squelching his irritation. "Sheriff, I was just about to call you."

"About what?"

"My dad had an old Camino pickup out in the barn. Somebody's stolen it."

Tommy Lee let tired springs slam the screen door shut and walked closer to Roger. "It's at Carson's Auto Repair. Your father was fixing it up for you." The sheriff looked at me for corroboration.

"That's right. We saw it this morning. Harold's done a nice job."

Roger rubbed a hand across his mouth, trying and failing to conceal the tremor in his lips. "Is that why you're here?"

"Yes," Tommy Lee said. "It's all paid for. Harold said just settle up for new plugs and points. But we're also here to look through the house and property for any clues as to who might have killed your father."

Roger Taylor eyed us skeptically. "I've started going through his things. Nothing strange so far. I'll let you know if something turns up."

"This is a police matter," Tommy Lee said. "We need to conduct a search in a methodical way. We have a warrant, but I'd like to have your cooperation. That might serve you well later on."

"What do you mean?" Roger asked.

"If we find your father was engaged in some questionable activities, it will be clear to all that you knew nothing about them."

Roger Taylor looked away, clearly weighing the sheriff's words. Then he turned to face us. "I didn't know anything about the Camino, right? You believe that was news to me, don't you?"

"It appeared so," Tommy Lee agreed.

"And I know nothing about how my father was running his business. So, you can come in and look for whatever you want."

We followed Roger into the front room. On the left, mismatched chairs and a threadbare sofa were set in a semi-circle around a stone fireplace. On the right stood an oval table that at one time might have been the family dining area. Now the surface was covered in boxes of assorted crackers and cookies that Rufus must have brought from his store.

"Where do you want to start?" Roger asked.

"Your father's bedroom," Tommy Lee said.

The interior layout of the house reflected the mishmash construction visible on the outside. We walked through an old kitchen with cracked linoleum flooring and a stained porcelain sink. The refrigerator looked like it was only one generation removed from an icebox used by my great grandparents. The first room beyond the kitchen was a den with cheap paneling and a single overstuffed recliner facing a wide-screen TV. I suspected the room might originally have been a bedroom before the other rooms were added.

A bathroom stood to the right and on the left a door led to a bedroom. But Roger walked through that room to a second one beyond it. The odd floor plan required a pathway that meant walking through one bedroom to get to another. Both rooms had unmade beds, and I assumed Roger was sleeping in the first one rather than take over his father's.

"This is it," Roger said.

Tommy Lee stepped past him. "Fine. Wait in the doorway. You can watch but don't interfere."

Roger retreated to the first bedroom. Tommy Lee slipped on latex gloves and I did the same.

"Check the closet," Tommy Lee said. "I'll take the dresser drawers."

I pulled a string connected to a bare bulb light fixture in the closet's ceiling and started sorting through clothes and personal items. The articles consisted of two cheap suits, one lightweight tan for summer and a charcoal gray for winter, a few dress shirts with fraying collars, and assorted jeans and sweatshirts.

I turned all the pockets inside out but found nothing. Four pairs of shoes lay on the closet floor: one black dress pair with worn heels, one pair of hiking boots, a pair of ancient Reeboks, and a pair of green Wellingtons. I reached into the toe of each shoe and discovered with disgust where Rufus kept his dirty socks.

Ball caps and rain hats filled a few shelves. I lifted each and found nothing underneath. The top shelf was wider, extending out over the rod holding the hanging garments. I stepped back to get a better angle on what might be up there. Rufus' height would have made the shelf easily accessible. The corner of a gray metal box was just visible. I stood on tiptoes but the box was out of reach.

I turned and saw Tommy Lee on his hands and knees, peering under the double bed. "You're taller than me. See if you can reach whatever's on the upper shelf."

As he got to his feet, the sheriff's knees cracked like dry branches. I stepped aside and glanced back at Roger. He seemed curious as to what might be stored on the shelf. Tommy Lee's fingers crested the top edge of the box, enabling him to slide it toward him until it dropped into his other hand.

He set it on the foot of the unmade bed. "Have you seen this before?" he asked Roger.

"Yeah. Dad used to collect pennies in it. I'd forgotten about it."

The box looked like something a small business would use for petty cash. It was about a foot long and eight inches wide. There was a keyed latch on the side and a small wire handle attached to the top.

Tommy lifted it a few inches. "Too light to hold many pennies now."

He set it on the mattress and pushed the latch's button. The top opened on squeaky hinges.

"He never kept it locked," Roger said. "The key was lost years ago."

Tommy Lee pulled out a bound stack of twenty-dollar bills. Then he pulled a second and a third. "I'd say his pennies have increased in value."

Roger's mouth dropped open. "Jesus. Do you think he stashed that away from the store? You know, in case of a robbery?"

"Maybe," Tommy Lee said. "But my guess is we're looking at five or six thousand dollars. Pretty good cash register reserve."

Roger shook his head. "Am I going to have to sort this mess out? What bills need paying? What supplies need to be ordered? Where the hell is his partner? That's what I'd like to know."

"So would we," I said. "Have you found his lawyer yet?"

"I just got a name from my mother this morning. During the divorce, her lawyer dealt with Bert Graves, whoever the hell he is."

"We know him," Tommy Lee said. "Call his office this afternoon and tell him I advised you to see him as soon as possible."

Graves was a second-tier attorney who operated solo and was known for taking any case that walked through the door or rode by in an ambulance.

From the box, the sheriff lifted several pages that had been folded in half lengthwise. Some were from a newspaper; some appeared to be plain white paper. He spread them out flat. The longest newspaper article was from the *Charlotte Observer* and dated last October. The story was about fraud in the food stamp program and documented cases in Charlotte and the eastern part of the state where investigators from the Food and Nutrition Services and the SBI had cracked rings of convenience and small grocery stores who accepted EBT cards for the purchase of off-limits items like cigarettes and beer. The worst offenders simply rang up items that never left the store and split the cash paid from the benefit account with the cardholder. That scam had all the trappings of what Rufus Taylor and Toby McKay had been doing.

The white pages were Internet reprints of similar stories from news sources around the country. Big busts in Detroit, New York City, and Trenton. The scams ran into the millions of dollars and I began to understand we weren't dealing with some nickel-and-dime corner store operation.

A smaller article from the Asheville paper last April was the most disturbing. A fourth-grade girl in rural Buncombe County had gotten off the school bus to find the headless body of her cat stuffed in the family's mailbox. The bus driver was just pulling away when he heard the child screaming. He stopped the vehicle and ran to help her. Then he called the police. The girl's father, a Buddy Smith, owned a small grocery store. He said he'd caught some older boys shoplifting beer the night before. He didn't know them, but believed they might have targeted his family for revenge. Smith was quoted as saying, "There's some sick people out there." Rufus or someone had circled the one line in the news story identifying the store as "Wilmer's Convenience Corner."

"There weren't any shoplifters," I said.

Tommy Lee gathered up the papers. "No. And it wasn't revenge. It was a message."

Our search of the rest of the property turned up nothing. We watched Roger count the cash in the metal box, gave him a receipt for it and the news articles, and took them as potential evidence. Although we had no direct proof linking the money and the El Camino restoration to earnings from the food stamp fraud, the temporary confiscation gave us some control over Roger.

We instructed him not to say anything about what we had found. His role was to follow the legal path for settling his father's estate and discover this new partner in the process. In the grand scheme of the murder investigation, the money and a restored pickup weren't items we'd refuse to return if their connection to a crime remained murky. Our objective was to find who killed Rufus and Sonny, not convict a dead fraud suspect.

When Tommy Lee and I arrived at Sonny's trailer, activity was winding down. The mobile crime lab was packing up and the head technician reported they'd lifted prints from the front door, the tool chest, the whiskey bottle and glass, and numerous knobs and open surfaces where the UV light revealed good images.

As Tommy Lee had predicted, the M.E. estimated the time of death to be between midnight and three a.m. The body had been transported to the morgue for a full autopsy. There was no exit wound, and the working theory was a light-caliber bullet had ricocheted inside the skull and caused extensive brain damage.

The small trailer felt claustrophobic and Tommy Lee asked Reece to step outside away from the forensics team. We walked to a storage shed about ten yards away.

Tommy Lee leaned against a wall of rough plank boards. "I covered Ferguson with a quick phone call. Any state boys show up?"

"No," Reece said. "Only who you requested."

"Good. Did you find any papers?"

"A utility bill and a bank statement were in a kitchen drawer."

"Nothing else? He didn't have a place for his truck or motorcycle titles?"

"No."

I looked around the driveway filled with police vehicles lined up behind Sonny's truck like they'd cornered it after a high-speed chase. "Where's the motorcycle? He must have finished working on it yesterday."

Reece pointed to the shed. "It's in there."

A sliding wooden door on overhead rollers covered an area large enough for a small tractor to drive through. Reece grabbed a wrought-iron handle and pulled the door to the left. A shiny black motorcycle with chrome pipes stood just inside.

"His bike's probably worth more than everything else he owned combined," Reece said.

I remembered the comment by Charlie the mechanic that Sonny would marry his motorcycle if he could. I walked around the sleek machine. A black helmet dangled from a chin strap looped around the handlebar. A black leather pouch sat on the rear fender just behind the seat. Double buckles sealed the flap closed.

"Did you check the saddlebag?" I asked Reece.

He flushed. "No. There was a lot going on."

I made no comment as I slipped on a pair of latex gloves. The metal buckles could yield a clean set of prints.

I found a pair of dark goggles, leather riding gloves, and a small weatherproof packet closed by a Velcro strip. Inside was the North Carolina Department of Motor Vehicles registration and the bike's title. There was also a folded piece of white paper. Scrawled in a mix of cursive and print handwriting was a list of names. They were not the names of people; they were the names of more than twenty stores. Two names jumped out at me: Taylor's Short Stop and Wilmer's Convenience Corner.

Chapter Eleven

When we returned to the Sheriff's Department, Tommy Lee immediately went to his office to call Ferguson and push for any information the SBI might have. The discovery of the list of stores, coupled with Pauline McKay's statements and Sonny's desire for protection, fueled the theory that Rufus and Sonny had been murdered, either under the orders of, or directly by, a person or persons running a network of food stamp fraud.

I, however, set the investigation aside and phoned Mom at the hospital for an update on Uncle Wayne.

"How is he?"

"Restless. Today wasn't a good day."

"Well, you knew he'd be anxious to get out."

Mom sighed. "He's running a fever and they've started him on a heavy dose of antibiotics."

My throat went dry. "Is there an infection in his brain?"

"No. A spot of pneumonia in his right lung. In addition to the antibiotics, they're coming in every two hours with breathing exercises and nebulizers to try to knock it out."

I felt a little better. Developing pneumonia in the hospital wasn't that uncommon. There's probably more bacteria and germs per square foot there than in a shopping mall at Christmas. But at Uncle Wayne's age, pneumonia was nothing to fool with. Susan said she and her medical colleagues often refer to it as the "old folks' friend" because it will take them when they're suffering from a prolonged terminal disease, sparing them pain and misery.

"I'm leaving the department now," I said. "Can I bring you anything?"

"I'm fine. You don't need to come." She spoke the words without real conviction. I knew she was worried about her brother.

"No. I want to see him. Tommy Lee and I are finished for the day. I can swing by the funeral home and be there in thirty minutes."

A pause. Another sigh. "Well, if it's no trouble, it would be nice to have Wayne's electric razor. I'd like to keep him looking as neat as possible."

"All right. Anything you need?"

"My knitting. It's in the canvas bag in the bedroom. I might as well be productive."

I parked behind the funeral home a little after five and saw Fletcher's Miata in the same spot it had been earlier. I felt a twinge of guilt that so much of the business of the funeral business was falling on him while my "part-time" deputy duties consumed ten and twelve hours a day.

I found him and his fiancée, Cindy Todd, sitting at the kitchen table. Cindy worked as a loan officer at the Bank of America branch a few blocks away. The petite, attractive woman was not just the perfect mate for Fletcher but gave him credibility with the locals. She'd grown up in Gainesboro and her mother ran the Cardinal Café, whereas Fletcher was a native of Detroit. Grieving families don't want to entrust their loved ones to strangers. Cindy's engagement meant Fletcher was now accepted as part of the town's family.

Seeing them at the kitchen table presented a believable image of what could come to be in the years ahead after my mother and uncle were gone.

"You okay, Barry?" Fletcher stood.

I realized I'd been staring at them.

"Yes, sorry. Thinking about something from the case."

Cindy rose and lifted Mom's knitting bag. "Your mother called and said you were coming by." She bent over and picked up a second bag. Mom's overnight valise. "I put your uncle's razor in here, as well as some clothes she wanted for herself."

"Thank you."

She handed them to me. "Fletcher told me about Sonny McKay. That's just terrible. I feel so bad for Mrs. McKay."

"I hope that was all right," Fletcher said. "I figured the word was out."

His comment reminded me that the murder hadn't generated media coverage. Tommy Lee had kept it off the scanners, but no one was denying what had happened. I remembered Melissa Bigham of the *Vista* was taking the two weeks after Labor Day off. Otherwise, she probably would have beaten the crime lab to the scene. "It's fine. We're just keeping it low-key. We're starting with forensic evidence. Afraid I can't say any more."

"Sure. We understand," Fletcher said. "And don't worry about anything here. Freddy's clear to work the next two weeks and Cindy's offered to help any way she can."

After eliciting a promise from Fletcher to let me know if things got crazy, I headed for Mission Hospital in Asheville. I phoned Susan and she insisted on meeting me after stopping at our house to feed Democrat.

I'd just disconnected when the cell rang again. The caller ID flashed "Archie." Tommy Lee was supposed to let him know when to initiate contact with Sonny. Had he heard about the murder or was he calling to put the now-defunct plan into action? Either way, I wasn't ready to deal with him. I let the call go to voicemail.

Uncle Wayne was asleep. The color I'd seen in his cheeks the previous day was gone. Instead, his pallid face looked tense and troubled. His fingers twitched and kneaded the bed sheet. His breathing rasped. A clear tube supplied a boost of oxygen to each nostril.

Mom was reading a book in the visitor's recliner. She set it aside and stood. "Here, let me take those."

She grabbed the valise and knitting bag from my hands and placed them on either side of her chair, building a nest with her possessions.

"How is he?" I asked.

"Fever's down to one hundred one. They're hopeful that the antibiotics are taking effect."

"Have they discussed putting him back in intensive care?"

"No. The treatment would be the same, and as long as he's breathing on his own, they'll keep him here."

"How about you? Are you getting any rest?"

"Enough. Hilda's waiting on me hand and foot." She smiled. "I actually find it easier being here rather than constantly having Hilda attempt to do things for me."

"Maybe I should stay at Hilda's."

Mom laughed and gestured to the recliner. "Why don't you sit? I know you've had a long day. Have Mrs. McKay and Sonny decided how to handle Mr. McKay's funeral?"

I realized Mom had been out of touch with the day's events.

"I'm fine, Mom. Why don't you sit? I have some things to tell you."

She gave a worried glance at Uncle Wayne and did as I requested. I told her about the murder, avoiding details. The tears came as she grieved for Pauline McKay—a woman who in less than a week lost both her husband and her son.

"Fletcher's being very consoling," I said. "He's helping her reschedule the funerals, and Freddy's available to assist as much as needed. So, I don't want you to worry."

She nodded. "I'll try. But it's hard not to. I sit here all day, looking at my brother and realizing neither he nor I will ever be any younger than we are right now. Time is moving into twilight for both of us."

"Mom, I'm sure he's going to make a full recovery. And you, you've got more energy than I do."

"Barry, I look at your uncle and I see an old man who I worry about going up and down stairs. I see myself facing a future with few options and a loss of control. Wayne will need rehab, possibly at home. I'll do what I can, but what I won't do is become a burden to you and Susan. You made one sacrifice coming back to help with your father. I'm not going to let you make another." She bit her lower lip and looked out the window. The sun sat low on the mountain ridges.

"Mom, you're not a burden. We'll get through this together."

"Yes. But I believe your uncle and I can make it work better for everyone if we move out of the funeral home."

A part of my mind heard her statement with relief. This was the logical, rational action I hoped she would take. But, a larger part, spanning from childhood, recoiled at the prospect, surprising me with its intensity. I'd not known Mom in any other context. To me, she was as much a part of the funeral home as the creaking floorboards or Formica kitchen table. Fletcher and Cindy were suddenly aliens invading a space I wanted to preserve.

"I made a call," she said. "To Alderway. I asked if they had any rule against a brother and a sister sharing a two-bedroom unit. They don't."

Alderway, a retirement community about five miles out of town, offered a continuum of options from independent living to critical care and dementia services. Several of Mom's friends were already there. As those places go, Alderway was safe, secure, and beautifully maintained. But my first thought was the nickname bestowed upon the complex. Black humor dubbed it, "Clayton's Waiting Room." In other words, Alderway was the last stop before our funeral home.

Three sharp taps sounded from the doorway. An elderly man brandishing a gnarled rhododendron walking stick entered.

"Reverend Pace!" Mom rose from the chair, thrilled to see the visitor.

"I'm so sorry, Connie. I would have come sooner but I was

out of town for the weekend." He opened his arms and engulfed Mom with a hug.

Reverend Lester Pace was a vanishing breed. Nearly eighty, he still roamed the hills serving a few isolated Methodist congregations as a circuit-riding preacher, although instead of a horse, he rode a Plymouth Duster. His worn jacket and string tie could have come from the Salvation Army and were probably as old as his car.

He'd preached at funerals my grandfather had conducted. A larger-than-life figure, he held himself above no man, woman, or child. With his weathered, lined face, white hair and piercing eyes, Lester Pace was a paradox of gentleness and ferocity. What he elicited from those who crossed his path was respect, which often grew into reverence. Far from the fire and brimstone image a first glance might create, Pace was a rugged shepherd tending a flock that lived on the margins. His very presence seemed to charge the air around him.

"Barry." Pace shook my hand and the calluses on his palm were like sandpaper. "You've got a full plate, don't you, son?"

"Yes, sir. It's all very tragic."

He nodded gravely, and then looked at Uncle Wayne. "What's his status?"

Mom repeated the latest on the pneumonia and treatment.

Pace leaned on his walking stick. "Connie, your brother's the strongest man I know. To stop Toby McKay with no regard for his own safety shows heart and courage. Those two things, plus the medical team, and God's power will serve him well. So, you have to have faith that whatever happens will be for the best."

The old preacher eased by us and went to the bedside. He laid his hand on Uncle Wayne's arm just above the IV and bowed his head in prayer. Mom and I stood in silence. I believed if anyone had a direct line to the Almighty, it was Lester Pace.

I heard footsteps behind us. Susan entered, and then stopped just inside the doorway. She held a bag from Lenny's Sub Shop.

Supper. I'd insist Reverend Pace join us. If Jesus could feed five thousand with five loaves and two fishes, we could stretch three sandwiches to feed the four of us.

It was during Pace's blessing of the subs that I thought about the people he served. These were the victims of opioid abuse, the proud but poor who needed Medicaid and food stamps to survive. These were the people who would turn to the Rufus Taylors of the region for credit. They were the ones susceptible to schemes for turning a food benefit into cash. Pace knew these people and would keep their confidence. But he also might offer guidance as to who could be behind what appeared to be a criminal enterprise. He would protect his flock from the wolves. Now was neither the time nor the place to broach the subject, but I decided a conversation with the good pastor could be valuable.

We left the hospital at eight-thirty. Uncle Wayne had awakened for a few minutes and seen all of us. He managed to croak out two sentences: "I ain't dyin'. Go on about your business." Those few words seemed to sap his strength and he went back to sleep.

Susan and I left when a medical team came in for the breathing treatment. Reverend Pace said he would take Mom to her friend Hilda's as soon as they were finished and Mom had told her brother good night.

Susan and I had driven separate cars, and I rode home accompanied only by my thoughts. The case retreated to the back of my brain as the impact of Mom's proposal to leave the funeral home launched a barrage of questions I should have been preparing for. How much would Mom and Uncle Wayne need to buy into a place like Alderway? What was the monthly fee? How could she access her equity in the property of the funeral home without hurting the resources and cash flow of our business? What would Uncle Wayne's share be and how much could he contribute? That question brought me to the sobering corollary—would Uncle Wayne even be here?

The case, Uncle Wayne's illness, and Mom's future were all swept from my mind when I drove up the driveway to our house and saw Archie Donovan's Lexus parked by the front porch. Susan pulled in behind me and I knew she was asking the same question: what was Archie doing here at nine o'clock at night?

The interior courtesy lights of the Lexus came on as Archie opened the door. Susan had turned on the porch lights when she'd swung by to feed Democrat, and Archie stepped up into their glow and waved like we were visiting him.

"Hi, Susan," he said with a nervous smile. "Barry, I left you a voice message but you must not have checked it."

"We've been at the hospital."

"Oh, of course." He stepped back to clear a path to the front door. "How's Wayne doing?"

"Not so well. He's contracted pneumonia."

"Gosh. I'm really sorry to hear that. Can I do something? Take care of the dog?"

"We're all right. What do you need?"

He glanced at Susan as if she might be a foreign spy.

"Would you like a glass of wine?" she asked him. "Or I could put on a fresh pot of coffee."

"No, thanks. I just need to talk to Barry a few minutes."

"Very well. But if you change your mind, I'll be up a little while longer." She unlocked the door and left it open behind her.

I appreciated her subtle reminder that it was late.

"You want to come in?" I asked Archie.

He walked to the front door and closed it. "Barry," he whispered, his voice quivering. "I heard about Sonny. Shot dead, right in his own bed."

"Yes. I meant to call you."

Archie's eyes were wide, reflecting the yellow cast of the porch lights. "If someone silenced Sonny, do you think they could be coming after me?"

"I don't see how. Sonny hadn't told you anything yet. No one knew you were planning to talk to him."

Archie looked away. His silence spoke a message that made my stomach turn.

"Archie. No one knew, right?"

"I didn't tell anyone about the food stamp scam."

"Who did you tell what?"

"I swore to keep it a secret."

"Then why the hell are you on my doorstep?"

Archie took in a staggered breath. "Because I'm afraid. I'm caught between professional standards of client confidentiality and what is probably coincidence."

"And you don't want to bet your life on a coincidence."

He nodded.

"Let's start with what you said."

"Well, this client had read my *Letters from a Gainesboro Jail* blog and asked me if I'd seen the man whose father attacked Commissioner James. Like you suggested, I said that Sonny wasn't in the next cell. Just that our paths had crossed."

"And?"

"I said I'd told him I was a robber because I didn't want someone like him knowing my identity. I said Sonny had been impressed and wanted to talk to me after his release. He had information that he wouldn't tell anyone else."

I could hear Archie telling his client those words, making himself seem important, the James Bond of Gainesboro.

"This was last night," I said. "When I called you and you couldn't talk."

"Yes." Archie paced back and forth on the porch. "But these people wouldn't have known Sonny or Toby. They were just curious."

"So, you tell them you're going to have a secret conversation with Sonny, and then during the night, Sonny's murdered. Did you say you were doing this on your own?"

He grimaced. "I said it was undercover work."

"For who?"

"I just said for the big boys."

"Jesus, Archie. The FBI? Why would you fabricate such an outrageous claim?"

"I never said FBI."

"Well, I don't think 'big boys' conjures up the image of the Laurel County Sheriff's Department. What guarantee do you have that your client didn't tell someone else?"

"Because I learned a secret from them."

"Them?"

"Yes. And their secret is more important than what I told them. That's why they wouldn't tell. At least I thought they wouldn't tell."

"Until you learned about Sonny."

"Like I said, I'm caught between client confidentiality and what's probably a coincidence."

"No. You're caught between client confidentiality and an obstruction of justice charge."

"Barry, I promised them. They asked me if our meeting was a privileged conversation like with a lawyer or a priest."

"You'd better find a lawyer and a priest," I snapped. Then the phrase triggered a memory—Janet Sinclair asking me the same question in our funeral home six weeks before.

I got up in Archie's face. "The Sinclairs. Your clients are the Sinclairs."

He jumped back like I'd jabbed him with a cattle prod. "How did you know?"

"Never mind that. Tell me this secret or I'm arresting you right now."

He looked over his shoulder at the front door as if Susan might be eavesdropping behind it. "Their identities," he whispered. "They're not who they say they are. They're in the Witness Protection Program."

Chapter Twelve

As soon as Archie told me the Witness Protection story, I called Tommy Lee. He insisted we meet immediately, and so at ten that night, Archie, Tommy Lee, and I sat in the great room of my log home and analyzed the veracity and implications of this unexpected development. Susan had retired to our bedroom, understanding the confidentiality of our conversation and knowing I would have done the same if one of her patients had dropped by for an urgent medical consultation.

I brewed a pot of coffee and set out a bowl of pretzels, giving Democrat a warning glare not to touch them. The dog whined and retreated to his cushion in front of the hearth.

Tommy Lee got right to the point. "Tell me how your stint in jail even came up with the Sinclairs?"

Archie rubbed his sweaty palms on his thighs. "The charity fundraiser. The Sinclairs made the ten thousand-dollar donation."

"You said you were going to get a certified bank check today. Why did they need to see you last night?"

"Mr. Sinclair called me yesterday afternoon and asked to meet. He apologized for calling on Labor Day, but said his wife had made the donation without considering their cash flow needs. They had every intention of honoring the commitment to the kids and that perhaps I could help."

"How?"

"He wouldn't say over the phone. He said it would be better if we could meet in my office."

"Were they a long-standing client?" Tommy Lee asked.

"No. I'd never met them before. Mrs. Sinclair had called for an appointment a month or so ago. It didn't get on my schedule and so I missed it. I apologized, but she never rescheduled."

"The Monday after the Fourth of July," I interjected. "The morning you met me about the float idea."

Both Tommy Lee and Archie looked at me with surprise.

"How come you remember that?" Tommy Lee asked.

"Because Janet Sinclair came to the funeral home to inquire about pre-planning for her and her husband. She showed up early claiming her insurance agent didn't keep a meeting."

"It wasn't my fault," Archie said defensively. "She requested the meeting the night before by leaving a message on our answering machine. I didn't get it till after you and I met, Barry."

"When did she make the funeral home appointment?" Tommy Lee asked me.

"That morning," I said. "My mother took the call before I arrived. I really didn't know anything before sitting down with her." I explained her strange request not to involve a New Jersey funeral home and to deal directly with the cemetery. I also said the cemetery had no record of plots owned by a Sinclair family.

Tommy Lee leaned forward in his chair and snagged a pretzel. "That's consistent with WITSEC." He used the short word commonly used for the program. "A new name severs all ties and they'll probably have to offer the cemetery some proof of their former identities."

"She said the surviving spouse would give instructions, or an attorney would provide the information in the case of simultaneous deaths."

Tommy Lee chewed the pretzel and chased it with a sip of black coffee. "If they were in WITSEC, the burial instructions probably give their real names, and your contact with the cemetery would create a lower profile than your dealing with a local funeral home. That would protect the surviving spouse." He turned to Archie. "But I don't understand why they confided in you."

"Like you said, new identities shut the door on the old. They told me the U.S. Marshals helped them get some assets moved into the new names, specifically bank accounts. Mr. Sinclair stressed they weren't criminals, but that he was an innocent accountant who discovered anomalies in a client's books who turned out to be laundering money for the mob. His testimony put some chieftains away but at the cost of being on a hit list."

"Okay," Tommy Lee said, "but what does that have to do with you?"

"Some assets didn't get transferred. Specifically, three insurance policies. A policy on the husband, another on the wife, and a second-to-die policy on both of them."

"Better explain that last one."

"It insures two lives but doesn't pay out till the second person dies. You get more insurance for less money because odds are one spouse might significantly outlive the other, and it mitigates what could be some health concerns if one of the two is a higher risk. They told me the beneficiary of that policy was the ASPCA. They're very charity-minded."

"Why don't they just apply for new policies under their new names?"

Archie looked at us like we couldn't understand that two plus two equals four. "Money. There's a lot of cash trapped in those policies. Each was a single premium and they dumped three hundred thousand in each. That means they paid enough so that no additional premiums are needed. The cash in the policy will grow tax-sheltered and unreported. The death benefit will be paid tax-free, and I don't know the face values but they might be two or three times the premium. But now they have no control over them. How do you make a claim when a strange name is on the death certificate? How do you borrow against the value or surrender the policy if your name no longer matches that of the owner?"

"Have you seen these policies?"

"No. They described them exactly the way I described them to you."

"So, you don't know the Sinclairs' original names?"

"No."

Tommy Lee looked at me and shook his head. "Somehow that just doesn't sound right."

"Well, it is," Archie exclaimed. "It's a great financial planning tool, if you remember not to piss off the mob."

I didn't doubt Archie's assessment. It sounded better than mechanic Harold Carson's advice to invest your money in a pickup truck. But I was getting the same vibes as Tommy Lee. "That seems like a lot of money for an accountant to earn."

"Evidently, his wife had a sizable inheritance," Archie said.

"What's his job now?" Tommy Lee asked.

"He's a manufacturer's rep for a line of sportswear. He said the marshals helped him get the job and he covers North and South Carolina and Georgia. Mrs. Sinclair helps him with his paperwork. The new life's going fine, but they'd like the financial security of owning those policies again. That's where they'll pull the ten thousand for the Girls and Boys Clubs."

"What could you do to help them?" Tommy Lee asked.

Archie grinned. "I came up with an option. I mean the policies are theirs. They should be able to get them back."

"You care to explain?"

His smile faltered. "I mean I outlined a possibility. I didn't tell them they should do it."

Tommy Lee grunted. "Sounds like this option has legality issues."

Archie shook his head. "No. Not since all the names are the same people. Look, you can't transfer ownership to another person without triggering a tax event. The insurance companies would report it. It needs to be an exchange involving the same individuals, like rolling over an IRA. But the Sinclairs can't do that because of their name change. So, I said they could form a corporation and list the owners or officers as themselves—and their old identities—four people. You can transfer a policy into a corporation as long as the original owners are corporate officers."

Archie stared at us like we should now see the obvious. Tommy Lee and I just stared back.

"So," Archie continued, "the Sinclairs set up a corporation. They can do that easily through an online service that will even file it with the North Carolina Secretary of State. They add their old identities as two officers and then file an ownership transfer to the corporation. The names match, the insurance company is satisfied it was a permitted transfer, and the Sinclairs are one step closer. Then they document that the old identities leave the corporation, but ownership stays with the corporation owned solely by the Sinclairs. They now have control in their new names." Archie raised his hands, palms up. "Problem solved."

I looked at Tommy Lee. I didn't know insurance regulations, but it sounded plausible.

Tommy Lee let out a long breath. "Impressive. But, Archie, you know what you've done?"

"Sure. Freed up ten thousand dollars for our kids."

"Maybe. You also explained how to launder hundreds of thousands of dollars."

Archie paled. "No. It was their money."

"But you don't know the source. You're trusting their word. These are the people you told you'd be talking to Sonny. If they murdered him, do you think they'd hesitate to lie about their finances?"

Archie ran the tip of his tongue over his dry lips. "Well, check with the marshals. They can tell you if they're innocent people."

"I'll tell you what the marshals will say. 'We can neither con-firm nor deny.' Marshals have one responsibility—to protect their witnesses. They won't tell you who's in the program and they won't even tell you if someone left the program. WITSEC participants sever all ties with their old world. To do otherwise voids their protection. Just by telling you, the Sinclairs violated the agreement. If I check with the marshals, they'll stonewall me. And I'm a fellow officer of the law. Then they'll go straight to the Sinclairs. Who do you think that loops back to?"

Archie swallowed. "Me."

"That's the way I see it."

Archie's gaze shot back and forth between Tommy Lee and me like he was watching a high-speed tennis match. "Well, what are you going to do about it?"

Tommy Lee shrugged. "Not my problem. You're the one who couldn't keep a secret. You're the one who bragged you were going to talk to Sonny. What are you going to do about it?"

"Send Gloria and the girls to her mother's in Weaverville. Demand round-the-clock police protection for me till you arrest these people."

"On what charge? Talking to an insurance agent?"

For a few seconds, Archie could only sputter unintelligible syllables, then managed to plead, "You've got to help me."

"Then here's what you're going to do: Nothing."

"Nothing?"

Tommy Lee leaned forward and set his coffee cup on the table. "You can send your family away, but keep it low-key. You go about your business as if Sonny's murder had nothing to do with you. How did you leave it with the Sinclairs?"

"They said they'd think about it and get back to me."

"What would your role be?"

"Get the paperwork from the insurance companies, help them fill out the forms, and then send it in."

Tommy Lee nodded. "So, you'll do exactly what they want. Your goal is to learn their real names. No less, no more. Can you do that?"

"Yes, sir."

"Good." Tommy Lee stood. "Keep us posted through Barry. If you need to meet, do it at the funeral home and stay clear of the Sheriff's Department. My guess is if they're going to take your suggestion, they'll do so within the next few days. If not, place a follow-up phone call. That would be natural and also you're expecting that ten-thousand-dollar donation."

Archie and I rose from our chairs.

"And if they renege on that?" Archie asked.

"Then let it go. You'll have done all you can."

"And you think I'll be safe?"

Tommy Lee stepped close and gently grasped Archie by his arm. "You will be, if you do as I say. And remember, the Sinclairs might have nothing to do with Sonny. The decision to kill Sonny could have been made earlier and have nothing to do with you. It sounds like their concerns go back to July before any of this happened."

"That's right," Archie said. "They wanted to talk about this back then." He looked at me, relief flooding his face. "Just like the funeral planning."

"Yes," I agreed. My mind jumped back to the day of my conversation with Janet Sinclair, Uncle Wayne's phone call from Forest Glen Cemetery, and Susan's setting of Robert Sinclair's broken leg. A possible connection flashed and I saw a new investigative path open. One that for the time being, I'd keep to myself.

Tommy Lee and I stood on the front porch and watched Archie's taillights wink out as he drove around the bend in my driveway.

"You going to check with the U.S. Marshals?" I asked.

"Not yet. Like I said, they'll neither confirm nor deny. They wouldn't tell me if they placed a mob informant next door to my house. I need to draw a few more cards before I play my hand."

"Like what?"

"Like the real identities of the Sinclairs. If Archie gets them to reveal their names on the forms for the transfer of the policies, I go in with the leverage to embarrass the marshals."

"Embarrass them?"

"Yes. They may have placed active criminals in my county. A big scandal broke last year in Arizona when a mob killer used his new identity to commit fraud across the country. He was an alleged real estate developer who took millions of upfront money, and then drove the projects into bankruptcy after pocketing the funds. It was a sixty-five-million-dollar debacle. The investors had no clue who they were dealing with because our own government fabricated a squeaky clean new identity and history for him."

"And the man was a killer?"

"Self-confessed. But his testimony brought down some mob kingpins, which made the prosecutors happy. Then the marshals protected him for being a witness, but who protects the public from him? Local law enforcement's never told that a career criminal has just settled in their community."

"And Robert Sinclair could be like this guy in Arizona?"

"Why not? I don't believe the Sinclairs simply ran out of time to change their policies before disappearing into the program. I think they were hiding money. Probably from the marshals themselves. Relocation support includes a financial stipend until the protected witness gains employment. They would want to qualify for as much as they could."

"But exposure could endanger them. I assume there's still a mafia bounty on Robert Sinclair's head."

Tommy Lee poked me in the chest with a forefinger. "That's the damn point. The marshals won't let that happen, so I'm hoping they'll tell me what I need to know. If it turns into a murder conviction, they'll drop the protection. Then if the mob bumps off Robert Sinclair, it's not on their watch. They can still tout they've never lost a witness while in their program."

Tommy Lee stepped off the porch and headed for his patrol car.

"You made a good point that Sonny could have already been a marked man," I said.

Tommy Lee turned. "I know. Robert Sinclair could be a wild goose chase. That's why our main areas for pursuit are the ballistics we've got, Rufus and Toby's financial records, and the trail of EBT card-use."

"And finding out who Rufus took as a new partner in the store," I reminded him.

"Yes. Roger needs to see the attorney as soon as possible. But enough for tonight. We'll start first thing in the morning."

"I need to be at the hospital."

"Oh, sorry." Tommy Lee walked back to me. "I should have asked how Wayne was doing."

I gave him a summary of my uncle's condition.

"You take care of your family first," Tommy Lee said. "In the morning, I'll just be pushing Ferguson and the SBI to expedite their findings."

I found Susan in bed reading *Southern Living* magazine. Democrat had flopped out on my side. He grudgingly hopped off when he saw me pull my pajamas from a dresser drawer.

"Everything all right?" Susan asked.

"Things have taken a strange turn. Tell me whatever you can about Robert Sinclair."

Chapter Thirteen

At seven the next morning, a uniformed state trooper stood outside the door to Uncle Wayne's hospital room. He held a paper cup of coffee in one hand and a pastry in the other. As he saw me approach down the corridor, he set the coffee on the plastic chair beside him.

I, too, was in uniform, and I trusted he freed his hand to shake mine rather than draw his service weapon.

"I'm Deputy Barry Clayton. My uncle is the patient. Is there some problem?"

He returned the greeting with a handshake and a smile. "Commissioner James insisted on seeing your uncle. He was released last night but is flying out from Asheville to Raleigh. A four-hour car trip would be too taxing, given his wound."

"Are you here because of further threats?"

"No. I'm here because the governor wants James to have an escort, at least till he's home."

"Am I free to enter?"

The officer glanced at his wristwatch. "Yeah. Please do. You might help hurry the commissioner along or we're going to miss the plane."

I knocked as I opened the door and found James standing at the head of the bed. Uncle Wayne was awake and either James or a nurse had inclined the mattress to a more comfortable sitting position. My uncle's color looked better and he smiled when he saw me.

"Here he is. The man I was telling you about. My nephew."

From the effusiveness of his words, one would think I'd discovered a cure for cancer.

The commissioner had his right arm in a sling and the bulge beneath his shirt indicated protective bandaging on his shoulder. Graham James was around sixty, a big-boned, square-jawed man who looked like he'd be as comfortable in bib overalls as he would in a tailored suit.

He extended his left hand. "Pleased to meet you. Your uncle says you're the Sherlock Holmes of Gainesboro."

"Obviously, he's delirious," I said.

"He'll get to the bottom of what happened, Graham. You wait and see."

Graham, I thought. Uncle Wayne and his new best friend were certainly chummy.

"I don't doubt it," James said. "Not if he takes after his uncle. Anything you can share with me, Barry? The SBI reports that the man Wayne stopped just flipped out."

I hesitated to answer. Ferguson had given the commissioner the story as far as his investigation had gone. And the SBI was being extremely cooperative so I didn't want to throw Ferguson under the bus. But it dawned on me that the Commissioner of Agriculture could be both an asset and an ally as our own case followed a trail into the world of food stamps and state-administered benefits. The USDA and James' agriculture department had to have a close working relationship.

"That's correct, as far as what we know regarding your attack. But there are some other elements that we are tracking that could reveal additional pressures that created Toby McKay's mental state. This isn't for public consumption, so I need both of you to keep the information confidential."

A politician loves nothing more than to get confidential

information. I didn't trust him not to leak it, or Uncle Wayne to remember it was confidential, so I restricted my comments to indications that Toby McKay might have been involved in a food stamp scam which further squeezed him financially. When he lost the second crop, he took it out on the commissioner as the symbol of his troubles.

"We're pursuing the food stamp fraud in connection to McKay and others. In fact, we might need your department's assistance as we dig further."

"Absolutely." With his free arm, James fumbled in his pocket for his wallet and awkwardly fished out a business card. "Have you got a pen?"

I pulled a ballpoint from my shirt pocket.

"You write. My left-handed chicken scratch will be illegible." He handed me the card. "I'm giving you my personal cell number. Day or night, you call if we can assist. I know many of the FNS investigators, if this thing moves into federal territory." He gave me the ten-digit number and I repeated it back.

Commissioner James turned to my uncle and patted him on the shoulder. "You're going to lick that pneumonia, Wayne, and then you're coming to Raleigh. That's an invitation from me and the governor. Bring the whole family. I don't care about your political persuasion. We'll have a good meal and a good time."

As he left the room, he whispered to me, "I want you to keep me informed on his progress. If we need to get him to a bigger hospital, just say the word."

I thanked him and promised to stay in touch.

"That man's a talker," Uncle Wayne said, as I returned to the bedside.

"What time did he get here?"

"I don't know for sure. The nurse had just been in, and she said it was six-thirty."

"I hope he didn't tire you out."

"No. It was good to see him." My uncle took a deep breath.

"It let me know I didn't simply kill a man. I saved a life. I can rest easier having seen that life in the flesh."

"And how are you feeling?"

"Weak as a newborn kitten. But the nurse said the fever broke during the night. Looks like I won't be family business quite yet."

I had to laugh. He sounded like he was apologizing for not being a customer of Clayton and Clayton.

Mom arrived a few minutes later and was ecstatic at her brother's progress. Dr. DeMint came by on his rounds and agreed that it looked like the worst was behind us. But, he said Wayne would need another day or two in the hospital and then a few more days in on-site rehab. DeMint wanted no chance for a relapse.

I had breakfast with Mom in the hospital cafeteria and then said goodbye. Rufus Taylor's service was at eleven and I decided I should cover the funeral home while Fletcher and Freddy Mott were up at Twin Creeks Baptist Church for the burial. I also had a call to place and I wanted to have the Sinclair file in front of me.

"Forest Glen. How may we serve you?"

The woman's voice sounded familiar but it had been almost two months since I'd made the original call.

"This is Barry Clayton. Clayton and Clayton Funeral Directors in Gainesboro, North Carolina."

"Yes, Mr. Clayton. We've spoken before, haven't we?"

"That's right. I had a question about the cost for opening a grave. But you said things were crazy and you called back later and spoke with my uncle."

A few seconds of silence followed. I could visualize her trying to reconstruct the phone calls.

"Yes, the day we had the excitement at the graveside service. I'm sorry I had to be so abrupt. Do you need that grave prepared?"

"No. I was just reviewing the file and thought I'd better double-check the information." I repeated the figure Uncle Wayne had entered in the estimate.

"That's correct," she confirmed. "And I remember now that I couldn't find the family's plots listed in the registry."

"Confusion on our end. Don't worry about it. I'm curious, since we both deal with a lot of funerals, what was so crazy that day?"

She laughed. "Have you ever had someone fall out of a tree?"

"No. That would be a first."

"Well, one of the mourners climbed a tree about forty yards away. Rumor was there was some kind of family rift and he didn't want to be seen. One of our gardeners spotted him. In his hurry to climb down, he fell. He gave a yell loud enough to be heard by those at the graveside. Then he ran, or rather hobbled, through the monuments to his car on the other side of the hill. Some of the men sitting under the funeral canopy got up and started chasing him, which caused even more confusion."

"They catch him?"

"No. He managed to get away. We don't know how long he'd been up there. The interment was at ten. One of those gravesides before the church service at eleven. When you called, we were dealing with the police."

"The police were there for a man in a tree?"

"The police were monitoring the attendees. The deceased was Bobby Santona, alleged head of the Santona crime family. He died in prison. Police speculated the man in the tree could have been taking pictures for some rival."

"Did he have a camera?"

"Not that anyone saw. And as far as I know, he was never identified. Our gardener was asked to look at mug shots. Either he didn't recognize the man or he was too scared to say he did."

"Are there a lot of Santona plots?"

"Oh, yes. They've got a big section with who goes where all

recorded. When a gang war breaks out, we can have multiple burials on the same day. I guess things must be calmer in North Carolina."

"Not really. I was once shot at a graveside service. I've got father and son gunshot victims to be buried next week. Some guy falling out of a tree would be a welcomed relief."

When I hung up, I looked at the notepad where I'd written "Bobby Santona." Was a jailed crime boss in Paterson, New Jersey, connected to our killings? Bobby Santona—Robert Sinclair. They couldn't be the same person, but they could be in the same family. I did an Internet search on Bobby Santona. He'd been convicted four years earlier on racketeering charges. One of the frauds involved tire disposal where his crew would pick up worn tires from trucking firms and then have an inside man process them through a New Jersey state-run facility without charging the firms the required fee. Instead, Santona would collect a fee lower than the state's. The trucking firms had lower expenses and Santona kept the money. New Jersey couldn't understand why tire disposal expenses were out of ratio with collected revenue. Then one of the family members was flipped by the FBI—not only on the tire scheme but other illegal operations as well. He was said to be close to the mobster's books and his identity was withheld from the press.

Robert Sinclair, on the day of Bobby Santona's funeral, needed treatment in Gainesboro for a broken leg. I logged onto Google maps and checked the travel time from New Jersey. Just under eleven hours. Susan got the call from the hospital twelve hours after the tree escapade. The trip was doable, although he must have been in a hell of a lot of pain. How much pain could you endure if you had a mob hit team pursuing you?

Another thought struck me. Was Janet Sinclair's sudden need to meet with Archie and me that July day fueled by her husband's return to New Jersey? Had he insisted on attending a funeral service despite her objections? Was that urgency rekindled by Toby

McKay's attack on Commissioner James? The connections were tenuous at best. I feared so tenuous that if we moved too quickly and telegraphed our suspicions, evidence would be destroyed and the Sinclairs could disappear. Following that trail had to be done quietly and secretly.

I printed out the information from the computer and took it to Tommy Lee.

His assistant Marge stopped me as I passed her desk.

"The sheriff's in with Special Agent Ferguson of the SBI. He said you should join them."

I looked at the closed door and then the pages in my hand. I didn't want to disclose the Santona possibility beyond Tommy Lee. "Marge, can I leave these with you? I'll discuss them with the sheriff after Ferguson leaves."

"You got it." She slid the papers into her top drawer.

"How long has Ferguson been in there?"

"Maybe fifteen minutes. No longer."

"Thanks." I knocked on the door and waited until I heard the familiar gruff, "Come in."

Tommy Lee and Ferguson were both seated, the sheriff behind his desk and the SBI agent in one of the two visitors' chairs. As I took a seat, I noticed a stack of computer printouts under Tommy Lee's right hand.

He patted them with his palm. "Sid was kind enough to bring these by in person. It's the ballistics report on the slugs from both murders. Rufus and Sonny were killed by the same gun. A twenty-two. No match to either man's rifle. Gas and powder burns on Sonny's entry wound prove the muzzle was placed directly against the skull, an awkward angle to use if the gun was a rifle."

"A revolver or semi-automatic?" I asked.

"We don't know for sure," Ferguson said. "There was no brass at either scene, but if the shooter fired a semi-automatic and then picked up the casings, it would look the same as if the shells stayed in the revolver's cylinder. If I had to guess based on the assumption that this was a professional hit, I'd say a semi-automatic. Burns on Sonny McKay suggest a suppressor, and that's not going to be used with a revolver."

"You run the ballistics through a database?" I asked.

"Yeah. No hits, either state or federal."

Tommy Lee leaned forward across the desk. "So, we've confirmed the same murder weapon which suggests a common motive for the two killings. That's no surprise. I've given Sid a copy of the list of stores we found in Sonny's saddlebag."

"I'll share them with the FNS investigative office in Raleigh," Ferguson said. "See what they know. It's a faster approach than asking to run the EBT transaction records for every store. None of us likes to feel we're on a fishing expedition for some conspiracy theory wild goose chase."

I wondered if Tommy Lee had shared Archie's revelations that the Sinclairs claimed to be in Witness Protection. I doubted he had, since they had no connection to Ferguson's line of inquiry.

"Thanks for your help, Sid," Tommy Lee said. "Whatever you can do to push this through the interdepartmental bureaucracy will be appreciated."

Ferguson slid back his chair and stood. "Well, we've got to stick together against the bureaucrats." He shook Tommy Lee's hand and then held onto it. "There is one possibility that I want you to watch out for."

"What's that?"

"What if Toby McKay attacked Commissioner James because he was ordered to? If he was in debt and threatened, he might have been coerced."

Tommy Lee smiled. "Who's offering conspiracy theories now?"

Ferguson dropped the sheriff's hand and shook mine. "I know it's unlikely, but even a blind pig finds an acorn once in a while."

"Or a one-eyed sheriff," Tommy Lee said.

We walked Special Agent Ferguson out of the department.

After goodbyes, I told Tommy Lee I had some new information. I picked up my Internet research from Marge and returned to his office. I repeated my conversation with the Forest Glen representative, the coincidence of Robert Sinclair's broken leg, and the death in prison of a New Jersey mobster named Bobby Santona. I gave him the copies of the newspaper articles of Santona's conviction and that someone close to him had betrayed him.

He read everything twice. "Do you know when the Sinclairs moved to Gainesboro?"

"No. I guess we find out when they bought their house. If it's more than four years ago, then we can rule them out."

"I'll send Marge to the courthouse to check the register of deeds. Even if it's within the last four years, I'd like to hold off and see whether Archie learns their names through his insurance scheme. That will be extra ammunition when I confront the marshals."

"What do you want me to do?"

Tommy Lee glanced at his watch. "It's one-thirty now. When was Rufus' funeral?"

"Eleven."

"See if you can track down his son. I want to know when he's seeing the attorney. Rufus' new business partner is still our most significant person of interest."

There was a knock at the door.

"Yeah?" Tommy Lee barked.

Marge stuck her head in. "Roger Taylor's here. He'd like to see you or Barry."

Tommy Lee looked at me. "So much for your tracking." He turned back to Marge. "Send him in. And then I want you to look up the residence of a Robert and Janet Sinclair. Find out from public records when they purchased it."

Tommy Lee and I stood, ready to receive our timely guest.

Roger Taylor came in wearing an ill-fitting charcoal gray suit that had to be from his father's closet. I realized he'd had no other option to wear at the funeral.

Without a word of greeting, he blurted out, "I just came from the attorney. He said my dad came in a few months ago and updated his will. He left everything to me, including the store. It's debt-free. There's no partner. No partner at all."

Chapter Fourteen

Roger Taylor was clearly happy with the news. His father had specifically named him as his heir and set up the business to cleanly transfer to him with no partner attached. Roger said the attorney, Bert Graves, was listing the restored Camino pickup and the discovered cash as part of the estate to be moved through probate as quickly as possible.

"I want to sell the store as fast as I can," Roger said. "Mr. Graves told me I need to get someone to keep the store open so it doesn't lose its value. I don't know nothing about running a store, so he's suggesting we find a possible buyer with a lease-to-purchase deal. You know, run the store for the estate until everything clears and I can sell it outright."

While Roger was talking, I was coming to grips with the no-partner setback. My theory that Rufus had been directed by some criminal element who had bought into his business had just evaporated. But if Rufus was doing the EBT card scam on his own, why had he told his son he had a partner? Was it to explain the cash influx, or was this partner silent, so silent that he didn't want his name appearing on any documents? If that was the case, Roger might soon find himself confronted by threats and intimidation.

Roger Taylor cleared his throat and looked uncomfortable. "Mr. Graves wanted to know why you had taken my father's cash. He called it liquidity that I'll need for legal fees and probate taxes. He wants to know what evidence you have that it's linked to any crime."

Tommy Lee nodded thoughtfully. "Well, Roger, we're in the middle of a murder investigation. The cash could have been the motive. Maybe somebody knew about it and tried to force your father to hand it over. Until I've had a reasonable amount of time to pursue our leads, that cash is staying locked in a safe in our evidence room. And if the store was as profitable as it appears, you might want to rethink your rush to sell it. Tell your employer you need a leave of absence. Show this community the Taylors don't turn tail and run."

Roger reddened. "Is that what you think I'm doing?"

"Well, you did say you didn't want to get shot. But I was thinking about all those friends and neighbors who shop at the store. What will they say? Someone murders your father and you don't stay around to push us to find the killer? You put some stranger in the business, assuming you can find someone, while you disappear?"

Roger ran his fingers through his hair. "But I've got a job. My boss man will fire me."

"Maybe. Or maybe he'll think differently if I tell him you're helping me with the investigation."

Roger's eyes narrowed. "What do you mean?"

"Your father told you he had a partner, right?"

"Yeah, but the partnership must not have worked out. My dad owned the store free and clear."

We were still standing. Roger's announcement about his meeting with the lawyer had catapulted us into the conversation without any of us sitting down.

Tommy Lee gestured to one of the guest chairs. "Have a seat, Roger. We need to talk."

We sat, Tommy Lee behind his desk and Roger and me side-by-side across from him.

The sheriff pointed a finger at the nervous young man. "Just because there's not a legal document doesn't mean someone else wasn't involved in your father's business."

"You mean like a silent partner?"

"More like an invisible partner," Tommy Lee said. "We don't know how silent he was when it came to dealing with your father. We don't know what kind of leverage might have been applied that doesn't show up in legal paperwork. Do you get my point?"

Roger shifted uncomfortably in his chair. "You're saying he might have crossed the wrong people."

"I'm saying he was gunned down by what looks like a professional hit. You don't know anything about that, do you?"

Roger threw up his hands. "Good God, no. I keep telling you my dad told me nothing about his business, other than he claimed he had a partner. And he only mentioned it once last year."

"Then your ignorance is your best protection. You run the store as the inheriting son and you might get contacted."

"By who?"

"That's the damn point. We want to know who. I'm sure any inquiry you get will be very low-key. You let us know. We take it from there. You're helping us find your father's killer, Roger. Isn't that important to you?"

His eyes teared. He nodded his head.

"Then I'll talk to your boss in Winston-Salem, and I'll speak to Bert Graves. But I don't want you to tell either of them what we're doing. I don't care that Bert is your lawyer, it's strictly between the three of us. I'll release the money and any claim on the Camino. And if there's anything I can do to waive estate restrictions, I will. You should start going through your father's records of accounts payable to find his suppliers. They'll be helpful because they want you to be successful so that you'll be a continuing client. Are we good?"

"What if whoever killed my father is watching me? What if they saw me come in here?"

"Anybody asks you, you came in because your lawyer told you to talk to us about the cash we found in your father's house. That's been resolved. From now on, you talk to Barry. You can do it through the funeral home. People will just think you're settling up your father's affairs." Tommy Lee looked at me. "Can you have Roger pay on some kind of installment plan so there's a record of an ongoing relationship?"

"Yes. That's no problem."

"And if I feel threatened?" Roger asked.

"We pull you out," Tommy Lee promised.

Roger was shaken, but he agreed to do it. Tommy Lee had him sign a receipt for the cash and then we ushered him out the back door.

"You think he's up to it?" I asked when we returned to Tommy Lee's office.

"Not if he gets severely threatened. Then I'll yank him immediately. But I think it will be a light approach, if anything. The smart move would be to leave him alone. That's why I don't think he's in any danger."

"Then why do it?"

"Because we're fishing. The more lines we have in the water, the better chance of a strike."

"What other lines have we got?"

Tommy Lee grinned. "I'm glad you asked that question. How would you feel about going on food stamps?"

I waited until Susan and I had finished supper and we were sitting on the back deck, enjoying the fresh air of a clear, mild evening. I was drinking Chardonnay. Susan, opting for Italian sparkling water, had poured herself a glass of Pellegrino.

I'd planned to talk to her about Mom's newly found resolve to move to a retirement community with Uncle Wayne, but that conversation could wait. Tommy Lee had created a new priority.

When I'd asked Susan the night before to tell me all she ethically could about Robert Sinclair, I'd shared our suspicions about her patient and how he could have broken his leg in Paterson, New Jersey. She confirmed that the injury might have happened as many as twelve hours earlier, but that it had set nicely and she'd released him from her care just last week.

"We've had no new information on the Sinclairs," I said, steering us into the topic I wanted.

"Nothing from Archie?"

"No. And it's not the kind of thing he can push. They'll either go for his idea or not. Or they might go for it but find some other insurance agent to handle it."

"I still don't understand how great an idea it is if one of them has to die to collect the money. I mean I understand why they have to get everything in their new names or else the policies are useless."

"The way Archie explains it, the ownership is the key, not the beneficiary. The owner can cancel the policy and take the cash value, which would create a tax event for anything earned above the initial premium, but then those taxes are settled and the money is clean and paid to the new name. But, the more likely scenario is the owner will borrow cash from the policy. That's not a taxable event. When the insured person dies, the death benefit simply pays off the loan and all taxes are avoided."

"Can Archie monitor the policies?"

"He might be able to if the Sinclairs make him the agent of record. But all this could be happening and still not tie into our investigation of the deaths of Rufus and Sonny. Right now we've got Janet and Robert Sinclair as persons of interest because Archie told them about his pending conversation with Sonny. We've got Roger Taylor running his father's store in the hopes that he might be approached by whomever is behind the EBT card scam. Tommy Lee now wants a third angle explored."

"What?"

"The list of convenience stores we found in the saddlebag of Sonny's motorcycle."

"Sounds like you'll need to go through a federal or state agency."

"That's one avenue, but do you think Tommy Lee is the kind of sheriff who outsources his investigation?"

Susan laughed. "Hardly."

"So, he's asked me to go undercover."

Her laughter abruptly ceased. "What?"

"He wants me to get an EBT card and use it at some of the stores in counties where I won't be recognized."

She set her glass on the deck beside her chair and turned to me. "I don't think that's a good idea at all. Two men were murdered."

"Which is why we've got to get to the bottom of this. Honey, that's my job."

Even in the evening shadows, I could see her jaw clench. I realized how both "Honey" and "that's my job" sounded so condescending. I changed tack. "I'll just be buying stuff. I won't be arresting or confronting anyone on my own. We're just looking for a way in. Tommy Lee hopes Archie, Roger Taylor, or I will catch a break and then he'll move with a full team. That could include the SBI, U.S. Marshals, and whoever else might have a jurisdictional claim. But first we've got to proceed with caution and discretion. At this point, Tommy Lee's fishing and we don't want to scare off the fish."

"At this point?" Susan repeated sarcastically. "Barry, that is the point. You're bait, and you don't know whether you're being dropped into a pool of guppies or sharks."

She picked up her glass of water and went into the house. Democrat padded after her. I guess even my dog was mad at me.

I took a healthy gulp of wine. Susan will cool off, I thought. It was my fault for not using the most tactful tone in sharing my new assignment. I would tiptoe around the eggshells our conversation had created and apologize for dismissing her concern.

I'd talk to Tommy Lee about any safeguards we might employ. The EBT card should be in my real name so I didn't have to remember an alias or worry someone might yell "Barry" in a store. I'd limit myself to counties the farthest away. And I'd have to improvise a subtle approach that didn't raise any suspicion I was an undercover cop.

I drained the wineglass and got up. I didn't want Susan and me going to bed with any anger smoldering between us. I'd bounce these ideas off her and ask for any additional suggestions. In fact, the argument actually made me feel good. It's hard to be angry when you know the other person's action was motivated by only one thing—love for you.

Chapter Fifteen

I met Tommy Lee in his office the next morning at seven. The Mr. Coffee pot was already half gone, letting me know he'd been working for at least an hour. He greeted me with a hot mug and a single photocopy of a list in his handwriting.

"We're accumulating moving parts," he said. "This isn't the big whiteboard like they have on the TV cop shows, but it's good enough for you and me."

I studied the page. At the top he'd written:

Archie Donovan?

The whole list read...

Archie Donovan?
Sinclairs—surveillance, Barry
Barry and EBT card
Roger Taylor?
EBT card records for stores and Toby McKay
Toby, Sonny, and Rufus financials
Santona crime family

I read the list a second time. "Why the question mark beside Archie and Roger?"

"Because there isn't much we can do about them. We can only react."

"What about setting up a check-in schedule? Not make it their decision when to report."

He nodded. "All right. Work out what's best for you. I guess the funeral home is still the logical choice."

"You've got me down for surveillance on the Sinclairs. Is that a solo gig?"

"I thought we'd get double mileage out of your undercover role. Archie says Robert Sinclair's a manufacturer's rep. If he travels, you can pick a couple of days at random to see if that's what he really does. And you can make EBT purchases if those travels take you near any of the suspected stores."

I set the list on his desk. "I want to talk about that. There are certain conditions I'd like to discuss."

Tommy Lee pursed his lips and gave me a penetrating one-eyed stare. "Conditions? What? You want combat pay?"

I wasn't going to throw Susan under the bus for worrying about me or even mention the discussion she and I had the night before. "No. Call them safeguards. I want to approach stores that aren't in adjacent counties. It reduces the risk of running into someone I know. And we should get the card in my name, just in case I do cross paths with someone who knows me. With our luck, it will be as I'm checking out."

"All right. We still have to work out the best way to get a card. You can't go applying through our local social services."

"I might have a way around that." I told him about Commissioner James' offer to help.

"Get on it right away," Tommy Lee ordered. "Stress that the fewer people who know about it, the better. What else?"

"Money. We need some way to fund the account."

Tommy Lee rubbed his palm across his unshaven chin. "Right. It's federal money administered by the state. See if James will kick in funds, if he has some discretionary pool that's part of the Department of Agriculture's own budget. I can add a little money. I'd prefer to fund the balance without actually drawing on federal SNAP money. God, a forest would be decimated just to create paper for the government forms we'd have to complete.

Much better if you have a card that links to an account outside the real system."

"Okay. I'll talk it through with James. Once I'm going to these stores, I'll want to let you know when and where I'm entering, in case I don't come out."

He shook his head. "No. Not me. I might be tied up. Make those calls to Marge, and if she's not in, Carol or whoever's on dispatch. Check back no later than thirty minutes after the call."

"That might be a little tight for a productive conversation."

"Forty-five, then. If we're taking safeguards, then make them effective."

"Which brings me to the trickiest part—how to make an overture to break the law." I picked up my mug of coffee, signaling the sheriff I was through talking and wanted his suggestions.

He smiled. "Far be it from me, a lowly county sheriff, to tell a big-city-trained officer how to run his infiltration."

Tommy Lee was teasing me about my experience as a Charlotte police officer before my father's illness brought me back.

"Then what you're telling me is you haven't got a clue?"

"Here's my advice, smart ass. Go into a store with the mindset to get cash or restricted items. You know you're breaking the law, so you'll appear a little nervous. That will make the play seem natural. A two-pronged approach might work. Mix in an item or two forbidden for purchase—a pack of cigarettes or six-pack of beer. See what happens. If he refuses, you can always say you forgot or meant to buy them with cash. If the purchase goes through, then a second approach could be to try to return one of the items for a refund. You could offer to accept less money if the return can be paid in cash rather than credited to your EBT account. Now he's making money and you're making money. Get several documented exchanges like that and then I'll come in and we'll try to flip him. Pressure him to give us someone higher up the food chain."

I stared at Tommy Lee for a few seconds. "For a lowly county sheriff, you're not as dumb as you look."

"I know. People tell me I couldn't be."

"I've got the store I'd like to target with those techniques."

Tommy Lee sat back and thought a second. "Man, I feel sorry for the guy, but you're right, he's probably the most vulnerable."

I knew Tommy Lee had zeroed in on the same target— Wilmer's Convenience Corner and the man whose little girl's cat had been ruthlessly slaughtered.

"He might be afraid not to work out a cash-split," Tommy Lee said. "You could be testing him, making sure he's complying with whatever ultimatum a dead cat represented."

"If he turns, we'll need to protect him."

Tommy Lee's face darkened. "I'm not going to have another Sonny McKay on my hands. I swear to God, I won't."

I said nothing and picked up the list.

The sheriff glanced at his wristwatch. "If you don't have anything else, I suggest you track down Commissioner James as soon as you can so we can get the EBT account rolling."

I did have one more request, the one Susan had insisted upon. "I want a gun. Not my service pistol but a small concealed weapon. Can you make that happen?"

"You'll have it this afternoon. Now go to work."

I went to my cubicle. Seven-thirty. No one else was in the bullpen. Activity would pick up in half an hour. I took the commissioner's card from my wallet. He said to call any time. He probably hadn't thought it would be early the next morning.

I used my cell phone rather than go through the department's switchboard. At this hour, voicemail was my likely destination, and I wanted James' return call to get to me as soon as possible.

To my surprise, a hoarse voice answered, "James here. Good morning."

"Good morning. This is Deputy Barry Clayton. Wayne Thompson's nephew. Sorry to call so early."

"No problem. I've been at my desk since six-thirty. You know how things pile up when you're away. How's your uncle?"

"Much better, thank you. Your visit perked him up."

"Say nothing of it. He's the reason I'm back at my desk. So, how can I help you?"

I briefly highlighted our plan for my undercover role and used Tommy Lee's line about decimating a forest to satisfy the federal paperwork if we ran my EBT card through the official Supplemental Nutrition Assistance Program.

The commissioner understood immediately. "Yes, coordinating that through SNAP would be a bureaucratic nightmare. Our I.T. people should be able to work that out. We'll stripe an EBT card with a routing number and account in my department. I'll authorize a thousand dollars. Keep me posted."

"Thank you, sir. Obviously, we're keeping this close to our chest. At this point we don't know who might be involved. What kind of turnaround do you need?"

"I'd say two days. I'll FedEx the card. You should have it Saturday or Monday. What name should I use?"

"Barry Clayton. I'm trying to keep this simple."

He laughed. "My philosophy, as well. KISS. Keep It Simple Stupid. Every successful politician's mantra. Good luck."

I thanked him for his help and he asked me to give my uncle his best regards. We rang off and I looked at Tommy Lee's list. My undercover work couldn't begin until I had the EBT card. There was only one item I could begin immediately. Surveillance on Robert Sinclair. I realized I hadn't heard Marge's report on the Sinclair house, either an address or date of purchase. I buzzed Tommy Lee.

"What is it now?"

"Commissioner James is already at work. Card will come with a thousand-dollar balance either Saturday or Monday."

"Great." His voice perked up with enthusiasm.

"Meanwhile, I thought I'd see if I can do a little shadowing of Robert Sinclair. Did Marge get the information for the house?"

"Damn. I've got a mind like a steel sieve. Yes, I forgot to share it. The Sinclairs bought the home three and a half years ago. That fits within the timeframe of the Santona conviction. It could take the marshals several months to get the Sinclairs permanent residency. During the grand jury hearing and trial, they would have been shuttled between safe houses."

"What's the address?"

I heard him rustle through some papers.

"2235 Dogwood Circle. That's in Arbor Ridge Estates, off Hendersonville Highway. There's no mortgage lien on the property, so they must own it free and clear."

"What would you think about tagging his car with a GPS tracker? We could use the one we had on Sonny."

"No. Not yet. We don't have enough for probable cause. I don't want to go to a judge till we've got a more compelling argument. Do the best you can by sight. At this stage, I'd rather you lose him than get too close. We'll ramp things up when Ferguson gets me the financials on Toby, Sonny, and Rufus, or if Roger or Archie come through."

"Okay."

"Remember, Barry, when you're fishing there's a time for action and a time for waiting. We're in the part I hate. The waiting."

Waiting. Two hours of sitting in my jeep at a side road about fifty yards from the entrance to Arbor Ridge Estates, waiting for either Janet or Robert Sinclair to appear.

I'd changed from my uniform into jeans and a polo shirt, driven by the Sinclair ranch-style house, and recognized the silver Mercedes Janet had parked at the funeral home back in July. The sedan was in a double carport with a space vacant for a second vehicle. That was at nine o'clock and Robert must have already gone to work.

Now it was eleven and Janet hadn't left and Robert hadn't returned. I'd phoned Marge and asked her to run the Mercedes' plate and see if that information led to the second vehicle. She discovered an Infiniti QX80 SUV registered to the same address. Both were leased by a company called Sinclairity Sales. I assumed Robert must have been a clothing rep who was basically self-employed and had set up a company structure for tax advantages. It might mean Archie's plan could be easily implemented if a corporation already existed that could add the names of their former identities as officers.

For surveillance, Arbor Ridge Estates provided ideal conditions. It wasn't a gated community and it had only one entrance. Unless I fell asleep, the Sinclairs couldn't elude my tracking expertise.

At eleven-fifteen, the silver Mercedes turned onto Hendersonville Highway and headed for Gainesboro. I pulled out and quickly accelerated to the speed limit. Between the curves and rising and falling hills, the car was visible for only short periods. I trusted that as we neared town and traffic increased, I could move closer with less chance of being observed.

At the first stoplight, she made it through the yellow, while I got trapped by the red. Then a unibody truck turned on the road obscuring all sight of her. When the signal cycled to green, I could only cruise slowly and search for the Mercedes among the on-street parking and off-street lots. No sign of the woman. For all I knew she could have driven through town and gone to Asheville. I gave up and swung through the Bank of America branch parking lot, taking the shortest route to the funeral home. On the backside of the building, out of view from the street, I saw her getting into her car. She'd been in the bank. In her right hand she held a manila envelope that was fairly thick and could have contained documents, cash, or both. In those few seconds, I took close notice of her wardrobe—lightweight khaki slacks and a pink blouse. And I made a decision to drop the tail and let her go on about her business. My best move now lay inside the bank.

Across from the row of teller stations, three glass-enclosed offices offered private spaces for financial consultations. Two were occupied by bankers with customers. Cindy Todd, Fletcher's fiancée, was in the third and alone.

She got up as she saw me approach and smiled broadly. "Barry, good to see you. Can I loan you some money?"

"You know we can always use money."

Actually, that wasn't true. The funeral home was marginally profitable, and I had my part-time deputy income and Fletcher had the backing of his family's large funeral home corporation, a corporation that held a minority stake in our ownership and allowed us to get a significant discount on our supplies.

"What can I do for you?"

I shut the door behind me.

The young woman's brow furrowed as she picked up the signal that this wasn't merely a social call.

"Right now I'm not your future husband's business partner. I'm a deputy sheriff and I'd like some information on whatever you might be able to tell me about one of your customers."

She gave a furtive glance out the glass wall, then moved to her chair behind the desk and sat. She indicated I should take one of the two guest chairs. "We have pretty strict rules of confidentiality. I'm not sure how much I can help you."

"This is a police matter, but I don't want you telling me anything that would get you in trouble with your supervisor. Just a few basic questions and you can decline to answer whatever you feel you can't say."

She nodded. "Okay, I'll tell you what I can."

I smiled, trying to put her at ease. "There was a woman who was just in here. She wore a pink blouse and khaki slacks."

"Mrs. Sinclair," Cindy volunteered.

"Yes, is she a regular customer?"

"She's in several times a week."

"Really? Is that kind of frequency unusual? I mean with all the online banking these days?"

"Not for a business with currency deposits."

"Of course," I said, as if I should have known that. "That's for her Sinclairity Sales company."

"I think that's the name. I've only helped her occasionally."

"For a loan?"

Cindy laughed. "I wish. Sometimes when we're not busy, we help the tellers. We schedule them according to customer flow patterns, but a normally less busy time can suddenly be swamped."

I looked over my shoulder at the counter across the lobby. Two tellers were on-duty, and each served a customer. "I guess that's why your walls are glass."

"Yes. We're trained to be aware of what's going on at the windows. In fact, when Mrs. Sinclair was here, I could see she was antsy. So, I helped her."

"Just a few minutes ago?"

"Yes."

"Deposits?"

"Not today. She has a safe deposit box. One of us needs to go in the vault with her. Just to sign her in. We don't observe what she's doing."

"Does that happen often?"

Cindy shrugged. "I really couldn't say. I've assisted her a few times, but I don't think it's as regular an occurrence as her deposits."

"What about a personal checking account?"

Cindy looked uncomfortable at revealing personal customer information. "Maybe. But I'd better not go into her records without clearance."

"Sure. I understand."

"We aren't her only bank," Cindy said, anxious to be helpful. "My girlfriend Tina Logan works at the Wells Fargo branch on the other end of Main Street. She said Mrs. Sinclair has an account there."

"How did that come up?"

"We were at lunch one day and ran into Mrs. Sinclair. We both said hello, and Tina told me afterwards that she was in her branch a few times a week."

"Really?"

"Yes. But that's not unusual. Business owners not only have separate accounts but often use separate banks to keep personal and company funds apart, especially if there are business partners involved."

"Do you know who any of her business partners might be?"

"No."

"Do you know Mr. Sinclair?"

"No. But that doesn't mean he's not on an account with her. Many customers just use the ATM for simple check deposits and withdrawals and rarely come in."

I wanted to ask Cindy who might be on the signature cards for any of their accounts, but knew that would take this conversation into an area beyond a casual chat.

"Thank you." I said. "Let's consider this just between us."

"Has Mrs. Sinclair done anything wrong?"

"Oh, no." I flashed my most innocent grin. "The truth is Mrs. Sinclair promised a ten-thousand-dollar donation to the Boys and Girls Clubs, but we haven't received it yet." That part was true. "I was hoping maybe she'd come in to make those arrangements. I saw her get in her car with a large envelope, and, you know, it's kind of awkward to put pressure on someone for a charity donation."

Cindy seemed relieved by the lie. "She seems nice enough. Maybe that's why she needed to get into the safe deposit box. You know, sell off some bonds or stocks."

"You're probably right. So, again, I wouldn't want her to think I was checking up on her. It's just that the Sheriff's Department was a co-sponsor of the fund drive."

Cindy zipped her lips. "Mum's the word."

As I drove away, I thought how nothing about Janet Sinclair's business at the bank was suspicious in and of itself. But why would a sales rep's company generate cash revenue to be deposited? I assumed Robert Sinclair would be paid a commission by check or wire. And what was in the envelope? That was at least a promising development because my guess and hope were Janet Sinclair had gone to the safe deposit box to retrieve insurance policies. Policies that she would be handing over to Archie Donovan.

Chapter Sixteen

After leaving the bank, I spent a few hours at the funeral home going through paperwork and catching up with Fletcher. I didn't tell him about my conversation with Cindy and would treat it as no big deal if she happened to mention it to him.

Fletcher told me the double funerals for Toby and Sonny McKay were going to be held at Twin Creeks Baptist Church on Monday. There would be only a brief graveside service and the turnout was expected to be small. Fletcher assured me that he and Freddy Mott would be able to handle it.

We were wrapping up our business talk at the kitchen table when he abruptly changed the subject.

"Have you ever priced an elevator or chairlift for the funeral home?"

The question was so off-the-wall I could only stare at him.

"I mean for your mom and Wayne. We all hope your uncle makes a full recovery, but if his balance is a little shaky, Cindy and I worry about him on the stairs."

I hadn't thought about one of those wall-mounted chairlifts, but it was a potential option. An elevator would be pretty expensive and require a good deal of construction.

"No, I haven't priced them." I decided to share Mom's declaration about possibly moving to the Alderway Retirement Community.

"That could be a good thing," Fletcher said. "Especially while they both have their health and can establish some social connections. We had a tough time convincing my grandmother to move to a retirement center. After three weeks, she was mad at my mother for not making her move earlier."

"Well, we'd need to work out the financing. The business leases the property from Mom, and I know she'll need to get her equity out."

Fletcher nodded. "That could be worked out. Why don't you get three independent appraisals? That way a fair offer can be made."

"But we have to decide if either you or I buy it, or we split it, or the business purchases it. What are the housing plans for you and Cindy?"

He laughed. "No offense but I'm pretty sure she doesn't want to live in a funeral home. Initially, we'll be in my rental house. When we buy, I'd like something like you have. Out of town and relatively secluded."

My house was a cabin built from materials salvaged from four historic log homes scattered throughout the Blue Ridge. I didn't build it. A psychiatrist from Charleston purchased five acres of mountain property, assembled the logs into a new structure whose interior contained all the modern conveniences, and then fell ill and had to sell his mountain dream. My place was unique and Fletcher was unlikely to find something similar unless he created it himself.

"But that doesn't mean we couldn't share ownership of this property," Fletcher said. "We'll see how things play out."

"All right," I agreed. "And I'll check on the lift. As a kid, I slid down that bannister. Might be fun riding up."

I left Fletcher and returned to the Sheriff's Department around three. Tommy Lee was in his office scanning through a document.

"Close the door and take a chair," he ordered. "Ferguson gave me the last six months of bank statements for Toby, Sonny, and Rufus."

"Anything stand out?"

"I've just given it a cursory read, but Toby's activity was minimal. An occasional cash deposit and a monthly utility check that often brought the balance close to zero. If he was getting any money from his EBT card, Rufus was paying him in cash. On the other hand, Sonny had regular deposits into his account every two weeks. The auto repair shop paid him by check and the amounts varied slightly. I guess because Sonny worked by the hour."

"Any indication that Harold Carson was paying him additional money under the table?"

"No. And looking at the six-month totals, Sonny earned more than would qualify him for food stamps. He was telling the truth when he said he told his father he didn't want any part of the scam."

"But he knew about it."

"The list we found proves that. And it's believable that he wouldn't turn in his father, especially if hard times forced Toby into his situation."

"What about Rufus?"

Tommy Lee flipped through some pages. "That's more interesting. He had two checking accounts, a business one for the store and a second for his personal finances. The business had a mix of deposits from the major credit cards, EBT card transfers, a few personal checks, and cash. Rufus paid himself a modest salary by check with the proper withholdings. He had some part-time hourly cashiers who were paid by check. Now, we don't know if he was also slipping them cash from the register. I wouldn't be surprised if that were the case and he was avoiding employer payments to Social Security and Workers Comp. After all, that's what he suggested Sonny work out with Harold Carson."

"You think there was enough cash floating around to account for what we found in his closet?"

Tommy Lee set the papers aside. "I doubt it. Especially since he spent a lot of cash on the pickup restoration. So he had to be siphoning off the phony EBT card income somehow. I think that's where the accounts payable come in. Lots of payments to grocery suppliers and vendors. We need to see if they are all legitimate. I'd asked for Ferguson to run the financials on all the stores on Sonny's list, but he claimed that was overreach and he couldn't get the approval to pry into so many private businesses for a fishing expedition."

"It is a fishing expedition."

Tommy Lee threw up his hands. "Of course it's a fishing expedition. That's what I told Ferguson. I'm fishing in a pond with three dead bodies. He was sympathetic but claimed his hands were tied without more proof."

"What about tracking the EBT cards in those stores?"

"Ferguson made the request and was told the FNS would get back to him."

"He had to go through FNS?"

Tommy Lee shrugged. "Food and Nutrition Services is a federal program. They had to be covered. I don't know which will be worse—they say they can't help us or they say they can. Their help always comes with a price, a price that at the minimum means they'll want to meddle in our investigation."

The intercom on Tommy Lee's phone buzzed.

"What?" he asked, letting the line stay on speaker.

"There's a gentleman here to see you," Marge said.

From the tone of her voice we knew the gentleman had to be standing right in front of her.

"I'm tied up with Barry."

"He says to tell you he's an investigator with the Food and Nutrition Services. It's important he speak with you."

Tommy Lee snorted an involuntary laugh. "What did I tell you," he whispered to me. "I'm betting on those dreaded words, 'I'm from the government and I'm here to help you.'" He turned back to the intercom. "Put the gentleman in Interview One. Barry and I will be there in a few minutes."

The sheriff stood. "If this guy's a jerk, I might tell him thanks, but no thanks."

"If anybody can recognize a jerk, it's you."

"I know. So just wait until you see your next performance review."

Our visitor was seated in one of the chairs on the interviewers' side of the table. I didn't know whether he'd done that by chance or whether he was used to conducting interrogations and took it out of habit.

He stood and we shook hands. He introduced himself as Collier Crockett. He wore the standard issue dark blue suit and American flag lapel pin. I guess he didn't want us to forget his FNS credentials were federal. If he wore that wardrobe during an active investigation in the mountains, he'd stick out like a ballerina at a square dance.

Tommy Lee sat beside him and I was left with the suspect's chair. As the sheriff and I had quickly discussed in his office, we said nothing further. We didn't even ask what he wanted.

After about thirty seconds of awkward silence, Crockett said, "I understand you're working a case involving SNAP benefits."

Tommy Lee shrugged. "We're working a double homicide and the motive might be entangled with use of an EBT card."

"And you asked for records of benefit charges at Taylor's Short Stop?"

"Yes. The location of the first murder."

"And now you want benefit transactions for roughly twenty more stores?"

"Through the auspices of the State Bureau of Investigation. Our case overlaps with the attempted murder of Commissioner of Agriculture Graham James."

"But I understand Special Agent Ferguson wasn't able to obtain the necessary authorization for such a sweeping request."

"Then we'll proceed with our own petition."

Crockett's smile morphed toward a sneer. He folded his arms across his chest. "That's not going to happen."

Tommy Lee crossed his arms. "Really? Who made you king of our investigation?"

"Nobody. Pursue your leads but the EBT cards are out of bounds."

Tommy Lee dropped his arms and leaned closer to the FNS agent. "Let's cut the crap. You're running your own investigation and you're afraid we're going to come in like the Keystone Cops and blow up your case."

"Your words, not mine, Sheriff."

"Well, here are some more of my words, Mr. Crockett. You can stick your case where the Carolina moon don't shine, and if I have to haul each one of those store owners into this interview room and ask them to bring their EBT records, I will. Two of my citizens have been murdered and I don't give a rat's ass whether that screws your case or not. Now, I might not be able to force them to supply their records voluntarily, but they'll know they are on my radar and I'll inform them whatever they say will be shared with the SBI. That is unless you climb down off of your goddammed high horse and give me a good reason I shouldn't."

The slick agent went as red as a stoplight. "You're trying to blackmail me," he said with a voice so constricted it was more of a squeak.

"No." Tommy Lee bent in even closer. "Read my lips. I'm pursuing my murder cases down any and all avenues. And if you're blocking my way, I'll do whatever I can to run you over."

Crockett was not only pinned in his chair by Tommy Lee's invasion into his personal space, he was also caught by the sheriff's piercing one-eyed stare. In an instant, it became a battle of wills as to who would look away first. I began to think I might have time to go out for a hamburger.

Finally, Crockett chose a way to save face. He kept his gaze fixed on Tommy Lee's good eye and said, "Let me rewind and start this conversation over."

The sheriff leaned back in his chair. "Okay. We're listening."

"I came to North Carolina about four years ago. Before that I'd worked in New York, New Jersey, and Chicago investigating food stamp fraud. Not the guy who sneaks a bottle of Thunderbird on his card or splits a couple of bucks with a store owner. We were breaking up more sophisticated scams—a network that involved food suppliers, in addition to benefit-recipients and corrupt store owners."

"How'd it work?" Tommy Lee asked.

"Legal purchases would be made and the store owner would get the EBT card's deposit into his account. But the sold products would be restocked. Or sometimes trucked to another store. Keep reselling the same merchandise that you've only paid for once. All EBT receipts were for legally qualified purchases. It's just that the cardholder got cash instead, usually fifty cents on the dollar. And we come down to economy of scale. Too much for a single store owner to organize and finance, but not for a proven business enterprise."

"Like what?" Tommy Lee asked.

"Like the mob. They can redistribute the food, enforce the store agreements with the store owners, and intimidate any wayward customers who might decide to blow the whistle. But that rarely happens because everyone at every level is breaking the law. Once a food stamp user accepts a cash payment, they are part of the conspiracy."

"How do you break it?"

"Get the goods on someone and try to flip them."

"Is that what you're doing here?"

"Well, most of my work was in eastern North Carolina. Undercover. But we were making progress here."

I remembered the newspaper accounts of the busts in that part of the state. I looked at the slick Mr. Crockett and tried to envision him blending into the small tobacco towns that made up the bulk of eastern North Carolina's population.

"How long have you been in this area?" Tommy Lee asked.

"About six months. We've had our eye on Rufus Taylor. His death was a setback."

"Had you turned him?" I asked.

"We were close. I don't know if there was a leak or Toby McKay's rampage spooked someone higher up. We have other things working. That's why I don't want us stepping on each other. I mean I could make a case that your murders should be folded into our investigation, but I'm not going to push for that."

"Because it would be over my dead body," Tommy Lee said.

Crockett smiled. "I believe you've already made that abundantly clear. So, my proposal is you let me take care of the big picture. You look at individual grocery stores where you think there's a link, but not do a sweeping request for information that could swamp you in data analysis but be business as usual for us. I promise you when we nail them, and we will, your murder charge will trump and you can go after them tooth and nail. How's that sound?"

Tommy Lee scowled. "Like I'm putting all my eggs in your basket."

"Maybe. But they're still your eggs."

The sheriff thought for a moment. Crockett was right about our being inundated with EBT receipts that we didn't have the manpower to examine.

"Then who do you think killed Rufus and Sonny?" Tommy Lee asked.

"Outside muscle. Probably Chicago. We found ties between them and the rings we busted down east. You know how it is, Sheriff. It's like squeezing a balloon. Control a bulge in one place and it pops out in another. I might be wrong but I think that bulge might have appeared in your backyard."

"So, you don't know for sure that the mob is even here."

"No. But unless your homicides are some Hatfield and McCoy feud, I'm betting we turn something up. I just want to make sure we don't stumble over each other in the process."

Tommy Lee looked at me. "What do you think?"

I didn't know whether I was supposed to play good cop or bad cop. So, I gave an honest answer. "Give Mr. Crockett his run with the overall EBT conspiracy. I'll follow up on local connections we have to Sonny and Rufus."

"That's fine," Crockett quickly agreed. "And let's keep lines of communication open. If I find a connection to your murders, you'll be the first to know."

Tommy Lee stood. "All right. Let's hope each of us gets justice served."

"Good." Crockett rose and shook Tommy Lee's hand. "Sorry I came on a little strong. I'm passionate about my work, and I respect that you are too. I look forward to working with both of you."

Tommy Lee escorted Collier Crockett out of the department. I went straight to his office, knowing he'd want to debrief the meeting.

"What do you think?" I asked when he returned.

"I think that if Mr. Crockett sent his DNA to ancestry.com it would come back ten percent human and ninety percent horse shit. He's either just starting and wants to pump us for all we know, or he's well down the road and doesn't want us getting any credit for his bust. But, I'm willing to play along where the EBT records are concerned. We probably couldn't get them, and the analysis could be beyond our capabilities. We'll see how forthcoming he is. Meanwhile, Commissioner James has your card coming and we keep to our original plan. Nothing's changed there."

He walked behind his desk and slid open one of the side drawers. He pulled out a holster attached to a thin nylon belt. "Here's the gun you asked for. It's a Kimber Ultra RCP II. One of the smallest forty-fives you can carry. Seven shot magazine and weighs only twenty-five ounces. Three-inch barrel so you'll need close range but it has the punch to knock someone over if you hit any part of the body. Shoot at least fifty rounds at the range so you're comfortable with it. I figure you don't want a shoulder holster. This rig works under your shirt and around your waist to fit the small of your back. The holster straps are Velcro so you just yank the pistol free. I can get you an ankle holster if you prefer."

I took the gun and rested it in the palm of my hand. "What's RCP stand for?"

"Refined Carry Pistol. Just a marketing term. But you're refined, right?"

"As smooth as Collier Crockett."

Tommy Lee groaned. "Oh, please."

My cell rang. I pulled it from my belt. "It's Archie."

"Better take it."

"Hey, Archie. I'm with Tommy Lee. What's up?"

"They came in." Archie was so excited the three words came out as one."

"The Sinclairs?"

I saw Tommy Lee's eyebrows arch.

"Yes. They have a company. Sinclairity Sales. Only now they've added two additional corporate officers. Do the names Robert and Joan Santona mean anything?"

"Indeed, they do." I put Archie on speaker and repeated the names for Tommy Lee.

"Where are you now?" Tommy Lee asked.

"My office. Do you want to see these papers?"

"Yes. But don't bring them here. Barry and I will meet you at the funeral home at..." he glanced at his watch "...at five."

"Okay."

"Archie," Tommy Lee said.

"Yes?"

"Good work."

"Thank you, Sheriff."

I disconnected. "That's an interesting development."

"Yes. But not conclusive of anything. Remember, we're following this lead because Archie told them he would be speaking to Sonny McKay. But if this operation is being run out of Chicago, then the plan to hit Rufus was already in the works. And the Sinclairs wanted this insurance work done back in July. We know that's a fact because Archie missed the meeting."

"So, what are you saying? That Toby's attempt on James and Rufus' murder just happened to occur on the same day?"

"I have to recognize it's a possibility. I just don't want us getting ahead of ourselves."

"What do you suggest?"

Tommy Lee sighed. "Well, we already have the SBI and FNS involved. Hell, we might as well bring in the U.S. Marshals. Next it will be the FBI, the Park Rangers, and the security guards at Walmart."

"Those guys are good. Could be a career move if you ever lose an election."

"Nah. I've got my heart set on Costco."

Chapter Seventeen

Tommy Lee, Archie, and I sat in the parlor with three untouched glasses of Diet Coke on the coffee table in front of us. The sheriff and I were in chairs, and Archie had his briefcase open on the sofa cushion next to him.

"The three policies are from three different insurance companies." Archie passed them to Tommy Lee. "I have brokerage arrangements with each, so what forms I didn't have on file I was able to download."

Tommy Lee gave the policies a quick look, trusting Archie to understand the meaning of all the fine print.

"They are what the Sinclairs described," Archie explained. "Joan Santona owns a policy on Robert Santona's life and is the beneficiary. He owns one on Joan and is the beneficiary, and the second-to-die policy is owned by Joan with the ASPCA as the beneficiary."

"Why does the wife own that one?" Tommy Lee asked.

"No particular reason. Statistically, she should outlive her husband. And since much of the premium came from her inheritance, she probably wrote the checks."

"How much coverage do they have?" I asked.

"Because of the actuarial tables, Robert Santona's death benefit is about fifty thousand dollars less than Joan's, but all three policies are just shy of three million in total face value and close to a million in surrender cash value."

Tommy Lee passed me the policies. "And the corporate papers?"

Archie lifted a document from the briefcase and handed it to the sheriff. "They've made changes by adding their former identities, Joan and Robert Santona, to the list of corporate officers. They also designated the death benefits to go to the company, Sinclairity Sales. That works out great because the Sinclairs are actually the sole owners."

I followed Archie's narrative and while I thought I understood, a question popped into my mind. "But the name of the insured would have to stay the same, right?"

"Yes. Otherwise, a different person has different health conditions and is potentially a different age, so changing the insured couldn't happen under the same policy. They'd have two choices. The owner could surrender the policy and get the cash minus the taxes due, or the owner could obtain a false death certificate for the Santona name and claim that person had died. To collect the second-to-die, both Santonas would need death certificates. Collecting the benefits gives them a lot more money and it comes into the company tax-free. That's harder to pull off. The insurance companies want a death certificate with a raised seal, not a copy. Some also want an obituary from the newspaper."

"Did the Sinclairs ask you about that?" Tommy Lee asked.

"Yes. Robert said it as a joke, but I think he was serious. I wouldn't know where to get a false death certificate, but since fake passports and driver's licenses exist, they could probably find a source somewhere."

"Would the false claim have to come through you?" I asked.

"It could, or the owner could deal with the insurance company's service center directly. Usually the agent of record is sent a death claim kit to assist the beneficiary. There's an ulterior motive. The company wants to keep us close to the money so we can possibly put the funds into another of their products, like an annuity."

"What did you say when they asked about the fake death certificate?"

"I laughed and said I knew they were still alive, and then there was a little bit of awkward silence."

I bet there was, I thought. Robert Sinclair was clearly angling to collect the full death benefit on all the policies.

Tommy Lee handed the corporate document back to Archie. I returned the policies.

"Those ready to go?" Tommy Lee asked.

"Yes," Archie said. "I told them I'd FedEx them tonight."

The sheriff checked his watch. "Then you need to do that. When's last pickup?"

"Six. But I can drive to Asheville if I miss it. Final pickup there is eight."

"It's five-thirty now," Tommy Lee said. "We'd better let you go. Anything else?"

Archie nodded. "Yes. Before I came here, I ran a history on the policies. Each was an aggregate of smaller ones consolidated within the same company. That's permissible. Each was originally purchased as three one-hundred-thousand-dollar contracts. They were all taken out within the same year, which is unusual. That was five years ago."

"Why would they do that?" Tommy Lee asked.

"Lower profile. Not as big an initial policy that might create more scrutiny. Funds could have been drawn from different banks without writing a big check. At least that's my guess. I backtracked this history after the Sinclairs left. They don't know I did so."

"Will the policy changes come back to you?" I asked.

"Yes. I believe everything will be turned around by the middle of next week."

"Good," Tommy Lee said. "Then I'll want you to mail them that completed paperwork. Avoid seeing either of them if you can. At least until we clarify what role, if any, they played in the murders."

Tommy Lee's concern echoed my own. "Did you get Gloria and the girls to Weaverville?" I asked.

"Yes."

"As soon as you get those documents back, you join them."

"Barry's right," Tommy Lee emphasized. "You'll no longer be their insurance agent, you'll be their loose end."

I used the funeral home's Xerox machine to make copies of Archie's paperwork. Then we sent him on his way, urging him to work away from the office. I knew he got the message when he handwrote instructions that the executed documents were to be returned to his mother-in-law's address. His secret mission was over and he was taking no more chances.

Tommy Lee reached for his Coke; the ice had all but melted. He took a long swallow and wiped his lips with the back of his hand. "What do you think?"

"We still don't have any connection between the Sinclairs and our murder victims. The insurance angle appears more relevant to their past lives than the activities of Rufus and Sonny. If Robert Sinclair is actually a rep for sportswear, it's not the kind of product that would put him in contact with grocery and convenience store owners."

"No, but his sales territory could overlap. I think we've got enough for us to make an unannounced visit on Luther Brookshire tomorrow."

"Who's he?"

"A U.S. Marshal in the Western District of North Carolina. His office is in Asheville, but I have his home address. Six-thirty ought to be late enough so that we don't appear rude."

"You're going to pound on a U.S. Marshal's door at dawn?"

Tommy Lee grinned. "Only if there's no doorbell."

At six twenty-five, Tommy Lee pulled into the driveway of a brick ranch in the Beaver Lake area north of Asheville and parked behind a dew-coated green Ford Escape SUV. I was holding a file with all the information we'd been able to gather on the Sinclairs—from the purchase of their home to the transfer of the insurance policies. We also had what information we could collect on the Santona crime family.

I'd worked late at the department going through law enforcement data banks, New Jersey newspapers, and whatever Internet sources seemed credible. What was most intriguing was the speculation that Bobby Santona's son, Robert, might have been murdered just before the older Santona was arrested. Or he had gone into hiding to avoid similar charges. We now knew both those conjectures were wrong.

As I followed Tommy Lee up the front walk, I noticed a bumper sticker on the Escape that read, "Semper Fi."

"Brookshire was a Marine?"

"Yes," Tommy Lee said. "An MP. He went into police work before becoming a marshal."

"You sure you want to wake up a Marine? Maybe you ought to phone and give him a two-minute warning. No sense waking up the whole household."

"He is the whole household. Luther and his wife split about two years ago. Casualties of the job."

I knew the long, irregular hours of law enforcement took their toll on a married couple. I'd vowed to Susan that if we ever headed down that path, the deputy duties would go. I'd bury bodies, not our marriage.

Fortunately, for Brookshire's neighbors, there was a doorbell and Tommy Lee didn't need to announce our presence with a booming knock. He pressed the button several times and we heard a corresponding buzz echo through the house.

"Hold your horses! I'm coming." The raspy, shouted words sounded like the speaker's first ones of the morning.

Tommy Lee bent over and picked up the newspaper lying by the threshold.

Luther Brookshire threw open the front door and squinted against the light. He looked to be in his late forties and wore a pale blue terrycloth robe loosely tied around his waist. His brown hair was streaked with gray and retreating from his forehead.

"Tommy Lee. What the hell's going on?"

"Training a new deputy how to serve papers." The sheriff handed Brookshire the *Asheville Citizen-Times.*

The marshal laughed in spite of himself. "You son of a bitch. Come in and I'll make some coffee. Although I doubt I want to wake up and hear whatever troubles you've brought to my doorstep."

While the pot brewed, Brookshire put on clothes. Then we sat around the kitchen table, and, after Tommy Lee and our surprised host caught up on old times, Brookshire asked, "What do you need? I assume you're working something that's crossed my path."

"Not something, somebody."

"Oh? Who?"

"Your friend Robert Santona and his wife, Joan."

Brookshire's eyes flickered slightly as he tried to fake a quizzical expression. "Is this the guy supposedly killed in New Jersey? I think his father was convicted on racketeering charges."

"No. This is the guy parading around my county as Robert Sinclair. The one who might have whacked a key witness in my murder investigation Monday night."

Brookshire nearly choked on his coffee. "You know I can't confirm or deny something like that."

"I'm not asking you to. I have the proof." Tommy Lee nodded to me.

I set the file on the table, opened it, and then slid the contents to the marshal. "He told an informant he was in WITSEC. Here are some insurance policies that he evidently hid back from your people and is now trying to get at the cash values. My informant also happened to mention the name of our witness, the witness who was executed in his bed that night."

Brookshire rapidly scanned through the documents. "Interesting. Let's say, hypothetically, Robert Sinclair is who you say he is."

"Who *he* says he is," Tommy Lee corrected.

"All right. Who he says he is. What motive would he have? Was your witness a threat to anyone else? Did this informant leak to anyone else?"

Tommy Lee gave Brookshire a broad-stroke summary of the food stamp scam case. He shared the network of stores, the threats to store owners, and the potential cover Robert Santona's job offers in that he travels throughout the region.

Brookshire shook his head. "All circumstantial. I don't hear anything that ties him to any wrongdoing. And if he is Robert Santona and you expose him, then his blood will be on your hands."

"Like I said, he is Santona. But neither I, nor Barry, nor our informant have said anything to compromise his new identity. He's done that to himself."

Brookshire waved a hand dismissively over the file. "What? Because his name appears on some policy and as an officer of an obscure company no one's even looking for?"

"No. Because Robert Santona went back to Paterson, New Jersey, for his father's funeral. He tried to hide in a tree, fell out, broke his leg, and then escaped from his pursuing family members by the skin of his teeth."

"What?" This time Brookshire wasn't faking his bewilderment.

"Yep. Barry's wife's a doctor and she set the broken bone. So, Santona alone shot to hell any little rumors that the marshals or the prosecutors started about his being a vanished murder victim. The only blood on my hands will belong to my informant if word leaks out that we know Robert Sinclair's true identity." Tommy Lee pointed to the file. "An identity we could have discovered only through those documents."

Brookshire stood and paced the kitchen. "Let's say Robert and Joan Santona are protected witnesses. What do you want me to do about it?"

"Nothing," Tommy Lee said. "Absolutely nothing."

Brookshire stopped and threw up his hands. "Then why the hell are you brightening my morning?"

"Look, Luther. If we start getting close to your guy and he is dirty—"

"He's not my guy."

"Okay. Hypothetically, if he is your guy and he knows he's screwed up, I figure he'll come running to you for help. I don't want you whisking him and his wife away into another set of identities. I don't know what damning information he gave on his father, but your WITSEC witness brought organized crime from Jersey to Gainesboro. And created a pile of bodies in the process. Bodies whose blood is on the hands of the U.S. Marshals. So, when he shows up, you'll tell him he's imagining things. Or if he's admitting to a crime, you, as a sworn officer of the law, will have to arrest him and turn him over to the appropriate jurisdiction. In other words, you'll hand his ass to me."

"All right, hypothetically speaking. But from what I've heard from…how shall I say it?…from unnamed sources, your theory overlooks one important fact."

"What's that?" Tommy Lee asked.

"Your food stamp scam demonstrates a very clever and creative mind behind it. Robert Santona has never been accused of being the brightest bee in the hive. So there's a good chance he has nothing to do with this whole thing. I don't want his blood on my hands because I didn't make that clear. An IQ that hovers slightly above room temperature isn't going to mastermind such a complex operation. That fact I can unequivocally confirm."

"All right," Tommy Lee said. "Then we'll also keep our eyes open for other bees."

"You do that." Brookshire's words carried the tone of an order, not a suggestion. "And if any of this heads back my way, I'd appreciate being in on the sting."

Tommy Lee shook his hand. "Then I guess we're done."

"Yes," Brookshire replied. "And you were never here."

Chapter Eighteen

We returned to Gainesboro a few minutes after eight. Friday morning traffic was light since most vehicles were headed into Asheville. During the drive, Tommy Lee and I laid out our plans for going forward. I'd try to get in position to follow Robert Santona, aka Sinclair, as he left his home. I'd also check in with Roger Taylor, and although Ferguson and the SBI had given us his father's bank statements, Tommy Lee thought it wise to see the actual books and any files of payables and receivables that Roger might find as he immersed himself in the convenience store's business.

My undercover role as a food stamp recipient would begin as soon as my EBT card arrived from Commissioner James. Then my next step would be to approach Buddy Smith, the owner of Wilmer's Convenience Corner.

As we neared the department, I asked, "Why didn't you press Brookshire for more information on what Robert Santona had provided that enabled him to enter WITSEC?"

"Because I pushed him as far as I could. He went as close to admitting the Santonas were in the program as I could expect. The marshals follow a strict adherence to protecting their witnesses' anonymity. Luther now knows I found the information elsewhere. I'll first pursue anything I can get on the Santona family and their operations in New Jersey. Lindsay Boyce will be good for that. Meanwhile, I think we should continue to refer to them as the Sinclairs. Less chance anyone could overhear the name Santona."

Special Agent Lindsay Boyce was resident agent for the FBI's Western North Carolina district. She was also Tommy Lee's niece.

Tommy Lee pulled the patrol car into his reserved spot. "If I think I need more than Lindsay can provide, I'll circle back to Luther. He left the door open when he said he wanted in on any sting."

"You trust him to put our case first?"

Tommy Lee opened the driver's door and then leaned back toward me. "Hell no. I'll give him a heads-up just as we start to move on Sinclair. Minimal lead time with little chance for him to jump the gun. Once we've made our bust, Luther will want to keep his hands off and trust me not to embarrass him or the marshals. He knows we're friends even though I think the WITSEC program is a mixed bag. It has unleashed violent criminals on unsuspecting communities. Robert Sinclair's not the first one to have gone back to a life of crime. So, I'm not counting on any help from Luther, not when I've got ace detective Barry Clayton hot on Sinclair's tail."

"Thanks for putting it all on me."

"You're welcome. You know the old saying."

I groaned as I knew what was coming. "I do. So don't say it."

He did anyway. "Barry Clayton. Undertaker. The last man ever to let you down."

I pulled onto the edge of the side road and parked where I'd been the day before. It was eight-thirty and the ground was free of morning mist, giving me a clear view of the entrance to Arbor Ridge Estates. I placed a quick call to Mom's cell phone. She reported that Uncle Wayne had a good night and was being transferred to the rehab floor later in the morning. They'd do an evaluation, prescribe a course of physical therapy, and hopefully have him ready for discharge early next week.

She dropped her voice to a whisper. "Your uncle's in the bathroom but I want you to know we had a talk last night."

"About what?"

"I brought up the subject of moving to Alderway. I put the need more on me. The physical strain of going up and down the stairs. I told him I'd had some near falls."

"You've had near falls?"

"No. But you know how proud your uncle is."

"Yes. I also know you never want to be a bother, so I hope you'd tell me if something like that was happening."

"It's not. But why not take proper steps while I'm in control?"

"What did Uncle Wayne say?"

"That he'd think about it."

The answer surprised me. I'd expected my uncle to build up an instant defense like when Mom pushed him to sell his house and move into the funeral home. But then I remembered she'd used the same argument, that having her brother live with her would be better for her safety.

"So, he might mull it over for a while?"

"I don't think so. A unit's available the first of October. That's less than four weeks away. Another one like it might not be available any time soon."

I wasn't sure what to say. Things were speeding up and I hoped Mom wasn't rushing a decision because of Uncle Wayne's condition. Before I could respond, a reflected flash of sunlight swept across my jeep. I looked down the road and saw Robert Sinclair's SUV turn onto the highway and head away from me.

"Mom. Sorry, I've got to go. Let's talk this weekend."

"Okay. But don't worry, Barry. It's going to work out." She hung up.

I started the jeep and jammed down the accelerator, spinning the tires as the vehicle fishtailed onto the blacktop. Within a quarter mile, I had Sinclair's charcoal Infiniti QX80 in sight. I braked to slightly over the fifty-five-miles-per-hour speed limit so as not to come up behind him too fast, but I dared not lag too far behind in case a truck pulled in between us, obscuring my view. I didn't want a repeat of what had happened when I followed his wife.

Sinclair turned right onto a two-lane road leading away from Gainesboro. His logical destination was I-26 running west to Asheville or east toward Charleston, South Carolina. Tracking him on an interstate would be easier than navigating traffic on a county road. With no traffic, I would stand out; too much and I could get stopped by a school bus or slowed by some farm vehicle that cropped up between us.

I knew Sinclair's territory included counties in both North and South Carolina, and so I wasn't surprised when he took the eastbound access ramp. Once on I-26, I stayed about a quarter mile behind, only drawing closer as we neared exits. We crossed the state line and headed into the interchanges around Spartanburg. I pushed the jeep closer to make sure I didn't get trapped in a wrong lane. He left I-26 for I-85 and then took I-585 headed into downtown Spartanburg. Trailing him through the city could be difficult as I didn't know the street patterns if we became separated.

We were on the outskirts when he pulled into a strip shopping center and parked in front of a store with a sign reading ActiveStyle. The show window featured manikins outfitted in tennis, golf, yoga, and other light sportswear. The variety appeared to exclude extreme sports or heavy-duty hiking and rock-climbing in favor of garments with more fashion-oriented designs.

I pulled into a space in front of a nail salon with six empty parking spots between us. Since I'm not much for manicures and pedicures, I waited in the jeep, angling to look across at Robert Sinclair as he climbed out of the SUV.

Climbed was the word because his short height meant the step down was more of a jump. I, of course, attributed his successful maneuver to Susan's surgical skills.

Sinclair couldn't have been over five-four with a rotund body that made him a matching bookend for Mayor Sammy Whitlock. He wore a yellow polo shirt over khakis, probably lines of clothing he represented. His black hair was thin on top and the light breeze lifted the errant strands making his round head look like an upside-down jellyfish. This was the man who scrambled up a tree? It must have been more of an overgrown shrub. I thought about his very attractive wife, Janet Sinclair, and what an odd couple they made. Maybe he wasn't so short and tubby when he was standing on his wallet.

He went to the rear of his vehicle and I saw that the hatch door had already opened. He grabbed a hanging bag and a briefcase, fumbled with his key fob, and clicked the remote to close the hatch and lock the car. Then he disappeared into the store.

In addition to the nail salon, the shopping strip housed a yoga studio, a Chinese restaurant that probably wouldn't open for hours, and a dry cleaner. I had no clue how long it would take Sinclair to present his wares so I was stuck without an option other than to stay in the jeep. However, ActiveStyle was an end store and I spotted a few parking places along the side. Moving the jeep there would put me in a less-visible position where I could still see the rear of the Infiniti. I parked facing out and waited.

It was nearing ten o'clock. Roger Taylor was probably at his father's store. I dialed his cell.

"Yeah," he answered.

"It's Barry. I need you to do something for me."

"What's that?" He sounded wary.

"When you go through your father's business papers, bring me any files or ledgers that document his accounts receivable and payable. We need to match them to the bank statements."

"I'm at his office now. The one in the back of the store. He's got a couple of old metal file cabinets. You know, the vertical ones. I was just starting to go through them."

My plan to have him bring any ledgers to the funeral home changed on the spot. "Is the store open?"

"No. I put a sign in the window saying we'd be closed till at least Monday."

"Good. You can go through whatever you need to, but don't throw anything out. I'll come to you tonight. Say, eight?"

"Okay. But why at night?"

"I'd feel better if you weren't seen with me. I'll park behind the store. Have the back door open."

"It's your party, Deputy. Just keep me safe." He hung up.

Ten minutes later, Sinclair loaded up his samples in the rear of the Infiniti and drove away. I followed him to four similar stores, all specialty retailers that weren't affiliated with national or regional chains. During his sales calls, he visited only one convenience store and it wasn't on our list. He pumped gas, went inside, and was out less than five minutes later with a jumbo drink, Slim Jim, and a package of Twinkies. Lunch in search of a heart attack.

We were south of Spartanburg when he returned to I-26 and headed for Gainesboro. I stayed with him until he took the exit closest to his home. I drove on to the main exit for Gainesboro.

Tommy Lee was in his office reviewing budget figures. He looked up as I knocked. "How'd it go?"

"If you need a new jogging suit, I can find you the best deals."

He rolled back from his desk and patted his stomach. "Make it a jiggle suit and I'll take you up on it. So, nothing suspicious?"

"No. Looks like he was doing his job." I gave Tommy Lee a detailed report including the observation that Robert Sinclair must have looked like a giant pear if he was indeed in the tree in the Paterson cemetery.

When I finished, Tommy Lee sat thinking for a few minutes.

"He might have things so well organized that he doesn't make collections like some mafia bagman," he said.

"Or at least doesn't make those rounds every day. He has to be successful enough in his job to keep his manufacturers with him."

"So, what do you suggest?"

"Maybe he handles the food stamp fraud on the weekends. I'll stake him out one more day and then move on to my undercover role when the EBT card comes."

Tommy Lee nodded. "All right. What about Roger Taylor?"

"I spoke with him this morning. He said there's an old filing cabinet in the store office. I'm going to look through it tonight at eight."

"You want me with you?"

"No. He's keeping the store closed till Monday. I'm going to park my car around back."

"If you're worried about someone seeing your jeep, why don't you let me drop you off? You can call me when you're finished."

His plan had merit, and I also knew he'd be anxious to learn what I'd discovered.

"Thanks. But I'd prefer to have dinner with my wife. It's been a hectic week."

"Then take her someplace nice," Tommy Lee ordered. "And call me after you see Roger Taylor."

With a short window for dinner, I could think of no place nicer than home. I stopped at Fresh Market and bought two ribeye steaks, lettuce and other vegetables for a salad, and a carrot cake, which I also counted as a vegetable. Then I chose a bottle of Malbec that I knew Susan would enjoy. This weekend she wasn't on call.

I beat her home, fed Democrat at five, and started the charcoal. I was tossing the salad when she arrived at five-thirty.

"What's going on? What have you done with my husband?"

"That debonair fellow has to work tonight. I'm here to see that your evening isn't a total loss."

She kissed me on the lips. "And when does my debonair husband get home?"

"He's meeting Roger Taylor at eight and it might be close to midnight." I gave her the plan to go through Rufus Taylor's business files.

"So, I'm afraid we have to eat earlier than usual. I've opened a bottle of Malbec to get you started."

"Are you having some?"

"No. Not when I've got to work."

"Then let's both have sparkling water. A full glass of red wine and a voluptuous woman will be waiting for you."

"Where are you going?"

She gave me an elbow. "In search of that debonair man."

We ate on the deck, the evening air was fresh and cool, and I regretted setting the appointment with Roger Taylor. I told her of the brief conversation with my mother and my uncle's willingness to consider moving to the retirement community.

"What would you think about moving into the funeral home?" she asked.

"You're kidding?"

"No. Maybe we should consider it."

I looked around me. The forest was alive with crickets. Dusk deepened the shadows and the stars would soon be bright in the dark sky.

"Don't you like it here? Do you regret selling your condo?"

Before our marriage, Susan had lived in a condo close to the hospital. She'd sold it six months ago.

"It's beautiful here," she said. "And the condo wouldn't have made sense. Too small and you have no family connection to it. I'm just saying that if we need to do something like that for your mother and Uncle Wayne, I'm willing to discuss it. I could put the equity from my condo sale into helping buy the funeral home from your mother."

Her proposal caught me completely off guard. I was touched by her willingness to help in a way even I hadn't considered.

"I told Mom we'd talk about it this weekend. Let's see what she's thinking before we suggest any possible options."

She reached across the table and squeezed my hand. "Fine. But I want you to know we're in this together. As a family."

She sent me on my way at seven with a kiss and a promise not to run off with my debonair double.

A few minutes before eight, I drove my jeep behind Taylor's Short Stop. I knocked on the back door. Roger opened it immediately.

"You been here all day?" I asked.

"Pretty much. I ran out for a burger at lunch. Even though the sign says closed, people saw my car and kept stopping to give their condolences." He smiled. "Guess we should have had the funeral here at the store."

"That's the way everybody knew your father."

Roger led me along a back aisle to the office on the other side of the restrooms.

"Anybody seem a little strange?" I asked.

"No. I had a couple truck drivers stop. You know, the guys who deliver snacks and soft drinks. I told them not to start restocking till next week."

He stepped into the small office. There was a desk with one rolling metal chair and a battle-gray file cabinet. On the floor behind the chair stood a small safe.

I pointed to it. "You know the combination?"

"No. I looked through the desk drawers, even pulled them out and turned them over hoping he might have written it down somewhere. I tried his birthday, my birthday, my mom's birthday. No luck. Guess I'll have to get the lock drilled out."

"What if I get a warrant to authorize us to search the safe? We'll get it open for you."

"But will you take whatever's inside?"

"Not if it doesn't relate to our case."

Roger was probably thinking of the cash we'd found in his father's closet and the possibility that the safe held a similar stash.

"And I could get a court order without your cooperation." I realized when we thought the safe hadn't been robbed, we'd ignored what might be its contents.

"Okay," Roger grumbled. "When will that happen?"

"Maybe tomorrow. Maybe Monday. I'll talk to the sheriff." I moved closer to the file cabinet. "Anything unusual in here?"

Roger pulled out the top drawer. "Nah. He's got copies of all the invoices by vendor, and they're in order with most recent at the front of each hanging folder. The middle drawer holds his checkbook and bank statements, and the lowest drawer has taxes and payroll records. Take a look."

He slipped by me and I looked at the top drawer. The first two folders were payables and receivables. There were no receivables. I guessed since he sold everything over the counter, there was nothing that he sent in the way of bills to others. Perhaps he kept the file for any vendor credits that he might be due. Payables held about fifteen invoices for grocery and other products stocked in the store. These were yet to be paid. I pulled the front sheet from a folder labeled "Aimes Distributors" and saw the invoice was stamped "paid" and a check number was handwritten under the invoice total.

I closed the top drawer and opened the one beneath it. I found the most recent bank statement, looked up the check number and saw that the amount matched the amount of the Aimes Distributors invoice.

I handed the statement to Roger. "Okay, here's what we're going to do. I'll call out the check numbers on the invoices and you tell me the amount posted."

"What are we looking for?"

"Anything that doesn't match." I flipped to the folder after Aimes. "Appalachian Brewers. Check number 1508."

"Two hundred dollars, eighty-five cents."

"Correct."

We moved through the recently paid invoices one at a time, each check matching the billed invoice perfectly. Then I found an invoice for Staples Sources. No total was on the invoice and the description was for miscellaneous non-perishables. That could be anything—canned goods, a quart of oil, a bottle opener, or suntan lotion.

"Find the most recent check to Staples Sources," I told Roger.

"I'll need the actual checkbook and stubs," he said.

I passed him the three-ring book and he flipped through backwards from the first unwritten check.

"Here's one from August twenty-first for four-hundred seventy-five dollars."

I looked at the date of the invoice. August twentieth. Fast mail service, if the bill was actually generated that day. The billing address for the company was a post office box in Spartanburg. Not impossible. I looked at the second invoice in the Staples Sources folder. This one did have an amount. Three hundred eighty-six dollars, thirteen cents. The date was August thirteenth with the check written on the fourteenth. The purchased items were identified exactly the same as on the first invoice—miscellaneous non-perishables. I continued going back through the bills. Where most of the others had been a monthly itemized statement, these were weekly and sent every Monday with payment made the next day. Rufus was certainly moving a lot of non-perishable items, or they were sitting on the shelf, being sold and resold as they were fraudulently rung up on the register and swiped for payment through the EBT system.

Staples Sources certainly deserved scrutiny. But how were the amounts paid determined? Some EBT purchases would be legitimate. Rufus must have had some system for tracking the illicit money that came into the store's bank account via the electronic transfer. I looked down at the safe. Would it contain those records? Or had Rufus Taylor's killer forced him to turn them over and then executed him?

Chapter Nineteen

I phoned Tommy Lee as soon as I left Taylor's Short Stop and gave him the information about the safe and the unusual number of invoices from Staples Sources. He agreed to seek a warrant to search the safe's contents and would authorize drilling out the lock. While he took charge of that aspect of the investigation, I would stake out the Sinclairs and see if Robert's weekend pattern included making stops at convenience stores.

Having no clue as to when Robert Sinclair might leave home on Saturday morning, I decided I should drive by his house to make sure I didn't sit all day at my surveillance spot only to see him return in the evening. So, at seven-thirty, I cruised slowly by his driveway. Both Janet's Mercedes and the Infiniti were in the carport. The SUV's hatch was open and a golf bag leaned against the rear bumper. One or both of them appeared to be getting ready to hit the links.

I returned to my spot down the road from the entrance to their neighborhood. About twenty minutes later, the Infiniti emerged on the main road and headed toward me. I ducked and peered beneath the steering wheel as the vehicle passed. Robert Sinclair was the sole occupant. I followed from a safe distance until he turned into the main entrance of the Gainesboro Country Club. The manufacturer's rep business must be successful. A Mercedes, an Infiniti, and a country club membership. The funeral business wasn't so lucrative.

Since I was neither a golfer nor a member of the club, I couldn't just saunter in and checkout Sinclair's golfing partners. I also couldn't sneak along the fairways, scurrying from tree trunk to tree trunk like some demonic squirrel.

I drove to a second entrance closer to the tennis courts, looped back toward the bag drop-off zone as if I'd come from another direction, and saw Sinclair lift his clubs out of the SUV and place the bag in a rack along the sidewalk. He waved to three men sitting at an outdoor table, each one holding a steaming mug of coffee. Their outfits, including Sinclair's, looked like the designer had combined every color from a palette labeled "neon."

Sinclair climbed up behind the wheel and drove to a parking area about fifty feet away. I exited through the main entrance and then circled in again from the tennis courts. Sinclair and his three buddies were at the table, talking and laughing as they waited for their tee time. They paid me no attention as I went to the parking lot and cruised by the vehicles. I suspected none of the luxury cars cost less than forty-thousand dollars. The Jaguar next to Sinclair's Infiniti had South Carolina plates and the bumper sticker—"I do it in ActiveStyle." Clients, I thought. Sinclair's on an outing with his clients. I suspected they'd play a round of eighteen holes and top off the morning with lunch and a round of Bloody Marys.

I decided to return to the Sinclair residence and keep tabs on Janet. If there was an innocent chance I could run into her at a grocery store or downtown shop, I'd speak to her. She'd originally contacted me at the funeral home so exchanging a few words or even striking up a conversation would be a natural thing to do.

Again, I didn't want to be waiting in my surveillance spot if she'd already left. I made a slow pass by her home and received an unexpected shock. Parked in front of the carport was a green Ford Escape with the bumper sticker, "Semper Fi." U.S. Marshal Luther Brookshire was in the Sinclairs' house. Was he warning Janet that we were investigating her and her husband? Why hadn't he done that by telephone? Unless he didn't want a record of the call.

I couldn't simply park in front of the house and I didn't want to confront Brookshire without consulting Tommy Lee. The wooded lots in Arbor Ridge were large enough that the trees provided privacy between houses. I drove about a tenth of a mile, turned onto a second neighborhood street and found a pull-off by a bold stream cascading down a twenty-foot rock face. The topography of this small section of Arbor Ridge couldn't support construction and was tucked out of sight of the nearest house. I parked on the shoulder and walked back.

Along the way I met an older couple and their Schnauzer. My presence wasn't suspicious as I looked like a fellow neighbor out for a morning stroll. However, the dog barked like I was Attila the Hun. The couple waved, and the man said, "Sorry. Grady thinks he's a Great Dane."

As I neared the Sinclair residence, I left the road and angled through the woods to where I had a good view of the carport. I settled behind a rhododendron bush and waited.

And waited. An hour passed. My legs cramped. The ground got harder. My phone vibrated once. A text from Susan.

FEDEX delivered card from Raleigh.

Good. I could start my role as Barry Clayton, undercover cop. Another hour passed. I stretched as best I could and used the time to review the case.

We knew a fraudulent conspiracy existed that linked convenience stores into some kind of organized network. Toby McKay's EBT card found in Rufus Taylor's possession and the list of stores Sonny had secreted in his motorcycle saddlebag supported that theory. The murders of Rufus and Sonny appeared to be fallout from Toby McKay's attack on Commissioner James. Someone had acted quickly to sever any traceable connection between Rufus and the person or persons behind the scheme.

Tommy Lee and I were looking at the Sinclairs because Archie had told them he was going to talk to Sonny McKay, and then Sonny McKay died that night. As the second murder victim, Sonny could have been a marked man already, but the Sinclairs and their admitted involvement in WITSEC certainly raised their profile in the case. Now the marshal who had all but confirmed the Sinclairs' status was in the house with Janet Sinclair. Was he telling her our suspicions or doing an investigation of his own? Tommy Lee said the marshals don't want to be embarrassed by someone in WITSEC engaging in criminal activities. Maybe by breaking the case first, Brookshire would mute the impact of such a revelation.

And then there was FNS investigator Collier Crockett. His ongoing efforts to build his own case meant he wanted us to go away. I understood his concern. He didn't want to see his work destroyed by other law enforcement agencies who set off alarms that could drive his targets to ground. My undercover work would have to tread lightly around the investigation Crockett had already mounted.

I heard the squeak of a screen door. I edged around the rhododendron to see Brookshire coming out directly into the carport. Janet Sinclair stepped into the open doorway. She wore one of those thick terrycloth robes you find in the closet of a high-priced hotel room. It was loosely cinched and her bare legs and feet protruded beneath its hem. She said something inaudible and Brookshire laughed and turned to face her. He slipped his hands under the robe and kissed her on the lips. If his job was to handle the Sinclairs, he was going all out with Janet.

"Well, that certainly complicates things." Tommy Lee made the one-sentence assessment as we stood behind Taylor's Short Stop.

Roger Taylor and a locksmith were in the office. With the

whine of the drill masking my words, I'd told the sheriff what I'd witnessed.

"It could just be an affair," I said. "Brookshire might not be mixed up in anything else."

"I can guaran-damn-tee you that bedding your WITSEC charge isn't in the approved marshals' playbook. If Luther showed such a lapse in judgment, then what else has he compromised?"

"What are you going to do?"

"Only thing I can do. Confront him face-to-face."

"You want me with you?"

Tommy Lee shook his head. "No. That would only make him more defensive. I'm going to use one of my more unscrupulous investigative tools—blackmail. I don't want to pull you into it."

"But what if he does something desperate? You'll have no backup."

"Oh, he'll know you were surveilling the Sinclairs. I'll tell him. But I'll also tell him if I don't check in with you by a certain time, you'll go straight to the FBI."

The drill whine ceased.

"Lock's out," Roger yelled from the back door.

Tommy Lee and I entered the store and crowded into the office.

"All right, Roger," Tommy Lee said. "Open the safe."

Roger yanked open the perforated door and we peered over his shoulder. No cash. Just two items. A ledger book about the size of a paperback novel and, beneath it, a manila envelope.

"Don't touch anything," Tommy Lee ordered. He rolled on a pair of latex gloves.

Roger Taylor backed out of the way and Tommy Lee retrieved the ledger. I gloved as well and he handed the book to me. Then he took the envelope. The interior was now as bare as old Mother Hubbard's cupboard.

I flipped through the pages. "Dates and amounts. Not large amounts. Mostly thirty to fifty dollars."

"Probably what was paid for by EBT cards," Tommy Lee said. "An accounting for how much the bogus charges amounted to. Then they would know how to split the take." He opened the flap of the unsealed envelope. "This is interesting."

He handed me the top sheet of several pages. It was a blank invoice from Staples Sources.

The sheriff flipped through the other sheets. "They're all the same. Rufus must have filled out the invoice with the appropriate total each time he wrote a Staples Sources check."

"Do I need to know all this?" the locksmith asked.

"No, Ed," Tommy Lee said. "Thanks. Send your bill to the department. And, Ed, this is confidential police business. Not a word to anyone."

"Anybody asks, I was here because you locked your keys in your car." He laughed. "Everybody will believe that."

As soon as the locksmith was out of earshot, Roger whispered, "Are you going to take back the El Camino and the cash?"

"No," Tommy Lee said. "But for your own safety, don't talk to anyone about this." He raised the papers for emphasis. "Got it?"

"Yes, sir."

"So, we're going with the original plan. Operate the store, but let me know if anyone approaches you."

I followed Tommy Lee out the rear of the store.

"Let's talk in my car a few minutes," he said.

I slid into the front passenger's seat. The sheriff started the engine and turned on the fan to circulate the air.

"I'm going to call Alec Danforth," Tommy Lee said. "He's the manager of the Gainesboro Country Club."

"Why?"

"If Robert Sinclair played golf this morning, he might have played golf last Saturday. Alec can access the tee times."

"Right. And Sinclair could have an alibi for the time of Rufus' murder."

"Yes. I should have looked into that as soon as Sinclair became a person of interest."

"We didn't know he played golf, and we focused on his job that covers similar territory to the footprint of the stores."

"Well, we know now," Tommy Lee said.

"Okay. What can I do?"

"Take the weekend off. That's an order. I'll update you later, and I'll let you know when I catch Luther at home."

"I'll probably be at the hospital with Uncle Wayne. So I'll be close if you need me."

"I won't. Now get out of my car and go see your family."

At a little after one in the afternoon, I knocked on the door of my uncle's small room in a rehab wing of the hospital. I entered to find him sitting up in a chair next to the window. Beside him sat Reverend Lester Pace.

The old preacher got to his feet. "Barry, take this chair. I need to be running along anyway."

"No. I'm good here." I sat on the foot of the hospital bed. "And I need to ask you something before you go."

"All right."

"But first, how are you doing, Uncle Wayne?"

"I'll be doing better when they let me out of this place. Nothing wrong with me. My head's so hard there's probably a pothole on Main Street."

"So, rehab's going well?"

My uncle waved his hand dismissively. "I'm running rings around the other contestants."

"Contestants?"

"Well, patients. The nurses have us play these games. Like bowling with plastic pins. I beat everybody."

Nothing like a little competition to motivate my uncle.

"At least the doc's moved up my release date to Monday, if everything goes well." Uncle Wayne shook his head. "Hard to believe it was only a week ago. Seems like I've been here a month."

"Was my mother in earlier?"

"Yes. Susan came by and picked her up for lunch. She said you were working. You learn why Toby McKay went nuts?"

"Making progress."

My uncle winked at Pace. "Secret stuff. Nobody's more close-mouthed than Barry." Then he turned serious. "Your mother said she talked to you about this Alderway nonsense."

I glanced at Reverend Pace. He gave a slight nod to indicate he was aware of the situation.

"I wouldn't call it nonsense," I said. "Not to her. I think the funeral home's become a burden to her. The stairs, the visitations."

"Come on. We both know it's me she's worried about. This whole thing started because I'm in the hospital."

"That doesn't mean she's not right to be worried."

"I know. I know."

Reverend Pace cleared his throat. "I told your uncle she might think she's doing it for him, but actually is worried about her own condition. Unlike this champion contestant here," Pace patted my uncle on the knee, "some of us feel our age."

"But are you going into some retirement home?" Uncle Wayne asked.

"Yes."

The answer surprised both of us.

"Alderway," Pace said. "It's affiliated with the Methodist church and as a fifty-plus-year serving pastor, I receive special consideration. I didn't want to tell you because I knew you'd be afraid to move there. You know I'd show you up in all the activities."

My uncle laughed. "You. A man of the cloth. Lying through your teeth."

"You can have the chance to prove me wrong then."

"Thinking about it," Uncle Wayne said softly. "Thinking about it."

There was a knock at the door. A nurse stepped just inside. "Mr. Thompson. Time for your afternoon session."

"What is it? Mountain-climbing?"

"Close. We've got a little obstacle course set up."

My uncle stood quickly, and then lost his balance and fell back into the chair. His face went scarlet.

"Now remember, we stand up slowly and then pause to get our equilibrium." The nurse came over and offered her arm.

Uncle Wayne sighed and let her help him to his feet.

"There we go," she said. "Now, escort me to the gym. It's not often I have the pleasure of walking arm in arm with such a good-looking man."

My uncle looked down at Pace. "I bet they won't be saying that to you at Alderway."

"Probably not. Especially if you're there."

Uncle Wayne patted the nurse's hand. "Come on, honey. Let's go set a record for this so-called obstacle course."

When they'd left the room, I asked Pace, "Are you really going to Alderway?"

"Yes. A small one-bedroom unit. I'll still tend my churches as long as I can drive without being a danger to others. But if the good Lord gives us three score and ten, then I'm well into overtime. Alderway will provide me with a community when I no longer can get around on my own."

"And my uncle?"

Pace shrugged. "He'll come to a decision in his own time. He doesn't like to feel that he's being railroaded. But if I were a betting man, I'd say his train's headed for Alderway. Especially if he feels like he and your mom are leaving you in a manageable position." He reached behind his chair for his rhododendron walking stick. "Well, I'd better take off." He paused. "But you said you wanted to ask me something."

"Yes." I pulled a copy of the convenience store list from my pocket. "You know this area as well as anybody. Can you tell me anything about the people who run these stores?"

Pace took the paper and studied it a moment. "Well, Rufus' store obviously. The Smart Mart in Mills River is owned by the Harris family. They attend my Pigeon River church. The others are a little far afield for me. I do know Buddy Smith at Wilmer's Convenience Corner."

"Really?"

"Yes, his wife, Elaine, grew up in the Oak Hollow congregation. A small church I'd rotate into once a month. She met Buddy Smith at a Bible camp when they were teenagers. Tough story."

"What do you mean?"

"A couple years ago, Elaine got leukemia. The childhood kind. High cure rate in children, but devastating to an adult. The medical bills were huge and Buddy had some cheap insurance with a very high deductible. The church had some fundraisers. Bake sales, car washes. Buddy even had a donation jar on the counter of his store. But Elaine died back in the winter. Left Buddy with his daughter, Norie. She must be about ten. It's been a struggle. I've been by to see them a couple times." He looked back at the list. "This reminds me I should check on them. The other stores, well, nothing stands out." He handed me the paper. "What's this about?"

I told him our suspicions that Rufus Taylor and Toby McKay had been tangled up in some organized network of food stamp fraud. How we'd found the news article about the dead cat and Buddy's story about the underage kids. We didn't buy it, especially when Wilmer's Convenience Corner appeared on the list.

"When did the cat incident happen?" Pace asked.

"Back in April."

"A couple months after his wife died."

"You're thinking Buddy got involved because he needed money for her care, and then tried to get out?"

"You're the detective," Pace said. "But these are hard times for a lot of people. Between the opioid epidemic and scarcity of jobs, people are desperate for cash. What can I do?"

"Whatever you feel called to do, but I'd appreciate your not telling him about me. I'm not looking to bust him. I just need to find out who's behind the operation. I've got a plan to do that without endangering him or his daughter."

Reverend Pace studied me for a few seconds. "I'll pray that God will be with you and that you'll prepare like He won't be."

Strange counsel from a minister. Strange, but wise.

Pace rose from the chair. "Call upon me for anything and at any time."

I stood. He hugged me. I remained standing until the echo of the tap from his gnarled walking stick faded from the hall. I took the more comfortable chair to wait for my uncle. My phone vibrated and the screen flashed Tommy Lee's cell.

"Yes."

"I'm pulling up to Brookshire's house. His Escape is in the driveway."

"You want to check back in forty-five minutes, like we agreed for me?"

"No. Where are you?"

"In my uncle's rehab room. He's in a PT session. I'm alone."

"Good. I'm going to put the phone in my pocket with the line open."

"You recording?"

"No. I want to be able to answer truthfully if he asks. Mute your phone so no sound comes from your end."

"Got it."

"Then do it now."

I hit the mute button and held the phone to my ear. My stomach tightened. If things went bad, I could only listen. Tommy Lee was on his own.

Chapter Twenty

I heard loud knocks. No doorbell for Tommy Lee this time.

"You again?" Brookshire's voice was muffled but understandable.

I boosted the level of my phone to the maximum.

"You asked me to keep you in the loop."

"So I did. Come in. You want a beer?"

"No thanks. I won't be staying that long."

Brookshire laughed. "Long enough to sit down?"

"Maybe." Tommy Lee's voice was devoid of any humor.

Springs creaked as the sheriff sat.

"Well, what is it?" Brookshire asked.

"We're staking out the Sinclairs. Robert played golf this morning. Janet, well, Janet had a visitor at home."

Silence. I thought for a second the call had been dropped.

Then Brookshire spoke, his voice a deep rumble with a hint of menace. "What are you getting at, Tommy Lee?"

"I think you know. A green Ford Escape parked in her driveway, and a Semper Fi sticker on the bumper. 'Semper Fi. Always faithful.' At least it wasn't on her car."

"Knock it off. And I'll thank you to leave now."

"Would you care to give me an explanation for my report?"

"Okay, okay. She and her husband are in WITSEC. The Santona family would get to them if they could, so be damned careful what you spread around."

"And you're her, dare I use the word, handler?"

"I'm their contact. She called me. She's spooked by these murders that look like mob hits. She's been jumpy since Robert made the harebrained attempt to sneak back to his father's funeral. I tried to calm her down. When I left, she was feeling better. End of story."

"I see. So, that's your explanation? You calming her down? Does she always wear a white terrycloth robe over nothing but her new identity? Do you always say goodbye with a kiss and what appears to be a strip search?"

"That's your word against mine and hers," Brookshire barked.

"Not against my word. My deputy was the witness. It's your's and Janet's word against his...and the pictures."

Pictures? Tommy Lee was really playing hardball.

"Pictures?" Brookshire echoed my own question.

"Great thing about these new cell phones. They're also high-definition cameras, and the files can be stored in the cloud immediately. An easy download to the U.S. Marshals' office in Washington."

I mentally kicked myself for not having the sense to have actually taken pictures. Tommy Lee's lie carried such devastating consequences for Brookshire that the marshal would either cave or try to kill him.

I heard rough scratches as Tommy Lee evidently lifted the phone from his belt.

"And if I don't report to Barry within the next ten minutes, he's been told to send the photos on. Then it's out of our hands, Luther."

"You son of a bitch. You're threatening me."

"I don't like being lied to. You're much more involved than you told us. I want to know everything about the Sinclairs and everything about your relationship with Janet."

"And in exchange?"

"The pictures won't exist. You have my word."

I heard the scraping sound as Tommy Lee returned the phone to his belt. Then a moment of silence.

Finally, Brookshire cracked. "All right, damn you. Robert and Joan Santona were placed here about three and a half years ago. I wasn't involved with their flip in New Jersey. Prosecutors handled that. They were admitted to WITSEC after giving up documents proving Bobby Santona, Robert's father, oversaw a major fraud conspiracy in the state's tire-recycling program."

Brookshire's statement matched what I had learned from the news reports of the trial.

"So, Robert Santona didn't have to testify in court?" Tommy Lee asked.

"No. The evidence was presented to the grand jury with the story it had been confiscated in a raid of Robert Santona's home. Actually, Robert and Joan knew the raid was coming. They had alerted the FBI as to the existence of the records."

"Why would they turn on the family?"

"Because the family discovered Robert and Joan had been skimming off the top. Joan actually kept the books. They might spare Robert, but his wife wasn't blood kin."

I remembered Brookshire's earlier comment that Robert Santona wasn't the smartest bee in the hive. That would be the queen bee. Queen Joan. And I felt I had learned the source of the money that had gone into the single premium insurance policies.

"So, Robert and Joan went into WITSEC before the arrests and trial?" Tommy Lee asked.

"Yes. The marshals pulled them out at three in the morning. We put the word out on the street that they'd gone to join Jimmy Hoffa."

"Do you have any reason to believe the Santonas, aka Sinclairs, are involved in any way with a food stamp scam?"

"No. Frankly, I don't see how they could even set it up. They're outsiders. Who would trust them?"

"It might not be about trust. It might be about fear."

"Okay," Brookshire conceded. "But who would fear them?

Look at Robert. That human butterball's not exactly an intimidator."

"How did they wind up in Gainesboro?"

"Janet thought out west would be too alien, but she was afraid to stay in the northeast. The North Carolina mountains seemed remote enough with a small town less likely to attract any of the people from their old lives. Then Robert had to go screw it all up last July by sneaking back for the funeral."

"Any evidence that he was trailed back to Gainesboro?"

"No. But the dummy didn't have the sense to use a rental car. He's pretty sure he got away from the cemetery before anyone read the license tag. But they could have seen the colors of the plate. And these two gangland-style murders have put at least a regional spotlight on Gainesboro. That's why Janet's been upset."

"How long has your affair been going on?" Tommy Lee asked.

"Only a few months. And that's all it is. Comfort and companionship. Tommy Lee, you don't know what it's like coming home to an empty house every night." His voice choked. "Janet's lonely too. Her husband's about as affectionate as a dead trout, and she's afraid to make friends because of her history. She and I…well, it just happened."

"All right, Luther. I'm taking you at your word, although the cop part of my brain is screaming you've shoveled in a lot of bullshit. Tell me this, and for God's sake, don't lie to me. Have you told Janet Sinclair anything about our investigation?"

"No. Not a word. I have a cop brain too. I might have used poor judgment in the affair, but I'd never compromise your case."

"How often do you see her?"

"When Robert plays golf. Sometimes during the week if he's on a sales route that we're confident will keep him away."

"Was Robert playing golf last Saturday?" Tommy Lee asked.

"No. He wanted to watch the parade. He and Janet weren't too far from the shooting. They left almost immediately. She dropped Robert at home, and then made an excuse to run an errand so she could phone me. She was worried she might show up in some cell phone video if it made the news. That's the kind of footage that can go viral."

"Sid Ferguson headed up the SBI investigation," Tommy Lee said. "Talk to him if you're concerned."

"I've looked through YouTube and Facebook. Mostly posts of the first responders. You're in some clips, keeping people back. I looked carefully and Robert and Janet never appeared."

Another pause, and then Brookshire added, "Your deputy. Shouldn't you phone him?"

"Did you hear everything?" Tommy Lee asked me the question as soon as he returned to his car.

"Yes. Do you believe him?"

"For the most part. Unless he's withholding damning information, he doesn't offer anything that links the Sinclairs to the EBT scam. All we have is Archie's leak to them the night before Sonny's murder."

"Does that change our approach?"

"No. I'm going to look into this Staples Sources company. Next week I might have you sit in the post office in Spartanburg to see who collects mail from the P.O. box."

"I forgot to tell you. My EBT card came this morning. If Wilmer's Convenience Corner is open tomorrow, I might drop by."

"So much for your weekend off," Tommy Lee said. "But, yeah, go ahead and get underway. Monday afternoon, I'll be at the double burial for Toby and Sonny. Pauline McKay called the department and asked for protection. I'd promised that, so I'll do it."

"You also promised to feed her chickens. You been doing that too?"

"Reece is on that assignment."

"Reece? Didn't he take that as an insult?"

"Nah. I told him he could have the eggs."

Mom, Susan, and I attended church Sunday morning. Afterwards, we went to Rockwells' Cafeteria, a Gainesboro fixture for over fifty years. Half our congregation was eating there and a steady stream of diners came by our table to ask about Uncle Wayne.

We took Mom back to the funeral home where she wanted to get ready for Wayne's return the next day. I'd forgotten to alert Tommy Lee that I couldn't stake out the Spartanburg post office until we got my uncle settled. Given the way hospital paperwork can be processed, his actual release time was anybody's guess.

I'd also wanted to have a conversation with Mom about her intended move to Alderway. Fletcher's suggestion to get three appraisals of the funeral home made sense, and Susan's offer to use the money from the sale of her condo meant we might be able to borrow enough funds for the shortfall with the existing lease to the funeral business covering the monthly mortgage payment. Fletcher's fiancée, Cindy, would be the first banker I'd approach. Of course, the wild card was still Uncle Wayne.

My unannounced family conference was short-circuited when Mom said she'd like to lie down for a few minutes. The barrage of well-wishers at church and lunch had been exhausting. She insisted that Susan and I should leave and enjoy our Sunday afternoon.

After Mom retired to her bedroom, Susan said, "You wanted to use that EBT card today, didn't you?"

"Yes. But I don't know if the store is even open. It's kind of a long drive for nothing."

"Did you check the Internet?"

I laughed. "You think a place called Wilmer's Convenience Corner is going to have a website?"

She pulled out her smartphone, rapidly thumbed the virtual keyboard, and then studied the screen. "No website."

"See."

"A Facebook page. 'Wilmer's Convenience Corner—If we don't have it, you don't need it.' They're open one to six, Sunday afternoons." She dropped her phone back in her handbag. "You can thank me tonight. And, Sherlock, you'd better change into some jeans and an old shirt if you want half a chance at pulling this off."

I found the store on the outskirts of Clyde, North Carolina, a small town two counties over from Gainesboro. Wilmer's Convenience Corner was indeed on the corner of Highway 23 and an unlined blacktop that wound through a warren of modest houses. It was the kind of place where kids would ride their bicycles for a Coke and a candy bar, and retired men would stop to chew the fat. There was one island of gas pumps and a single pump by the left corner of the white concrete-block building that dispensed kerosene.

A man in his mid-thirties was pumping gas into an old muddy Bronco. I parked along the side of the building, and, as I walked to the front door, he gave me a nod that was nothing more than an acknowledgment of my existence.

A thin man with tired eyes sat at the front counter. Behind him on a stool was a red-haired girl of ten or eleven. Her nose was in a Baby-Sitters Club paperback, and she didn't look up when the bells tinkling above the door announced my entry.

The man spoke the universal line—"Can I hep ya?"

"Just picking up a few things. Y'all take EBT cards, don't ya?"

"Yeah, for qualified purchases."

I glanced at the door to the man at the Bronco. "Oh, these will be qualified, all right."

I picked up a green plastic hand-basket and started walking the aisles. The Bronco's engine roared to life and the gas customer drove away. Now it was just the three of us.

I chose some bread, a box of breakfast cereal, a can of pork and beans, and then some items that weren't covered by SNAP benefits. I picked up a small bag of dog food, a roll of paper towels, dishwashing detergent, and then I hit the cooler for a six-pack of Budweiser.

I carried my purchases to the counter. "I'd like a carton of Winstons too. I flipped open my wallet and laid the EBT card atop the box of cereal.

"Some of these items don't qualify, sir."

I ignored him and turned to the girl. "How's the book, Norie? I hope it has a happy ending for everyone."

The child looked up at me with a smile that transformed into confusion when she saw a total stranger. She glanced at her father.

A tremor ran through his body. "Sorry, but they don't qualify." The words came out as a nervous whisper.

"Oh, Buddy, I'm sure they do. Go ahead and ring them up, and then they can find their way back to the shelves. The usual split is fine." I looked back at Norie. "Didn't mean to interrupt your reading. Your dad says you're a smart girl. He's very proud of you."

"Thank you," she said, obviously aware that something wasn't right.

"Oh, and I'll need the receipt, Buddy. You know, just a routine audit to make sure what you report and I report are the same."

He gave a barely perceptible nod and began keying in the prices. The total came to sixty-three dollars and seventy-six cents. I gave him my card and he swiped the stripe. A few seconds later the machine spit out an approved slip. The item prices matched but he'd changed the codes to nothing but approved products. I realized the normal procedure might have been nothing more than ringing up a phantom sale. On the other hand, Buddy Smith probably read my behavior as a test, a test he was desperate not to fail.

He handed me thirty-one, eighty-eight—half the purchase total. "Have a nice day," he murmured.

"Sorry to make you restock this time." I left him with the pile of groceries.

Once in the jeep, my stomach unknotted. Still, I felt godawful. Scaring that poor man and his child. I dreaded the next step which would put Buddy Smith in a vise. I'd be back with my deputy credentials, and after a repeat performance, threaten to take him into custody. But that could wait a day or two. I wasn't going to do that in front of his daughter. I'd make the bust while she was in school.

On the way home, I phoned Tommy Lee.

"You did well," he said. "Let's plan a return visit on Tuesday morning."

"Okay, but after the girl's at school."

"I understand."

"And then, after we get my uncle home tomorrow, I'll go to the Spartanburg post office."

"No, you won't," Tommy Lee said.

"I won't?"

"Funny thing about that post office. I'm on my way back from Spartanburg now. I decided to ride down and check it out. Even though the post office is closed, you can still get to the boxes. Except the P.O. box on the Staples Sources invoice, 8009, doesn't exist. The highest number is 8000. Those checks were either picked up at the stores in person or mailed to another address. I guess we're back to your new friend Buddy Smith and the hope that each week he's writing a check to Staples Sources."

"That's one avenue," I said. "Yet, the checks are being cashed at some bank, if not in Spartanburg, then it could be anywhere in the country. But if this is a local operation, they might keep it here. What do we need to do to get account names?"

"I can get a court order. Or I could first ask my lead investigator to use his winning smile and charm the information out of every bank contact he knows. So, be sure and brush your teeth, you charmer, you."

Chapter Twenty-one

Sunday evening, Susan and I sat in our customary chairs on the back deck with Democrat stretched out at our feet. I'd opted for a beer; she chose sparkling water over wine, citing seven o'clock surgery the next morning. I'd briefed her on my encounter with Buddy Smith and his daughter and she'd agreed with my efforts to shield the girl as much as possible.

"You think they're in any danger?" she asked.

"Not at the moment. I made my approach when it was just the three of us. He'll continue whatever the established practice is. If we succeed in getting his cooperation, then things could change. I'd want to make sure the girl was someplace out of harm's way."

"Did you have your gun with you this afternoon?"

"Snug in the small of my back. But I don't think I have anything to fear from Buddy Smith. The man was terrified by whom he thought I represented."

"I don't know about that," she said skeptically. "Don't underestimate what people will do to protect their children."

Democrat lifted his head and growled. I heard the crunch of tires on gravel.

"Who could that be?" Susan asked.

"I don't know." I laughed. "Archie's supposed to be out of town."

"Let's go see." She rose from her chair. "I'll put on a pot of coffee."

We went to the door, Democrat leading the way. Through the front windows, I saw a gray sedan behind my jeep.

"That looks like Sid Ferguson's car. He's with the SBI."

I was wrong. The driver's door opened and a man in a dark suit stepped into the glow of the front porch lights.

"It's the food stamp investigator, Collier Crockett. This is definitely police business."

"Then I'll put on the coffee and take Democrat and a book to the bedroom. Let me know when he leaves."

I stepped onto the porch. "Good evening, Collier."

"Clayton," he snapped. "Just what the hell do you think you're doing?" His jaw was tight and his eyes narrow slits. Whatever he thought I'd done was driving him to either slug me or have a coronary on the spot.

"Standing on my porch. On my property. And if you don't ratchet down that tone I'll have to charge you with trespassing."

He stopped at the bottom of the porch steps and looked up at me. "You think you're cute, don't you? We'll see how cute when I report you blew an undercover operation months in the making."

"Fine. Then we'll counter with how you obstructed a murder investigation by withholding information and leaving us to find our own way. If that screwed up your case, then you only have yourself to blame. Last time I checked, murder trumps fraud every time."

"I warned you to stay in your own county. I'm running a multi-state investigation. An investigation that you've jeopardized."

I realized what had set him off. "Buddy Smith. Wilmer's Convenience Corner."

"Yes. I've been working on him for several months. Since a terrible incident with the girl's cat. He's low on the food chain, but I'm sure he knows who's above him. He just hasn't gotten comfortable enough to talk. Now you've really spooked him."

"Were you tailing me?"

"No. Buddy called me right after you left. He thought you'd been sent to sniff out if he was turning sides. Now he's clammed up on me. If I bust him, it could send everyone else underground and we don't have all the players pegged yet." He stepped up on the porch closer to me. "So, do you understand how your fishing around is unraveling our whole operation?"

"We weren't fishing. We were targeting a very specific lead."

"Yeah? What was that?"

What the hell, I thought. He needed to know Tommy Lee and I weren't Laurel and Hardy. "A company we believe transfers the funds from the EBT deposits to whoever's running the fraud. A company called Staples Sources. I pushed Buddy Smith to sell me non-qualified items to get some leverage and see his accounts payables. See if Staples Sources was one of his suppliers."

"Why Buddy?"

"We found a list of stores tied to Toby and Sonny McKay. Buddy's was one of them. We also learned about the dead cat and thought that made him a more likely target."

Collier Crockett took a deep breath and seemed to calm down. "And why Staples Sources?"

"We found a number of blank invoices from the company in Rufus Taylor's store. He was evidently filling them in to pay whatever was the share of the week's illegal take that he owed his partners. We've confirmed the address of the company is bogus. Haven't they popped up on your radar?"

Crockett shook his head. "No. We've been concentrating on the EBT purchase side. I remember the company name but they seemed legit. This is the first I've heard about blank invoices."

"What did you tell Buddy Smith about me?"

"He gave me your name since it posted on your transaction. First time I've heard of an undercover operative not using an alias. Anyway, I told him to ignore you. I said if it was a test, then he'd passed and you wouldn't be back. I tried to leverage your visit as another reason he should trust me. I can protect him against you."

"Then if I see him again, I'll let him know I'm a deputy. That we're working together."

Crockett scowled. "He's my potential source. Whether you're a good guy or a bad guy, you're going to spook him. He's nervous enough when I dress down and drop by for a chat."

"We've got our own case to solve. I'll speak to the sheriff, but as far as I'm concerned, any lead is fair game. But thanks for the heads-up. We'll be careful."

He pointed his finger at me. "Be more than careful, Clayton. Buddy Smith is entangled with some bad people. You could get him and his little girl killed."

He pivoted on his heel and returned to his car. I watched him spin the tires on the gravel backing up, then lurch forward, spewing stones in his wake.

At seven-thirty the next morning, I phoned Tommy Lee and gave him the details of my confrontation with Crockett. "I told him I'd talk to you, but that I didn't see us limiting our investigation."

"I agree," the sheriff said. "But we should go easy. Crockett has a point about too much attention being paid to Buddy Smith. Let's see what we can learn about Staples Sources. I'll talk to Crockett and work out some information exchange. When are you headed to the hospital?"

"I'm leaving now. My uncle's supposed to be released at eleven. But don't count on me till mid-afternoon."

"Okay. And I'm tied up with the McKays' funerals. I'll ask Marge to do an Internet search on Staples Sources. Maybe we can come at them that way."

"Maybe, but the prospect doesn't seem very hopeful."

"I know," Tommy Lee commiserated. "We could be hitting a dead end and have to see where Crockett's case leads. I'm beginning to think the Sinclairs are a red herring. We're reading too much into them because of WITSEC."

"We're reading too much into them because we don't have anything else. Damn it, Tommy Lee, all we have to show for our efforts are three fresh graves in the Twin Creeks Baptist Church cemetery."

As I feared, Uncle Wayne's eleven o'clock discharge didn't happen till twelve-thirty. I offered to buy lunch from the cafeteria, but my uncle said he didn't want to spend another minute in the hospital. So, we made a run through a Wendy's drive-through and took food back to the funeral home.

I pulled to the rear entrance where there were fewer steps onto the back porch and into the kitchen. All was quiet. Fletcher and our assistant, Freddy Mott, were at the McKays' burial service.

Uncle Wayne didn't refuse my arm as he shuffled inside. Mom pulled a chair out from the kitchen table and he eased himself into it.

He looked around. "You know. This place is really quiet when nobody's here."

Mom and I looked at each other. Such an obvious statement was merely the preface to some other thought.

"Kinda sad," he continued. "When this place isn't a home. What will we call it? A funeral house? And the kitchen. I won't be cooking any more family meals here. Guess we'll have to call it the break room, like it's part of some office complex."

"Don't be silly," Mom said. "How many meals did you cook here?"

"Sandwiches, Connie. I made a lot of sandwiches."

Mom laughed. "Oh, Wayne, only you would lament over a home-cooked sandwich." She set the Wendy's bag on the table beside him. "Now eat your store-bought one."

My uncle chuckled and pulled out a cheeseburger.

After we ate, I helped Uncle Wayne upstairs. We had to stop on the landing a moment for him to catch his breath.

"I tell you, Barry, getting old ain't for sissies."

"No one ever accused you of being a sissy. The trick is to be sensible. Don't do too much too soon."

He tightened his grip on my arm. "Don't worry. I'll take the steps one at a time."

On the second floor, he dropped my support and walked down the hall to his room. It had once been mine. I followed him in and was surprised to see he hadn't changed it. The shelves still held the model ships and planes I'd built with my dad. Framed pictures displayed family vacations, some with Uncle Wayne, some without.

"I can box my stuff up and give you more space," I said.

My uncle sat on the bed and looked around. "No, I like it. Reminds me of when you were a boy." His eyes moistened. "Reminds me of when I was a boy. Not so long ago, Barry. You'll see. It all flies by in the blink of an eye."

I heard Fletcher's voice downstairs and left my uncle to rest. Mom was pouring him a glass of lemonade when I entered the kitchen.

"How'd it go?" I joined him at the table and Mom set a plate of cookies between us.

"As well as expected. Small crowd. Didn't have enough pallbearers to bring both caskets out of the church at the same time." He shook his head. "If I never do another double funeral again, it will be too soon."

"And Pauline McKay?"

"She seemed numb. The sheriff stood with her and her sister Nelda. He was going to escort them back to Pauline's house. She's tired of hiding out in Canton and wants to return home. I think he was going to check the locks and give her some security advice."

I hadn't thought about Pauline McKay in a few days. Perhaps enough time had passed that she was no longer considered a threat. I hoped so. We couldn't force her to stay in hiding.

"I know you can't talk about a case," Fletcher said, "but are you making any progress?"

"We're finding some dots. Now we need to connect them."

My phone vibrated. I checked the screen. The number was for the Sheriff's Department switchboard.

"Sorry, I've got to take this."

I rose from the chair and walked rapidly out to the privacy of the backyard. "This is Barry."

"It's Carol. Are you at the funeral with Tommy Lee?"

"No. What's up?"

"Do you know a Luther Brookshire?"

"Yes. He's a U.S. Marshal."

"He called the department asking for Tommy Lee. I told him the sheriff was at a funeral and couldn't take a call. He asked for you. I can patch him through."

The phone clicked.

"Deputy Clayton?" Brookshire's voice was tense, the words clipped.

"Yes. What's wrong?"

"Janet Sinclair just called me. She arrived home to find Robert dead in the carport. I'm on my way there now."

"Dead? How?"

"Shot in the head. He was executed."

Chapter Twenty-two

I didn't bother to go to the department or change into my uniform. I sped to the Sinclairs as fast as I could, the jeep's hazard lights flashing and horn blaring in a desperate effort to clear the road. I called Carol our dispatcher back and told her to send EMTs to the Arbor Ridge address. I also asked her to make sure she saved the number that would have registered Brookshire's call. I wanted to know where he'd been when he phoned.

Then I called Tommy Lee. "Robert Sinclair's been shot and killed."

"Where?" he asked.

"His carport. Janet found him, called Brookshire, and he called for you. Carol passed him to me since you're with Mrs. McKay. I'm on my way. Carol's alerting EMTs and recording time and number of Brookshire's call, in case you want to pull a GPS location."

"Good thinking. I'll send out two deputies to help. Also, I'll contact Lindsay Boyce and request their forensics."

"You're bringing in the FBI?"

"Yes. We're dealing with WITSEC, and the marshals are going to go nuts. So much for never losing a witness. I want to deal with a friendly federal face. You secure the scene. I'll be there as soon as I can."

Janet Sinclair stood in the front lawn of her house and stared up into the trees. One arm was stretched across her chest with her hand clutching her opposite shoulder. The other hand held a cigarette that she puffed like it was a deep-sea diver's air hose. I appeared to be the first responder and parked the jeep on the narrow shoulder in front of the house, leaving the driveway clear for EMTs and forensic units. I got out and tucked the Kimber pistol in the small of my back.

Janet flipped the cigarette away and ran toward me.

"Mr. Clayton, Mr. Clayton," she cried hysterically. "They shot him. The family shot him."

She surprised me with a fierce hug, head against my chest. "I was afraid they'd come back for me. They left the White Rose of Santona."

"The what?"

"Their signature. By the body. Luther will know."

I let her sob a few minutes, and then took her shoulders and gently pushed her away. "I need to check the scene. Why don't you wait in the house? Luther Brookshire will be here soon. He's the one who called me." I hoped the mention of the marshal would calm her down, although at this point a dead husband, an adulteress wife, and her lover would be an unusual combination at a crime scene. I hoped my fellow deputies and Tommy Lee would arrive first.

I took her arm and steered her toward the front door and away from the carport. I couldn't see the body, but the trunk of Janet's Mercedes was open and a torn bag of groceries lay at the left rear corner of Robert's SUV. Several cans of food had rolled to the edge of the sloped driveway. To my eye, the story appeared to be that Janet had returned from the grocery store, lifted the brown paper bag from the trunk, and then rounded the back of Robert's vehicle headed for the door in the carport. I guessed the body was close to the front of the car on the driver's side. She didn't see it until clearing the large SUV.

We stepped up on the small front porch. The door was

unlocked and I opened it. "Wait here while I check inside." I crossed the threshold and pulled my pistol free.

The home had a formal living room, expansive kitchen, den, and a master bedroom on the first floor. Folded clothes were spread out on the king-sized bed where either Janet or a housekeeper had left them. Three bedrooms and two baths were upstairs. One of the bedrooms had been converted into a home office. Both a laptop and a desktop were on a credenza behind a wide desk. We would want to go through both and any external drives that might exist. I holstered my gun and returned to the front door.

"It's all clear," I said.

She sniffled and wiped her eyes with her fingers. "Is there anything I can do?"

"Whatever makes you the most comfortable. Brew some coffee. Have another cigarette. There'll be a lot of people here soon."

She nodded and withdrew into the living room.

I circled back and noted a dented can of corn and a shattered bottle of ranch dressing on the concrete driveway. Inside the ripped bag, I saw a box of elbow pasta and a jar of tomato sauce. Other items were underneath, but what I found most important was a receipt trapped under the pasta. I picked it up, noticed that the date and time stamp placed her in the grocery store less than forty minutes ago. I stuck the receipt in my pocket to add to whatever evidence might be forthcoming.

I moved into the carport. Robert Sinclair lay on his back by the front tire. The driver's door was closed, so he must have stepped out, shut the door, and was either surprised by or familiar with his killer. There was no way the scene I viewed distinguished between the two possibilities. What was indisputable was the bullet hole in his forehead and two red splotches on his blue polo shirt. Blood flow had been minimal, indicating he'd died instantly. The method was a classic hit—two to the body, one to the head.

Next to his face lay a long-stemmed white rosebud. A statement? A signature?

I returned to my jeep and pulled an evidence-collecting kit from the back. It included latex gloves and clear evidence bags. I also grabbed a small flashlight.

I went in the Infiniti from the front passenger's side. A super-sized soda cup was in the center console holder. Some files with stores names on the label tabs were on the passenger's seat. A Snickers candy bar wrapper was wadded on the floor. I used the flashlight to peer under the seat. Nothing but wires for the position control.

The backseat was clear on the right side. I shone the light into the rear storage area. The golf clubs I'd seen on Saturday lay diagonally across the carpet. Spiked golf shoes were beside them.

Robert Sinclair's body blocked access to the driver's door, and I didn't want to move it even a few inches until forensics and the M.E. had cleared it. But I could get in the back door behind the driver. The floor mat was clean. I bent down, half in and half out of the car, and reached under the driver's seat. My gloved hand encountered a book and what felt like a tube. I placed my cheek on the rear mat and angled the flashlight so that the beam threw directly underneath the seat. It was a book. But the metal tube was a suppressor mounted to a semi-automatic pistol pointed straight at my face. I carefully lifted the gun and sealed it in an evidence bag. Through the clear plastic, I could identify it as a Beretta 92FS twenty-two caliber. The same caliber that killed Rufus Taylor and Sonny McKay.

I did the same with the book, but not before flipping through several pages. It was a ledger of columns filled with numbers. No words, no cursive handwriting. Sections were divided under five-digit headings. I suspected one of those five-digit codes stood for Taylor's Short Stop. Another for Wilmer's Convenience Corner. I was holding the master accounts for the network of stores engaged in the food stamp fraud conspiracy. I would probably become FNS Investigator Collier Crockett's new best friend.

I stood back from the car and looked down at the body sprawled before me. Robert Sinclair, aka Robert Santona, had received justice dispensed by his own family with bullets and a flower while his own weapon lay less than three feet away.

The sounds of sirens wailed ever louder. I turned and walked down the driveway, ready to wave the cavalry into position.

Deputies Reece Hutchins and Steve Wakefield had quickly established a perimeter. We knew the activities of police cars and vans would soon attract the neighbors.

Tommy Lee arrived about ten minutes ahead of U.S. Marshal Luther Brookshire, which gave me the chance to show the sheriff what I'd discovered beneath the driver's seat.

"For the time being, we keep these items to ourselves," he said.

"Robert's death is our case?"

He gave a wry smile. "Up until my niece yanks it away for the Bureau. I know Lindsay well enough that she's not going to let an interstate mob hit go to her Podunk uncle. She knows me well enough to know I won't back off until I'm sure we got the man who killed Rufus and Sonny."

I nodded, and then saw Brookshire's green Escape skid to a stop in front of my jeep. "Your buddy Luther's going to want a piece of the case as well. His protected witness got whacked."

"He's already had one piece too many. But I'll play nice. Let's go hear Mrs. Sinclair's statement before Luther has a chance to coach her. He can sit in, but it's our investigation."

Tommy Lee hurried to intercept the marshal as he ran up the lawn. I went in the carport door and through the kitchen to the living room where I found Janet standing in front of a bay window. If she'd brewed coffee, she wasn't having any. One hand held a cigarette, the other a glass of whiskey.

"We're going to need a statement now, Mrs. Sinclair."

She turned to me. "Can I give it to Luther?"

"He can sit in, but right now your husband's murder is our jurisdiction."

She sighed and took a healthy swallow from her glass. "Funny, isn't it? Me coming to you for those funeral arrangements. I didn't know you were a deputy. Guess you'll be doing double duty when we meet about getting Robert back to Paterson."

"We'll do that later." I glanced around the living room. There was a plush white sofa and expensive-looking wingback chairs in matching navy blue upholstery. I gestured to the sofa. "Why don't you sit with me? The sheriff and Marshal Brookshire can take the chairs."

She stubbed out her cigarette in an ashtray on an end table by one of the chairs and joined me on the sofa.

Tommy Lee and Brookshire came in through the front door. The marshal was clearly agitated and looked like he could barely restrain himself from running to her.

"Janet! Are you okay?"

"Yes," she said calmly. "I was at the grocery store. I guess the killers didn't want to wait for me. So, what now? Identity number three?"

"Yes. I'll get you out of here tonight."

Tommy Lee held up a hand. "Before anyone goes anywhere else, we need to learn what happened here. Marshal Brookshire," Tommy Lee said formally, "you're welcome to sit in, but right now this is our case and Barry and I will do the questioning. Why don't you sit over there?" The sheriff pointed to the wing-back chair farther from Janet.

Brookshire complied, sitting on the edge of the cushion and still clearly agitated.

Tommy Lee took a notebook and pen from his pocket. "Go ahead, Barry."

I angled myself on the sofa to face her. "Why don't you tell us what happened today? Walk us through from the time you woke up to when I arrived."

"Well, I slept till around seven-thirty. That's when I usually get up. Robert was already gone. He's an early riser and he had some appointments in Murphy."

Murphy was a town in the most western tip of North Carolina and nearly two hours from Gainesboro.

"Did you speak to him?" I asked.

"No. He's sweet to get up quietly and not wake me." Her voice caught. "I didn't even get to tell him goodbye." She glanced in the direction of the carport where her husband lay on the concrete floor. Then she looked at Brookshire. "Luther knows how close we were. How much I loved him."

Brookshire shifted uncomfortably. He knew that we knew the truth.

"And so you got up," I said, trying to keep her focused.

"Yes. Robert had started the coffeemaker. I turned on the *Today Show* and had a cup with a bowl of yogurt and fruit. Then I started some laundry. Now that I'm not working, I try to keep to a schedule and Monday is laundry day. Most of Robert's clothes are perma-press. They're samples of the casual wear and sports lines he represents. I touched up a few items with the iron and by then it was nearly ten. I was getting a little cabin fever and knew I had to buy a few things for supper. So, I decided to treat myself to an early lunch at the country club and then do my shopping."

"Did you meet anyone in particular?" I asked.

"I joined some women I occasionally play bridge with. Linda Albany and Chrissy Perry. They'll confirm my story. I ran by the bank, stopped at Ingles and picked up pasta, tomato sauce, greens for a salad, and a few other items I needed. Robert said he'd be back mid-afternoon, and we'd talked about squeezing in nine holes of golf so I didn't make the grocery shopping a prolonged affair. It was probably about two-thirty when I started for home. Robert had texted me that he was getting off the interstate. I replied that I was at the grocery store."

"What time was that?"

She thought a moment. "I was in the produce department. I guess around two-fifteen. The time stamp should be on my phone."

"So, you didn't speak to him."

"Correct. When he said he was exiting the interstate, I knew he was about ten minutes away. I expected to be home about fifteen or twenty minutes after him, change clothes, and then we'd take his car. His clubs were already loaded."

"All right. And did you come straight here from Ingles?"

She swallowed and then nodded. "It must have been around ten to three. As I expected, his car was here. I pulled to the right, where I always park. I popped the trunk and carried the single bag. Usually he'll come out to see if I need help, but I assumed he was probably changing back in our bedroom. I walked around his car..." She stopped and caught her breath. "I walked around the back of the car and saw him lying there. I dropped the bag and ran to him. I thought he'd had a heart attack. Then I saw it."

"It?" I prompted. "The bullet wounds?"

She shook her head. "The rose. The White Rose of Santona."

"Yes. You mentioned that. What is it?"

She looked at Brookshire. "I'd rather Luther tell you. He knows more than I do."

Tommy Lee and I stared at Brookshire, waiting for him to pick up the story.

He leaned forward in the chair. "First, I need to get something out in the open. Robert and Janet Sinclair were in WITSEC. Their former names were Robert and Joan Santona."

So, Brookshire was going to play it straight, I thought. He gave no acknowledgment that we'd already discussed their true identities.

"Thanks to their cooperation with the FBI, prosecutors were able to convict Bobby Santona and some of his key associates of racketeering. We took Robert and Joan into Witness Protection and spread the rumor that they'd been abducted and killed. You see, Robert is Bobby Santona's son and his role in the conviction of his father would be unforgivable."

"Why did he turn?" I asked.

Brookshire looked at Janet. She gave a slight nod.

"There were some funds that went missing," Brookshire said. "Accusations were leveled at Robert and Joan. Robert became fearful, especially for his wife's safety. We offered them a fresh start."

And in exchange for Robert's betrayal of his own family, Joan, aka Janet, started an affair with her handler. But I kept that thought to myself.

"And the rose?" I asked.

"It's never been proven, but the story is that whenever an informant or enemy of the family is killed, a white rose is left as a calling card. Some of the mob hits of the other families are more gruesome. Severed genitals, missing fingers, sliced-off ears. You get the picture. Warnings to anyone who would dare cross them." Brookshire sighed. "Looks like Robert didn't heed our warnings."

"What do you mean?" I asked.

Brookshire looked at Janet. "Tell him."

"Robert went back to Paterson for his father's funeral. He wore a disguise, if you can believe it. Fake beard. Glasses. I told him he was crazy. That was why I came to you about funeral arrangements. I was afraid his violation of the marshals' rules would lead Robert's family straight to us. I begged him not to go. When he insisted, I urged him to keep at a distance. I didn't mean for him to climb a goddammed tree."

"And he came back with a broken leg," I said. "My wife treated him."

"Yes. I wanted to contact Luther immediately. I thought we'd have to move again, but Robert insisted he'd gotten away before anyone saw his car." She looked at Brookshire. "I guess he was wrong. Dead wrong."

"Don't worry," Brookshire said. "We'll get you resettled."

I looked at Tommy Lee. He nodded for me to continue.

"When you found your husband's body, did you go in the house?"

"No. I was afraid. I called Luther and told him what happened. He suggested I get in my car and drive into town, but I couldn't just run away leaving Robert like that. Luther called back a few minutes later and said you were on the way. I waited in the front yard where you saw me."

"Why didn't you go to a neighbor's house?"

She shrugged. "I wasn't thinking that clearly. We really don't know our neighbors. And I thought if anyone was waiting for me, they would have shot me as soon as I got out of the car. Like they did Robert."

"But you didn't go into the house," I said.

"Well, I wasn't one hundred percent sure, was I?"

"But the doors were unlocked. Both the front and the one to the carport."

She gave me a humorless smile. "One of the nice things about living down here. We never lock our doors. Back in New Jersey, our house would have been stripped before we reached the main road."

"You left your doors unlocked, but your husband carried a pistol."

Her eyes widened. "He what?"

"I found a pistol under the driver's seat."

"That's news to me. Luther, did you know about it?"

"No," the marshal answered. "Maybe he carried it because he traveled so much."

"Did he have a permit to carry?" I asked.

"I don't know," Brookshire said. "It's the first I've heard of it."

"How much do you know about your husband's business?"

"He was successful. He liked his clients. We have a climate-controlled storage unit where he keeps his samples. We're not rich but we're comfortable."

"How's he paid?"

"He has a base salary and then a commission schedule."

"Is he ever paid in cash?"

"Not that I know of."

"A joint account?"

She shook her head. "He has a business account, then we have a joint account, and I have an account of my own. I pick up seasonal work with H&R Block. My background's accounting. That's how Robert and I met. A continuing education class."

"How long had you been married?"

"Had," she repeated, recognizing everything about her husband was now past tense. "Thursday next it would have been fifteen years. We were going to Kiawah Island to celebrate." She covered her eyes with one hand. A shudder visibly ran through her body.

"How much longer do we need to go on?" Brookshire asked.

"Till we've covered everything." Tommy Lee flipped through his notes. "Did you ever travel with your husband?"

"No. The mountain roads make me carsick, and there was nothing for me to do."

"Did you ever meet any of his customers?"

"A few times. Robert would have dinners or cocktails at the club. I attended when it was a spousal event."

"So, you were alone most days."

"Except during tax season. Then I go into the H&R Block offices. Sometimes here, sometimes Asheville. It depends on where I'm needed."

"And tax season is when?"

She smiled. "Longer than it used to be. Now they want me mid-January through April fifteenth. Three times they've asked me to take a full-time job." She paused. "Maybe I'll need one." She looked at Brookshire. "Wherever I wind up."

Not if Archie got the insurance policies changed, I thought. The woman could live anywhere in style as long as she collected before WITSEC gave her a new name.

"Barry also found a ledger book," Tommy Lee said. "It was under the seat with the gun. Do you know what it contains?"

Janet shook her head. "It would have to be for his work. Maybe orders or payments due. Do you think Robert was involved in something illegal?"

"We don't want to just assume that the killer came from the family. If Robert was involved in something illegal, then he could have had other enemies."

Her jaw clenched. "My husband is dead in the carport, the Rose of Santona by his side. He helped bring his own father to justice and now you're accusing him of a crime. Something like this food scam thing."

I glanced at Brookshire. His face turned red.

"They're not accusing you of anything," Brookshire said. "We're all trying to do our jobs. To protect you and to find your husband's killer."

Janet Sinclair buried her face in her hands. "I know. I know."

Deputy Reece Hutchins stepped into the living room. "Special Agent Boyce is here, Sheriff. She and her forensics team."

"Thanks. Barry and I will be right out."

"You brought the FBI?" Brookshire exclaimed.

Janet's head snapped up. "Why?"

"Because if this White Rose of Santona is the real thing, we've got an interstate murder of a federally protected witness. The FBI has resources way beyond our department. They're our best hope of finding your husband's killer."

Her eyes narrowed. "Then bring them on. If my Robert's going into the family plot, I want as many of his despicable relatives going into the ground with him."

Chapter Twenty-three

Tommy Lee told Reece to wait in the living room with Brookshire and Janet Sinclair while he and I briefed Special Agent Lindsay Boyce.

We found Tommy Lee's niece in the carport. She had gloved and booted and was bending over the body with a member of her forensic team.

"When you get a chance, Agent Boyce," the sheriff called, "Barry and I will be at my patrol car."

She looked over her shoulder. "Be there in a sec."

Tommy Lee and I walked to the bottom of the driveway to where he'd parked on the opposite shoulder. We both leaned against the front fender and watched the techs work.

"Are you going to hold anything back from Lindsay?" I asked.

"No. We'll give her everything, including Brookshire's affair."

"What does she already know?"

"I briefed her over the weekend about the Sinclairs and the potential that they could be linked to our food stamp scam. She wasn't that familiar with the Santona case in New Jersey, but she was requesting the file. If she's got it, I doubt she's had time to do much with it. But she'll run with this investigation. A dead, supposedly protected, witness will be high-profile in the Bureau."

"What happens to us?"

Tommy Lee shrugged. "Ballistics will either show Robert

Sinclair was killed by the same weapon as Sonny and Rufus, or it won't. The same can be said for the gun under the driver's seat."

"And if nothing matches the ballistics from Sonny and Rufus?"

"Then we press on. But Lindsay will take over Sinclair's murder because the non-match with our murders lends credence to a professional hit out of New Jersey. Likewise, if the gun under the seat isn't a match for us, then it means we've got another player in the game. If it is a match and Collier Crockett can get Buddy Smith at Wilmer's Convenience Corner to either confirm that Sinclair had threatened him or that a section of numbers in the general ledger matches what he was reporting, then I think we are done. The deceased Robert Sinclair will be our killer. Then Crockett can mop up his end as he identifies and arrests complicit cardholders and store owners."

Tommy Lee looked back at the carport. "Here comes Lindsay. Let me lead and you can fill in whatever I miss."

The Special Agent in charge of the FBI's Asheville resident agency cut an impressive figure as she walked toward us. Trim and fit, she wore her dark blue pinstripe suit like she was some Wall Street executive, yet her short brown hair was still long enough to bounce with each stride. Her pale blue eyes sparkled in the late afternoon sun, and with her back to her colleagues, she flashed us a brilliant smile.

"So, Uncle, you ask me to do a favor for you on Saturday and then dump a body on me on Monday. I can hardly wait till tomorrow. What's next?"

"What's next is you're wrapping up my case. Barry found a pistol and a potentially incriminating ledger book that were hidden under the driver's seat."

"Guns N' Roses. So, are you keeping the gun and giving me the rose?"

"No, you get the whole package, provided you run me an expedited ballistics report."

"Okay. That it? A gun and a ledger?"

"And a surviving WITSEC alum who's getting the ultimate in protective coverage."

Boyce arched an eyebrow. "Do tell."

For the next twenty minutes, Tommy Lee gave her a detailed briefing that ran from Toby McKay's assault on Commissioner James through our interview with Janet Sinclair. Then she walked with us to get the evidence bags locked in my jeep.

"All right. I'll keep the chain of custody secure on these puppies." She turned to me. "I may need a statement from you if Brookshire gets caught up in this mess. I'll also run a cell trace requesting the location of Brookshire's call to the Sheriff's Department."

"May I make a suggestion?" I asked.

"Please," she said. "Any suggestions from you are welcome. Now, from Uncle Tommy Lee, well, that's a different matter."

Tommy Lee ignored her.

I pointed to the clear bags protecting the gun and ledger. "I know you'll go over both of these for fingerprints, but when you do forensics on the victim's vehicle, check the floormat under the seat."

"What am I looking for?" Boyce asked.

"I'm curious as to the pattern of gun oil."

Boyce nodded. She knew what I was getting at. Every well-maintained firearm is frequently cleaned and oiled. Trace residue should appear on the Infiniti's carpet.

"So, if it looks like the oil pattern is fresh with no other trace, the gun was laid there," she said.

"Planted there," I corrected. "Odd that there's no holster, but not odd if Sinclair felt like he needed to be able to grab the pistol quickly. If you find lots of oil traces in a broad pattern consistent with the gun shifting during travel, then I'll feel better. Otherwise…"

Boyce looked at Tommy Lee. "Gee, I wonder who should be wearing the sheriff's badge?"

"What do you mean sheriff?" Tommy Lee said. "I was thinking the same thing about your FBI shield."

We left the scene about six as dusk was settling in. I phoned Susan from the jeep and asked if she'd started dinner. It was one of those nights where I felt like a pizza and a couple of beers. She'd just gotten home and said a pizza sounded wonderful. She'd make the salad if I'd pick up a plain cheese on one half and then whatever I chose to pile on the other. Mushrooms and pepperoni were my leading candidates.

It was another crisp fall evening and although we ate at the dining table, I slid open the sliding glass door to the deck and let the breeze blow through the screen. All the ambience of the outdoors without the bugs.

I devoured all four of my slices and looked longingly at one of Susan's plain cheese. "You know I've still got beer left in my glass. I try to make pizza and beer finish together. Like eating ice cream and cake. You, on the other hand, just have water, and after I bought you the nice bottle of on-sale Malbec."

She laced her fingers together and rested her chin on her hands. "Oh, poor dear, we can't have that. Go ahead and take the food out of our mouths." She gave a mysterious smile that signaled something else was going on.

"Our mouths? Who are we now? Queen Elizabeth?"

"No. You should make a better deduction than that." She picked up her wineglass of sparkling water and toasted me. "My Prince Charming."

My throat went dry. Clues clicked into place. Susan's sudden switch from wine to water. The Mona Lisa smile. "You're not?" My pulse quickened with unanticipated excitement. "We're having a baby?"

Her smile broadened. "No, silly. We're not having a baby."

And just as suddenly, my unexpected euphoria vanished, leaving only unexpected disappointment.

Susan kept her glass aloft. "We're having babies."

The rollercoaster of emotions within that ten-second span made the car jump the track. Maybe I blacked out. Maybe my mind soared to some other astral plane. The next thing I recalled was Susan standing beside me.

"Barry, are you all right?"

"All right? I'm ecstatic. But are you sure?"

Susan and I had decided the past spring we were ready for a family. We'd not done anything special but rather let Mother Nature take her course.

"I suspected it, but didn't want to say anything till I was sure. I got confirmation today."

"Two?"

She laughed. "Two strong heartbeats. That Mother Nature, what a sense of humor."

"How far along?"

"About eight weeks. I'd rather wait a few more before we start telling people."

I scooted back my chair and stood, my knees a little wobbly. "Shouldn't you sit down? How about the sofa?"

"Barry, I feel just as good as I did three minutes ago. Maybe you should sit. Finish your beer and the pizza."

"Beer? This calls for champagne."

"You may call for it but no champagne will answer. The closest we have is your beer and my sparkling water."

"Then that works for me." I lifted my beer. "To the most wonderful mother-to-be."

She raised her glass. "And to the calmest father-to-be. Either that or he might have to be tranquilized before these babies come."

We talked till midnight. When I was changing for bed and emptying my pockets, I found what I'd forgotten—the folded receipt I'd plucked from Janet Sinclair's torn bag of groceries. It should have gone in with the gun and ledger, especially since the time stamp could exonerate Janet by providing an alibi for the time of Robert's death.

I was careful to hold the receipt by a corner edge and take it to the kitchen where we kept zip-lock bags. Before securing it, I made a closer examination. The listed items included the elbow pasta, tomato sauce, ranch dressing, and produce I'd seen scattered on the concrete. And there was another purchase, one I hadn't seen, one that proved Janet Sinclair a liar.

Chapter Twenty-four

"Ice cream? You woke me up over a missing half gallon of ice cream?" Tommy Lee's gruff question warned me that he didn't view my discovery with the same "smoking gun" implications that I did. At least not a few minutes after midnight.

"She clearly lied," I argued. "She said she didn't go into the house but I bet you dollars to doughnuts she left the other groceries for show and put the ice cream in her freezer."

"Did you inventory the items in the dropped bag?"

"No," I conceded. "But I saw them scattered and I don't think there was enough room for a half gallon in what little space remained in the bag."

"That still doesn't change the time stamp on the receipt. Unless she had someone shopping for her, she could have come home, found her husband, and gone into shock. People do mundane things in traumatic situations."

"And people do calculated things when they can callously step over a dead body to enter their house to save a five-dollar carton of ice cream."

"All right," Tommy Lee said. "I'll cover Lindsay in the morning. She took possession of everything at the murder scene. Be in at seven and we'll sort out priorities. Anything else you want to tell me while I'm still awake?"

I wanted to shout I was going to be a dad twice over, but I

yielded to Susan's wish to delay. Besides, I didn't particularly want my news mingled with a conversation about murder.

"No. Sorry to bother you. It's probably nothing."

"What the hell, Barry. Everything starts from nothing. I'm just cranky in my old age."

"When were you not?"

He hung up on me.

At six-fifty the next morning, I walked into Tommy Lee's office wearing plainclothes and carrying a bag with two egg and sausage biscuits from Bojangles'. "Peace offering. No more late night phone calls."

He grabbed the bag. "Don't make promises you can't keep. Any more insights strike you during the night?"

"Nothing I can work on. I wonder if we're missing something and the WITSEC status and food stamp scam are more closely related than we thought."

"How so?" Tommy Lee mumbled, his mouth full of biscuit.

"There's a high degree of organization to this fraud operation. What if Robert Sinclair was still tied to the mob?"

"But he put his old man away."

"Yes. And there are competing factions within every family. What if someone in the family or more likely a rival family wanted old Bobby Santona out of the way? They entice Robert to give up the evidence. But they can't guarantee his safety so who better to protect Robert and Janet than the U.S. Marshals."

"That's a stretch," Tommy Lee said. "A lot of hypotheticals. And what's in it for Robert?"

"Right under the nose of Brookshire and the marshals, Robert runs the food stamp scam. The mob sets up shop in the mountains."

"So why the hit?"

"Robert generated too much attention. Not from his ill-conceived return for the New Jersey funeral but for the executions of Rufus and Sonny. They sever the ties by killing Robert."

"And walk away from the whole operation?"

"It was probably going down anyway. Collier Crockett's infiltrated the network. He might be able to turn Janet Sinclair. She'll claim ignorance, of course, but he might find some leverage."

"Like a missing half gallon of ice cream?"

"No. Although that does bother me. I was thinking more about money. We haven't followed that trail. We don't know where it leads."

"If the gun under Robert's seat matches the one that killed Sonny and Rufus, then I think our case is closed. But, share your theory with Lindsay. She can get to the financials."

I remembered Cindy's comments at Bank of America that Janet Sinclair also had accounts at Wells Fargo. Someone was cashing the checks Rufus had been writing to Staples Sources. Maybe that was Janet.

"What are you planning for this morning?" I asked.

"Back to paperwork and budgets. Nothing to do until Lindsay runs her tests and we get the M.E. report."

I pulled the zip-lock bag with the grocery receipt from my jacket pocket. "Pass this on to Lindsay."

"Give it to her yourself. Why don't you go to her Asheville office and have a sit-down? Frankly, I think your mob theory is farfetched, but no sense shutting down a line of inquiry over my misgivings. Besides, the expense won't be coming out of my budget."

"Thanks for your unwavering support."

He laughed. "Sure. Take an unmarked rather than your jeep. I'll spring for the gas. You still carrying the Kimber?"

"The pistol's in the jeep."

"Take it. We still might have a killer in the area who thinks you know more than you do. Keep your gun closer than Robert Sinclair kept his."

Tommy Lee called his niece at home and the special agent agreed to meet me at her office at nine. The FBI's resident agency was located in the Federal Courthouse in Asheville. Security was tight, and a little before nine I had to produce my credentials and declare the concealed Kimber before I could proceed to the second floor.

I'd been in the FBI office several times with Tommy Lee and knew his niece would give a fair evaluation of whatever I presented.

I accepted a cup of coffee and sat across from her in the small conversation area in a corner of her office.

She had exchanged her navy blue pinstripe pants suit for a charcoal gray one. Her blue eyes were bright and focused on me with undivided attention.

I pulled the zip-lock bag protecting the receipt from my jacket pocket. "I have a confession to make. I picked this up from the grocery bag yesterday and forgot to give it to you. I don't know if the medical examiner's time of death will be specific enough to clear Janet Sinclair, but combined with the time of her call to Luther Brookshire, there's a good chance this will corroborate her alibi."

"In your possession the whole time?" Lindsay glanced at the receipt and then laid it on the coffee table between us.

"Yes."

"Good. Since the Bureau is heading up the investigation, we'll get an official statement from you while you're here."

"There is one thing about the receipt that struck me as strange."

She picked it up and re-examined it. "What?"

I told her about the ice cream and that I suspected Janet had taken it from the bag and put it in the freezer. "That undercuts the statement she gave us," I said. "She claimed she never entered the house after finding the body."

Lindsay nodded. "That's what she told us in our interview."

"Why would she lie?"

"Who wants to be known as the wife more concerned with saving her ice cream than losing her husband?" She smiled. "Unless it was sea-salt caramel."

"Is Janet still in the house?"

"No. We took her into protective custody."

"With the marshals?"

"No. We have a safe house. I'm keeping her away from the marshals until we make sure Brookshire's not involved. As it is, he's on shaky ground because of your discovery of his affair with a married witness. He's being cooperative and I'm not looking to make him the centerpiece of a case without grounds. I've expedited the requests for cell records and ballistics, including Brookshire's service weapon. I'll also send someone by the Sinclairs' house to check the freezer for the missing ice cream. Then I'll raise the statement discrepancy with Janet Sinclair."

"What about the ledger?"

Lindsay Boyce set down the grocery receipt and picked up her cup of coffee. After a sip, she said, "Not sure what to do with that. We weren't involved in this food scam thing. FNS Investigator Crockett has already contacted us about needing that as evidence for his case. Given the white rose, odds are this is a payback hit from the Santona family. Joan Santona aka Janet Sinclair will get a third identity and the case will go cold. That's my fear."

"Let me float one other theory, but be warned," I said, "it's a stretch."

She laughed. "At this point, I'd even look at a theory involving aliens and a mothership."

So, I told her my thoughts that Robert Sinclair had betrayed his father for a rival faction, used the marshals as the best protection available, and then flagrantly set up his scam with the backing of mafia organization and expertise. "We never got a chance to trace the money trail of Rufus Taylor's checks to Staples Sources. You might want to explore that option."

"Isn't Crockett doing that?"

"I told him what we've found but I didn't hand over the Taylor ledger. I guess I should give that to you or him."

Lindsay pursed her lips as she thought it over. "Hold onto it till we get the ballistics report. If there's no ballistics match to the gun in Robert Sinclair's SUV, then you might need to follow that lead yourself. We should know a lot more by the end of the day." She took another sip of coffee. "How did you get interested in the Sinclairs in the first place?"

I told her about Archie Donovan's plan to enable the Sinclairs to access the cash values of the insurance policies that were still in their old names. And how, in true Archie fashion, he'd bragged about being in the cell next to Sonny McKay and that he was going to meet Sonny the next day.

"And then Sonny turned up dead," Lindsay said.

"Yes. Whether that was planned before Archie talked to the Sinclairs or as a result of that conversation, we didn't know. We had to check it out."

"And the ledger you found in Robert Sinclair's car is the missing link between him and the food stamp scam."

"And the gun might be the murderer's signature."

Lindsay Boyce looked out her second-story window and thought a moment. "Do you know if Archie Donovan's name-change paperwork went through?"

"I don't. He hoped by mid-week, so either today or tomorrow. You're looking at Robert's death in light of the benefits that can now come to Janet Sinclair?"

"Yes. There's a hell of a lot in the policies' cash values. I doubt she'll want a new identity until she gets that money. If there's no link between her and the crimes her husband might have committed, then she'll collect it all."

"Another layer of motive," I said.

"Too many layers. You're right about following the money. I guess we'll need to work with Collier Crockett and see where this food stamp scam takes us. If you're right, it could lead back to New Jersey."

"Any suggestions for what I should do in the meantime?" I asked.

"Assume your case is still going to be open and keep working it. We might intersect, but you go with your leads and don't worry about stepping on my toes."

It was good to hear her say those encouraging words, especially since that was my intent all along.

"Then can you photocopy the ledger book I found yesterday?" I asked. "And I'll have Tommy Lee send over a copy of what we discovered in Rufus Taylor's safe."

Special Agent Lindsay Boyce set down her coffee and offered her hand. "You've got a deal. I'll give you paper to write your statement while I take care of copying the ledger."

About twenty minutes later, I signed several handwritten pages documenting what I had discovered upon arrival at the murder scene. Lindsay Boyce handed me a thick manila envelope containing the photocopied ledger pages and walked me down the hall where we found a familiar face waiting in the small lobby.

"Deputy Clayton." Collier Crockett extended his hand. "I understand you broke open my case."

"That he did," Lindsay Boyce said. She and the FNS Investigator also shook hands.

"Well, I just happened to show up first," I said.

He laughed. "Most of the time, that's what it's all about." He eyed the folder in my left hand. "That for me?"

"No. It's some information for the sheriff."

"I'll go over what I have for you," Lindsay Boyce said. "And I want to share some interesting theories Barry's developed."

"All right." Crockett's tone became serious. "But the EBT fraud is still in my wheelhouse, just so we all understand."

"And I've got a dead federal witness," Lindsay stated. "I suggest we let Barry get on with his duties while you and I discuss how to move forward."

"No problem." Crockett turned to me. "I hope this wraps up

your case for you. If I come across anything relevant, I'll be sure and shoot it your way."

"Thanks." I left the two federal agents to battle over their turf.

I'd parked in the Otis parking garage across the street and before heading back to Gainesboro, I decided to follow up on the question Lindsay Boyce had posed about Archie and the paperwork. I hadn't spoken to him since he'd joined his wife and daughters at his mother-in-law's.

"Barry?" He answered his cell on the first ring.

"Everybody okay?"

"Yes, but I'm about to go crazy wondering what's going on. Janet Sinclair called me this morning about her husband. She's scared to death and wants to get her money before she goes into hiding."

"She's in a safe house," I assured him.

"Yeah. A room at the Renaissance Hotel in Asheville?"

"How do you know that?"

"She told me. She called from the bathroom while the shower was running."

"What's the status of the policies?"

"Everything is good to go. I got the confirmation the owner-ship has changed to the company. We'll drop the Santona names from the listed officers and leave only Sinclairs." He paused. "Now it will just be Janet. She wants the death certificate and the beneficiary and cash surrender forms."

"Beneficiary? Doesn't the name of the insured still have to be Robert Santona?"

"It does."

"How's she going to use a Robert Sinclair death certificate to collect on the death of Robert Santona?"

"She told me the marshals would straighten it out. I just need the death certificate and claim forms."

She's going to use them to create a forgery, I thought. Change the name from Sinclair to Santona.

"How are you going to get them to her?" I asked.

"I'm supposed to text her. She'll tell me where to leave them. A friend will pick them up."

A friend? I wondered if Janet was still in communication with Luther Brookshire. Was he the marshal that would enable Janet to collect the death benefit that would be much higher than the cash value? He certainly could arrange a name change on a death certificate.

"But I told her the documents haven't come back to the office yet," Archie said. "I didn't want her to know I'm in Weaverville. I expect to get them here later this afternoon."

"So, you could wait until tomorrow to deliver them?"

"Yes. And I need to get the death certificates from Fletcher. I spoke with him a few minutes ago and he expects them later this afternoon. I'll be so glad when this is over. All I want is to get the ten thousand dollars from Janet Sinclair for the Boys and Girls Clubs and be done with it. Barry, never encourage me to do something like this again."

Me? Encourage Archie? "I won't. You can count on it. But do me a favor. Let me know what Janet Sinclair arranges to get the death certificate and forms."

"Sure. You want me to give her your number?"

I took a deep breath and suppressed my better judgment. "No, Archie. This is our secret. It's even more important than when I told you not to tell anyone about your conversation with Sonny. Remember how that turned out."

"Don't worry. I've learned my lesson. Mum's the word."

We disconnected. I looked at the manila envelope on the seat beside me. Soon Collier Crockett would be trying to decode those records; Lindsay Boyce would be searching through Robert Sinclair's bank records. At the moment, both were still viable avenues for my investigation and I had no other leads. I pulled out of the parking garage and headed for Gainesboro.

Chapter Twenty-five

I found Cindy Todd alone in her glass-walled office in the Bank of America branch. She spotted me immediately as she must have been watching the lobby for any congestion in the teller lines. She waved and I beelined straight for her open door.

Cindy stood up from her desk, her face pale as parchment. "Barry, Fletcher told me about Mr. Sinclair. I can't believe such a thing would happen in our town."

"I'm afraid so. Can we talk a few minutes?"

"Yes." She motioned me to a guest chair.

I first closed the door and then sat across from her.

"Is this about the Sinclairs?" she asked.

"Yes. You're going to get a visit from the FBI."

Cindy's eyes widened. "Have we done something wrong?"

"No. But they'll come in with warrants for the safe deposit box, account records, and anything else tied to Robert Sinclair. Janet Sinclair is being held in protective custody for her own safety, but if she should come in here before the federal agents, I want you to call me immediately."

"She was just here yesterday. I waited on her myself."

"What time?"

"A little after noon. One of the tellers was on lunch break and another called in sick. I covered a window for about thirty minutes."

"What did she do?"

Cindy wet her lips, uncomfortable with my question.

"Cindy, this is a murder investigation. You're going to have to cooperate with the FBI, so you may as well start with me."

"She got a cashier's check for nine thousand dollars from the Sinclairity Sales account."

"How much did that leave?"

"I think it was around a thousand dollars and some change."

"So, she could have deliberately kept it under a ten-thousand-dollar withdrawal."

"I guess so," Cindy said.

"Had she ever withdrawn that much before?"

"Maybe. I don't wait on her that often. We'd have to go back through the records. I think most transactions are commission deposits and then transfers to the Sinclairs' personal account. As I said before, sometimes there are cash deposits as well."

"Who was the payee on the cashier's check?"

"She wanted it made out to cash. That's a little unusual. Most of the time the payee is someone who wants to know the check is good."

"Anything else?"

"She also went to her safe deposit box. I saw her leave with a couple of manila envelopes under her arm."

"Taking things out, not putting them in like the other day?"

"That's correct."

Janet Sinclair's actions didn't necessarily mean she was involved in her husband's murder. She had a history of reacting to perceived threats. Her July visit to the funeral home and her concern for the life insurance policies had been triggered by her husband's ill-fated, secret attendance of his father's funeral. She also could have been aware of Robert's criminal enterprise and been spooked by the spate of killings, anticipating the jeopardy created for her and her husband. Was she organizing a financial life raft for both of them, or was she bailing out on her own? Or with someone else?

"You said Janet had an account at Wells Fargo," I said.

"Yes. Where my friend Tina works."

I looked at my watch. It was a few minutes before eleven. "Do you think she would meet me for lunch?"

"Maybe. She usually goes early. Sometimes she skips the meal and runs errands."

"Would you do me a favor and call her? An introduction from you might put her at ease."

Tina Logan didn't have time for lunch but agreed to meet me at eleven-thirty for a cup of coffee at the Cardinal Café. I used the extra time to phone Tommy Lee and brief him on my conversations with Special Agent Boyce and Cindy.

When I'd brought him up to date, I asked, "Do you want me to report to Lindsay?"

"No. Let's wait till she gets us the information from her forensics team. If Janet's at a safe house, then she's not a flight risk. What's your plan after you meet Tina?"

"I thought I'd make an unannounced visit to Buddy Smith at Wilmer's Convenience Corner. I hope he'll have some records like Rufus Taylor did. Lindsay gave me photocopies of what we think is Robert Sinclair's master list. Can you also scan and send a photo of Sinclair that I can show him? The one on his driver's license is certainly preferable to anything taken at the crime scene."

"You're stepping on Crockett's toes," Tommy Lee warned.

"Crockett never said he'd successfully flipped Buddy. Maybe showing the photo to the man and telling him that Sinclair is dead will take away his fears. At this point any other stores in the fraud network are of no interest. Crockett's welcome to them all."

"All right. Go ahead. We've got a pair of murders. That's two aces in my book. Lindsay's got one, while Crockett's only holding an EBT card. He's not even in the game."

At eleven-twenty, I slid into the back booth at the Cardinal Café. I wanted to beat the lunch crowd and claim the spot that offered the most privacy. I'd told Tina Logan what I was wearing so she had no trouble finding me as soon as she entered.

Tina looked to be in her mid-twenties, an attractive African-American woman with a bright smile and slim figure.

I stood to greet her.

"Deputy Clayton?"

"Yes. But I'd prefer you call me Barry."

"And I'm Tina."

I gestured for her to sit on the booth bench across from me. Helen Todd, owner of the cafe and Cindy's mother, immediately came to us with a pot of coffee and two cups.

"Well, Tina," she said. "Couldn't find a better lunch date?"

"I'm a new diet," I said. "Women see me and lose their appetites."

They both laughed.

"Oh, Barry's not so bad," Helen said. "And he's married. His wife's trained him well." She set the pot on the table. "I know y'all want to talk, so I'll leave you to it. If you decide you want something else, just holler."

She left and Tina grabbed two packets of Sweet 'N Low.

"How long have you known Cindy?" I asked.

"A couple of years. I moved here from Asheville for my job. I met Cindy through our book club."

"As she told you on the phone, I'm working on an investigation tied to yesterday's murder of Robert Sinclair. Cindy told me his wife Janet also has an account at your branch."

She nodded, and then shook her head. "I can't believe it. Mrs. Sinclair must be devastated."

"Yes. Right now the best thing we can do is find out who killed her husband."

"Why do you want to know about their banking?"

"Standard procedure." I tried to make it sound like it was no more unusual than finding out their age. "And you might be asked some similar questions by the FBI."

"I'd much rather talk to you."

"Thank you. Let me assure you the agents will be very courteous. But I thought this would be a more relaxed setting."

She took a sip of coffee. "I don't know how much help I'll be."

"Did you know Mr. Sinclair?"

"No. I never met him. I only knew his signature."

"His signature?"

"The endorsements on his checks. Evidently, Mr. Sinclair set up the account over three years ago. That's before I came. It's in his name along with a DBA name."

"DBA?"

"Doing Business As. The account number that is tied to Mr. Sinclair receives deposits to a doing-business-as company name."

"Sinclairity Sales," I said.

Tina shook her head. "No. His account was for Staples Sources."

Her words struck like a flash of lighting, illuminating the path from Rufus' records of bogus EBT charges to the master ledger in Robert Sinclair's car to the deposits in a bank account named Staples Sources. We could potentially trace funds from Rufus to the final deposit, but the stronger case would come from Buddy Smith and his testimony as to exactly how he was threatened into participating.

"Did these checks always come made out to Staples Sources?" I asked.

"Yes." Tina thought a moment. "Although once Mrs. Sinclair brought in several checks in an envelope that was addressed to that Sinclairity Sales you mentioned. The double S caught my eye."

"Double S?"

"Sinclairity Sales—Staples Sources."

Barry, you idiot, I thought. I'd never noticed the alliteration.

"Do you remember the address on the envelope?"

"No. But I'm pretty sure it was their home address. I could look it up."

So, the dummy invoices that transferred money from fraudulent EBT card purchases had a phony address, but the stores mailed their payments to the Sinclairs in envelopes addressed to Robert Sinclair's legitimate company. A double layer of insulation. Staples Sources sounded like some grocery supplier. A simple audit probably wouldn't look past the invoices and canceled checks.

"What payments went out of the Staples Sources account?"

"A few times Mrs. Sinclair made withdrawals by a check her husband had written to cash. I can review the statements when I get back to work."

I remembered Cindy Todd said Janet sometimes deposited cash into the Sinclairity Sales account at Bank of America. Something Janet denied. Were the cash withdrawals an untraceable way to get money from Staples Solutions into their personal accounts?

"Yes," I said. "Please review the statements."

Tina looked at me with concern. "This is okay, my talking to you?"

"Yes, but I wouldn't want to cause any internal policy problems between you and the bank. When the FBI comes, don't mention we talked unless they ask. Believe me, they'll find your information very useful." I handed her my card with my cell phone number. "Call me once you've checked that account."

"And if Mrs. Sinclair comes in again?"

"Help her. You've got no reason to treat her differently."

She nodded, reached for her purse, and opened it.

I held up my hand. "Coffee's on me. Thanks for making the time."

"You're welcome." She slid out of the booth and left.

Helen came over and I ordered a grilled ham and cheese sandwich. I needed to eat and to chew over what Tina Logan had told me. We now had the provable link between Rufus Taylor's checkbook and Janet Sinclair's deposits. Also, Rufus' itemized list of the amounts of the fraudulent EBT purchases could be examined against Robert Sinclair's master ledger. I wanted to find those connections, and then, armed with that confirmation, visit Buddy Smith at Wilmer's Convenience Corner where I hoped he'd confess to a similar setup. If he could identify Robert's face as the person who intimidated him, our circle would be complete.

I returned to the Sheriff's Department and booked one of the conference rooms where I could work undisturbed. I spread out the ledger we found in Rufus Taylor's safe, his checkbook stubs, the photocopies of the book from Robert Sinclair's Infiniti, and a legal pad for jotting down any notes.

I started with the last page of Rufus' entries and then worked backwards through Sinclair's ledger looking for a match. Each page had a five-digit number as a heading, a list of dollar amounts, and their total sum. About five pages in, I found a page with numbers identical to Rufus' last page, including the total amount of four-hundred-seventy-five dollars. I noted the heading number 00027. I flipped forward till I found the number recurring again. This page total was three-hundred-eighty-six dollars and thirteen cents. Both numbers matched checks Rufus had written to Staples Sources.

I flipped through the master ledger and found twenty-four unique coded headings in all. Probably the identifying numbers for the individual stores in the fraud network. We had store names from the list I'd found in Sonny McKay's saddlebag, but without the key, I had no way of knowing which store corresponded with which heading without going through each store's fraudulent purchase records. And those records might be destroyed once Sinclair's death went public. If there was a key sheet, it wasn't in any of the materials I had. Could Special Agent Lindsay Boyce have missed it when the book was copied?

I called the Asheville office of the FBI and was put through immediately.

"What's up?" she asked.

I told her I'd matched sums on Rufus Taylor's checks to records in the book from the murder scene, but that I couldn't decrypt how the heading numbers identified the stores.

"Sorry I can't help you. I express-shipped the book to Quantico for analysis right after I made copies for you and Crockett."

"Where's it going after that?"

"If nothing seems relevant to our case, it will go to Crockett. Maybe he can figure out that key."

"Do me a favor," I asked. "If the lab results yield something promising like prints or DNA, have the book come back to me. We are talking about a double homicide."

"You know Crockett's a federal investigator. He won't want it going to a local sheriff. He wasn't too thrilled when I told him I'd given you a copy."

"Why?"

"Because he's a tight ass who fears you'll screw up his case. I told him he's lucky I held onto the book long enough to make him a copy and that it didn't go to Quantico last night."

I shared her assessment of the FNS investigator, but I had an ace to play. "All right. Who would you rather face? Tight ass Crockett? Or your hard ass uncle, Tommy Lee?"

She laughed. "Okay, you'll get your damn book when we're through with it. I did send the gun and Sinclair's floor mats to Quantico last night. I expect to hear something back this afternoon. A murdered federal witness gets everyone's attention."

I thanked her for her help and disconnected. No sooner had I laid my cell phone on the table than it rang.

"Barry Clayton," I said.

"Deputy Clayton. It's Tina Logan."

"Yes, Tina."

"Sorry to be late getting back to you. We were slammed after lunch."

"No problem. Have you had a chance to look at that account?"

"Yes, sir." Her voice dropped to a whisper. "It's empty."

"What?"

"The funds were wired out yesterday afternoon. Nearly half a million dollars."

I stood up from the table, too agitated to sit. "Wired where?"

"The Cayman Islands."

Chapter Twenty-six

"And you're sure about the time?" The speakerphone in the middle of the table vibrated as Special Agent Lindsay Boyce asked the critical question.

Tommy Lee had called her from the conference room where I'd spread out the ledgers, check stubs, and Staples Sources invoices from Rufus Taylor's store.

"Yes," I said. "The bank employee told me the funds had been wired out at four-fifty-five yesterday afternoon. We know Janet Sinclair was with you. Did she slip into the bathroom with her phone or have access to a computer?"

"No," the FBI agent insisted. "You handed her over to us at four-fifteen, we interviewed her for approximately an hour, and then took her to a safe house."

"The Renaissance Hotel in Asheville," I said.

"How did you know that?"

"She called her insurance agent, Archie Donovan. She's getting the death benefit and the cash values out of some insurance policies."

"Not if she murdered her husband," Lindsay said sharply.

"And your evidence to charge her?" Tommy Lee asked.

"From what Barry says, we've got her fingers all over the Staples Sources bank account, whether she wired out the money or not."

Tommy Lee shook his head, a fruitless gesture in front of a speakerphone. "She can say she thought the checks were all part of her husband's businesses. He signed them, she deposited them. She had no idea he was doing anything illegal. And she has an alibi for when the funds were transferred."

I thought of another argument. "If Janet was guilty, why let me discover the ledger book in the car? That's what her attorney will profess."

"But we know it was to take you off the case," Lindsay said. "You have your killer and your investigation is closed. The gun and ledger tie him to the murders."

Something began gnawing at the back of my brain. "Who told her we were investigating food stamp fraud?"

"What do you mean?" Tommy Lee asked.

"Yesterday, when we spoke with her in her living room, she said, 'Something like this food scam thing.' It was when she thought we might be accusing her husband of a crime. We hadn't mentioned it, but Brookshire looked uncomfortable as hell when she said it."

Tommy Lee drummed his fingers on the table. "When did Brookshire leave the scene?"

"He left around four-thirty," Lindsay said. "I pulled him aside, told him I knew about the affair, and that we would be handling protection for Janet. We argued and he left in a huff."

"I guess we were with the techs in the carport," I said. "I don't remember him going."

"That gave him twenty-five minutes to either use his smartphone or access a computer," Lindsay said. "If he and Janet are not only lovers but also conspirators, then he could have had all the passcodes and account numbers to facilitate the wire transfer."

"What do you suggest for a next step?" Tommy Lee asked her.

"Do Janet and Luther know we know about the bank accounts?"

Tommy Lee looked at me.

"I haven't told them."

"Then let's do nothing about the accounts," Lindsay said. "I'll put a tail on Luther Brookshire and we'll give Janet freedom to use her phone and move about. I'll even tell Brookshire he can start the process for putting her back in WITSEC. We'll see if they start communicating with one another."

We heard someone call Lindsay's name.

"Hold a second," she said, and she muted her phone.

"That's not a bad plan," Tommy Lee whispered. "If Brookshire is involved, he'll want those store owners to get rid of any records of the fraudulent payments so there's no way to match the master ledger. We might not be able to tie him to Sinclair's murder, but some of those store owners might be able to identify him."

The speakerphone clicked on.

"I've just gotten results in from Quantico," Lindsay said. "I'll fax the report, but here's the basic information."

I grabbed a pencil and my legal pad.

"The ballistics test confirms the gun matches the one used in the murders of Sonny McKay and Rufus Taylor. However, the bullets retrieved from Robert Sinclair's body are from a nine millimeter."

"What about prints on the gun?" I asked.

"They match Robert Sinclair's. However the lab tech added a note. The preponderance of the prints are from the left hand."

"Do we know if Robert was left-handed?" Tommy Lee asked.

"Yes," Lindsay said. "I asked Janet Sinclair that question yesterday, anticipating we'd want to make sure someone hadn't tried to place the prints after he died. But the key word is preponderance. The tech notes only left-hand prints—on the gun, on the magazine, and on the cartridges. Have you ever tried to load a magazine with one hand?"

"Someone knew he was left-handed and overdid it," Tommy Lee said. "Obviously, Janet knew her husband was left-handed, as would Luther Brookshire, given his close connection during their relocation in WITSEC."

"And, Barry, your concern about the floor mat paid off. The only gun oil was on the spot where the pistol lay. That's a pretty unlikely circumstance given curvy mountain roads. Both the ledger and gun would have slid around to some measurable degree."

"So, Janet Sinclair is either a hapless pawn or a coconspirator," I said.

"Well, she couldn't be her husband's killer," Lindsay declared. "We ran down the surveillance video from Ingles and confirmed she was in a register line at the time on the grocery receipt."

I thought how Luther Brookshire had described Robert Sinclair. That an IQ hovering slightly above room temperature isn't going to mastermind such a complex operation. "Sounds like Robert Sinclair could have been a dupe in this whole thing. And if the murderer was a hitman from the Santona family, why bother to plant the pistol with Robert's prints? He'd just want to waste the guy, leave the rose, and be gone."

Tommy Lee leaned closer to the speakerphone. "Lindsay, have you tracked Brookshire's location for when Janet called him yesterday?"

"Yes. He was on your side of Asheville. He could have removed the battery from his cell phone, traveled undetected to kill Sinclair, and then powered back up in time to receive Janet's call when he was safely away from the crime scene."

Tommy Lee sighed. "Well, if nearly a half million dollars is now out of the country, is there a danger Brookshire's a flight risk? Either solo or with Janet?"

"I don't know about Brookshire," I said, "but I don't think Janet's going to walk away without collecting the money from the insurance policies. If she can get the death benefit as well as cash values, we're talking more than a million and a half. As far as she knows, she's not a suspect."

"Then let's leave it that way," Lindsay said. "We'll let her stay in the safe house, but give her a loose rein. I'll tell Brookshire I've reconsidered and that as soon as we check out a few things from her statement, the marshals can have her back."

"Sounds good," Tommy Lee agreed. "Barry, what's your next move?"

"I think if Brookshire's part of the EBT conspiracy and he planted the ledger book, he'll want to make sure the store owners destroy the matching records. He might instruct them by phone, or if he's concerned about being tapped, visit them in person. I'd like to see Buddy Smith at Wilmer's Convenience Corner and show him a photo of both Robert Sinclair and Luther Brookshire. I've got Sinclair's. Lindsay, can you e-mail me one of Brookshire?"

"Sure," she said. "And I'll throw in one of Janet. Never underestimate a woman's deceitfulness."

Tommy Lee laughed. "That's my niece. Calls 'em like she sees 'em."

"And what I want to see is this case closed," Lindsay said. "Especially if we've got a dirty federal marshal."

I remembered that Wilmer's Convenience Corner wasn't convenient around the clock. Buddy Smith closed at seven during the week. If I was going to have a confrontation with him, I preferred to arrive nearer closing time and wait till we could talk in private.

As it was late afternoon, I phoned Susan at her clinic to let her know I'd be late for dinner.

"How are you feeling?" was my opening question.

"I'm fine, Barry. I don't want you treating me like I'm sick for the next seven months."

"I know. I know. I guess I'm just getting used to the idea."

"Don't worry. I'll whine when I want to. What's up?"

I gave her the status of the case and told her I'd be home late. Wilmer's Convenience Corner was about forty-five minutes away.

"Is this undercover?"

I realized I wasn't sure. Collier Crockett had come to the cabin angry at what he saw as my interference, but he said that he hadn't given away my identity. Maybe I could demand

Buddy's records claiming to represent Sinclair or Brookshire. If that didn't work, I'd show my creds and tell him I was working with Crockett and the FNS.

"I'll play it undercover at first," I told Susan.

She took a deep, audible breath. "Please be careful. Two little ones are going to need their father."

Her words hit hard. I wasn't one for taking unnecessary risks, but now the prospect of leaving Susan a widow with two infants shocked me with its unanticipated magnitude.

"I will, dear. We're close to wrapping this up. In a few days, everything will be back to normal."

"Barry, you know our normal will soon be changed forever."

"And I can hardly wait. Love you."

"Love you too." She hung up.

I sat for a moment, second-guessing my plan. Buddy Smith had his own little girl to protect and she'd be home from school. So, I'd play my role easy on the threat level, either as a criminal or a deputy.

Next I phoned Fletcher at the funeral home and learned he had the death certificates for Robert Sinclair.

"Have you told Archie?" I asked him.

"No. I just picked up ten copies from the town hall fifteen minutes ago."

"Good. I'll call Archie. Leave them on my desk in case he wants me to run them by tonight."

I immediately dialed Archie's cell phone. "Have you heard anything more from Janet Sinclair?"

"Yes," he said. "She called at noon asking for the insurance forms and death certificates."

I could hear Archie's young girls laughing in the background. "Where are you?"

"Still with Gloria and her mother. Do you think it's safe for us to return home?"

"Not yet. A day or two at most. And I have the death certificates from Fletcher and you can contact Janet Sinclair. But,

Archie, tell her you'll just drop them off at the Renaissance Hotel. Don't meet her or this unknown friend alone."

A few seconds of silence passed. "You think she killed her husband?" His voice sounded like he was being strangled.

"No, I don't. She has an ironclad alibi. But there are things and people still at play. Someone might be watching her, so I'd rather you keep your distance."

"So, should I drive into Gainesboro now?"

Weaverville was an hour away on the north side of Asheville. That meant Archie had to come in and then turn right around. Wilmer's Convenience Corner would be a much closer rendezvous. "Archie, do you have all the policy information with you?"

"You mean like the companies and the numbers?"

"Yes."

"Of course. I downloaded the forms and I've pre-filled everything out. All Janet has to do is sign and either mail or FedEx them and the death certificate."

"And where will the checks come?"

"To that company. Sinclairity Sales. The one we rolled the ownership into when we added their Santona names. The address of record is their home."

Janet had left the Sinclairity Sales bank account open, which meant she would need to collect her mail, or, if there was an accomplice, have that person pick it up. Then the checks could be deposited, and if our theory was correct, wired to the Cayman Islands.

"Good. We'll meet near Asheville. I'm interviewing someone at Wilmer's Convenience Corner." I gave Archie the address. "Just be there around five to seven and wait in your car. Maybe pump some gas if you need it, and then park at the edge of the lot if I'm not there yet. Try not to be late. They close at seven."

"And where do I drop the forms off at the hotel?"

"At the front desk. Phone her after you're back in your car. If she wants to change the mailing address, tell her she can't because it's not the address of record."

"Okay. Then I'll see you at Wilmer's Convenience Corner. Six fifty-five."

"Yes. Just do everything exactly as I said and you'll be fine."

Archie laughed. "When have I ever not listened to you, Barry?"

Only whenever I'm talking, I thought.

Chapter Twenty-seven

I was in the jeep, headed for my rendezvous with Archie and a possible confrontation with Buddy Smith at Wilmer's Convenience Corner. On the seat beside me were two folders: one with three copies of Robert Sinclair's death certificate and the other with individual photos of Luther Brookshire, Robert Sinclair, and Janet Sinclair. I felt confident that if Buddy recognized any of the three people, he would break and I could get Lindsay Boyce to place him and his daughter Norie in an FBI safe house.

The drive gave me an opportunity to review the scenes of the case, one by one, like placing pieces of a puzzle together when you're not sure what the final picture is going to be.

Toby McKay had had a failed apple crop and gotten in debt to Rufus Taylor. He'd forfeited his EBT card as a forced method of repayment. All of the cash generated by its fraudulent purchases was either being kept by Rufus or split with the organizers of the scam food stamp network. Then Toby lost a second crop and suffered an emotional breakdown. But instead of going after Rufus and the conspiracy, he targeted Commissioner of Agriculture Graham James, whose department had destroyed his tainted apples and forced him into his dire circumstances.

Rufus was murdered less than an hour later. One certainty—his death wasn't a coincidence, not when Toby's EBT card was discovered in his wallet. Toby's son, Sonny, showed up drunk at the hospital that night, trying to see Commissioner James, ostensibly to explain his father's actions. He wound up in a jail cell next to Archie, who took on the ridiculous alias of Brad Pitt and learned that Sonny believed his own life was in danger. Reluctantly, Tommy Lee agreed to let Archie continue his charade with Sonny, but Archie, being Archie, bragged to his clients, the Sinclairs, that he was playing a crucial role in the investigation of Toby McKay's attack on the Commissioner of Agriculture. Sonny was murdered that night, and with the same gun that killed Rufus Taylor.

We had statements that Janet Sinclair left the Apple Festival parade soon after Commissioner James was attacked. She could have called someone, like her lover Luther Brookshire, or gone after Rufus herself. She knew Toby's action would trigger an investigation that could lead back to Rufus. With him dead, ties to the large-scale fraud would be severed.

But we found cash and articles in Rufus' closet that pointed to a broader conspiracy, and the newspaper report of the slaughter of a little girl's cat led to Wilmer's Convenience Corner, a store on a list that Sonny McKay must have intended to share with Archie, aka Brad.

We also had the definitive link between checks Rufus Taylor wrote to Staples Sources and the deposits Janet Sinclair made on behalf of her husband. Or the more likely scenario that Janet had been forging his name from the start. Once the possibility arose that Janet Sinclair killed Rufus, then her execution of Sonny McKay became an easy leap to make. The gun was the same. And the likelihood existed that Sonny would have let down his guard if a pretty woman knocked on his trailer door late at night claiming to have car trouble. But Sonny had drunk himself into a stupor and a simple break-in was all she needed.

If we assumed Janet's guilt brought her lover Brookshire into the picture, then he could have killed Robert, or all three, for that matter. He'd been close to Janet and her husband, guarded their identities in WITSEC, and could have been both seduced and enticed by Janet and the food stamp conspiracy. She'd probably witnessed the Santona family organize something similar in New Jersey.

Planting the gun and ledger on Robert pegged him with both the murders and the food stamp fraud. The signature White Rose of the Santonas diverted the focus from North Carolina to the New Jersey mob and created the impetus for Janet to be given a new identity within WITSEC. She and Brookshire could then follow the money out of the country. Between the insurance and the wire transfer, they could live very well, indeed. It was all an impressive plot if we hadn't had the breakthrough with the bank accounts and the overreach of making sure the gun in Robert Sinclair's car reflected his left-handedness. They'd been too clever for their own good. And now the potential testimony of Buddy Smith would be the final piece of the puzzle.

My cell phone vibrated. I glanced down to see the call was from Tommy Lee.

"Where are you?" he asked.

"About fifteen minutes out from Wilmer's Convenience Corner. What's up?"

"You and I had a visitor come by the department who wanted to talk to both of us."

"Who?"

"Luther Brookshire."

"Really?" I felt my heart rate jump. "A confession?"

"Partly. A confession of stupidity for getting involved with Janet Sinclair. But his main concern was that we believed him when he said he would never undercut our investigation. Yesterday, he picked up on what you did. That Janet Sinclair knew we were investigating the EBT scam. He realized he would be the first person we zero in on as the leak. He swears he never mentioned anything to her about our case. And he thinks she killed her husband."

"And you believe him?"

"Let's say it gives me pause. I've known Luther a long time, but sex and money are powerful motivators. He claims Janet made the first move and the affair's been going on only a few months."

"Isn't that what you'd expect him to say? It's a preemptive move because we know he's tied to her."

"Yes, but because we know he's tied to her, why would he say he thinks she killed her husband? Why even go there?"

Tommy Lee's question stopped me. If Brookshire accused Janet, she'd only drag him down with her. And we hadn't put any leverage on Brookshire yet. It wasn't like he was copping a plea. "I don't know. It's something to think about."

"Here's hoping your conversation with Buddy Smith sheds some light. If he identifies Luther, then his mea culpa about the affair is nothing more than an attempt to throw us off. But the timing of the affair is interesting."

I understood what the sheriff meant. "It started about the same time as Robert went to his father's funeral and when Janet first sought to change the insurance policies. She wanted to keep Brookshire close. He was her WITSEC guardian."

"And the source of a new identity," Tommy Lee added.

"But if not Luther Brookshire, then who? We know she had to have an accomplice."

"Unless Robert really was hit by the Santonas."

"But that makes no sense with a planted gun and ledger."

"I know. I wanted you to have this information before you talk to Buddy Smith. Keep open the possibility that Luther is innocent of everything except being seduced."

We disconnected. I quickly ran through the scenes I'd constructed. If Janet hadn't learned of the EBT investigation from Brookshire, would she have brought it up herself? It wasn't common knowledge. A switch threw in my brain. A perspective shift projected the case from a whole new angle. The EBT scam wasn't common knowledge. Sid Ferguson of the SBI and Lindsay

Boyce of the FBI hadn't been aware of it. That was odd because an FNS investigator was usually paired with one or the other as a case progressed.

What had Collier Crockett said about his background? Chicago, New York, New Jersey. A tingle started in the back of my neck. Was Luther Brookshire the first person Janet Sinclair had seduced? Crockett had broken up rings in eastern North Carolina, but only the occasional single store in western North Carolina. He could have come across the Sinclair operation, but instead of busting it, he could have joined it. The network would have been protected. Even the ledger book from Robert's SUV would have been handed back to Crockett. Or if Janet and Crockett went as far back as New Jersey, he could have set the whole thing up down here. Brookshire said Janet was the one who wanted WITSEC to locate her in the North Carolina mountains.

I was only minutes away from Wilmer's Convenience Corner. It was too late for me to get a photo of Crockett e-mailed to me. I had to meet Archie. I had to intercept Buddy Smith as he was closing the store. But I'd give him a verbal description of Crockett and maybe get a positive ID from a photograph later tonight.

The other businesses near Wilmer's had closed for the evening. The small grocery store was open but as I drew closer, the light on the gas pumps went out. It looked like Buddy might be closing a few minutes early. I drove by and then made a sharp turn into the lot out of sight of the front windows. Less than a minute later, Archie pulled his Lexus next to me headed in the opposite direction and we lowered our windows so we could talk without getting out.

He gave me an okay sign. "I got here early, bought some gas, and then parked at a tire store one building over."

I handed him the folder with the death certificates. "There's three in there. Wasn't sure if she needed one for each policy."

He shook his head. "Just the one for the death claim, but good to have the extras. I guess she really is going to try to change the name from Sinclair to Santona. If I'd known they were crooks, I never would have suggested the whole plan."

"And we might never have known what was going on."

Archie sighed. "Yeah. That's some comfort. Just so you know, there's a little girl in the store. Looks like she's doing her home-work."

"I know. She's the owner's daughter. Thanks. I'll check in with you later."

Archie hesitated. "You sure you don't need me?"

"It's just a conversation. You go on to Asheville."

He raised his window, gave a wave through the glass, and eased back onto the two-lane highway.

I slipped the Kimber pistol into the back holster, waited for an oncoming car to pass, and then stepped out of the jeep. I checked my phone to make sure it was still silent, and then opened the app I needed.

Bells tinkled as I opened the store's front door.

"We're closing in a few minutes." Buddy Smith's voice came from one of the aisles. He stepped into view, a broom in his hand. His face went pale when he saw me and he laid the broom against a display of Hostess snacks. His gaze went immediately to his daughter, who was writing in a notebook at the end of the checkout counter.

I held my hands out, the folder in the right one. "I don't want any trouble. I just want to talk and show you some pictures."

Buddy Smith held up his own hands as if to push me away. "No. I've been told not to talk to you." He sidestepped around me and went to his daughter.

The girl looked up from her homework, fear plainly visible in her eyes.

Buddy put his hands on his daughter's shoulders. "You're trying to muscle in, and we won't be intimidated. Not anymore."

"That's what you were told? I was muscling in?"

"Yes. So get out and I won't tell that you came back. It's for your own good."

"I'm a deputy sheriff."

He eyed me skeptically. "Right. Then you'll let Norie go." He stepped back. "Leave your books, honey. Run up to the house. I'll be there shortly."

The girl hesitated, clearly reluctant to leave her father.

"Go!" he ordered.

She scooted off the stool and hurried by me. The bells jangled and the door slammed. Buddy Smith moved closer to the cash register.

"I'm with the Laurel County Sheriff's Department. All I want is for you to look at these photographs." I stepped toward him.

His hand disappeared beneath the counter and then reappeared gripping an old, tarnished thirty-eight revolver.

"Whoa," I said softly. "There's no need for that. I can show you my ID."

Buddy pulled back the hammer. "Keep your hands where I can see them." His voice quivered and the gun shook. I hoped there was a lot of play in the trigger.

"Whatever you say. But at least take a look at what's in the folder. Why would I bring pictures if I meant to do you harm?"

"Spread them out on the counter and then step back."

I did as he ordered. He looked at them in short glances, afraid to take his eyes off me for more than a few seconds.

"Nope. I don't recognize none of them."

His own facial reactions supported his words.

"Then tell me this. Do you know a man named Collier Crockett?"

Again, the blank stair.

"He's about forty. Black hair going gray at the edges. Sharp dresser."

His eyes widened slightly. "No. I don't know no one by that name."

I nodded. "Fine. I'm done here. I didn't mean to scare you or Norie. She's a lovely girl." I smiled. "My wife and I are having twins. I hope they're as nice as she is."

Buddy Smith's chin trembled and his eyes teared. He lowered the gun as the tension left his body.

The door burst open, ripping one of the bells from its mounting. Sheer panic flared on Buddy's face. I turned around.

Little Norie stumbled into the store, her arm wrenched behind her back. A pistol was jammed against her temple. A pistol held by Collier Crockett.

"Mr. Callahan, no!" Buddy wailed.

"Set the gun down, Buddy." The menace in Crockett's voice curled my blood. He kicked the front door closed.

Buddy uncocked the revolver and laid it on the counter. Norie whimpered.

"Slide it to the far end," Crockett ordered.

Buddy complied.

"I have to congratulate you, Buddy. You've caught yourself a real fish." He turned to me. "And you, Deputy Clayton, you just couldn't keep your nose out of my case, could you? That's why I've been following you."

He moved the pistol away from Norie's head and pointed it at me. "Buddy. Frisk him. Run your hands up each leg and check under his shoulders and his waist."

"There's a gun in the small of my back."

Buddy pulled the Kimber from the holster and set it on the counter.

"Frisk him anyway," Crockett said.

I spread my legs and held out my arms to make it easier.

"It's over, Crockett. We've found the bank accounts, we've got the money trail, we've got the evidence that you murdered Robert and then overdid it with the prints and placement of the pistol. Whose gun was that? Janet's?"

"She freaked out when Toby McKay went nuts. First killed Rufus and then Toby's son."

"And if she went down, you'd go down. So, what are you going to do now? Kill us all?"

Crockett didn't answer. He looked at the photos on the counter. "What are those?"

"Pictures. I was hoping Buddy could make an ID. He couldn't. He didn't give you up."

Crockett kept his grip on Norie's arm and motioned with the pistol. "Hold them up one at a time, Buddy."

The store owner lifted Robert Sinclair's photo, then Janet's, followed by Brookshire's.

"What's Brookshire doing with them?" Crockett asked.

"We thought he might be part of it."

"Why?"

"Because he's having an affair with Janet."

Crockett flinched like I'd slapped him. "He's what?"

"Having an affair. Do I need to spell it out? Janet wants to make sure she gets her new WITSEC identity. After all, everyone's supposed to think the Santona family is after her. Then she and Brookshire will leave the country and catch up with the wired funds and the insurance money. I guess you'll be left here holding the bag. And after you wired the money for her. I tell you there's no justice, is there?"

His eyes narrowed. "What insurance money?"

"You mean you didn't know about the million and a half dollars she's walking away with since you so conveniently murdered her husband?"

Crockett's face turned nearly purple with rage. "You're lying, you son of a bitch."

"Really? Didn't she tell you she met with an insurance agent? Archie Donovan. That's where she heard Sonny McKay was about to talk about your little EBT card fraud. That's what set her off again, right?"

Crockett's jaw clenched. I knew I'd pushed the right buttons, but I'd overplayed my hand. He knew that I knew he'd been played for a fool. In a flash, I saw what was coming.

My fear was confirmed when he said, "Bring me your revolver, Buddy."

"Don't do it. He's going to shoot me with your gun and then murder you and Norie with mine."

"Shut up." Crockett moved the barrel of his semi-automatic back to Norie's temple. "Bring it, Buddy. Hand it to me butt first and I'll let your daughter go."

Buddy walked like he was about to collapse. He picked up the old revolver, holding the barrel in his left hand.

"Daddy, don't," Norie whispered.

Buddy's face went hard. He grabbed the gun with his right hand. Crockett whipped his pistol from the girl's head and aimed it at her father.

The explosion was deafening. Not from the gun, but from the front door and wall exploding as a car smashed through it. Glass and splinters flew from broken windows and boards. Crockett spun around and fired shots indiscriminately into the windshield of the vehicle. Norie fell to the floor as I jumped for the Kimber and racked the slide just as Crockett wheeled back around. I fired three shots as fast as I could pull the trigger. The impact of the forty-five caliber slugs into Crockett's chest drove him back like he'd been hit by a train.

Dust hung in the air like fog. I ran to Crockett and kicked his pistol clear. His eyes were open, seeing nothing.

I turned back to Buddy. He was kneeling, embracing his daughter in a smothering hug. Both were crying.

I stepped over the debris to the driver's side of a mangled Lexus. Archie Donovan fought through a deflated airbag and practically fell out of the car. He looked up with blood streaked across his face.

"Archie, are you hit?"

He coughed. "I fell across the seat after the airbag smacked me." He looked up at the windshield. Bullet holes showed where Crockett's shots had penetrated just above the steering wheel. "Sorry, Barry. I didn't do what you told me."

I helped him to his feet and did the unthinkable.

I hugged him.

Chapter Twenty-eight

Wilmer's Convenience Corner looked like a war zone. Blue, red, and orange lights flashed from vehicles filling the parking lot and running along the highway's shoulder for a hundred feet in either direction. EMTs, Buncombe County deputies, and firemen dotted the scene. Buddy Smith's neighbors from the houses on the ridge behind the store stood on a perimeter the police had cordoned off. The murmur of their whispers was like a steady buzz of insects.

Archie had had the presence of mind to call 911 before his crash and a horde of Buncombe County law enforcement quickly arrived on the scene. I'd raised Tommy Lee, who in turn contacted Lindsay Boyce. She and her FBI team were nearer and it seemed like no more than twenty minutes before she appeared, making it clear to the Buncombe County Sheriff that this was a federal investigation.

Buddy Smith and Norie were together in the back of an ambulance. Both had suffered minor cuts and bruises from flying debris. Archie's nose had swollen from the airbag's impact and he had a gash on his forehead that required a few stitches. Miraculously, I was unscathed.

Lindsay Boyce requested Tommy Lee, Archie, and me join her in her SUV for a briefing on what happened. She would speak with Buddy Smith and Norie after they'd been removed from the trauma of the scene.

Lindsay and Tommy Lee sat in the front seats with Archie and me in the rear.

"Okay, Barry," Lindsay said. "walk us through what happened."

I opted to let my story be told directly. I retrieved my cell phone, opened the record app I'd started before entering the store, and we heard Crockett convict himself and Janet with his own words.

"This is good," Lindsay said when I stopped the recording with the sound of Archie's car crashing through the store wall. "Really good."

"Yes," Tommy Lee agreed. "But it would be better if we could get Janet Sinclair incriminating herself as well."

"Any ideas?" Lindsay asked.

"Have the agents who are minding her said anything about this event?" I asked.

"I don't know. Why?"

"We get Crockett's phone and see if he had any e-mail or text correspondence from Janet. If so, we contact her as Crockett. Arrange a meet. If she comes to him, we've further nailed down that they had a relationship. Maybe even have Archie drop off the insurance forms as originally planned. She might pick them up and try to give your agents the slip. I mean, she knows the Santona family didn't kill Robert, so she's got nothing to fear."

"Worth a shot," Tommy Lee said.

"I'll check my agents," Lindsay said. "If Janet doesn't know, I'll make sure she's isolated from any news." Lindsay twisted in her seat to face Archie who sat directly behind her. "Why did you stay?"

Archie nervously wiped his palms on his pants. The magnitude of his action was beginning to sink in. Especially the bullet holes in the driver's side of the windshield.

"I pulled out of the parking lot and about fifty feet down the road a car passed me going the other way. I wondered if the driver would think it suspicious if he saw Barry going into the store as it was closing. So, I slowed and checked the rearview mirror. The car kept going but then suddenly turned into the lot of the closed tire store. That's where I'd been waiting for Barry. I pulled onto the shoulder and killed my lights. In a few minutes I saw a man walking near the gas pumps. A little girl ran out the front door of the grocery store and the man grabbed her. He dragged her inside. I turned my car around and eased back with the headlights off. I stopped out of sight of the front window and got out. I crept up beside the front door and could hear everything. You heard what Crockett said. It was clear to me he could start shooting at any time. I ran back to my car, made the 911 call, and then used the only weapon I had. My Lexus."

"That was quick thinking," Lindsay said. "Are you still game for taking the insurance forms to the hotel?"

Archie looked at me and shrugged. "Yeah, but what if she happens to come down to the lobby and I look like this?"

"Just leave them at the front desk," I said.

"Okay, but there's another problem?"

"What?" I asked.

"I need a ride."

Archie rode to Asheville with me in the jeep. I'd placed a quick call to Susan to tell her I was okay and Archie did the same with his wife Gloria. We weren't sure what names the news media might be mentioning, but we didn't want our families worrying.

Special Agent Lindsay Boyce had been assured by her agent at the hotel that Janet had no knowledge of the incident at the store. She was watching a movie on HBO. Lindsay had found a text message on Crockett's phone that read,

at 302 Renaissance.

The number matched Janet's hotel room and Lindsay verified that the sending cell phone belonged to Janet. It was the same number from which she'd contacted Archie. We would send the ruse message from Crockett's phone after Archie delivered the forms to the front desk. Since she was expecting them, we didn't want any delay to alarm her.

We'd just entered Asheville on I-240 when I had a call from a number I didn't recognize. I started to let it go to voicemail, but with all the actions swirling around us, I decided I'd better take it.

"Barry, it's Luther Brookshire."

"Yes, Luther. I'm kind of tied up right now."

"I understand. I'm watching the news. Are you okay?"

"Yes. Thanks. Tommy Lee said you came by the department."

"So you know I had nothing to do with this."

"I do."

"Did she kill Rufus and Sonny?"

"That's what Crockett said. He was in it with her."

"That's the FNS investigator, right?"

"Yes. We think they were in it together from the very start. And they were lovers."

Brookshire's voice choked. "She played me for a fool. And I made a fool out of the marshals."

I didn't say anything. My unspoken thought was that Brookshire was correct. She had played him for a fool, she'd played Robert Sinclair for a fool, and I felt certain she was planning to ditch Crockett and take all the money. *La femme fatale.*

"Don't worry, Luther. We'll get her. I've got to go." I hung up before he could say anything else.

I parked the jeep in a ten-minute loading zone at the hotel. "On second thought, Archie, don't leave the forms at the front desk. Ask that they deliver them to room 302. We don't want her coming down where she might see a newscast in the bar."

"Got it." He grinned. "This time I'll listen to you."

He was back in five minutes. "Now what?"

"Now I take you to Weaverville and your wife and girls."

After Archie was reunited with his family, I phoned Tommy

Lee. It was nearly eleven, but he was still with Lindsay at the FBI office.

"What's the plan?" I asked.

"Why don't you head home and get some rest?" Tommy Lee said.

"Oh, no. You made me your lead investigator on this thing and I'm seeing it through."

"Okay. I'm staying at the Aloft. I'll book you a room. Lindsay and her agents will take Janet into custody in the morning. We'll be observers."

"Did you send Janet the text?"

"Yes." Tommy Lee chuckled. "My niece is quite devious. She wrote, 'trouble with the wire transfer. Need to see you! Over Easy Café. 8AM.'"

The Over Easy Café was a popular breakfast spot a few blocks' walk from Janet's hotel.

"Good," I said. "She might not come for Crockett but she'll come if she thinks there's a snag with the money. Are you going to make it easy for her to slip out?"

"Yes. Lindsay has one female agent with Janet. She'll just happen to take a shower around twenty to eight."

"And we'll be where?"

"Lindsay's sending a van for us at seven-fifteen. We'll be watching through its tinted windows from across the street."

"All right. I'll see you in the lobby of the Aloft at seven-fifteen."

The room was available when I arrived. I was afraid I'd have trouble falling asleep, the way my mind was racing. I stripped, tried to shake the dust from my clothes, and then took a hot shower. I set my phone alarm for six forty-five and put my head on the pillow. The next thing I knew the alarm was chirping.

The van was in position by seven-thirty. Lindsay had brought two thermoses of hot coffee and some sweet rolls. The plan was to take Janet at the front door. But the concern was that as vicious as she'd proven to be, we didn't want any altercation to break out that could injure an innocent bystander. The Over Easy Café was so popular that a line usually formed about fifteen minutes before opening time.

Around ten till eight, an Asheville police car, siren blaring and lights flashing came speeding past us. We didn't think much of it until two minutes later when a second cruiser raced by.

"Uh, oh," Lindsay muttered. "I don't like this." She turned to an agent in the front passenger's seat. "Henry, walk back toward the hotel along the route Janet should be taking."

Five minutes later, his voice crackled over the comm set. "A woman's body's been found behind the hotel. I believe she's our target."

"Copy that." Lindsay slid open the side door. "Gentlemen. Shall we?"

We showed our IDs to the police officers who were setting up a perimeter around the body. They were very curious how the FBI had showed up so quickly, but Lindsay offered no explanation other than the victim was a federal witness.

Janet lay on her back along the single-lane road that ran between the hotel and the historic Thomas Wolfe House. Blood splotched the front of her light-blue coat. An oozing wound marred the center of her forehead. Even in death, her face held an expression of total surprise.

Beside her head lay a single white rose.

"How could the Santonas find her?" Lindsay asked.

"Check her phone," I suggested.

Lindsay borrowed a pair of latex gloves from one of the officers and rummaged through the purse beside Janet's waist. She found the phone.

"What am I looking for?" she asked.

"Any text containing the hotel information. Like what we found on Crockett's phone."

Lindsay thumbed through the texts as Tommy Lee and I huddled around her. "Here's the one to Crockett," she said. "I recognize the number." She continued to scroll. "Here's another."

"That's Archie's phone," I said.

"And here's a third."

I pulled my own phone from my belt and checked my messages. The number matched. "That belongs to Luther Brookshire."

"How will we prove it?" Lindsay asked.

"You won't," I said. "You can canvas every flower vendor in the area to see who bought a white rose, but I suspect he might have just paid someone to buy it for him. What's the time on that message?"

"The night before last. When we first booked her into the hotel."

"Or maybe he tipped off the Santona family," Tommy Lee said.

"Maybe," I conceded. "Ironic that the marshals never lost a witness in WITSEC and here's the second within three days. And possibly shot by the marshal handling her."

"No," Tommy Lee said. "The marshals will claim they voided their protection the day Robert Sinclair went to that New Jersey funeral. Their record's intact."

Lindsay nodded. "So, what now?"

I looked down at the body. "Now I call a cemetery in Paterson, New Jersey."

Chapter Twenty-nine

"Then on Friday afternoon, Commissioner of Agriculture Graham James announced the formation of a task force involving his department, the SBI, the FBI, and FNS to track down and prosecute all who might be part of the fraud ring Collier Crockett and Janet Sinclair created." I picked up the wineglass by the leg of my chair and took a sip. "And now you're up to date."

Melissa Bigham leaned over and turned off the digital audio recorder on the low table between us. She, Susan, and I sat on our back deck. Democrat lay at Melissa's feet. It was late Sunday afternoon. Janet Sinclair had been shot the previous Wednesday, and Melissa had returned from her vacation in the Caribbean yesterday to find one of the biggest stories in Gainesboro's history happened while she was gone. To say she was as angry as a wet hornet doesn't begin to describe her wrath.

As an attempt to pacify her and the *Gainesboro Vista*, Tommy Lee had authorized an exclusive interview with me. I'd suggested drinks and dinner at the cabin. I was counting on Susan to prevent any bodily harm. Bodily harm to me.

"Okay," Melissa said flatly, "so, off the record, who do you think killed Joan Santona, aka Janet Sinclair?"

The sheriff and I had agreed there would be no speculation on Luther Brookshire's guilt while the FBI investigated Janet's murder. And I'd kept Brookshire out of my story because his affair had no bearing on the key events.

"All I can say is we found a white rose beside her body. Whether it was a Santona hit or someone else casting that suspicion, I don't know. Anyway, that case is out of our jurisdiction."

She frowned. "Come on, Barry. Surely you have an opinion."

"Well, I will say that we've learned Collier Crockett had investigated food stamp fraud in New Jersey when the Santonas were suspected of being involved. My speculation is that Crockett and Joan Santona met then. She was already skimming from the family, and that's why she turned over evidence that got her and Robert into WITSEC. Robert was so infatuated with her that she could manipulate him to do anything. As far as we know, he was happy repping his sportswear lines and playing golf. His signature that the FBI found on checks and deposit slips appears to have been consistently forged by Janet. I believe Robert really didn't have much of a clue as to what was going on."

"And you think Janet and Crockett planned to leave the country?"

"I think Janet did. Crockett could have wound up someone she used and discarded along the way."

"Any update on Buddy Smith and his daughter?" Melissa asked.

"He's turning state's evidence. I expect he'll get a light sentence and probation. His store was barely making ends meet and when his wife got cancer, he got involved with Crockett, only Crockett called himself Callahan. Lindsay Boyce believes Crockett used a false name with every store owner as another layer of protection. In his investigations, he'd find ones who were taking cash out of customers' EBT cards and threaten to report them if they didn't start splitting the take. Staples Sources was the shell company and the corrupt store owners wouldn't be audited since Crockett was the lead investigator."

"Did he kill the little girl's cat?"

"Yes. After Buddy Smith's wife died, the medical bills ceased. Buddy wanted out. The dead cat was a message. I think a judge will be sympathetic to what the poor man went through."

"And it sounds like at the end, he was going to defend you, rather than give his gun to Crockett."

I flashed back to the grim look of determination that transformed Buddy's face from fear to resolve.

"Yes. But I'm afraid Crockett would have shot first."

Melissa smiled for the first time. "Except for Archie."

I nodded. "Except for Archie."

"And here's my threat to you, Barry Clayton. If something like this ever happens again, promise me you'll track me down even if I'm on Mars."

"Or what?" I asked.

"Or I'm running this story under the headline, 'Archie Donovan, Junior, saves Buryin' Barry.'"

Susan laughed and raised her glass of sparkling water. "To Archie."

"To Archie," I repeated. For once, the words didn't stick in my throat.

Over six weeks later, Thursday, the first of November, dawned chilly and clear. At eight o'clock, Susan and I stood on the front porch of the funeral home and watched the moving van turn off Main Street into our parking lot. I put my arm around her waist and patted her tummy. The baby bump seemed to be growing daily.

We'd loaded the truck the previous day after getting Uncle Wayne and Mom settled in their apartment at Alderway. Both had been over the moon when we'd told them about the twins. Mom was already anxious about what the grandchildren would call her, and Uncle Wayne regaled us with tales of how they needed a set bedtime like when he grew up on a farm and had to get up early for chores. My bachelor uncle, the expert on child-rearing. Our only livestock was going to be Democrat.

"Your mom called a few minutes ago while you were out back," Susan said. "She and Uncle Wayne are on their way with ham biscuits and orange juice."

"Did you tell her we're fine?"

Susan laughed. "Now what good would that have done? She said she wants the movers to have something to eat. You saw how they loved those cookies yesterday."

That was my mom. See a person, feed a person. The local movers were doing triple duty: moving Mom and my uncle, moving Cindy and Fletcher, and moving Susan and me.

Not since high school had I lived in the funeral home. Susan and I agreed the two-bedroom cabin would be cramped quarters and it was Susan who convinced me that the funeral home with four bedrooms was a ready-made option. We took the money from the sale of her condo, also sold the cabin, and paid Mom a fair appraisal. Fletcher and Cindy bought the cabin before it went on the market and the movers got all the business, plus cookies and biscuits as a bonus.

Trailing the van was a Chevy Malibu of several years vintage.

"Oh, no," I groaned. "I wonder what this is about?"

"Who is it?" Susan asked.

"Archie. He bought a used car because his insurance company says he wrecked his Lexus on purpose."

"But he saved three lives."

"Don't I know it. Lindsay Boyce and the FBI are getting involved. They're working the angle that Crockett and Janet caused him to total his car. The FBI may manage to have the Sinclairs' assets impounded. Archie could wind up with Janet's Mercedes or Robert's Infiniti, if Archie doesn't die of old age before the government paperwork is completed."

Archie parked on the far side of the moving van. He got out, waved, and then pulled two wrapped boxes out of his backseat.

He stacked them under his chin and walked toward us without being able to see his feet.

"You'd better go help him," Susan said. "We don't need to test our new homeowner's policy if he trips."

I met Archie at the edge of the sidewalk and took one of the packages.

"Thanks, Barry. I can't stay, but Gloria and I wanted to get you something for your first day in the funeral home. Can't believe you're living here. It's like old times."

He stepped up on the porch and smiled at Susan. "And how are you doing, little Momma?"

"I'm good, Archie. How's the family?"

"Terrific. Everything's terrific."

"Well, that's terrific," I echoed.

"Come on in," Susan said. "Have some coffee."

"Thanks. These are for the kitchen anyway." Archie stepped around her and led the way into the house.

Susan and I looked at each other. She shook her head as if to say, "Only Archie."

He set his package on the kitchen table and I placed the second one beside it. They were wrapped in pink and blue paper.

"Go ahead. Open them."

Susan took one and I took the other. In less than a minute, we were looking at identical boxes with a picture of a yellow booster seat on the sides.

"What do you think?" Archie asked. "We got this color because we don't know the genders, but you'll need them for when the twins are old enough to sit at this table and eat their peanut butter and jelly sandwiches."

Archie punched me gently on the arm. "Huh, buddy? Just what this funeral home needs. New life." He laughed at his own joke. "And if they're boys, I've got the perfect names."

I cringed.

He punched me harder. "Archie and Barry."

Author's Note

Secret Undertaking is a work of fiction, but elements of the story are based in fact.

The U.S. Marshals Service is charged with operating the Federal Witness Protection Program, or WITSEC, as it is known. In contacting the U.S. Marshals for information, one quickly learns that all aspects of their procedures for relocating their witnesses are closely guarded. "Neither confirm nor deny" is their prevalent answer. However, they referred me to the book, *WITSEC: Inside the Federal Witness Protection Program* by Pete Earley and Gerald Shur, the man credited with creating WITSEC. Although the Marshals neither confirm nor deny its accuracy, the book is a fascinating revelation of the program's history.

WITSEC was instrumental in decimating the mob, but an unintended consequence has been those occasions when relocated witnesses have used their new, squeaky-clean identities to return to a life of crime. Local law enforcement is not made aware of their presence in their communities. That tension between invaluable testimony for the prosecution of major criminal enterprises and the protection of those witnesses who are criminals themselves is real and created the underlying conflict for my story.

Likewise, the urban and rural abuse of the Supplemental Nutrition Assistance Program (SNAP Food Stamp Program) is also documented fact, but I wouldn't want the crimes depicted in my story to undercut the tremendous benefit that SNAP provides. Although fraud exists, it is a very small percentage of an overall program that offers vital assistance to millions of low-income individuals and families. It is a key component of our social safety net, and the USDA aggressively investigates and prosecutes those who would subvert it.

Acknowledgments

Special thanks to retired Mecklenburg County Sheriff Chipp Bailey for his insights into the U.S. Marshals' insulation of relocated witnesses from local law enforcement. Also I'm appreciative of what information the U.S. Marshals Office of Public Affairs was able to share regarding WITSEC. Thanks to my brother Arch de Castrique, insurance and investment guru, for devising the Sinclairs' policy scheme.

I'm grateful to my editor Barbara Peters for her guidance in developing the story and to Robert Rosenwald and the staff of Poisoned Pen Press, who turn stories into books. Thanks to the many librarians and booksellers who introduce my stories to readers and to all who spend time with my characters.

Finally, I'm grateful for my family—Linda, Melissa, Pete, Charlie, Lindsay, Jordan (and canines Grady, Belby, and Norman), who make reality even more fun to experience than fiction. Thanks for creating such a wonderful world.

To see more Poisoned Pen Press titles:

Visit our website:
poisonedpenpress.com
Request a digital catalog:
info@poisonedpenpress.com

		Optimistic and spontaneous	Considerate and with understanding	Reflective and correct
MANNER	Businesslike	Visible	Sensitive	Formal
WORK-STYLE	Hard-working Ambitious Professional Effective Exact	Committed Personal Flexible Stimulating Articulate	Personal Relaxed Friendly Informal Low-key	Structured Organized Specialized Methodic Succinct
WORK PACE	Fast and decisive	Fast and spontaneous	Slow and consistent	Slow and systematic
PRIORITIZES	The task and the result	Relationships and influence	Retaining good relationships	The task and work method
AFRAID OF	Losing control	Losing prestige	Confrontation	Making a fool of oneself
BEHAVES UNDER PRESSURE	Dictates conditions and asserts oneself	Attacks and is ironic	Backs down and agrees	Withdraws and avoids
WANTS	Results	Inspiration	Stability	Quality
WANTS YOU TO BE	Straightforward	Stimulating	Kind	Exact
WANTS TO BE	The one who decides	The one who is admired	The one who is liked	The one who is correct
IS IRRITATED BY	Inefficiency and indecision	Passivity and routines	Insensitivity and impatience	Surprises and whims
WANTS TO HAVE	Success and control	Status and flexibility	Calm & quiet and close relationships	Credibility and time to prepare
BEHAVES	Businesslike	Elegant	Friendly	Law-abiding
LIVES IN	The present	The future	The past (when everything was better)	One's own thoughts
RELIES UPON	Gut feeling	Recognition	One's self	Specialists
DON'T LIKE	Sitting still	Being alone	Unpredictability	Hurry

Surrounded
by Setbacks

ALSO BY THOMAS ERIKSON

Surrounded by Idiots
Surrounded by Psychopaths
Surrounded by Bad Bosses (and Lazy Employees)

· · · ·

Surrounded by Setbacks

Turning Obstacles into Success
(When Everything Goes to Hell)

Thomas Erikson

ST. MARTIN'S
ESSENTIALS
NEW YORK

First published in the United States by St. Martin's Essentials,
an imprint of St. Martin's Publishing Group

SURROUNDED BY SETBACKS. Copyright © 2021 by Thomas Erikson. Translation copyright © 2021 by Rod Bradbury. All rights reserved. Printed in the United States of America. For information, address St. Martin's Publishing Group, 120 Broadway, New York, NY 10271.

www.stmartins.com

Library of Congress Cataloging-in-Publication Data

Names: Erikson, Thomas, 1965– author.
Title: Surrounded by setbacks : turning obstacles into success (when everything goes to hell) / Thomas Erikson.
Other titles: Omgiven av motgångar. English
Description: First U.S. edition. | New York, NY : St. Martin's Essentials, [2021] | "Originally published in Sweden by Forum in 2020"—Verso. | Includes bibliographical references and index.
Identifiers: LCCN 2021016088 | ISBN 9781250789518 (hardcover) | ISBN 9781250838933 (international, sold outside the U.S., subject to rights availability) | ISBN 9781250789525 (ebook)
Subjects: LCSH: Success. | Goal (Psychology)
Classification: LCC BF637.S8 E7413 2021 | DDC 158—dc23
LC record available at https://lccn.loc.gov/2021016088

Our books may be purchased in bulk for promotional, educational, or business use. Please contact your local bookseller or the Macmillan Corporate and Premium Sales Department at 1-800-221-7945, extension 5442, or by email at MacmillanSpecialMarkets@macmillan.com.

Originally published in Sweden by Forum in 2020.

First U.S. Edition: 2021

10   9   8   7   6   5   4   3   2   1

Contents

Part II. Creating Lifelong Success, or How to Win Every Time

When It All Goes to Hell

WHEN IT ALL GOES WRONG

Sometimes it just happens. Things go bad. In a big way.

You're about to celebrate your daughter's graduation with a party in the backyard; the family has prepared for this for months, fifty guests have arrived, and suddenly the heavens open, the rain pours down, and the whole affair is ruined.

When you check the balance of the equity fund the bank recommended so highly and realize that your financial advisor really didn't know more than you. Now you're broke—again.

When you realize that the presentation you've been working on for several weeks, the one that is going to catapult you directly to the corner office, was on the other USB stick.

When the house you've dreamed about since you were a kid finally comes on the market, but the bank says no.

When you've just reestablished contact with an old friend, only to learn that he only has six months left to live.

When you're walking down the sidewalk one fine morning and happen to put your left shoe right into a pile of dog shit.

When your worst enemy in the company gets the top job you thought had your name on it.

When you just open your eyes in the morning and everything goes wrong.

Sometimes you feel as though you're surrounded by setbacks, obstacles, and adversities. Little ones and big ones. And each time, you're overwhelmed by a feeling of hopelessness.

You've picked up a book with a slightly depressing title. But this book isn't really about setbacks. It's about how you can deal with what you perceive as setbacks, and instead learn to achieve success. Life is what it is; it's more a question of what you make of it than of what happens around you.

Like a wise person once said: it isn't about what happens to you, but about how you deal with it.

This planet can be a tricky place to live. A wonderful place, too, but nevertheless a rather weird one. And we aren't always great at adjusting to the circumstances.

Some people manage to get through life fairly well without serious damage, but nobody manages to completely avoid difficulties and setbacks. Some people only have to deal with minor irritations. And then there are those who get such a rough deal from life that it makes you wonder why the powers above don't descend and give them a helping hand. They get hit so hard that you wouldn't want anyone to suffer that way.

Despite unimaginable difficulties, some of these people do keep going. How? What is their secret? Why don't they just lie down and give up?

Somewhere I heard an expression that stuck in my mind: "If you find yourself in a rowboat way out at sea—by all means say a prayer, but start rowing toward land at the same time."

That's a good approach to difficulties and setbacks in life. Sometimes you need to hope that it will get better, but you also need to act.

And here we have one of the most important keys to dealing with setbacks and building your path toward success: you have to do something.

THIS BOOK DOESN'T CLAIM TO BE TOTALLY COMPREHENSIVE

There's research that can confirm much of what I am going to share with you. I will refer to some of it, and at the end of the book you will find a list of books to read on many of the subjects that I'll discuss.

A lot of what we're going to look at is based on my own experiences. Experiences that I've spent years trying to understand myself. I've also observed the journeys of others I've encountered over thirty years of professional life.

The approach that I share in this book has saved me from serious problems on more than one occasion. It's given me the ability to pitch unpleasant experiences overboard, retain my focus, and keep rowing my boat.

So has everything gone perfectly? Certainly not. I make my own mistakes and end up in trouble, just like everybody else. Even in situations where I really should have known better, I've sometimes managed to mess things up all by myself. And sometimes the world doesn't go my way at all. A few situations come to mind:

- When I was ten years old, my family moved hundreds of miles away from everyone I knew.
- I misjudged the willingness of a potential client to do a deal, and that carelessness meant a missed contract for a *lot* of money.
- On one occasion, I wrote a grumpy letter of complaint to my employer (the biggest business bank in Scandinavia).

The letter went right up to the CEO, who phoned me and gave me what for.

- At first, nobody was interested in the original Swedish manuscript of *Surrounded by Idiots,* my first book. About twenty publishers said no. Some of them rather brutally. I had to publish it myself.
- After the publication of my first book, I was pursued by a malevolent stalker.
- I've gone through two divorces.

Of course, this list of failures, setbacks, and difficulties could be far longer. Nevertheless, I've succeeded with some things. And you can read about the methods that have helped me in this book. You'll learn how to:

- never forget where you're going in life;
- not worry about what other people think of you;
- know which people really wish you well, and who doesn't;
- learn from every setback, so that you won't run into a brick wall again;
- stay on track, even when the people around you are doubtful;
- turn a setback into a success;
- stop wasting your time on the wrong things;
- deal with your fears;
- achieve long-term success without giving up on the way.

KNOWLEDGE IS NOT POWER

That familiar old expression "Knowledge is power" is indeed deceptive. Knowledge is *not* power. The world is full of enormously well-educated people who (if we're being honest about it) aren't doing particularly well. People with all the right letters before and after their names. They know just about everything and can quote every possible theory, but they don't even have power over their immediate environment.

So what is knowledge? Well, knowledge is *potential* power. If you use it, that is.

It makes no difference what you know and what you are capable of doing. Not even if you have an IQ higher than anyone south of the North Pole. However well-read you might be, and whomever you may have listened to, whichever books written by the world's cleverest people you may have read—it makes no difference.

No. Difference. At. All.

What you are *capable of* is beside the point. What you *know* is irrelevant. The only thing that matters when it comes to dealing with obstacles and creating success is what you actually *do*.

In the United States, 44 percent of all doctors are overweight (*Newsweek*, October 2008). I haven't managed to find any equivalent statistics for the Swedish medical profession, but all the doctors I've met are definitely not in the best shape. How can that be? They know better than anyone what you should eat and that you should exercise regularly, and they've seen all the sad effects of being overweight and smoking. Nevertheless, many of them also have challenges with their health. It doesn't add up.

This kind of thinking may determine what you do with the content of this book. You can always nod and say, *Yeah, so what?* Or say, *I don't believe that*. Or you can test it yourself. You won't know whether it works for you until you've given it a try.

The problem is bigger than that. We tend to stick to our normal ways of thinking, even when new insights come our way. Ideas that we've lived with for a long time, perhaps many years, aren't easy to let go of. Sometimes we need to change perspective.

Recently, I heard that the definition of "intelligence" shouldn't be how high your IQ is, but rather your ability to neutrally observe something that doesn't fit in with your existing picture of the world and actually take it in. And even change your own opinion on the issue.

YOUR RESULTS ARE ALL THAT COUNTS

We don't really need loads of new ideas to achieve success and to deal with setbacks. Perhaps as you read this book you'll find yourself thinking, *Meh, I've heard this before!* When that thought crops up, because it will, I want you to ask yourself three questions:

1. Are you doing it today?
2. Have you mastered it?
3. Do your *results* show that you have mastered it?

If you say that you already live an active, healthy life, I'm going to believe your waist measurement, not your words. If you claim that you're in full control of your financial situation, I'm going to rely on your bank statement, not your words. If you say that it's easy for you to apologize to others, I'm going to look at how your relationships work, not listen to your words.

Does that sound tough? Maybe it is. But if you want to start an interesting journey toward a bright future, I can promise you some interesting insights.

But remember: knowing something is not the same thing as doing it.

THE RESULTS WILL TAKE THEIR TIME . . .

A warning might be appropriate here. In some of the chapters, you may start wondering whether the author is completely crazy and think that I'm a workaholic with no personal life or ability to enjoy life at all. You may be tempted to close the book and think that you are never, anyway, going to get anywhere if this is what success requires.

To you, I want to say the following: when I describe how I spend my time, I do so knowing that I have things to achieve and goals to reach. Later on, when I talk about how it's a waste of time to watch TV, it's based on the understanding that that time does nothing to actively contribute to your goals. As general entertainment, there is nothing wrong with TV.

The tips and the ideas I present are only relevant for those who want to get more out of life than they do today. They're for people who want to reach a certain goal within a particular time frame. During calmer periods of life, things will likely look different.

You might find my advice unreasonable but remember that I'm talking about achieving long-term success. The purpose is to give you the tools to move you forward and prevent you from staying stuck where you are, treading water. When I talk to you through the book, I do so assuming that you want to move ahead in life. So I'll tell it like it is and assume that you're looking for change.

But remember this: you won't get six-pack abs in thirty days. Probably not even in six months.

You won't be offered a cool management position just because you finished your final exams.

That dream boyfriend or girlfriend won't waltz around the corner just because you're a nice guy.

You won't become financially independent in five minutes. Perhaps not even in twelve months. It's going to take longer than that.

Or like the financial genius Warren Buffett has said, "No matter how great the talent or efforts, some things just take time. You can't produce a baby in one month by getting nine women pregnant."

On the other hand, time passes regardless. Why not do something good while we wait?

PART I

The Best Way to Deal with Setbacks, or Everything That Can Go to Hell, and What You Can Do About It

. . . .

1

It's Not Them. It's . . . You

Do you want to avoid setbacks as much as possible and instead experience as much success as you can? In one respect, you're just like everybody else: you want to lead a good life.

I think that all of us deserve a good life. You, me, and everyone else should be given the chance to have a good life from the moment we find ourselves here on Mother Earth. Life is so short, in some cases little more than a few decades. But regardless of whether you will live to age 50, 60, 75, or—why not—110, I think that you deserve to have a good life during the time you're here. Even though the planet is presenting us with more problems than we had perhaps foreseen, even though the world is not always a beautiful place, and regardless of the fact that our society sometimes feels totally sick—we have a duty to make the best of what we have.

To achieve these delightful possibilities, there's really only one thing you need to do. Forget long lists with endless action items; put aside all that good advice. You don't need to sit down in a corner and meditate, start analyzing your dreams, have a vision, or become a world champion at a single thing. No, there is only one thing you need to do for good fortune to come to you. If you do this single thing, then everything will sort itself out.

Are you ready?

The only thing you need to do is to take 100 percent responsibility for yourself.

Now.

The single most important factor for avoiding problems and creating a bright future for yourself is the ability to take responsibility. Nobody is ever going to achieve his or her dreams without accepting full responsibility.

When I say responsibility, I mean it in a positive sense. Not a burdensome responsibility for the failings of others, or responsibility for the development of society. Or responsibility for global conflict. Or taking on responsibility for whatever mess your boss made without ever getting a "thank you." No, I mean the responsibility you take for yourself and for your own life. And this is where many of us have a lot to learn.

You are no doubt a responsible person in many respects. I am sure you take care of your family, you're loyal at work, you don't subject yourself to unnecessary risks, you stick to the speed limit in school zones, and so on. Absolutely.

But sometimes it goes wrong anyway.

Let's say that somebody got a nice bonus last month. And her way of celebrating was to spend the whole evening out with the girls on the town.

The result: they had a really great evening, but she's just as broke as before. Short-term pleasure, instead of a sound life in a long-term sense. And that's a problem. All of us know this, but we still fail to do the right thing. For various reasons, we hide the truth from ourselves. And we don't always take responsibility for our situation.

We'll try again:

Somebody got a nice bonus last month. She invested the money in a sensible equity fund, which has now started to increase in value.

The result: she's increased her assets and will continue to do so. Suddenly we have a positive result because she was a great deal more responsible.

Let's look at the three types of responsibility you need to take.

The First Responsibility: *Everything That You Do*

Your responsibility is basically never-ending.

What does that mean?

It means that everything you *do* is your responsibility. Your actions, regardless of whether they are evil or good, are entirely your responsibility. Even if someone else asks you to do a particular thing, the decision to *do it,* and *how* you do it, is your responsibility. When your partner asks you to do something that you find repulsive, then it's your responsibility to say yes or no. If your boss asks you to do something that you don't think is really right—it can be something morally wrong or ethically questionable—it's your responsibility if you actually do it. It makes no difference that she demanded that you do it. Some people would have said no. When your children nag you about privileges and treats they think they have a right to, and you give in even though you know that it's entirely wrong, that was your responsibility. To blame your decision on possible consequences won't work. Other people would not have agreed.

If you're angry about your rotten sales figures at work, while simultaneously ridiculing the outside consultant who is trying to show you a better way of doing business, well, then you're responsible for having refused to listen to good advice.

When you drive through a red traffic light because you thought you would get through in time, you're responsible for all the potential catastrophes that may arise as a result of your decision. You can tell yourself you didn't "see" the light change because you were so worried about being late to pick up your child from school. But tell that to the police officer who stops you two hundred yards down the road. Or to the dad of the child you nearly ran over.

If you sit too long with your cell phone in your hand in front of the TV and are completely unaware of your teenager's nervous anxiety before the school dance tomorrow, that, too, is *your* responsibility. It doesn't make any difference that you felt that you simply had to watch this cute cat play piano. It was *your* choice to give priority to your cell phone rather than talk with your child about her worries.

If you wake up on a Saturday morning after the most raucous after-work gathering in modern history, with a hangover of epic proportions, that's your responsibility. The fact that you've gone to an after-work happy hour every Friday for God-knows-how-long doesn't matter; *you're* the person who decided to go. Trying to explain this away to yourself or your partner by saying, *Everybody else drank too much, too,* doesn't cut it. It was you who lifted the glass to your lips time after time. The hangover is completely and entirely your own responsibility. Telling your family *I can't drive you to the football game because I "don't feel too well today"* is completely transparent. Nobody falls for it.

A blockhead brought some donuts to the office; you ate two and your diet is all messed up. Come on! Who decided to eat those donuts? Whose body was affected? Your work colleagues'? No, it's your waistline that is now challenging your clothes budget.

You can't claim that she did this, so I was forced to do that. No, no. You made an active choice, that is what you did. Necessary or otherwise, you are the one who made the choice.

You can always control your own actions.

If you save money and invest wisely and become economically independent before reaching the age of forty, that is also your responsibility. And you can definitely take the credit for it. It works both ways.

Everything *you* do is *your* own responsibility.

You Either Create or Allow Everything That Happens to You

To avoid setbacks and achieve real success, you need to accept that you are the person who governs your own life. This attitude is far from new, and not everybody agrees with it, but let me show you some examples. When I say that you "create" what happens, I mean that to a great degree your own actions influence the result.

If you step into a bar in the wrong part of town on a dark night, walk up to four beefy dudes with shaved heads and tattoos all over their faces, who have been drinking beer since four o'clock in the afternoon, and say, "Goodness, I've never seen anything this ugly," then you'll know perfectly well why you ended up in the hospital.

But here is an example that's harder to take in: You stagger home every evening after working overtime again. In a comalike state, you force yourself to eat dinner while—in total silence—you think horrible thoughts about your boss. After that, you vegetate for hours in front of the TV and are bombarded with news about murders, acts of terrorism, corrupt politicians, and doomsday prophecies about our climate. You're so stressed and tense that it feels like it's impossible to do anything else. Like, for example, go for a walk together with your partner, or play with your kids for a while before their bedtime. Your partner wants to talk to you about important things, but you're too tired, so you bluntly say that you need to rest. After three years of this familial bliss, you come home late one evening to a silent, empty house. Your partner has left and taken the children, too. Perhaps there's a note in the kitchen: *You don't love me anymore.*

A simple truth: this, too, was a situation that you were involved in creating. It just took a bit longer to realize it.

The Second Responsibility: *Everything You Don't Do*

It's easy to forget that you are also responsible for everything you *do not* do.

Every time you know that you ought to go for a walk instead of pour a glass of wine, it's your responsibility. It doesn't matter whether you "forgot" or deliberately avoided it (in other words, just couldn't give a damn). Similarly, if you see somebody who needs some help at work, something that you could do in five minutes, but you choose to look the other way because it isn't actually your job, then that's your responsibility. Your decision to be a less-helpful colleague will always be your responsibility. You will discover the consequence of that choice the day you're the one who needs help.

Every time you press "snooze" on your alarm instead of getting out of bed and reading a book for half an hour, it's your responsibility. Every time you don't listen to your partner because you think that you already know what she or he is going to say, it's your responsibility. If you get a flirty text from a female colleague and you avoid telling her it isn't okay because you're married, then you've made a fool of yourself. Your ego has nothing to do with it. A failure to make things clear is your responsibility.

None of these are things that you can blame somebody else for. In your heart, you know that I'm right, even though all of us sometimes hide behind apologies and empty excuses. Defense mechanisms are indeed natural. They're there to protect us from possible dangers, but they aren't much use when they simply trick us into thinking that we have done the right thing, when really what we have done is wrong.

Sorry? You were late for the meeting because the printer was being used by somebody else? But who chose to wait until the absolute last second to print those damned documents? Who chose *not* to plan ahead?

What did you say? Your team didn't do what they should have, and now your boss thinks you messed things up? But who was it *didn't bother* to follow up with his team?

If you should study but don't study, and instead play computer games for six hours, then you only have yourself to blame. It was you who *couldn't care less* about studying, and now the exam is coming up regardless.

You didn't follow up on your threat of turning off the internet if the kids didn't start tidying up after themselves, and now your home looks like a war zone.

You never demanded that she come with you to the therapist, so now your relationship is worse than ever.

You refused to participate in the company's in-house training program because you assumed you already knew everything, and now the newly hired twenty-three-year-old has been named the Manager of the Year and is well on his way to becoming your next boss.

You attended a seminar and learned all about the DISC method and its four colors. But despite the fact that you now know that your Yellow behavior means that you're careless with details, you did nothing to correct it. Now you've messed up the contract with the company's biggest client, and your boss's boss wants to talk to you about your future at the firm.

You never got around to taking your dogs to training classes, and now all three are totally out of control.

You need to realize that in none of these situations are you a victim of anything but your own passivity. You said nothing, you demanded nothing, you waited too long, you never said yes or no, you never tried anything new. Instead, you just sat there.

It's not nice to hear it, I know.

Seeing the Warning Signs in Time

Very rarely does lightning strike out of a clear blue sky. Oftentimes, we need to train our ability to react to the warning signs that precede unpleasant events. You might feel there's something in the air: you see something strange, somebody makes a stray comment, your gut says something is off. But sometimes we choose to put the warnings aside and don't notice things like:

- your repeated headaches every Sunday night before work;
- your teenage son's endless absence from the dinner table;
- your belt that seems to have become too short again;
- the weird sound from somewhere under your car;
- that strange alcohol smell you notice on someone;
- the lipstick smear on a shirt collar;
- your boss's odd look when you make suggestions.

And so it goes on. But sometimes you do need to act when you feel that something isn't quite right. If you have that feeling, do something about it. If your partner comes home late every Tuesday after work, that's a pattern that needs to be handled, however unpleasant it may be. Confront the person, because that is how successful people act. They don't wait passively and hope that it will blow over. They raise the point of concern and ask for feedback. Of course, nobody loves negative feedback or hearing bad news, but once you get it, you can act. It's better to know about a problem than to go around in ignorance. When the shoe finally drops, it will be much worse than if you had raised the problem early.

You know that I'm right. You can feel it in your entire body, can't you?

WHY DON'T WE DO ANYTHING EVEN WHEN WE SEE THE YELLOW LIGHT?

Why don't we react to things that look a bit weird or sound strange? It's about risk. We don't want to risk what we have, so we accept some things that we shouldn't accept. There's a danger in confronting people around you. Going to your boss and telling it like it is sometimes requires courage. Dealing with unpleasant things with your partner can be unbelievably frightening.

We've seen the warning signs. But we often pretend that we haven't seen anything, since that's so much simpler. We keep quiet to avoid confrontation, conflict, and the risk of discovering an unpleasant truth.

For many years I went around with an uneasy feeling in my gut about certain people, both in my personal life and at work. But I learned to escape from the uncomfortable feeling of deceptive denial and to address even very difficult behaviors in others. And I've never reverted to pretending to be satisfied when in reality I'm not. You can do the same.

Stop living in passivity and start acting to achieve the life you could have. Don't stay on in a bad relationship. You'll only become bitter. Don't remain in a job you detest. Nobody is going to thank you for it. Ditch your bad eating habits. It's your body that is suffering, nobody else's.

There are no rights to claim. The world does not owe you anything. You, and you alone, can change your own situation. Nobody is going to do it for you.

Stop putting things off or turning a blind eye to reality.

Accept this simple fact: *you're responsible for everything you* don't *do*.

But it doesn't stop there.

The Third Responsibility: *Your Reaction to Everything That Happens*

What happens to you is often in large part your responsibility. At this point, many people get irritated and claim that *it wasn't my fault that the traffic was chaotic and I was thirty minutes late for my interview for a new job. How the hell can that be my responsibility? It isn't my fault!*

Uhmm, well, even if it wasn't you who ran over that deer near the crosswalk that stopped all the traffic for five miles in every direction, it was you who didn't allow for potential mess-ups on your way to the interview. It was you who didn't allow sufficient time to deal with unpleasant surprises. And it is you who reacted with anger at the traffic chaos.

This is important. Even if you didn't create the incident in question, you are responsible for how you reacted to it. The fact that you're now angry for having been delayed on your way is your responsibility. If you look around at the lines of cars, you'll see quite a lot of people sitting calmly in their cars and listening to music or just enjoying a moment's relaxation. Some people have chosen to appreciate the moment of silence during their day. It's just another way of approaching the situation.

It rains on everybody—rich, poor, short, tall, thin, fat, young, old. The question is: Who makes a fuss about it and acts like it's the end of the world, and who accepts the rain and starts to collect the water?

To avoid the feeling of continuous setbacks bombarding your life, you need to realize that you are (and nobody else is) responsible for how you react to what happens. There is always an alternative reaction.

Note that I'm talking about everyday things and not about how you react if, for example, somebody close to you tragically dies. But you're smart enough to distinguish between the small difficulties of life and the true tragedies.

The problem with not taking responsibility for one's reactions is that everything becomes impossible. Oddly enough, the same laws of nature apply to all of us. While you and I might grumble about how the state of the economy is terrible, somebody else is making a fortune under the same conditions. If your excuses about your boss, the company, and all the idiots around you were true, then nobody would ever succeed at anything.

Ingvar Kamprad would never have founded IKEA and established stores across the world. Spotify would have never gone beyond an idea on a piece of paper. The Rockefeller family would be destitute. Stephen King would never have written a single book. We would never have heard of Greta Thunberg. Barack Obama would never have been America's first Black president. None of the major religions would have been founded. Microsoft, Google, Volvo, Tesla, or Apple wouldn't have existed at all.

Even though we all have many of the same limiting factors around us, those factors only seem to restrict certain people. Some people don't understand that what they're doing is impossible. They just go out and do it anyway.

It's not about what happens around you; it's about what you choose to make of it. Unfortunately, many of us unconsciously restrict ourselves with our limiting thought processes and with self-destructive habits. We ignore useful feedback; we fail to continually develop ourselves; we carelessly waste a lot of time on lots of stupid things; we help to spread meaningless gossip. We eat far too much unhealthy food; we don't bother to go to the gym; we spend money we don't have on things we don't need to impress people we don't like. We don't bother to invest in our future; we avoid necessary conflicts; we neglect to speak important truths to people around us; we don't ask for help when we need it—and then we wonder why life doesn't go the way we wish it would!

Unfortunately, many—far too many—people live their lives exactly like that. And when they encounter setbacks, they always have an explanation (or rather, an excuse) for why everything went to pot. But the fact that you're sitting in the same boat as everyone else is cold comfort, is it not? Why not at least get a little boat of your very own?

You can manage your own reactions much better than you think.

You missed your flight. Tough. You swear and grumble. That's your choice, in that case. Of course, you can be angry, disappointed, shattered, destroyed.

You can also choose to go back to why you missed the plane in the first place. Perhaps you overslept? Left home a little too late? Had no margin of time. Why did that happen? Er, you pressed "snooze" three times because you were too tired. But why were you so tired? Because you stayed up too late the night before.

Now you can choose a completely different reaction: lucky for me I now know that if I'm going to get up early the next morning, then

I need go to bed before ten o'clock. An important insight. And above all: *your own choice.*

You can change your way of thinking, change your way of communicating with others, change the images inside your head. You can definitely change your own behavior, regardless of whether you are a Red, Yellow, Green, or Blue (more on the color profiles later!); you can adjust your behavior to the circumstances. These are things that only you have control over. Unfortunately, many of us are stuck in our habits, in our bad habits. We're stuck in our repetitive reactions to our partner, our children, our boss, our employees. And to the rest of the world, too, for that matter.

In some strange way, we rely on predictable reactions that seem to happen outside our control. We need to regain control of our own thoughts, our inner dialogue, our dreams, and our behavior. We can't continue as we always have, because then we'll get the same results we've always gotten. And believe me when I say that very few people want that.

THE THIRD PSYCHOLOGIST

Taking full responsibility is not a new idea. In fact, we find it in the work of the greatest psychologist of all time, a man many of us have never heard of.

Freud and Jung had a contemporary colleague who is not nearly as well known as they are. Partly because he didn't care about whether he was going to be remembered, and partly because his ideas were more important than the man himself. He established concepts like the "inferiority complex"; he invented conversation therapy (nowadays seen as self-evident); he analyzed how family constellations and family dynamics influence children; and he thought that not only the past but also the future ought to play a part in therapy. Today he's almost forgotten, but you will find his ideas in every modern form of therapy.

The man we are talking about is Alfred Adler. Freud taught that what you experience within yourself has been caused by factors outside you. If you had parents who treated you badly, then you'll always be a victim. The trauma in your childhood will leave its mark on who you are. You are, so to speak, condemned from the very start. Adler had a different take.

Adler didn't agree with that at all. He thought that it is you, yourself, that creates the feeling of trauma. He didn't deny that there are nasty parents, and he didn't ignore the fact that a person is obviously affected by being treated badly during childhood. But he was of the opinion that you can choose how you look at your history. Portraying yourself as a victim can benefit you. You get sympathy from those around you. People will become involved in your well-being. Which isn't bad for somebody who was born into the world with unloving parents. But do you really want to be a victim?

Within psychology, during the last ten years or so, many have started to question the value of digging too much into people's pasts. In many cases, it's like scratching at scabs that are in the process of healing. This is a major and relatively little-researched area, but progress is being made, and psychotherapy is now leaning more in Adler's direction than in Freud's.

It's not easy to liberate oneself from the past. All of us have some "baggage" that weighs us down. But once we've managed to liberate ourselves, we're free of it. The past shouldn't have so much importance in people's lives. It doesn't even exist, apart from inside our heads. What's done is done. The question is: What should happen now?

Clinging to the past won't change what has happened, but it may affect the future, and often in a negative way.

THOUGHTS VS. EMOTIONS

We are emotional beings who make decisions, even very big ones, based on feeling. But that is not the same thing as being governed by our emotions. You will certainly be able to recall situations in which, for example, you've lost your temper and the results weren't great. But what would have happened if you'd been able to control that anger?

Anger is not always negative, but on the occasions when it doesn't lead anywhere constructive, it would have been better to be able to control it. To loudly scold a waiter because he spilled coffee on you might feel good for a moment, but a better approach would probably be to deal with it as calmly as possible. I can promise you that the service will be better if you succeed in controlling yourself.

What comes first, thought or emotion?

If you think about it, you'll probably find that the thought comes first. In most cases, the thought triggers the emotion. The emotion, on the other hand, is commonly what triggers action. We've all heard that response from people who have done the weirdest things. Why did you do that? It *felt* good. But if you can manage your thoughts in a rational manner, you won't need to be a victim of your emotions every time.

There's a story about two brothers who grow up with a father who drinks and fights and can never keep a job. He supports himself with petty theft and goes to prison time after time over the course of his sons' childhood.

One of the sons grows up to become a drunken habitual criminal. When asked how his life turned out like that, he answers, *With a father like that, what else could I do?*

The other brother leaves home, studies, gets a top job at a bank, and marries the prettiest girl in the district. He brings up three wonderful children. When asked how his life turned out like that, he answers, *With a father like that, what else could I do?*

The same background. Different ways of dealing with it.

How does that happen? If we were always victims of our past, we would always react similarly to the same events. That's a completely impossible idea.

Sure, we're all unique individuals. But you can definitely choose how you think about a particular event and draw different conclusions. The reflection *My dad was a drunken bastard, and the last thing I want to do is be like him* will create a very specific feeling of revenge. And that in turn will lead to specific actions.

But the thought *My dad was a drunken bastard, and the apple never falls far from the tree* is going to create a feeling of resignation. And that will in turn lead to extremely destructive actions.

Becoming a victim—of your tough childhood, destructive parents, being bullied, being born with dyslexia, chronic morning fatigue on your mother's side, poor health, obesity within the family—is absolutely understandable. But when you come across a person who is trapped in the past, think about this: What does this person gain from retaining the feeling of hopelessness? Because there can be something beneficial from remaining in the role of victim. Sometimes you need to look closely to really see it. And understand it.

WHY A WALKER ISN'T ALWAYS FOR THE BEST

If I had bad grades at school—regardless of the reason—I can always insist that I'm not clever enough to learn new things.

If I was overweight as a child, I can always blame my weight on something wrong with my hormones, and there's no point even trying to stop eating pizza.

If I was bullied in school, I can always mention that at my workplace and get lots of sympathy and attention.

If I have the slightest headache, I can make a big thing of it and have people wait on me hand and foot.

I've seen an example of that among my acquaintances. An elderly lady uses a walker and hobbles about unsteadily every time family members are at home. Concerned about her frailty, they visit often and help as much as they can. When nobody is at home, she whips around the house without the slightest difficulty. (The neighbor sees her through the windows).

This lady is not evil or mean or grumpy or demanding. She has simply settled into a sort of victim mentality. She might not even be aware of it. If anyone were to confront her, I guess she would deny it.

If you want the attention of relatives—why not try getting it in a positive way? There are alternatives.

The crux is that if you can deal with your emotions and act from the point of view of the here and now instead of being confined to the past, you'll be a considerably more liberated person. If you're worried about your finances, it's because in your mind you can imagine a huge pile of unpaid bills. The more you think like that, the worse you'll feel. Changing your way of thinking about your personal finances might not pay your bills, but it can—read: should—give you ideas for how you can increase your income, for example.

3

No More Excuses!

An end to all excuses and alibis! They lead nowhere. I wish I could say that I've completely stopped making excuses myself, but naturally that wouldn't be true. Like everybody else, I sometimes fall into the trap and think up excuses for why project Z didn't work out as it should, even though I know that I was the person who did things wrong.

Making excuses is a human trait; it's part of the defense mechanisms that our consciousness uses to protect us from the tough reality we sometimes find ourselves in.

But even though it's a human trait, it's a waste. Excuses never lead you forward; they simply cement your current position. If you're content with that, no problem. But that's rarely the case.

WHAT ARE EXCUSES?

Excuses can be found in any situation in which you point at causes other than yourself. You can't blame unpleasant events on the weather (rainy or cold), on the state of the market (too weak), on taxes (too high), on wages (too low), on your boss (too unfair), on your partner (not understanding enough), on company policy (too easygoing and permissive or too hard and inhumane), on your children (too badly brought up), on your parents (too demanding or too easygoing), on your work tasks (too boring), on school (not interesting enough), on your teachers (not good enough), or on a thousand other things.

But you know what? Setbacks—what we sometimes just call real life—will come your way regardless of the circumstances. Even if all the things just listed were perfect, something would still go completely wrong. And it will always be about you. If you want success instead of setbacks, you need to accept your own role in the whole process. You need to accept and recognize the reality of the situation.

It was you who ate all that junk food.
It was you who accepted the job offer.
It was you who stayed in the same job year after year.
It was you who chose to believe what they said.
It was you who ignored your own intuition.
It was you who abandoned your old dream.
It was you who bought that unnecessary stuff.
It was you who didn't take care of it.
It was you who decided to do everything yourself.
It was you who said yes to the dogs.
It was you who thought the thought, who created the emo-
    tion, who made the choice, who articulated the words.

And that is why you are where you are right now.

The true measure of personal maturity is to take full responsibility for what happens. And excuses or alibis—they don't belong there.

AN END TO YOUR GRUMPY COMPLAINING

The same thing applies to grumbling and complaints. It's often point-less to criticize the state of things. On the one hand, nobody wants to listen to your dissatisfaction; on the other, it rarely changes the situation.

A person who has made his or her way through the worst life can put in one's path didn't do it by sitting around and grumbling about how terrible everything is. Intellectually, you know I'm right. But you, just like me, are sometimes stuck in the habit of focusing on negative things at the wrong moment.

Complaining about various circumstances is not the same thing as thinking negatively. Thinking negatively is worrying about what is going to happen and painting imaginary, horrifying scenarios.

The complaining that many people indulge in is more of a bad habit than an actual defense mechanism. And it's a habit we've learned at home or at work. There are more than enough people around you who are professional complainers for you to be able to improve your skills simply by listening to them. But that is a skill you really don't need.

There's an interesting psychology in complaining. When you complain about something, it means that you think there is some-thing better elsewhere.

Think about it. If you complain about your boss, it means that you believe there are better bosses. If you complain about the food, it's be-cause you suspect that someone else is eating better. If you complain about your job, it's because you believe that other jobs are more fun.

If you complain about your partner, it means that somewhere deep inside you genuinely believe there are better partners in the world. But I'm fairly certain that if your partner was the last man or woman on the planet, you'd complain a lot less.

When I exhort you to stop complaining, of course it doesn't mean that you should just accept injustices. If you've got problems at home, then it's probably a good idea to raise the issue and try to have an intelligent and constructive conversation. If your coworkers are lazy incompetents, then you need to talk. Naturally, you must be able to give each other some less-pleasant feedback now and then. I'm not talking about avoiding or turning a blind eye to unpleasant things.

What I am against is the sort of complaining that doesn't lead anywhere.

An example: your partner often comes home a little late for dinner. That makes you irritated and grumpy. Perhaps you're the one who has made dinner, and now it's cold. You have a bit of a spat, but then you sit down and eat in silence. The next evening, the same thing happens. But do you ever change anything? Do you try to understand and solve the problem? Why does she come home so late?

Or you complain that you never have enough money. The state raised taxes, so now you have less in your wallet. You're deeply dissatisfied. You talk to everybody and anybody about this dreadful injustice. But, at the same time, you spend at least that same amount a month on lottery tickets or at the casino.

You complain about your poor health, but you don't quit smoking.

To complain is to keep going on and on, "sawing sawdust," as lecturer Jörgen Oom called it. A very fitting expression. What is the point of sawing sawdust? There's nothing left to saw.

Besides, we tend to complain about things that we actually can do something about. That's what is so strange about it. We complain about each other, about ourselves, about the results we achieve. But we have bigger problems. Take, for example, gravity. Everything you let go of, falls to the ground. That's such a pain! But have you ever heard anybody complain about the gravitational force?

To summarize, we often complain about things we could easily do something about but have chosen to refrain from changing.

Why?

Simple. Change involves risk. The greatest risk is being ridiculed by others, to hear that you're wrong, to fail, to need to climb outside your comfort zone. All of those are unpleasant things, so we stay where we are. And complain. Because then it at least feels like we're doing something. But that is a misleading picture of reality.

IF WE TURN THE WHOLE THING AROUND

If we look at the list earlier in the chapter we can actually turn all the sentences around. You could quite simply . . .

> . . . start eating more nourishing food;
> . . . say no, even when some people try to get you to say yes;
> . . . dare to say no to the wrong job;
> . . . leave a job you hate;
> . . . not blindly trust everyone and anyone;
> . . . listen more to your own gut feeling;
> . . . stick with, and work for, your dreams;
> . . . not go shopping with money you don't have;
> . . . take better care of your belongings;
> . . . ask for help;
> . . . learn how to train your dogs;
> . . . read a self-help book and actually try out the ideas.

All of that is in your control, isn't it? You could change everything in just a few minutes, simply by changing you own attitude.

AM I AN OLYMPIC-LEVEL NONCOMPLAINER?

While writing this, I'm on the thirteenth floor in a hotel room in Oslo. I've been here for just over twenty-four hours, because last night I gave a public lecture nearby. My room has been incredibly noisy ever since I arrived—other guests talking, hotel staff wheeling trolleys past my door, the clink of glasses, some unbelievably bad music that never stops. It was after 11 P.M. when I got back to my room, utterly exhausted. I slept horribly. I've rarely been in a hotel room where I heard so much noise.

Now the core of the problem: What have I done to change my situation? Answer: nothing. I only have myself to blame. I could, of course, have gone down to the reception desk after fifteen minutes of noise and requested a better room, one that wasn't next to a busy major road where everyone was driving past as noisily as possible. But I didn't do anything about it. So, no, I'm not free from this meaningless behavior. Instead, I texted my wife and complained about how noisy it was in the hall. As if she—hundreds of miles away—could affect the situation one little bit.

Which leads us to another interesting problem.

WE COMPLAIN TO THE WRONG PERSON

Have you thought about how many people have the rather strange tendency to turn to somebody who is not involved in the situation and who is unable to influence it in any way?

A lot of people turn to their work colleagues and complain about their partners. Then they go home and complain about their work colleagues. Why? Because it's simpler. It's fairly low-risk to complain to somebody else instead of confronting the person concerned. Asking your boss to plan the project better so that you can avoid having to work on Sundays demands more than just raising the same issue with your wife. Asking for a change of behavior at home is a great deal more difficult than moaning about it to your lunch companion at work.

This meaningless complaining is something we should replace with clearly expressed wishes for changes. If you find yourself in a situation you aren't satisfied with, do something about it or get the hell out of there, and do it quickly. Agree to work more on making your relationship work, or ask for a divorce. Make an effort to improve your working conditions, or get another job. Regardless of what you choose, there will be a change.

Yes. It's far easier to say this than to do it. But complaining will get you nowhere. It will only make you bitter.

WHAT DO YOU COMPLAIN ABOUT?

It's useful to look for patterns. What follows is a simple table to help you to identify what it is that you complain about and when you do it. When I did this exercise a couple of years ago, I discovered that it was in certain settings and with certain people—two former colleagues to be exact—that I became a real whiner. We criticized the government, the weather, the economy, the company, the clients, the bosses, the useless organization, the training program, the company policy, and everything else under heaven and earth. There was no end. Ugh. I didn't like what I saw, and I finally broke the pattern.

What the complaint was about	What triggers the complaining?	Can I do anything about the problem? If so, what?
My own pitiful finances	Every time bills need to be paid	Get some extra part-time work, talk to my boss and negotiate a raise, offer to take more responsibility, reduce my expenses

The weather	Every winter morning when the iced-over wind-screen needs scraping	Nothing, or move farther south, or build a garage
A persistent stomachache	An hour after every dinner	Think about my diet; perhaps I eat too much of one type of food or have too much heavy food too late in the evening

I realized that this storm of complaint normally took place on Mondays at lunch. So I stayed at my desk on Mondays and took a boxed lunch that I ate at my desk. When colleagues A and B wanted me to come to lunch, I just pointed at my lunch box. And after a few weeks, the pattern had been broken. (I assume they managed their Monday misery sessions in my absence.)

As you can see from the table, the most important question is: What can you do about it?

How Did It Go? What Did You Write Down?

Perhaps it was difficult to think of anything. That might be because you don't reflect on your complaints until you're actually in the act. So pay attention to your own behavior in the coming week. You don't need an app. No excuses (such as not having a pen!). Jot a note on a piece of paper or on your phone when you notice yourself complaining.

The whole point of column three is that if there isn't anything to write there, then *there really isn't anything to complain about*. Just think how much time you saved!

If, however, there's a whole list on the far right, then suddenly you'll have a comprehensive plan of action that will help you actually deal with things that are worth complaining about. A collection of small irritating moments can devour all your energy. You might as well solve all those annoying tiny problems on this list.

At one office I visited, ten people complained that the trash can in the kitchen was placed too far from the sink. But none of them had taken the radical measure of moving it ten feet closer. It sounds utterly ridiculous writing that, but it's an actual example.

If the items on your list are not worth dealing with, then we have a different situation. Because then they're *not worth complaining about*.

Getting stuck in these negative tracks can totally disturb your mental focus and make all the setbacks you encounter feel bigger and more serious. So just drop these little irritants. Easier said than done. Ignore them if they're not worth dealing with. Be a bigger person than the people who complain about utter silliness. Be above that. Move on.

THERE IS ALWAYS SOMETHING TO COMPLAIN ABOUT

Does it even matter if you take responsibility for your life? What difference does it make if some of us complain, grumble, and make excuses? The world will continue roughly the same as usual, anyway.

Uhmm . . . well. If you accept full responsibility from now on and are prepared to behave in a 100 percent adult manner, then an interesting thing will happen: you will become the sole owner of your future. Only you can decide how things will go for you in life. And that's fantastic, isn't it?

Think how wonderful it would be to be independent of others. To not have to make excuses, blame others, point your finger, and name scapegoats other than yourself.

Perhaps you believe that you already do take full responsibility. You look after your family, you keep the flag flying high at work, you look after yourself and your health. I believe you. Absolutely.

But if I could sit on your shoulder for a week, I bet that I would hear you mumble and grumble about one thing or the other and subconsciously blame every imaginable factor other than you yourself. If it isn't the damned traffic, then it's the price of gas. Or the income tax. Or the government. Or the other party. Or it's raining at completely the wrong time. Why is it so sunny? Perhaps you're irritated with your boss. Or the whole company. They're all idiots. You're the only one who understands.

Sure, there may be problems at your workplace, but full responsibility means that you quit finding reasons for why you don't always do the best you can. There are no shortcuts.

Accept that, and arrange your life according to the fact that you own your own decisions. Sure, that can be a burden, but most of all it's liberating. Because now there are no other obstacles than what you can actually influence—yourself. All limitations are gone.

ANYONE CAN OPEN THE MOST COMPLEX LOCK

For the sake of simplicity, from now on I'm going to assume that you really *want* to bring about a change in your life, whatever that may be: your health, your finances, your relationships, your career, your education, your desire to travel, your wish to work as a volunteer, your hobby, or whatever. The fact that you're still reading means you want something more in life.

But remind yourself throughout this book that what you do or don't do is your responsibility. Not mine. Not your mom's. Not that of your boss, husband, wife, or children. Your responsibility.

Remember that nobody becomes successful because of what they know or are capable of or say. It is only the actual *doing* that is going to count.

Somewhere or other I picked up the phrase "Anyone can open the most complex lock in the world; they just have to have the code."

So let's make sure that we give you as many digits as we can.

SUMMARY

Everything you do or don't do is your own responsibility. Being able to take *full* responsibility is the only sign of personal maturity that really counts.

You are also personally responsible for your own reactions to what others do or don't do. Remember that a thought often comes before an emotion, and that emotion comes before action.

The advantage of this approach is that you, if you choose it, will be in possession of your own future. You decide how your life is going to develop. Others will have considerably less power over you.

It's a bit unnerving, in a way. It means that you're going to need to take a few more risks than you would otherwise.

But at the same time, it's absolutely fantastic. Because this approach gives you lots and lots of possibilities. With your new attitude, you can change the course of events and you have an incredible future ahead of you.

If you are going to complain—talk to somebody who can do something about the situation. Even better: if there's something to complain about, try to solve the problem yourself. By all means, tell people around you what you've done. Don't boast about it, but few people are more appreciated than those who solve existing problems.

4

From Minor Problem to Serious Crisis in Three Minutes

Professional problems, hopeless challenges at work, setbacks in your relationships, mess-ups related to bringing up children, personal problems that never seem to come to an end, physical problems, overweight or underweight, financial problems, family and relatives, neighbors, conflicts of every type, plus more—the list can go on and on. Life consists of a whole host of setbacks. Sometimes it feels as if you're surrounded by problems.

Problem after problem, problems that are only interrupted by one *crisis* or another. Problem, problem, problem, *crisis*! I first heard Brian Spencer say this, and it's so true. Everybody you meet has either just gone through a crisis, is in the middle of a crisis, or is on the way to a crisis. They just don't know it yet.

Is this good or bad news?

SO WHAT CAN WE DO ABOUT
ALL THESE SETBACKS?

So what should you do when you crash-land? Pull your hat down over your eyes and hope that everything will simply disappear? Or should you learn how to deal with the mess?

Since it's impossible to completely avoid crises and setbacks, you might as well learn how to deal with them. We have to accept that the world works like this.

What's most important here is that you don't assume the wrong sort of responsibility. Absolutely give others a helping hand with their problems if you can. That will be appreciated, and it will show that you're a good person. But don't assume responsibility for everybody else. They are adults and sometimes need to be responsible for themselves, too. They will learn how to deal with their own setbacks.

ARE THEY REALLY SETBACKS—OR IS IT LIFE?

One thing always bothers me: I'm not sure that we're always dealing with setbacks.

In order to deal with the obstacles of life, it's a good idea to have a strategy, but also be aware that a strategy is not everything. You need to keep track of your own frame of mind. Because often we create obstacles inside our own heads. We build up a mental picture of catastrophe—even though the solution is actually extremely simple. Sometimes all you need to do is pick up your telephone. And realize that it wasn't even a problem at all.

It can be beneficial to have perspective on potential problems. Having the wrong grout color on the backsplash above your kitchen sink is hardly the end of the world. It can easily be fixed, after all.

When I coach people one-on-one, I realize that many of them want to prepare themselves so well that they will completely avoid unpleasant surprises. This attitude often results in perfectionism taking over, and nothing happens. To avoid driving into a ditch, they perfect and polish their ideas for so long that the initial purpose is completely lost.

A farmer prepares his field the best way possible. He plows it, fights weeds and undesirable insects, spreads fertilizer, and sows seeds. He waters and works hard from morning to evening. The crop grows. He follows the crop carefully, waters a bit more. He worries about his crop but watches it grow nevertheless.

The day before he goes to harvest, there is a freak hailstorm that flattens the whole crop.

Everything is destroyed. All his work has been in vain.

Whose fault is it?

Answer: nobody's.

But, you might exclaim, *that isn't fair! The farmer worked so hard!* Yes, sure. It is horribly unjust. Absolutely.

But this is something that all of us are going to meet with—injustices. And that is how things are. How the farmer deals with the situation is up to him. He can choose to roll up his sleeves and make sure that when the next harvest comes around, he will have his revenge against the weather gods. Or he can give up and sell the farm. It all depends on his attitude.

If you want to completely avoid problems and crises and every type of setback, then you'll have to spend the rest of your life hiding in a corner. Pull a blanket over your head and hope for the best.

The rest of us can give you food, we can protect you, we can keep you warm and make sure nothing dreadful happens to you. All you need to do is to stay under that blanket and never leave your comfy corner.

You might well live to be one hundred years old without any major problems. I really don't know.

But what a life . . .

WHEN EVERYBODY NEEDS TO BE PERFECTLY HAPPY ALL THE TIME

Nevertheless, there seem to be many people in our society today who try to protect themselves from everything. Everything, absolutely everything unpleasant must be kept at bay.

We should obviously avoid problems as much as possible. Naturally, we should vaccinate ourselves and make sure that we wear bike helmets. We should use the seat belts in our cars, and we should protect our houses from burning down by blowing out all the candles when we leave the room. Perfectly reasonable measures to deal with life in a cautious manner. The instinct for self-preservation should be there, and you shouldn't take stupid risks.

But in some people I perceive a sort of obsession with getting rid of all types of setbacks in life.

Everybody must like me.

My boss can't criticize me in the least.

If my body isn't exactly perfect, then my life is over.

My neighbor's car is always going to be fancier and nicer than mine.

My children always have to receive top grades at school.

My summer vacation must be perfect, not to mention the holiday break. Everybody must glow with delight, or else it's a total disaster.

My husband/wife/partner must always like everything I
do—all the time.

And I must be happy and carefree from morning to evening,
every day of the week, otherwise life is hardly worth
enduring.

We should love our jobs every second of the day.

Our sex life should always be a heavenly explosion of bliss.

Some of these unrealistic expectations might come from social media infiltrating our innermost emotional life. By scrolling up and down in various feeds on the internet, we're all presented with the perfect lives of other people, their brilliant successes in life, and their wonderful relationships and family life. I doubt anyone exists who is completely immune to that type of input. We forget that nobody posts pictures of the family's squabbles, the burnt Sunday roast, or Uncle George after too many drinks.

THE BENEFIT OF ADVERSITY

It's my absolute conviction that a setback is something positive. It's like a muscle that you want to strengthen. If you put it under stress, it will become stronger. If you never exercise it, it will wither away. To make yourself stronger, you need to push your mental muscle.

One example is of course the pendulum. To make it swing in one direction, you first have to accept that it will also swing in the other direction. You can't make a pendulum swing in only one direction and not the other. It will swing in both directions regardless of what you would prefer. It follows a law of nature.

To make it swing in the direction you want it to, the positive direction, you will have to reckon on the fact that it is also going to swing in the wrong direction, the negative one.

Success demands that you be prepared for the risk of meeting setbacks.

My own theory is that this is what leads many people to give up far too early. They love life when it swings in the right direction, but dread when it goes in the opposite direction. And, as usual, if you want to avoid risks completely, then you're hardly going to get anywhere in life.

If you don't go out hunting for what you want, then you're never going to get it. If you don't ask, then you won't get any answers. If you don't work your way forward, you'll always remain sitting in the same place.

If you don't shoot, you won't hit the target. If you don't propose a business deal, you won't sell anything. If you don't apply for that dream job, it will go to somebody else. If you don't ask that boy on a date, nothing will happen. I know you've heard this hundreds of times, and you realize that it's true.

And yet . . . so many people tend to sit down and bide their time. Wait.

Because it's horrible knowing that something can go wrong. Risks are unpleasant. Ask me. For a long time, I did this myself.

But the people at the top of the mountain, they didn't fall into the trap. They got there under their own steam. Of course, they had help in various ways. But they didn't end up on top by slouching in front of the TV and making other people successful.

WHY DO WE GIVE UP TOO SOON?

Why do you give up? Why do you let go and just float along? You know that nobody is going to leave a treasure chest on your front steps. We know that we aren't going to wake up one morning in April looking good and in great physical condition if we don't do anything.

It depends on us, and only us. We understand that we need to take responsibility for our lives, and we're prepared to roll up our sleeves and do what's necessary. And even so, many fantastic plans just capsize. Why?

There are a lot of reasons for that.

It was too hard. It wasn't worth it. Nobody has faith in me. I don't have faith in myself, either. To be honest, other things seem so much more fun. It takes too long, and I don't have the patience to wait. I can't remember why it was so important. Anyway, it's not important anymore.

It's just too much. Life can't just be work. I don't see any results. What if I'm wrong? Everyone says that I should drop it.

I think that I'm pretending that I still want to do it. And so on.

HAVE YOU EVER GIVEN UP?

Of course you have. A fitness goal you had: losing weight is the most common, but putting on weight can be desirable, too. Building muscle, perhaps.

Learning something new. Golf, Spanish, keeping your desk neat. Getting out of bed in the mornings. Stopping procrastinating. Reading more interesting books. Trying an alcohol-free month. Starting to save money. Spending more time with your children. Refraining from clutching your cell phone every minute you're awake. Taking evening classes so you can apply for more advanced jobs.

It might be a failure in your relationships. Getting your partner to really understand why you say those things. Or getting your partner to read your thoughts. Persuading Auntie Greta to abandon her negative attitude. Convincing your best friend to stop talking about himself or herself. Or finding a partner when you want to have somebody to share your life with.

Why not talk shop? There are lots of setbacks to indulge in at work. Building your own business and earning a pile of money to be able to impress your old pals. Making a career. Doubling your income. Learning a new skill to improve your employability. Starting to take responsibility for your own development. Not whining about your boss when you come home in the evening, because your family just can't face hearing it anymore. No longer using the excuse that you love your job and giving notice to quit and leave your useless boss.

You've tried a whole pile of these things, haven't you? But then stopped. Why did *you* just let it drop?

Deep inside you are the answers you need to dig out and be brave enough to look at.

What would it be worth for you to learn to see why you gave up, and know how you can avoid that next time?

SUMMARY

Setbacks, problems, and crises are everyday fare for most of us. You can always find yourself knocking your head against some wall or other. The more we accept that setbacks are a part of life, the easier it will be to put up with that life. Sometimes it goes well, sometimes less well. It's nobody's fault that this is how the world works. But you need to accept the circumstances under which all of us live.

You can't protect yourself from everything. So training your ability to deal with the hardships of life is the best way forward. Pay attention to your thoughts. Your thoughts govern your emotions, not the other way around.

The Four Development Phases: Dodgy Dynamic

Just because something feels difficult, it doesn't necessarily mean that it's a setback. Sometimes it's just a question of different phases in life that we must go through. The realization that ups and downs are there all the time can be liberating. It isn't your fault; this is simply how the world works.

There are a variety of reasons why we sometimes, despite the best of intentions, don't manage to make any headway with seemingly simple challenges in everyday life. It's not always our own fault that the road feels steep. But you can't simply blame the fact that it's tough and give up—that's the complete opposite of taking responsibility. We do, however, benefit considerably from understanding what happens when things go totally wrong. Look at the following image.

This is a model that was originally created by Paul Hersey and Ken Blanchard in the mid-1970s, one that has since spread across the world. They originally examined how children learn new things, and in the process they discovered that adults often acted in exactly the same way.

Hersey and Blanchard wanted to find out how a person progresses from being a happy amateur to a full-blown professional. What

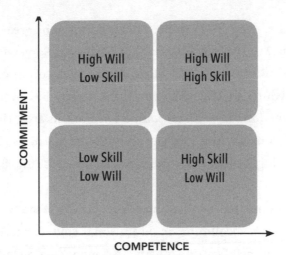

phases does one go through? They, like most of us, had noted that some tasks were more difficult to carry out than others. Even if you started doing a particular task with great enthusiasm, you could find yourself stuck before you knew it. But how does this happen?

They looked partly at the competence of the particular individual—that is, whatever specific knowledge or ability the person has that applies to the situation—and partly at the commitment to a specific task. Commitment was then divided into motivation (do I want to?) and self-confidence (am I capable?).

THE FIRST PHASE—HIGH WILL, LOW SKILL

High commitment (motivation + self-confidence) but low competence (for this specific task).

When You Start Off Full of Energy but Without Really Knowing What You're Doing

When you start a completely new task that you really want to do, you're motivated and you feel very confident about dealing with everything that needs to be done. This is going to be great fun. How hard can it be? Just get going, full speed ahead! Somewhere at the back of your mind you do, of course, know that you've never done this before, which should make you think twice. But even if you're aware that you don't have much competence in this area, that doesn't worry you too much. You just get on with it regardless. Why? You have such a high degree of commitment! Everything feels good, right?

This can be related to just about everything. Finally starting a new exercise class, beginning an educational course, changing your diet, learning Finnish, getting a new job, embarking on that big DIY project at home, planting a hedge, reading an important book that is going to help you make progress in your career.

It's a lovely phase. Everything feels really great, even though you subconsciously might have a creeping awareness of the fact that you don't really know what you are doing. But you just go for it anyway.

THE SECOND PHASE—LOW WILL, LOW SKILL

Low commitment (motivation + self-confidence) and low competence (for this specific task).

When Nothing Works and You're About to Give Up

When you've busied yourself with your task for a while, it's not uncommon to discover that things aren't quite so simple as you previously thought. What should have been extremely straightforward turns out to be more complex. It doesn't turn out like you expected, there are no results, and everything takes far too much time. And it's hard to find the joy in something that isn't going smoothly.

Note that this can be about anything from doing your DIY project at home, to going to the gym, to sticking with your most recent New Year's resolution. What was at first inspiring is now just a burden. Everybody else except you seems to know how to do it. This isn't what you had in mind, and there is no end to the problems.

Most of all, you feel confused. Was this really such a good idea? Perhaps you should return to your usual old routines?

And herein lies the great danger. If you don't know that you now find yourself in a natural but perhaps not especially pleasant phase, there's a risk that you'll simply abandon your big plan. The going is just too rough. And you can add yet another failure to all the others. Not what you needed just now. This is the reason why many gardens are full of unfinished projects, why some houses are "partially" renovated (why some of the baseboards are missing), and why there are so many unused gym memberships in people's wallets (and closets full of almost-new workout clothes).

It's a natural phase, and all of us end up stuck now and then. The challenge is not to give up too soon.

THE THIRD PHASE—LOW WILL, HIGH SKILL

Low or medium-high commitment (motivation + self-confidence) but high competence (for this specific task).

When You Start Seeing the Light at the End of the Tunnel but Still Hesitate

If you keep on struggling—and resist that acute desire to just drop the whole thing and arrive late at work, throw your hammer in the trash can, and burn your Finnish dictionary—you'll notice that even though it's still quite an effort, you are actually, little by little, learning. It's about looking for good news and celebrating small victories.

If you don't give up, it's going to get easier after a while. Keep working at it—going on a run in the morning, studying in the evening, taking on some extra projects at work—and you'll notice how the pressure slowly eases up. You gradually regain your motivation because task after task is going to go more smoothly. Things become a bit easier. You start to see results, even though they're still too small to satisfy you.

Your self-confidence is not yet sufficiently strong for you to be immune to setbacks. There's still a risk that you'll give up, because your self-confidence is not firmly established.

THE FOURTH PHASE—HIGH WILL, HIGH SKILL

High commitment (motivation + self-confidence) and high competence (for this specific task).

When It Finally Looks Like You're Going to Manage to Go the Distance

In the end, it's going to work out. Since you're not a person who gives up easily, you've struggled on through everything as best you could. You've clung firmly to your plan and meanwhile have learned loads about what works and what doesn't work. Your knowledge and motivation have increased—your self-confidence has returned. Now everything feels good again, and you might even find it hard to understand why you were so discouraged before. From this vantage point, it's easier to see that you needed to make your way through all the phases to attain that "flow." Now you have what I call momentum. It doesn't require nearly as much energy to keep on track.

HOW LONG DOES THIS PROCESS TAKE?

No one can say how long it will take between the first and the final phase. This depends on many different factors. But what's important is that you understand that this is a logical process that takes place virtually every time you try something new. Setting off at full speed at the beginning simply indicates keen commitment to the task, and there isn't anything negative about it. One thing or another is going to happen en route, and these things are going to slow you down; this is part of the process.

An important point: there is nothing wrong with you.

You react negatively to setbacks, and that can lead to frustration. As you're learning how to move forward, your commitment will return. You just need to keep your faith that this will happen.

There are studies about this aspect, and it's clear that if you've lost your motivation and perhaps your self-confidence—the second phase—then the next step is to rebuild your confidence. It's hard to feel confident when you know that you lack competence for a particular task. As your skills develop, you'll start feeling better again.

As usual, there's no rule without an exception, but you should also know that if you find yourself completely stalled, the solution is fairly simple: go back to basics, learn the job from beginning to end. Don't cheat. Don't take any shortcuts. Don't ignore the task and dump it on somebody else. You're going to feel much more confident and self-assured once you master this.

SUMMARY

The most important conclusion here is that it's impossible for you to feel the same amount of motivation and self-confidence in everything you do. Even though the model I've just described can vary from person to person, and even though the degree of difficulty of the task you undertake affects how long it will take, you can see how every new endeavor will follow this pattern of waxing and waning confidence and motivation.

We've all been there. On Monday we start off at full speed. Things are going to happen, oh, yes! On Tuesday, our energy level has dropped markedly, and on Wednesday everything is just an impenetrable darkness. But on Thursday, it feels a bit better, things start moving along. And by Friday you find yourself beginning to smile. This is a natural process.

I want to emphasize: not everything you do can be fun and motivating *all* the time. There are many people who only follow their gut feeling and devote their time to what is fun. I'm not saying that you should only do things that are difficult, and force you to struggle 24/7—no, not at all. But if you show interest only in things that feel good and enjoyable, then you are doing things only in the first and fourth phases.

This means two things, both equally bad: if you start new things— the first phase—and encounter a challenge and give up, you will never learn how to master new situations. You will reach phase two, and come to a full *stop*. Then perhaps you'll start something else new—in phase one—which you will in turn drop as soon as the going gets rough. You will simply switch between phase one and phase two. You will add a long row of failures to your mental CV. Not good.

The other thing is that if you want to feel entirely secure all the time, then you will only do things you are already capable of—the fourth phase. In other words, you're never going to challenge yourself by trying something new. Instead of testing slightly new paths in your life, you'll stay in your own comfort zone and continue to do the sort of things you feel good at.

That would put you in an especially unfortunate cul-de-sac. It works for a while, then all development and growth come to a halt.

Which Setbacks Are the Absolute Worst?

It's naïve to imagine that life can be perfect all the time. To achieve that, you would probably have to get your very own planet.

In order to get a little perspective, let's make, in a very unscientific way, a ranking scale of the petty troubles in life.

Assuming that the newspapers are right: within fifty years, Earth is more or less going to burn up and all life will die out. If we don't accept the fact that we messed up the world big-time, then it will soon be over. That seems like roughly the worst-case scenario, so let's give the potential end of the world the maximum 100 points on the list of things that can go wrong.

If the end of humanity is the highest rating on the catastrophe scale, how many points would we then give to, for example, the Second World War? The greatest and perhaps worst war in history. Around seventy million or more dead as a result of the global disaster that Hitler caused. That's nowhere near the absolute end, but it is a horrific catastrophe. So how many points do we give to the Second World War? 80 points?

What about the First World War then? However simplistic it may be, we could compare the two wars—so perhaps 70 points in comparison to the Second World War. "Only" ten million dead.

Listing other wars, and in comparison, all of them—regardless of their brutality and evidence of human evil—will probably be ranked lower than the two world wars. But let's give all wars 50 points on the list of catastrophes, because war is always horrible.

What happens if we take a look at other types of catastrophes? Where does the tsunami in Southeast Asia in 2004 land? It was an enormous tragedy. Entire towns were swept away, and houses, cars, people. The number of dead was just over 230,000. But compared with the Second World War, which lasted six years, the concentration camps, the carpet bombing of countless cities, human torture, hideous crimes against humanity . . . should we give 30 points for the tsunami, perhaps?

Nature is nature; we don't control it. But the things we do to each other, we do control those. A person killed by a natural disaster is a different sort of tragedy than one killed by another person.

Corruption, abuse of power, the fact that there are so many psychopaths at the top of lots of different organizations across the world? Perhaps that ranks as high as the tsunami. Perhaps higher, in fact—I think I would give that list 40 points.

And we can go on and on like that.

Compared with the troubles listed above, how would you rank your fiercely held opinion that your mayor is an idiot? Maybe 4 points. That you missed the bus one Tuesday in April doesn't rank at all on this scale.

OUR OWN PERSONAL CATASTROPHE SCALE

Instead, let's look at our own—extremely personal—scale of setbacks. Dying would be just about the worst that can happen to you—90 points. Yes, there are worse things. Your child killed in an accident? That's 100 points. It's hard to imagine anything worse than something happening to your children. Or being attacked and robbed and almost killed in the process. Again, a missed bus scores at a ridiculously low level. But let's put aside the catastrophes for a minute. What should be on your list of trials?

You are fired from your job.
Your company goes bankrupt because of the recession.
You make a fool of yourself because you can't handle
    alcohol.
Your car is stolen the day before your family road trip.
Your garage burns down, and the electricians who put in the
    faulty wiring didn't have any insurance.

These are examples that we can relate to. These things are unpleasant to have to deal with and yet can happen to lots of people every year.

If you have your own business, bankruptcy is among the worst scenarios you can imagine. You'll have to fire people you like and care about. You're personally responsible for the bank loan. Your bank informs you that they are expecting you to pay them over $100,000.

For somebody who is employed, the equivalent nightmare is losing your job, perhaps in the middle of a deep recession. There are no other jobs available. Your future is looking bleak.

You have debts but no income. You can't pay your mortgage, so you and your family will be forced to move to a tiny apartment. You'll have to sell your private car so that it won't be repossessed. Your company car—that's just history now. Perhaps you have three children who don't really understand why they won't be going on vacation this year. The summer cottage—forget it. You'll have to cancel your gym membership, and none of you will even be able to afford any take-out food for the next three years. Your children continue to grow. Affording new clothes for them turns into a total nightmare.

Then we've got the social "freezing out"—which is not uncommon. You and your family don't fit in with your peers anymore. The other people in your circle of acquaintances won't want to be "infected" by your misfortune, and soon the invitations to dinners and birthday parties have disappeared.

After fourteen years in the banking world, I also know that a dodgy financial situation is one of the toughest factors to deal with in a relationship. Quite often, the relationship will crack after a while, because partners usually end up blaming each other. The frustration has to find some outlet.

So now you're broke, unemployed, have a damaged marriage, and unhappy children. You might start the habit of drinking a little more often that you ought to. Who knows whether your children will even stay with you under these circumstances? You're going to end up severely depressed and might not want to get out of bed again.

At this point, it's best that I explain something: I'm not a horrible pessimist! I do firmly believe in positive thinking over negative thinking, but we definitely need a measure of realism in our lives, right?

HOW MANY POINTS WOULD YOU GIVE TO THE FOLLOWING (VERY REALISTIC) SCENARIOS?

The chain of events described above is far from unique. There are millionaires who have had to leave their homes and lost everything because of poor judgment.

If we consider the scenario of a lost job and a destroyed life to be your personal world war, and rate it at about 80 points on the catastrophe scale, then where should we rank the everyday minor dilemmas, the sorts of things that you have to deal with in an ordinary week? How many points would you give to the following trivial incidents:

- You didn't get your kids to school in time.
- The florists didn't have any pink lilies you had your heart set on. They only had white ones.
- Your neighbor's cat pissed in the kids' sandbox—again.
- A work project means that you have to work late three nights in a row because you wasted time during the day doing completely irrelevant things.
- A rabbit bulldozed no fewer than three gigantic craters in your beautiful lawn.
- Your lying colleagues have been far more successful in their careers than you.
- You messed up a potential business deal with a client.
- Your wallet seems to leak. It looks like you won't be taking that European vacation with the guys next year.
- You're troubled by a bad back despite having done everything the doctor told you to do. Lost weight, started working out, got a massage, etc.
- Your son is not performing well at school.
- Your daughter is being bullied at school.
- Your elderly mother is ill, and you don't know how much longer she has left. This really is hard to deal with.
- Your partner doesn't kiss you good night anymore. He or she might not even love you anymore.
- You might not love your partner, either.
- You have to wait for an agonizing *three* seconds for your favorite webpage to load, rather than the expected *one* second.
- You received paralyzingly few likes on your latest Instagram post.

- Your boss thinks you are an idiot.
- Some days your children agree with your boss.
- You were blocked in at the parking lot and had to wait an excruciating seven minutes before the grade-A idiot came out of the store.

I'm not trying to make fun of these smaller, mundane troubles, but if we don't put things in perspective, we're not going to manage life very well. I don't mean that these small things are unimportant, but in relative terms they are still . . . well . . . small.

On the other hand . . .

EVEN SMALL THINGS CAN CREATE LARGE PROBLEMS

Have you been bitten by a bear? No? I thought not.

How about bitten by a mosquito, what about that?

Precisely. It's the small things that bother us in our everyday life. If we don't learn how to deal with those irritating everyday incidents, we're going to run into problems when we try to tackle the big things. If we can't handle missing the bus without feeling furious, how are we going to deal with a lecture from our most important client? If we lose it when the boss asks us to work a couple of hours extra, how are we going to manage when our children get bullied at school?

In bygone days, an empty gas tank when I was in a hurry to get to the airport could drive me crazy. But I learned that these small bothersome moments serve as a little reminder that life isn't going to be simple—ever. Besides, whose job is it to keep track of how much gas there is in the tank . . . in *my* car? We're back to the question of responsibility again.

The small things are important because they prepare us for the big things. And if somebody has protected you from all those minor irritations . . . well, er, if you've never met with real opposition in your life, then you're going to have endless challenges when real problems do indeed show up. Because they are going to. We can be quite certain of that.

It's like a sort of vaccine. You get a little dose, you learn how to deal with it, and when the proper infection arrives, your immune system is ready for it. Small, everyday problems help us grow strong and resilient for harder things.

THE SPOILED CHILD'S LIMITED POSSIBILITIES TO SUCCEED

People who are frustrated by helicopter parenting often point out that children also need to be prepared for life. They argue that we do teenagers a disservice when we protect them from every unpleasantness in life. In the end, it will rebound and cause trouble: if you're totally unprepared, then the rebound might be especially hard. Because when you get your first job, your mother isn't going to be there to protect you.

But on the other hand, some people argue in favor of the idea that children should be children for as long as possible, and I understand this viewpoint, too. I once wished that I could protect my (now-adult) children from all the evil in the world. The problem is that I can't. The only thing I can do is to try to protect them from the very worst of it, while also letting them confront what I think they can manage on their own. I'm not saying that I was the perfect parent by any means, but both of them seem to manage excellently by themselves, so something must have worked out okay.

Sure, it would be lovely to have a rosy dreamlike existence without any challenges or problems, right? In which everything is great and someone serves you ice cream and fizzy drinks every day without you ever putting on weight. You can have a glass of wine every evening without it affecting you in the slightest. It doesn't matter whether you get anything done at work or not. You get a raise automatically and regularly. The sun shines every day and you're always happy.

I'd also like to live in that fantasy world. It would be very nice.

The sad truth, however, is that such a world doesn't exist. In my opinion, it's pointless to strive for something that is impossible to achieve.

When you think about it, up until now you've actually survived 100 percent of your very worst days in life. You're doing great.

SUMMARY

There are setbacks and there are setbacks. You can deal with them by putting them in perspective. Accept that they come, but make sure that you don't act like you're on the edge of a precipice of despair every time something negative happens.

By stepping back a bit from every situation, you can more easily judge what's right in front of you.

It can be useful to bear in mind the simple "five-plus-five rule": if something won't make a difference in five years' time, then don't spend more than five minutes being upset about it.

7

Your List of Setbacks

Put together a list of your own setbacks. List the obstacles you've encountered in life, so that you have a sense of your own baggage. You don't need to dig too deeply or start obsessing over or wallowing in every trial, but it can be a good idea to know what the situation really is. You might come to the conclusion that your life has actually been rather good so far.

Here is an aid to help you create a simplified table of your setbacks. It's designed help you get a quick overview of your setbacks and things you've experienced in your life so far and to put these in perspective. There's a sample ranking scale on pages 66–67. You can choose what events you list and how you rank them.

Remind yourself of what your life has looked like. The list can have as many items as you want. You could use one hundred, or just thirty things. If you want to list every missed bus since the 1990s, it might be a bit longer.

When you look at this simple list, you may notice something. Look at everything you've managed to survive without giving up. You must be a strong person!

Sure, some things have cost you dearly. Absolutely, you've been knocked around, and it can hurt. I understand. But here you are, nevertheless. And that's fantastic! It can be a powerful thing to remind yourself of the adversity you've already gone through. It's easy to forget.

It's easy to create a list of your own. Write down the obstacles and difficulties that immediately come to mind, using the line that corresponds with a point score you think is appropriate.

My points	Setbacks
100	
95	
90	
85	
80	
75	
70	
65	
60	
55	
50	

45	
40	
35	
30	
25	
20	
15	
10	
5	

THOMAS'S LIST

Strangely enough, my childhood was so easygoing and free from trauma that I'm almost ashamed to admit it. The trouble came later in life. To give you a helping hand, I've created my own list here. Hopefully this will help you fill in your own list. But remember that we're all unique. Things that I consider to be problems and identify as notable obstacles are ones you might laugh at. (Something to note: in writing my list, it turned out that I'd forgotten a couple of major incidents. My interpretation: if something doesn't come to mind, it's likely no longer significant.)

Thomas's List of Setbacks

My points	Setbacks
100	
95	
90	Losing my mother
90	Resuscitating my two-week-old son with mouth-to-mouth
85	Chronic sleep problems for more than thirty years
80	Car crash; I was still inside as it started to burn
80	Came close to being completely burned out—on a leave of absence for three months
75	High-speed car crash; the car was totaled
75	Victim of a psychopathic stalker for six months
60	My manuscripts were refused by publishers for twenty years
50	My books didn't sell particularly well when they were eventually published
45	Second hernia operation, when I almost fell off the operating table in panic
45	Car crash; ended up with a whiplash injury
40	Robbed in a bank and was forced into the bank vault with a gun pointed at me
30	Berated by the CEO of the company I worked for after I wrote a stupid letter to the board
30	Media attack orchestrated by various psychologists because of *Surrounded by Idiots*
25	Allergic to furry animals, dust mites, pollen
20	First hernia operation
15	My daughter's heart murmur when she was a child

15	Car crash, but nothing serious
15	Lost all my friends when I moved to Stockholm
15	My parents' divorce when I was in my late teens
5	My girlfriend dumped me in my first week of military service

As you can see, the setbacks in my life are fairly typical. This very simple technique helps me see things in perspective. I've taken a few hits and have both highs and lows. Knowing that I've survived all these things, I'm confident that I can also deal with whatever else comes my way.

It's important not to wallow in these things or make them the subject of daily conversation.

REFUSING TO BE DEFINED BY OBSTACLES

Peter is a good friend of mine who has struggled with dyslexia his entire childhood and adolescence. Many years ago, he chose to not see it as a shortcoming. It wasn't easy, but now he's written several books, all of them much appreciated by their readers. What did he do? He accepted the fact that it would be harder for him to be an author than it would be for somebody who didn't have dyslexia. He refused to define himself by his diagnosis. He worked hard and succeeded *despite his diagnosis*. Or, as he says, *thanks to* his diagnosis. Without dyslexia, he wouldn't have had anything to battle against.

When I asked Peter how he would rank his dyslexia on the scale of setbacks, he thought it over very carefully. At first he didn't want to put it on the list at all, because the dyslexia has led to lots of good things. But in the end, he allotted it 25 points, because of course it was pretty tough for him at school with unsympathetic teachers who thought he was a bit thick. Nowadays we know better, but thirty-five years ago much less was known about dyslexia.

Peter's reasoning is important. Because, like me, he has always dreamed of becoming an author, the dyslexia was an important motivator for him. It was the thing he was determined to beat. He wanted to prove to himself that he could write, *despite* the dyslexia.

The world is full of such examples. No matter what your situation, if you look around you, you'll certainly find lots of similar life stories.

SETBACKS OR POTENTIAL POSSIBILITIES?

As we think about Peter's example, it's interesting to consider whether what we consider obstacles actually are obstacles. Sometimes we interpret a situation completely wrong. Or our thinking is just a bit too narrow. What one person would call a fantastic possibility, another person would say is useless. But what I would call a setback, perhaps you would see as a possibility. On the face of things, you might see a situation one way, but sometimes it can be a good idea to reflect a little longer on what a particular event can mean.

A good practice—regardless of your first reaction to a particular event—is to ask yourself: What about the situation am I overlooking? Are there any other possible interpretations of this situation? Are there any benefits or positive sides? Of course, there aren't always, but surprisingly often there are positive aspects of a seemingly depressing experience.

Looking at my own list, this is extremely clear. For an author, it's awful to have your manuscripts refused, and I received hundreds of refusals over twenty years. This monumental setback just went on and on, proof that I shouldn't write books. On the other hand, I chose to keep at it because I've always liked writing. In retrospect, I know that those rejections forced me to polish my writing, to develop and become better.

During those twenty years, I didn't think like that; I was just as disappointed and angry as you would imagine. But in retrospect I know that the refusals led to something positive. The first ten books I wrote, which were never published, gave me enough training to be able to express myself so that people understood me. I wasn't published as an author until I was actually ready.

Let's look at some fictional examples.

The Setback

Your boss gives you even more to do. Just piles work on your desk. What a bastard.

The Potential Possibility

Or . . . perhaps she sees that you have potential and is confident in your skills? Soon your career will take off.

The Setback

You miss the bus by a demoralizing five seconds. Now you'll have to wait for nine minutes.

The Potential Possibility

On the next bus you bump into an old friend whose telephone number you've been trying to find for months. Now you spend a great evening together.

The Setback

Your partner wants you to go on a trip together, but you don't want to go. Your first reaction is irritation and anger.

The Potential Possibility

On the other hand . . . perhaps it means you'll get a much-needed break from everyday life, have some time for each other, and enjoy experiences that can boost your relationship.

The Setback

Your son never stops pestering you about the new hockey gear he wants. You can almost see your credit card melting from the financial stress.

The Potential Possibility

But . . . with the right coaching, perhaps your boy will be the next Wayne Gretzky. He'll be able to buy you a new house in a few years.

The Setback

The new owners of the company you work for want to restructure, and you're going to be made redundant after twelve years of faithful hard work. Your career looks bleak.

The Potential Possibility

But . . . the new owners will pay you twelve months' severance when you leave, so you'll have a chance to start up that little business venture you've been toying with. Soon you'll have both the time and money you need.

Of course, you don't need to be naïve. Sometimes bad news really is bad news. If I step into a heap of dog poop on the pavement, my shoes might well be destroyed. If my phone is stolen at the restaurant, that's going to be a headache. But actively looking for potential possibilities even in awkward or undesirable situations leads—more often than you think—to more interesting lessons and new experiences.

What do you have to lose?

A lot of people think that positive thinking is silly, and they don't believe it works at all. But there are useful possibilities and positive outcomes in places we're not used to looking. We just need to step back a bit to see them.

Many of the most advanced inventions we use today have their origins in advanced failures.

Only you can decide how you should react to what happens around you. You already know that, and you've heard it before. I want to remind you that how you react to your situation is your responsibility. Oftentimes, we need to work to put things in perspective. We can accept that sometimes things are going to go totally wrong, but at the same time we can sometimes overestimate the severity of the situation.

So let's go back to your list of setbacks.

Put this book down, and try this:

Look at the situations, one by one. And choose just one to start with.

Go back to that time in your memory and accept that it was an unfortunate experience. Don't focus on the misery, but instead spend a few minutes reflecting on the positive effects of that event.

This is an exercise that I sometimes use when I do one-on-one coaching, and many people just completely dismiss the idea. Getting stuck with a job you didn't ask for can only be negative, they say. There's nothing positive about your child doing poorly in school, they say.

I respect these attitudes. Not all bad things bring something good with them. But more times than you think, they actually do. So add a little realism to your list. Try this exercise for each item on your list of setbacks. I wouldn't be surprised if half or more of your obstacles also moved you forward in a valuable way.

Even really difficult things can create positive effects. A woman I worked with many years ago was devastated by the death of her mother. But after a painful period of mourning, she realized that she wanted to put more effort into her relationship with her father. She did so, and they had a better relationship during his final twenty years than they'd ever had before.

It's easy to sound dismissive or flippant when advising people to look for the positives. But by taking a few steps back and looking at a situation as objectively as possible, we really can gain important insights. This strengthens us and prepares us for the future.

The setback	The potential possibility

SUMMARY

Even though all of us encounter adversity, it's wise to have perspective. Since we're governed by our emotions, we can react more strongly in the heat of the moment than is really justified.

Take a step back and look at each obstacle in turn.

Was it really as negative as you first believed? And is there actually anything positive hidden here?

If you think about the greatest benefit you gained from a seemingly hard situation, is there an element of gratitude for having had that experience in your life? Look at what it gave you.

Do We All React to Setbacks the Same Way?

Obviously, different people react in different ways to different types of problems. Besides, we react differently on different occasions. The situation, your mood, and other difficulties or opportunities you may be experiencing at the same time can change how you perceive a situation. People are decidedly different in this area.

What you're interested in, your motivational factors, your driving forces, your unique situation, and more all influence what you choose to consider a setback.

If somebody blocks your car in a parking space when you should be halfway to the airport, I can make allowances for your cursing. But if somebody blocks your car in a parking space when you've just won a huge amount of money on a lottery ticket, then I doubt whether you'll be that put out. The same event, different circumstances. So it's clear, we're never going to be able to completely chart out or predict how we react to trying circumstances.

Just remember one thing: obstacles often bring out our less-flattering sides. Few people look forward to a setback.

Besides, all of us have different experiences. If we compare ourselves with Nelson Mandela, we'll probably look a bit unimpressive when it comes to handling adversity. Spending more than twenty-five years in prison for your political views would have crushed most people, but not him. He was finally released, and he didn't react the way people thought he would. Instead, he turned the other cheek and was elected South Africa's first black president.

THE DISC MODEL

I use the widely known DISC model (dominance, inspiration, stability, compliance) to describe dissimilarities in behavioral patterns. There are lots of other methods, but this model covers most of what you need to know just now. I've associated each of the four behavior profiles with a color—red, yellow, green, and blue—to make the system simple to use and easy to remember.

There are an endless number of factors that affect how a person functions, and in this book I will deal with two of them: a person's behavioral profile and a person's development level.

If you've read my previous book, *Surrounded by Idiots,* you'll soon be getting a short refresher course on the basic behavior types.

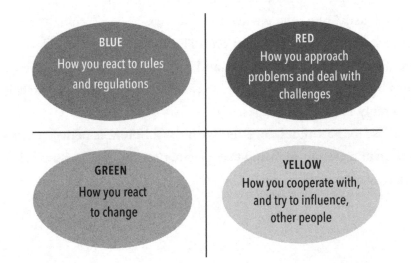

Red, the task-oriented and extroverted color, is governed by an ability to deal with problems and difficult challenges. The tougher the scenario, the better. If something goes a bit too smoothly, the Reds almost become suspicious. What's the catch? Why is it so easy? It should be hard; it should be difficult. You have to put in some work. It might even need to be a bit painful. Pain makes you strong. Reds like a fast pace, action, and having lots of things going on.

If Reds are focused on being active, then yellow, the extroverted and relationship-oriented color, is about integrating. These are the people who always have to convince everyone else to see things their way. They can't leave the room until everybody agrees with them. And they see sunshine even when it's raining. The Yellows also like a bit of action.

Green, the relationship-oriented and introverted color, is about an unwillingness to change. A lot of green in someone's behavior profile indicates a desire to maintain the status quo. Greens won't be in favor of change, even if it's absolutely necessary. These are people who say things like "It was better before," or "The grass isn't always greener on the other side." New ideas are summarily dismissed: everything is working nicely the way it is, thank you very much.

And lastly, blue, the introverted and task-oriented color, is about appreciating rules and regulations. The Blues follow the rule book and always know what is right and proper. They read the instructions before they even open the box with that new IKEA bookshelf. Preferably in three languages.

These four attitudes, together with the differences between introversion and extroversion and task orientation and relationship orientation, lead to certain specific behaviors.

WHAT KIND OF BEHAVIOR DOES THIS LEAD TO?

When we look at how these behavior types play out, we start to see clear differences in every respect imaginable. On the following pages you can see a number of specific qualities relating to a particular color. Remember, however, that there are exceptions. There are always exceptions. It's complicated to understand human beings.

Here are a few points to remember about the DISC model:

- Everything about an individual's behavior cannot be explained with the DISC language.
- There are also other models that explain human behavior.
- There are more parts of the jigsaw puzzle than just "the colors" to map various behavioral patterns.
- The DISC model is built upon psychological studies. It is used across the entire world and has been translated into forty languages.
- Historically, there are similar models in different cultures, e.g., the theory of the four temperaments, which originally came from Hippocrates, who lived in antiquity, approximately twenty-five hundred years ago.
- About 80 percent of all people have a combination of two colors that dominate their behavior. About 5 percent only have one color that dominates their behavior. The rest are dominated by three colors.
- All-Green behavior, or Green in combination with another color, is the most common. The most unusual is all-Red behavior, or Red in combination with another color.
- There may be differences in behavior between the sexes, but I do not focus on the gender perspective in this book.

	RED	YELLOW	GREEN	BLUE
APPROACH	Energetic and direct	Optimistic and spontaneous	Considerate and understanding	Reflective and correct
MANNER	Businesslike	Visible	Sensitive	Formal
WORK STYLE	Hardworking Ambitious Professional Effective Exact	Committed Personal Flexible Stimulating Articulate	Personable Relaxed Friendly Informal Low-key	Structured Organized Specialized Methodical Succinct
WORK PACE	Fast and decisive	Fast and spontaneous	Slow and consistent	Slow and systematic
PRIORITIZES	The task and the result	Relationships and influence	Retaining good relationships	The task and work method
AFRAID OF	Losing control	Losing prestige	Confrontation	Making a fool of oneself
BEHAVIOR UNDER PRESSURE	Dictates conditions and asserts oneself	Attacks and is ironic	Backs down and agrees	Withdraws and avoids
WANTS	Results	Inspiration	Stability	Quality
WANTS YOU TO BE	Straightforward	Stimulating	Kind	Exact
WANTS TO BE	The one who decides	The one who is admired	The one who is liked	The one who is correct
IS IRRITATED BY	Inefficiency and indecision	Passivity and routines	Insensitivity and impatience	Surprises and whims
WANTS TO HAVE	Success and control	Status and flexibility	Calm and quiet and close relationships	Credibility and time to prepare

	RED	YELLOW	GREEN	BLUE
BEHAVES	Businesslike	Elegant	Friendly	Law-abiding
LIVES IN	The present	The future	The past (when everything was better)	One's own thoughts
RELIES UPON	Gut feeling	Recognition	One's self	Specialists
DOESN'T LIKE	Sitting still	Being alone	Unpredictability	Hurry

- The DISC model does not work for analyzing ADHD, Asperger's syndrome, borderline personality disorder, or other diagnoses.
- There are always exceptions to the concepts I outline in this book. People are complex—even Red people can be humble, and Yellow people can listen attentively. There are Green people who deal with conflict because they have learned how to do so, and many Blues understand when it's time to stop tweaking the details.

WHAT THE FOUR COLORS WOULD DEFINE AS A SETBACK

When we look at the four colors and their interests, we see some interesting patterns.

People who are predominantly Red in their behavioral profile are just waiting for problems, even though they don't know what the problems are. They have a sort of constant battle-readiness, even though they live in the here and now. They don't plan for problems, but they deal with them if they have the audacity to show themselves.

People who are primarily Yellow think a bit differently here. These positive individuals live mainly in the future, where everything is bright and delightful, which means that they can be totally surprised by possible obstacles. They can end up in over their heads. Just like the Reds, they don't really have a plan, because the setbacks were not exactly expected.

Folks with profiles dominated by Green often walk around with a constant ache in their stomachs because they know—from their imaginary experience—that the bubble is about to burst. Somebody is going to mess up, and there will be big problems. This often leads to a certain passivity in order to avoid making things worse, even though nothing has happened at all.

Finally, people who are mostly Blue are risk analysts from birth. They function exactly the opposite of Yellows. Here, the attitude is that just about everything can go totally haywire, so you should use every imaginable safety net and protective measure to keep catastrophe at bay. The result is that they need forever to accomplish anything. It takes time to protect yourself from everything.

But what do they react to? Do the colors get upset by the same thing? How does a Yellow view a setback, compared to a Green? Let's take a look, and see what we can expect from those around us.

How Reds Define Setbacks

It's very valuable to understand what Reds see as setbacks, because that is where they will direct all their energy . . . and it's a good idea not to stand right in the line of fire.

What does a Red person view as an obstacle? Interesting question. For obvious reasons, they don't exactly back away when problems arise, and they're generally well prepared for everything to go sideways. Reds might be the most realistic when it comes to accepting the world as it is. My argument that everyone is affected by problems and crises is nothing new for the Reds. They already knew that.

Since they like speed, action, and to achieve (the best) results, everything that stands in the way of that is a setback.

If a Red boss wants to increase profitability by 2 percent, then too low a turnover and too high costs will be different facets of the same problem.

If a client doesn't want to buy from the Red salesperson, then that client will symbolize the obstacle—not the fact that the salesperson was poorly prepared or not properly updated.

And if your Red neighbor wants to build his garage right on your property line, then your "no" will be a big setback. After all, it prevents him from having his way. *Your* problem is that *you* are now the obstacle to his goal.

Everything that slows down the process is a problem. Everything that means the Red doesn't win. Setbacks are the same as losing: not sealing a business deal, being abandoned by your spouse, having your salary reduced, not being elected as chairman of the homeowners association (loss of power). Anything that means the Red loses control of the situation—their very greatest fear—is a setback.

How Yellows Identify Setbacks

If you remember Yellow behavior, then you'll recall that these people are more relationship-oriented than the Reds. Yellows have an interesting perspective amid all their infectious positiveness. In effect, they see only possibilities and positive outcomes, so it can be a bit of a shock when something goes wrong. What happened? This was going to be a great success!

The most devastating setback is anything that affects the Yellow's ego, like making a fool of yourself in public. Being loudly reprimanded by your boss in front of the whole department might be worse than being quietly fired on a Friday afternoon.

Far-fetched? Perhaps, but Yellows will always be sensitive to events that make them look unsuccessful. Appearances can be the most important thing for them.

Social ostracism. Not being chosen for the football team. Not being invited to the neighborhood's big block party. Seeing colleagues going to lunch together without even being asked if you're hungry. Being left by your partner. Naturally, nobody would think that was ideal, but the Yellow will be destroyed.

Anything negative about the Yellow as a person will be the greatest kind of adversity for this color.

How Greens Recognize Setbacks

Greens can spot obstacles anywhere. They have an introverted side that the Reds and the Yellows both lack. This means that a lot happens under the surface without others perceiving it. Greens consider disagreements and resistance to be setbacks. Any form of conflict is bad news.

This is challenging because conflicts are found everywhere. It's impossible to avoid them. You can't go through life without ending up in conflict with other people or even with yourself. Greens will often be troubled by inner conflict between what they ought to do and what they want to do. Greens don't have the same type of energy as the Reds and Yellows.

When Greens get scolded, they might not react as strongly as Yellows would at that particular moment, but they will remember the injustice for a very long time.

Like Yellows, Greens are relationship-oriented, but a Green lacks the strong ego of a Yellow. This means that Greens can face obstacles in a group setting in particular. Greens won't consider their own personal gain, but will consider the group's success or failure. Team sports work well for Greens because people compete together, but if it goes badly for the team, then Greens will suffer even more deeply than if the failure was theirs alone.

The Blues' Rational Definition of a Setback

When we look at how Blues consider obstacles, we see exciting patterns. As I mentioned earlier, they have their own way of critical thinking, which means that they're not really surprised by anything. When it all goes wrong, Blues will soberly nod and think, *Yep, exactly what I expected*. It will just confirm how they know the world works.

If I wanted to joke about this, I'd mention that old cliché about pessimists being happy when everything goes sideways, because then they're finally proven right. But perhaps it isn't quite that simple.

Obstacles can be defined as everything that doesn't follow the plan. This is slightly ambiguous, because the Blue expects that the plan won't be a sufficient defense against all problems. But when things do start to deviate from the plan, those things become—by definition—a setback.

The Blues love being in control, not of the situation or of other people—that's Red behavior—but they want to have total control over all the details. However, the larger the project, the more unlikely it is that they'll achieve the desired degree of perfection. If they aren't given sufficient time to make the plan so flawless that it would essentially execute itself, well, that, too, might be something they'd consider a trial.

An easily overlooked but important aspect of Blue behavior is that the Blues hate to make fools of themselves. And if they do that by, for example, missing details, being careless, or not having had time for proper quality control, then it's a particularly bad situation. The Blues will go out of their way to avoid precisely that.

Even if they aren't especially relationship-oriented and aren't the most emotional people you've come across, they react strongly to what they see as faults. If their failings are revealed to others, they might not react emotionally, like a Yellow whose ego has been wounded, but they will grind their teeth and be deeply ashamed of their carelessness.

And if you're the one who revealed their mistake, well, then you're the problem in the Blues' book. And that is not good news.

SUMMARY

I'll remind you again that the four colors are a simplification of how we humans behave. We are very often a combination of several colors, but I guarantee that you will be able to use this system in your own life.

How Each Color Reacts When Things Go Wrong

Let's have a look at what the DISC model says. As you read, see if you recognize yourself in these descriptions.

THE REDS' REACTION WHEN EVERYTHING GOES DOWN THE DRAIN

Now hold tight! People with a lot of red in their profile—it doesn't have be just red, but could also be red in combination with another color—expect that life is going to cause them problems. As I've mentioned, they have a pronounced competitive streak and aren't afraid of things getting a bit rough. And very often they have more energy than the rest of us.

But naturally things still sometimes go wrong even for these turbo-personalities. The Reds react in two ways when things get tough. They "get to work on it," or they "sneak away from it."

They might sound the trumpet to attack whatever is standing in their way and conquer all opposition. Setbacks in relationships, for example, are often dealt with in this way. They throw out the rule book and will resort to virtually anything when their weapons have been sharp-ened. It's about winning, about being right, about seeing the other party give up. Because this is about a victory for the Red. Charming? No, but that's the truth of it.

When it comes to concrete issues or problems to be solved, Reds activate everybody around them. There is a battle to be fought! Ev-eryone needs to roll up their sleeves to remove the roadblock in the path of the general progress. Here we have effective project leaders who make sure that everybody has plenty to do.

Being in a bad mood is the rule rather than the exception for Reds. The Red often displays aggression, directed not only at the problem or situation, but at everything and everybody that's in range when things get hot. When the battle is over, there might be little more than splinters left. For the Red, this is of lesser importance; even a scorched-earth victory is a victory.

The other Red response—to "sneak away from it"—is slightly less common, but it happens. It means exactly what it sounds like. The Red simply ignores what has happened and turns to something else. We don't know what exactly triggers this reaction. During all the years I have studied Red behavior, I haven't really succeeded in working out why Reds sometimes just shrug their shoulders and ignore the whole thing. I can't find a clear pattern, beyond the fact that they weren't really interested from the beginning. Like everyone else, Reds can have good or bad days that can influence their reaction. But most likely this is how they respond to things that they feel aren't worth fighting for.

If they hear some bad news at work, something that might affect the Red significantly, but it comes from a complete idiot, they can ig-nore it without the slightest difficulty. Reds have the ability to ignore things that they don't think are worth wasting energy on.

Obvious strengths: the Reds are fairly tough and can deal with adversity well. They see it as a true challenge, and they are willing to fight to the bitter end because they don't particularly care what everyone else thinks of them.

THE YELLOWS' REACTION TO
A DEEPLY UNFAIR EXPERIENCE

The Yellows have an especially positive basic attitude that is a very good defense against all injustices in life. When yellow is combined with other colors, this applies to a varying degree.

One of the Yellows' keys strengths it that they are always looking for possibilities. There is no opening they don't find to help them negotiate their way through an obstacle. If there is an exit, they will find it. But they also have well-developed defense mechanisms that shield them from the harsher blows of life. If, for example, a client doesn't want to put in an order, they can quickly explain it away with the rationalization that it was the wrong client anyway. Even a direct insult might be brushed off as the other person's problem: they didn't know any better. The Yellow shakes off defeat as easily as you change your shirt.

Besides, they will—as usual—share the burden with others, since they never stop talking. Everybody around them is going to know what is going on.

Relationship problems are often handled with the Yellows' dubious gift of the gab. They are sparkling communicators who can turn any conversation to their own advantage. And it's going to sound good, too. (It's not a coincidence that many salespeople have a lot of yellow in their profiles).

What's interesting about Yellows is that they can react extremely strongly once the bad news hits them. For a moment, they'll feel awful, especially if somebody else witnesses their difficulty. Sure, they can go around with a collection bag to gather all the attention and sympathy they're owed, but if the situation looks really bad, it will damage their egos. Not good. And then they'll feel like shit. In the days following the setback, the Yellow will "rewrite" the experience in his or her head so that it isn't quite so bad. This, too, is a defense mechanism that helps for the time being, but it doesn't solve the problem in the long term. If a really Yellow person gets to ponder a problem long enough, then the setback will eventually be rebranded as a victory.

The Reds' desire to fight through a problem isn't as pronounced in Yellow behavior, which can limit Yellows' development in the long term. They struggle on and have lots of energy, but on the whole they are more sensitive than the Reds. It depends somewhat on their individual driving forces, but the Yellows might very well give up if they think it isn't worth the struggle.

The Yellows' strength in dealing with setbacks is their unbroken positive way of looking at the world. They will always find something to laugh at, which cheers them up and helps move them along.

THE GREENS' WAY OF DEALING WITH THIS COLD, CRUEL WORLD

The Greens—depending upon how much green there is in their profile—tend to struggle with setbacks. They might not be natural fighters, and they function better when daily life moves at an ordinary pace. They can become extremely worried by seemingly small things. They view setbacks as a part of life, but they are extremely exhausting for people who only want a bit of peace and quiet. This often leads to a Green's passive behavior. After all, there's less risk of being knocked around if you stay at home and pull the curtains.

They are (just like the Yellows) fairly sensitive to major setbacks when they encounter them, but (unlike the Yellows) they don't forget as easily. They simply have a better memory than the Yellows. Negative experiences, like getting a reprimand from the boss, or being obliged to work late when you've planned a relaxing evening in front of the TV, or finding that the bill from the mechanic is not going to be cheap can whirl around inside the Greens' consciousness for months. They tend to brood, until the problem has grown into an enormous obstacle.

As for relationship problems, the Greens are actually extremely good at dealing with these. They are, after all, natural relationship types, and are very good listeners as well. However, their fear of conflicts can sometimes lead to difficulties. If they are caught up in a difference of opinion, it can be very difficult for them to deal with. It's harder for Greens to handle setbacks in which others are involved than it is to manage problems that only affect them.

As Greens are fairly natural introverts, a lot of their energy comes from within. Unfortunately, this includes both positive and negative energy, so when a bad experience whirls around inside their heads it is continually intensified until things look absolutely hopeless. A serious adversity, like being fired or losing a close friend, can lead to burnout. This means that Green people might need help to get themselves back on track.

On top of it all, Greens tend to view everything as a setback. It doesn't need to be anything more serious than an empty toothpaste tube in the morning; the day is wrecked. What a Red or Yellow person would never perceive as a problem can completely paralyze a Green individual, leaving them anxious 24/7.

The Greens' strength in dealing with adversity is that they're good at getting others involved. They get help and make sure that they have support from important people in their lives.

THE BLUES' ANALYSIS OF INEVITABLE SETBACKS

The Blues have an interesting approach when it comes to obstacles. Since they are brilliant risk analysts, they will (as I've mentioned) likely have foreseen most things before they happen. All that a major setback actually does is confirm that the Blue was indeed right. *This project was doomed to failure. Why did we even start this adventure in the first place?*

Blue people are perceived as pessimists for a reason. They are forever looking for things that can go wrong, and when things finally do go bad, they're almost happy to have been proven right.

It may seem contradictory, but they often react very calmly to most things, even when there's been a major snafu. Blue people try to actively distance themselves from their emotions—even though no one is completely emotionally neutral, they do it better than the other colors—and look at the situation. What has actually gone wrong? How did it happen? Who is responsible and what does the presumed solution look like? Sorry, that should be *solutions* (plural), because Blues need at least three different alternatives to decide among.

They tend to solve all problems and setbacks in the same way, even when they concern relationships. In that regard, they're seen as somewhat "clinical" by those around them. They create lists of what has gone wrong and see everything in terms of "facts," because that feels logical. The problem is that more emotional individuals think that the Blues are idiots who can't handle emotions.

That is a misconception. The Blues understand emotions, even though they camouflage their own, and they will definitely remember every individual's different reactions. But they will argue logically, even when confronting relationship issues, which more often than not makes things worse, because they have little respect for touchy-feely stuff and general yammering. It will make them withdraw completely. And more than any other color, the Blues like their own company.

It's simpler to deal with task-oriented issues. These can be broken down into their constituent parts and analyzed. This takes time, but Blue behavior does lead to a brilliant problem-solving ability. The Blues' stamina is fantastic, and if they've decided to cross a mountain of resistance, then they are going to do it. The only real risk is that they'll run out of time.

Since they are masters at making plans, they're going to draw up long lists with next steps. Just like with Red behavior, the Blues consider it natural to meet with opposition, but whereas the Reds try to destroy any obstacles in their way, the Blues will methodically pull every obstacle apart bit by bit.

Yet (and this is something to consider when you have a Blue person in your vicinity) Blues are more interested in the process itself rather than in achieving a goal. The path itself is going to be more important than the destination. The Blues' extremely long-term perspective can mean that they consider setbacks interesting problems in themselves, which can be resolved when they get there by way of something on their list.

In short, Blues' strength in dealing with setbacks is that they analyze objectively and don't get too emotional. They take the time necessary to turn the ship—even if it is going to take a very long time.

SUMMARY

How we behave in the face of setbacks is contingent on the particular situation as well as other personal qualities. Driving forces, development levels, mood, competence, general motivation, and self-confidence all influence how we confront and manage problems when they arise. The DISC model—like all other similar models—has its weaknesses in giving a 100 percent accurate description of how a particular individual functions under stress. But it can help us understand the most basic constituents of someone's behavior.

I am fairly certain that you recognized a couple of examples in those descriptions. And they can give you some clues as to how you should consider the setbacks you will encounter.

My own experience is that it's possible to learn to deal with setbacks. One of the best pieces of advice I've ever received is to try to look at the situation as it really is. Not to make it bigger or smaller based on an emotional response, but to simply consider what happens as neutrally as possible.

Easy to say, but not so easy to do. It's easier for the task-oriented profiles, the Reds and the Blues, than for the Greens and the Yellows, who are more person-oriented. There is no value judgment in this, but Reds are often successful because of their resilience in the face of adversity.

Every setback you've had in life is feedback from the world you live in. You need to learn to see how useful that is. Take it for what it is. Always learn from your mistakes. A cliché? Perhaps it is. But you can learn from other people's mistakes, too. Realize that you are not the center of the universe.

How Does the Author of This Book Deal with Setbacks?

As you've already seen, I've met with some daunting obstacles in life. I've encountered everything imaginable, from burning cars to media storms. The ranking I listed in chapter 7 shows how I felt about each of these various situations. On the whole, setbacks that are personal and related to relationships were much more difficult for me than things that were connected with my work. The same might be true for you.

A REALITY CHECK

So am I good at dealing with setbacks? One of my methods for handling setbacks and adversity is to accept that they are a part of life. I know from my own experience that it's impossible to escape them totally, so I've stopped even trying. I do the best I can as an author, lecturer, husband, and dad. I don't count my blessings in advance. But I also don't plan on negative experiences. If they come along, then that's that.

I've found it valuable to distinguish between situations that I *can* influence and stuff I *cannot* influence. When it comes to taking responsibility for myself, I practice what I preach.

Things I can influence include:

- what I do;
- what I refrain from doing;
- how I react to what I can't influence.

As an example, we can consider the media storm that my book *Surrounded by Idiots* caused at home in Sweden in 2018. The book was about the basics of the DISC model, the four colors, and served as an introduction to behaviors and everyday psychology. I wanted to spark people's curiosity about these subjects, because I believed that there were far too many unnecessary conflicts in our everyday lives due to ordinary, simple misunderstandings. So I used a suitable model and wrote a book. That seemed fairly low-risk. After all, the DISC model had existed and been used the world over for more than forty years. Something like fifty million analyses have been carried out in about forty languages. Regardless of what you think of such a method, it was out there. And many people had used it.

After the book had been on sale in Sweden for almost four years (and sold close to one million copies), some people had become so irritated by it that they decided something had to be done.

A handful of my competitors—lecturers, authors, and consultants, many with training in psychology—did their very best to publicly attack the book and me personally. There weren't many detractors, but they were impressively loud.

Of course, that wasn't enjoyable. Like everyone else, I prefer it when people like and appreciate what I do.

On the other hand, the criticism was not unexpected. *Surrounded by Idiots* had become so popular that criticism was unavoidable. The book was everywhere. The critics were harsh: the book was stupid, meaningless, a waste of paper. As for me, I was a fraud with limited intellectual capacity who didn't know what I was talking about. Why didn't I just go away?

So how did I handle this?

My Responsibility: What I Did

I took action where I could. I read the criticism until I understood what the heart of the complaint was. Via several newspapers and radio shows, I presented my own arguments and rebuttals. The critics were right on a couple of points. In the early editions of *Surrounded by Idiots,* I had been a bit careless with some of my wording, and that could lead to misunderstandings, so I corrected that for future editions. But we talk about details.

That was all I could do. I also continued to work on new books and on my lecture material. I continued to spread knowledge about behavior and everyday psychology. My calendar was so booked up with speaking engagements, I couldn't do anything else.

My Responsibility: What I Didn't Do

I also got to choose what actions to avoid. When more critics joined the chorus of complaints, I was aghast. But since I couldn't do or say anything to change their opinions—they, of course, had every right to their own opinions—I simply did not respond. And I stopped reading what they said. That was my way of dealing with what I couldn't influence.

My Responsibility: How I Reacted

I could also govern my own reactions. I chose not to react to what certain aggressive critics said. Since I have experienced major crises in life, I wasn't extremely affected. The positive reactions from my readers easily outweighed the voices of a few critics. My inbox almost exploded with supportive cheers that drowned out any criticism.

Obviously, I wasn't completely impervious. Sure, it was unpleasant to have others put words in my mouth, but I saw no reason to correct all these fantasies about me or my books. People who want to find fault will always look for it. The same people will, incidentally, be reading these words, too, and be sharpening their pencils to hack away at this book as well.

While certain critics became more and more irate, I reminded myself of why I do what I do. I want people to explore how we communicate with one another, and be curious about acquiring greater self-awareness.

But, and this is important: I don't have any ambitions to convince people who aren't interested. I don't force my opinion onto anybody else, nor should you. If people don't want to listen—then simply walk away. If you think a book is bad—put it aside and pick up another one.

My message to you is: try to establish a levelheaded response to things you can't influence anyway. It takes too much energy and focus to worry about what other people might think.

As Winston Churchill said, "You will never reach your destination if you stop and throw stones at every dog that barks."

LEARNING FROM LIFE

You can gain important insights from your setbacks. When people attack you instead of disagreeing with your message, when they demean themselves with a personal attack instead of having an objective discussion, then you know that their position is rather weak.

You don't need to worry about it. It says far more about them than about you.

MY COLOR PROFILE

As I write in *Surrounded by Idiots,* people with different behavioral profiles react to bad news in different ways. Reds tend to not listen until the end, get angry, and then launch a counterattack.

My red column is high. Very high. A lot of people don't realize it, because I know how to keep it under control when necessary. That requires active effort, and sometimes my control fails when I let my emotions gain the upper hand. Ask anyone who knows me well. I'm not always super-nice to deal with. But that's also one of the main reasons why I've learned to think before I speak or react.

The Yellows are quick to feel insulted, and become dejected in response. Getting personal criticism can hurt a Yellow person badly, because it goes right to the heart. It doesn't look good; What is everyone going to say? Falling off a pedestal is probably the worst thing that can happen to Yellows. Their egos suffer quite the blow. Luckily, the Yellows have well-developed defense mechanisms, so they brush off most stuff fairly quickly. And within a couple of weeks, everything is back to normal.

My yellow column is also quite high. I recognize myself in the description of how criticism can sting, but only if it comes from people I care about—basically, my family. That can hurt. And sometimes I take up a defensive position and try to make myself look better. Immature. Yes, I know.

Individuals with a lot of green in their behavioral pattern are very sensitive to criticism and take almost everything personally. It's easy to crush a Green person if you're really nasty. Greens are offended by almost everything, and often are hard on themselves without any external help. Also, they have an irritatingly good memory for injustices.

My green column is, on the whole, nonexistent. My apologies.

Blue behavior is interesting because the Blues simply distance themselves from the matter. They are task-oriented analysts who are fully aware of facts and details. They can stare at you with a completely blank face while you rant and rave. Then they'll ask you to put that in writing, because they want to go through what you said in peace and quiet. That way they can break down your arguments to bits.

My blue column is just as high as my red column. This is the behavior I lean on when people around me rush ahead and don't know what they're doing. Some people have learned to appreciate this, but others think it's a real pain that I remember every single word from the last meeting.

SUMMARY

Again, this is not an exact science. People are complex, but even with as simplified an analysis as this one, you can begin to understand more of your own reactions and perhaps find explanations for why you feel a particular way.

Remember that even though you're not responsible for what others say to you or do to you, you are responsible for how you choose to react.

I suppose that was my way of saying, *Think positively.*

But what if it's just not possible to think positively? What do you do then? You'll find the answer in the next chapter.

11

Our Tendency to Focus on the Negative

Let's reflect for a moment on why so many of our life experiences can be perceived as obstacles.

We've all been there. You might be driving in the car somewhere and suddenly everyone slows down. For reasons unknown, you find yourself in traffic, and it is not moving. You can't see an accident or anything causing the problem. You're stuck there for an hour. Suddenly the line starts moving. Slowly, slowly you crawl along, swearing.

When you reach the place where the traffic jam started, there's still nothing there. No broken-down car. No fallen branch. No explanation. Except for one thing . . .

. . . The most beautiful sunset you have seen in all your life leaves you, and thousands of other motorists, speechless.

Unbelievable, isn't it?

Unbelievable is putting it mildly, because that is never going to happen. There is never going to be a sunset so beautiful people stop their cars. On the other hand . . . if there had been a major car crash, then we'd certainly slow down and have a good long look. *Is that a leg that's sticking out? I think I saw some blood.*

HOW OUR BRAINS ARE PROGRAMMED

If we ask neuroscientists, they'll explain that it's how we're wired: we're forever looking for problems and risks, because that increased our chances of survival once upon a time when we were living in the wild. The short version is that our consciousness is always on the lookout for things that have the potential to go wrong. There's nothing wrong with you. Your brain is programmed to function this way. If it hadn't been, perhaps mankind would have died out long ago. If we hadn't seen the danger lurking around us forty thousand years ago, we might have been a very short-lived species.

Nowadays, there are fewer benefits to this problem-spotting behavior. But we do the same thing regardless. That is one of the reasons why the media works the way it does. It shocks us with huge headlines proclaiming this or that catastrophe. Good news hardly has any place in today's newspapers. Why? Because doomsday headlines generate more clicks online than good news. Writing about war, murder, death, climate disasters, and catastrophes catches our attention far more than reading that the sun shone and somebody got a new job.

I was something of a news junkie for many years. After listening to several news reports in the car on my way home from work, I simply had to get home before six o'clock to watch the news on TV. Then the other news program at seven thirty. After that, a break until the longer news show at nine o'clock. Just before going to bed, I filled up with the late-night news. By the time I got into bed, I was updated on murders, terrorist acts, wars, conflicts, economic crises, fraud, and natural catastrophes.

In retrospect, I don't have a good explanation as to why I sucked up so much (bad) news. I was stuck in a habit. In the end, I succeeded in breaking the habit, and that is one of the best things I've done.

Nowadays, you have to have an almost inhuman focus in order to avoid getting caught in a negative spiral. After surfing the internet and completely losing your faith in humanity, you have to drink a bottle of wine and munch a box of chocolates to reacquire a degree of hope.

Not watching the news was a way for me to keep my mind clear and unmuddled. If something really serious happens, I hear about it one way or another.

MORE ACTION = MORE MISTAKES

Our own mistakes can create painfully negative thought patterns.

If we consider the most successful people we can imagine, they're all extremely action-oriented. Many of them hate small talk; they don't want to hear delightful plans or talk about everything that *might* happen. They want to know what *is* going to happen.

So they act. Shoot first, ask questions later. That leads us to an interesting observation.

Even though some people take action more quickly and more frequently, it doesn't always end up for the better. Of course not. Sometimes our reactions are both quick and wrong, to put it mildly. The speed of the decision alone means that these doers make more mistakes than other people.

They will sometimes be scorned for this. The psychology is interesting here, because making mistakes and making a fool of yourself is viewed very harshly today. Everything must be perfect; nothing must look bad or careless. Perfectionism has spread.

Making mistakes is, of course, a pain. It can create setbacks and leave you sick to your stomach. But it's also unavoidable to sometimes make mistakes; this is part of a learning process. Mistakes and errors are simply feedback that tells you this particular thing didn't work, try something else.

Never making mistakes means very little learning of new knowledge. There is almost nothing that teaches you more about a particular thing than doing it wrong from the start. And yet many people are hesitant.

You shouldn't risk your job or your marriage in the name of making mistakes, but accept that mistakes are a necessary obstacle you can't avoid.

WHAT ARE YOUR WORST MISTAKES?

Time for a little exercise. Write down your worst mistakes in life, the times that you really made a fool of yourself or perhaps did something shameful. Not your setbacks, because those can be things that were unrelated to your own actions. No, this is about choices you have made yourself—a list of mistakes.

You don't need to show the paper to a single soul. You don't need to post your list on a billboard for all to see. But describe your own behavior fully and in detail. Be really honest about it. It's not enough to just think about a particular situation, because your brain is going to protect you from the unpleasantness and will conjure up lots of defense mechanisms.

As an example, you could write:

I was going to ask this girl to dance, but I was so bowled over by her and extremely nervous, I had a few drinks before I did. Unfortunately, it was more than just a couple, and when I finally got up the courage to talk to her, she noticed my breath and said no thank you.

Now you can write down what you learned from this:

Drinking alcohol is not only good for your self-confidence, it's also effective at frightening away girls with good taste. I'll have to find another way to build up my courage next time.

Another example might be:

The boss asked at the morning meeting if everybody was satisfied with the new organization system, and then (in front of the whole group of twenty-five people) I chose to complain about the negative aspects of the new system and criticize the boss for certain decisions. Unfortunately, afterward I was called up to his office and was reprimanded, my judgment was questioned, and now I realize that I've ended up on his shit list.

So, what did you learn from this?

I learned that even when the boss asks for some honest feedback, I should express myself carefully and respectfully. Considering his ego, I should always give negative feedback when it's just the two of us, instead of doing it in front of the whole team.

So, what do you say? Shall we try it? Devote a few minutes to this before you go on reading. I guarantee that you'll find useful insights when you consider the lessons you can learn.

My mistake	What I learned from it

As you can see, making mistakes is not all negative. There's a lot of knowledge to be gained here. Once you discover that you've made a mistake, big or little, you'll find that this is an opportunity to learn new things, to adjust your behavior or change your attitude, or whatever it might be.

As usual, this is easier said than done. You need to train yourself so that you consciously improve your ability to approach mistakes in this way. It might take a while before it comes naturally, but that doesn't mean you should stop trying. Just like learning to drive, it's difficult at first. But after a while you don't even think about everything you do behind the steering wheel. You just do it.

Don't let a fear of mistakes paralyze you. That would be the very worst mistake of all.

Welcome to Laterville!

Imagine that you've had a phenomenal idea. You've thought up something truly valuable. Perhaps it's a business idea; perhaps it's something that could jump-start your career; perhaps it's as simple as starting that DIY project you and your partner have dreamed about for so long.

STARTING . . . SOON

This idea is so brilliant and so urgent, it's so important and so critical to your future . . . that you simply have to think it through just one more time.

You need to wait for the right opportunity. Maybe the weather could be better. Later on might be a good time to roll up your sleeves. When you feel stronger, more rested, more motivated. When the planets are aligned or when the recession is over. When taxes are lowered or prices raised. Yes, soon . . .

So you put this brilliant project aside for future use. Now and then, you'll remember your idea, but it never feels like the right moment.

Or you don't have time. Or it's hard to determine whether it really is a good idea or not.

And after a while, you don't think about it anymore. Now it's gone. It has disappeared into eternity and gone to the graveyard of good intentions.

You don't even notice that you have moved to a place called Laterville.

WHERE IS LATERVILLE?

Laterville is inside every person. All of us have an address there. We run away to Laterville when we should do a particular task but don't feel like it at the moment. This is where we wait, waffle, plan, think. And remain passive.

In Laterville, everything looks just great on the surface. Everything more or less works as it should, and nothing really seems to need to be changed. There is a deceptive calm. There is no hurry, no stress. It's where you can be yourself awhile. Nothing is especially important here. You have what you need and you're not living a bad life. On the contrary, you're comfortable, really comfortable. So there's no hurry. Everything is going to happen—later. The problem with Laterville is primarily that you feel satisfied here.

WHO DO YOU MEET THERE?

The other inhabitants of Laterville, of course. They don't think that there's much of a hurry, either. They agree that it's time to take things easy and reflect on life before you throw yourself into something you don't even know much about. They, too, have ideas and ambitions. Drawers stuffed full of them, in fact. They are not shy about talking about their grandiose plans. They're absolutely going to use all those wonderful ideas. But later. Much later. In Laterville, everybody speaks the same dialect. And it is a very disheartening tongue.

> *That great idea I had in May, I'm going to write it down—later.*
> *Yes, sure it's time to start visiting the gym—later.*
> *I'm really going to start putting some money aside for that*
> *   project—later.*
> *That training course sounds interesting. I'm going to apply for*
> *   a place—later.*
> *At last, my dream job opened up! Of course I'll call the boss of*
> *   the company—later.*
> *Now I really am going to visit my mother—later.*
> *We should start having date nights, my partner and I—later.*

The problem with Laterville is that it's an incredibly large town. A gigantic metropolis. In fact, Laterville is almost unnaturally overpopulated. The majority of all the people you've ever met have an address of their own there; they often visit and meet in gardens, at cafés, at lunch spots, or at home with each other—and discuss everything that they are going to do later in life. They sit and dream awhile.

I'll do it later.

Always later.

Later.

Later.

Later.

Often they don't even do that. They just do what they've always done. And that's why they get the same results that they've always gotten.

But not you. Oh, no, you have ambitions. You want more.

IS IT POSSIBLE TO GET AWAY FROM LATERVILLE?

If you want to move away from the paralyzing situation in Laterville, you need to sell the house you have there. Put it on the market. But that's the least of your problems. I promise you, the house isn't going to be on the market long before someone makes an attractive offer. Because a lot of people want to live there. They really like it in Laterville. It's an insidious place and far too easy to be drawn to.

Few of the inhabitants in Laterville are ever going to succeed at anything extraordinary. That doesn't mean that there aren't any honest taxpayers here, certainly not. A lot of them work hard, don't fool yourself. And there's nothing wrong with working hard. But their true ambitions and even their dreams are hidden under a sluggish, indifferent veneer of imagined satisfaction. Once these people have moved to Laterville, they behave as if they've left life behind them. Some are just waiting to retire.

This isn't about folks who have been physically exhausted from manual labor or years of hard work; that's a different situation, and as a society we should support them.

I suspect that so many look forward to retirement because they don't *want* to work. But why don't they? Because they don't feel like they're doing anything meaningful. Their present jobs don't give them anything. Their workplaces are dysfunctional, their bosses are bastards, and their coworkers are (to be honest) not much better. Why would anybody want to keep working there? Or maybe they only stay because of their coworkers, but the work itself is meaningless.

You might as well just buy a ticket to Laterville, where you can sit at the latest trendy café and grumble about the government, taxes, prices, companies, immigration, the weather, football, TV, or whatever you want as long as you don't need to take responsibility for your own situation.

WHAT IS LIFE LIKE IN LATERVILLE?

Slow. There's a striking fact about Laterville: leaving this place is not something you do just like *that*. You've surrounded yourself with people who support you in doing absolutely nothing. Otherwise you'd disturb things far too much. It's fine for you to be yourself, but if you stand out too much and give the impression of being unique in comparison with the rest of the inhabitants, then problems will come your way.

This is where you'll meet people who think it's way too wasteful to spend extra money on fresh produce, but who don't think twice about spending the same amount on snacks and beer.

Saving a hundred dollars a month is unthinkable for your neighbors in Laterville, but drinking or smoking up the same sum every week doesn't present a problem.

Fifty dollars month for a gym pass? Forget it. Sixty dollars a month on cable is, however, perfectly acceptable.

This is where you'll also find folks who think it's a waste to spend money on a weekend seminar or an educational program to help them grow and build their future, but who strangely enough buy the latest Gucci belt for three times as much.

In Laterville there are block after block of people who would never invest in their own businesses, but who would gladly pay that amount for an iPhone 88, or whichever version we're on. Because, you just *have* to have one.

But there are other priorities, too. Time works the same way here as it does everywhere else. Even here, there are twenty-four hours in a day.

In Laterville, you have neighbors who never have time to go to the gym. Because three to five hours a week is actually a lot of time. Nevertheless, they manage to fit in three hours of TV—every day.

In Laterville, you'll bump into acquaintances who think it's a hopeless project to find time to read, but who, for some reason, manage to squeeze in a couple of hours on Facebook, Instagram, and YouTube—every day.

Unfortunately, we also have parents who think it's too expensive to put aside some money for their daughter's college fund, but who can afford to travel to Thailand every year—on credit, with 20 percent interest.

If you ask your neighbors how to achieve your goals, the majority will have nothing to say. Goals? What do you mean? Walk up and down the street. Knock on the doors. Ask everyone who opens, *What are your goals in life, and what are you doing to get there?* They probably won't even understand the question. Let alone have an answer.

To put it bluntly: in Laterville, everyone is on their way to . . . nowhere.

I realize that this can sound elitist. But remember: I'm not saying that the inhabitants of Laterville are less worthy or important. That isn't what this is about. All people are important. It doesn't matter who we're talking about. Everybody has the same right to everything in our society. I am not saying this as a cliché, but because that is what I truly believe. Everybody should have the same opportunities.

But I am saying that their attitude to the world around them and to their own possibilities and goals is not going to help them move forward in life. They are missing the opportunities in front of them.

Do you really want to live in Laterville? Forever stuck in an environment where all that counts is the here and now, where future possibilities make up a cloudy vision that nobody really thinks about?

No, you don't want that. Because there are alternatives.

YOU'RE JUST AS WELCOME TO WINNERVILLE

Ah! Winnerville! This is a place with considerably fewer inhabitants than Laterville. And that means the prices are much higher, but oddly enough, there is always a rapid stream of people who move in here, too. And anybody is welcome to build a house here in Winnerville. Because there is lots of open land here.

People who live their dreams reside in Winnerville, people who make an incredible effort to realize their visions and who dream big. Who aren't afraid of all the work that is involved in realizing their dreams. Who, when their neighbor buys a nicer car, immediately go across and congratulate them on the purchase and ask to go on a test ride with them. And think to themselves that perhaps they, too, ought to work hard so that they're able to afford such a nice car.

Here you are inspired by the success of others instead of intimidated by it. You would never scorn somebody's dreams or ambitions to go further. Instead of explaining why an idea won't work, your neighbors in Winnerville will immediately say, *Great idea. How are you going to make it happen?* And they will often offer to help you.

Here people see possibilities. They dare to believe in change, but accept that you must work for it. They realize that a serious plan for the future needs to involve more than five lottery tickets every Saturday. Everybody in Winnerville has worked to get there. Nobody got there via an inheritance, or won their way in by chance.

In Winnerville, they know that not only millionaires are self-made. They understand that everybody is self-made. But only the successful ones admit it.

WHAT DO THE STREETS OF WINNERVILLE LOOK LIKE?

Winnerville is where all the successful entrepreneurs live. The elite athletes. The managing directors and authors and doctors and lawyers and businessmen and everyone who has been successful in their particular spheres. The best in any field you can think of all live here.

But the single nursing assistant who—despite the fact that she must support her ailing mother—manages to put aside a little for the future also lives here.

The refugee who refused to give up after his job application was rejected 784 times and who now works at the local bank lives here as well.

The person with dyslexia who, after being labeled as stupid during twelve years at school, now runs his own business with two hundred employees has also built a lovely home here.

In Winnerville, amid the new IT billionaires, you will find the author who, after a half lifetime of refusals, managed to get published.

You'll find the swimmer who won the local championship despite the fact that she has no arms.

The woman who after years of abuse found the courage to report her husband to the police and who is now brave enough to leave the house after it gets dark—where does she live? In Winnerville.

Anybody could be your neighbor in Winnerville—from the person who was refused a bank loan to start his business and instead got an extra job as a cleaner at night to save enough money and now owns a chain of thirty gyms with one hundred employees . . . to the cancer patient who was told she had no chance of survival and five years later is busy training for the New York City Marathon.

THIS IS WHERE ALL THE PEOPLE WHO BELIEVE IN THEMSELVES LIVE

In Winnerville you'll find everyone who has chosen to believe in themselves rather than listen to others. Those who refused to believe that it was impossible, and now stand there stronger than even they themselves dared hope.

Winnerville is a wonderful place to be. When folks get together in the evenings, they don't talk about other people. They don't gossip about who said what about this and that, who divorced whom. They talk about ideas, possibilities, and they always have the future in clear focus.

They don't talk about problems and they don't complain very much. Instead, they discuss how things could be improved.

Naturally some worries are aired, and in Winnerville you can often find people who have suffered adversity in life. But the interesting thing is, since they live in Winnerville and not Laterville, they always get up again when life knocks them down. That might also be why they ended up in Winnerville. They don't carry all the world's woes on their shoulders. They accept that sometimes they're going to lose, and they learn from their mistakes. Instead of banging their heads into the bricks that are thrown at them, they build staircases and bridges.

And they don't laugh at others who've met with misfortune. Instead, they give them a helping hand, because they know that the next time it might be them who are in need of help.

To put it briefly, in Winnerville people are happy, quite often just as happy as in Laterville. And I wouldn't be surprised if they actually feel a lot better.

IDEAS IN WINNERVILLE

Imagine the following scenario: For several years you've observed that your department is lacking in certain ways. This or that system doesn't work perfectly, and you've talked endlessly with your colleagues about why nobody does anything about it. A lot of time has been wasted debating the problem, particularly whose fault it is that the situation came about in the first place.

But one morning you wake up with an idea. Suddenly you see the solution! Why didn't you think of that before? Of course, you don't have all the details completely worked out quite yet. You're not sure how to go about it. But you feel in your whole body that you have just stumbled across something very important. But how do you launch the whole thing? Start something on your own? This is new territory for you.

Imagine that you raise the question with a good friend in Winnerville. Perhaps a neighbor. You describe the whole situation, share about your idea, and voice your justifiable fears.

Your neighbor is going to say that you should give it a try. It sounds like an excellent idea. When you say that you've never done anything like this before, he'll point out the obvious: nobody who tries something for the first time has done it before.

When you say that you're worried that you don't have enough money to move forward, he talks about how he started his own business. For three years the family didn't have a car, he says. Now they have three cars, and all of them have British names. They didn't go on vacation, they didn't even go to the movies. But today he runs a flourishing business with lots of employees. He lives in the prettiest house on the street, and his children see him more than ever because he can afford to be at home three days a week. And they travel wherever they want, when they want.

Perhaps you mention to this successful neighbor that you don't know how you will find the time. He asks you how many hours a week your ordinary job takes. When you say forty, he'll laugh and say, *Well that's excellent—you're free Saturday and Sunday! Not to mention all your weekday evenings. And with less time in front of the TV, you can always start on a small scale. Just go for it,* says your friend.

But what if it goes completely sideways? you say.

Yes, that could happen, says your friend. *But then you'll have gained experience if it does.*

Besides, since he knows how hard it can be to build your own business, he offers to help. He encourages you to ask whatever questions you might have. If he can help you, he'll be happy to. Because however busy he may be, he can always find a little more time. Your friend in Winnerville knows how to handle time.

That's another thing about the people of Winnerville. They help one another. They don't sit and smolder enviously about their neighbor's new car. No, they understand that it's important to build networks. Who knows, perhaps you will repay the favor someday?

Try it! What's the worst that can happen?

. . . AND IN LATERVILLE . . .

What would happen if you woke up that same morning in Laterville? Same company, same background, exactly the same irritation at the failings in your workplace. And the same brilliant idea has just appeared in your head.

Full of energy, you describe this business idea to your friend while you drink your Friday beer. Because it's finally happy hour and he wants to unwind, he listens with only half an ear. But once he understands—perhaps you work together—that you have a good idea, he says helpfully:

But you're not an entrepreneur! You work in the office/storeroom/ outdoors.

But it's a great idea, isn't it? you counter. He immediately wonders how you're going to finance the whole thing. It sounds like you will have to invest lots of money. Your own money. Waste of time asking the bank. They don't lend money to small businesses, anyway. Everybody knows what the banks are like. Damned bloodsuckers. You can lose everything. Have to sell your house. Think about your family. Don't do it.

Now you'll have to listen to a story about somebody's brother-in-law and a terrible interest rate, but after that you try again.

Your friend insists that it isn't going to work, because if it had been a good idea, then somebody would already have done it. Ergo, it must be a bad idea. Now let's have another beer.

Your buddy confides in you that you need to have contacts and connections to get anywhere. Without the right network, the project is doomed. Who do you even know? While you search for an answer, he blurts out, *Somebody has to actually buy what you sell. Have you sold anything before?* No? Just as he thought.

Now you, too, start to think that the idea sounds stupid.

But your friend hasn't finished with you yet. He gives you the coup de grâce.

How would you find time to do all the work required? You already do some overtime, and you need to give yourself a bit of free time. If you insist and say that you think it would take five years to become really successful, he's going to laugh his head off.

Five years! Are you crazy? Then you'll be five years older than today!

The fact that by then both of you will be five years older regardless of what you choose to do with your time doesn't bother him. He doesn't think that way. He is too problem-oriented. He can't see the goal. There is no vision. His thinking is far too narrow.

Instead of supporting you and helping you think up solutions, he tells anyone at the bar who will listen what an idiot he works with. By the time everyone has finished laughing, you'll regret that you ever mentioned that stupid idea.

They're right. Since you've never succeeded before, what makes you think you'd succeed with this project? What were you thinking?

Note: Your friend at the bar in Laterville might be intelligent, friendly, a good dad to his children, hardworking, a well-educated fellow, and a faithful taxpayer. That isn't what this is about. It's about his narrow thinking. His attitude is wrong. He sees only problems and doesn't want you to succeed.

He restricts you and provides all the arguments you'll ever need to put off your brilliant idea.

The next morning, your idea is put aside and forgotten.

But . . . two years after the thought: *Shouldn't somebody do something about this problem?* flitted through your head, you see an advertisement for exactly that same thing. Somebody has solved the problem exactly the way you imagined and is now in the process of building a future for herself based on that one idea.

And then you are going to regret not going ahead. Oh boy, are you going to regret it.

All of this might sound a bit harsh. I realize that. And perhaps I've really annoyed you now.

Good. Because I want you to react. And keep on reading.

Because I have a confession to make: for many years, I lived in Laterville.

My Life in Laterville

I had a big house in Laterville. A posh address. A typical Laterville neighborhood. No one in the family was suffering. We were doing okay. But not much happened. I rarely thought about the future. Instead, I acted based on what would happen next week or possibly next month. And, sure, it worked. We had food on the table.

What's really unnerving about this is that I don't know when I moved into Laterville. I don't have any clear memory of how I ended up there. When—after a series of random events—I finally moved out, I realized the truth. I turned around and looked at the place where I had spent the first forty years of my life.

Everyone who's known me for a long time knows that I've always worked a lot. Worked hard. I've never had an issue with that. I'm happy to arrive at work a bit early and stay at it past working hours. Work the odd Sunday now and then. That never bothered me. It was about taking responsibility and doing what was right. Everyone who knew me in those days would probably say that Thomas Erikson worked hard. But did he work smart?

When I think back to how many years I wasted working without any clear direction, I can get really angry. At what, you may ask? At myself, of course. It's no one else's fault that I ended up in Laterville, where life is on cruise control and ordinary is good. I moved there of my own free will.

Or, to be more specific, the lack of my own will.

Perhaps I wasn't actually unhappy in Laterville. I just . . . was.

There's no one to blame other than myself. When I try to figure out what I was thinking, all I can say is that I probably didn't think at all. I didn't have a plan for anything. In fact, I didn't take any responsibility at all.

Although that's not right, either, when I think about it. Just like most of my neighbors in Laterville, I planned my vacations in far more detail that I planned my career. Or my life, for that matter.

Let's look at that sentence again:

I planned my vacations in far more detail than I planned my career.

WHAT HAPPENS WHEN YOU DON'T PUT ON YOUR THINKING CAP

I'll avoid saying something clichéd, like, *You have lots of vacations but only one life,* but you know that's true.

Why didn't I take life more seriously? There's no intelligent answer to that question. In some moments, I think back to my childhood, and, God help me, my friendly and totally supportive parents were simply . . . too kind. Sometimes I wish that they'd given me a kick in the pants and demanded a little more.

But it doesn't make a difference how it happened that I worked hard year after year without a larger plan or any true direction. I suspect that I did it because everybody else did it. My parents did it, all my relatives did it. Everyone I ever knew did exactly the same thing. We were busy working without thinking about the future.

During my adult life, I've had lots of brilliant ideas, thousands of sparkling fantasies and possibilities. But I never picked up the shovel and started to dig to see what was there.

Because that wasn't what you did in Laterville. You just worked, picked up your kids from school, ate dinner, watched TV for a while, and then went to bed.

Good night.

I didn't have any goals for myself. If anyone had asked me where I planned to be in five years, I would have laughed and just waved the question away. Five years, are you crazy? How could I possibly know that?

Because in Laterville they never ask questions like that. They look sideways at everyone who doesn't stick to the norm. They call entrepreneurs "workaholics." People who stay in good shape and go running every morning for an hour are "gym freaks." People who say "no thanks" to an extra glass of wine are "killjoys." They glare at anybody who stands out and has a good career, or who earns a lot of money or rises in status.

How do I know all this? Well, I did it myself.

THE ANNOYING EXAMPLE OF THE
SNEAKY SOCIAL CLIMBER

Once one of my neighbors replaced his car at the same time that he bought a huge new motorcycle. A Harley-Davidson to be exact. It must have cost him a ton. Rumors around town also said that the whole family had gone on a Mediterranean cruise. How disconcerting! The family lived in a house roughly the same as the one we lived in. They had led a completely normal life up until this new state of things. And I suddenly noticed that he irritated me when he waved cheerfully from across the street. Didn't he suddenly look a bit stuck up? My own smile was definitely pasted on.

Why was that?

The guy could now afford nicer things. And, in secret, that disturbed me. I'm not proud of it—it makes me look like an envious bastard—but I did compare myself to him.

Over dinner, we speculated resentfully about how it had happened. How could the neighbors suddenly afford both a new car and a motorcycle? And how come they were off on vacation all the time? His wife hardly ever left the house! How was all of this possible?

I guessed that his windfall was probably inherited money. If it wasn't an inheritance, it could only be a lottery prize. What other explanation could there possibly be? Because he couldn't have earned it, surely. Not with the way he looked. Or with the education he presumably had. And since I'd talked with him, I knew that the guy wasn't particularly smart. He had a bit of a one-track mind, even though he wasn't exactly stupid.

Is there anything more irritating than a person who you know is less smart than you does better in life than you? It's infuriating.

Then they moved away.

Phew!

What a relief it was when I saw the moving truck pull out of their driveway. At last I could relax a little. Soon, the balance in the Laterville district was restored. A different, ordinary—and hopefully deep in debt—family moved in. Life returned to normal. Those happy, lucky social climbers had only made people feel bad.

Later I learned that the wife had started an online business and sold dog food. That was probably where their extra money came from. That was in the days when the internet was fairly new, and nobody really knew where it was going. But instead of thinking *Aha, that's the explanation,* I found it even more annoying. I'd thought about starting a business on the internet. Only later.

My frustration wasn't about them, not really. While I burrowed deeper into the bedrock of Laterville, this family pushed its boundaries. And managed to do well enough to upgrade their lifestyle a bit.

What did I do? I was thinking. Waiting for the right time. I wasn't exactly planning, but I put all sorts of ideas neatly on a shelf where I could look at them when I had time. I was so smart that it was bound to work out. As soon as the right opportunity turned up, I'd be on my way. Everything would sort itself out—later.

This family had an idea, put it into practice, and found success.

And here comes an important insight: The universe couldn't care less who intends to do what. All that counts is what you actually do.

The most complicated combination lock in the whole world can still be opened by someone. You just have to have the right code. If you have the combination, your background, your last name, or your education doesn't make any difference. All that counts is what you *do*.

In Laterville, there's far too little constructive thinking. Life just trundles along. And when somebody does do something, the rest of us try to explain why they probably should have refrained from doing it. If they don't listen, and they end up in the ditch, then we can point a finger at them and say I told you so. And if they, to everybody's dismay, become really successful, then we hope that they move the heck out of here as soon as possible.

WINNERVILLE OR LATERVILLE?

The great thing about your future hometown is that you are in charge. The decision to test your wings is entirely in your hands. It's up to you. And you know it.

You can choose how you will see the possibilities that are right in front of your nose.

If you don't want to tell me or anyone else just now, put down the book and go into the nearest bathroom. Look at yourself really closely in the mirror and say out loud in a firm voice:

I choose to live in Winnerville.

That's it. Now you've made a decision that I want to congratulate you for. From now on, nothing is going to be like it was before. The world is at your feet.

You can, of course, also say to yourself in the mirror, *I choose to live in Laterville.* That's fine by me. What's important is that you make an active choice and don't just let things fall where they may while you surf the internet for the latest football scores.

What's so great about *that* Laterville decision is you can now close this book and save several hours of your time. This book is written for those who want to get away from Laterville and find a nice place in Winnerville. Give the book to somebody who wants to get somewhere.

Or keep on reading and see what can happen when you actually pack your boxes and move from one place to the other.

A shark in an aquarium will never reach its natural size. Its growth will always adjust to the environment it's living in. If you release the shark into the sea, it might not grow into the size of the one in *Jaws,* but it will get a great deal bigger than in the aquarium.

The same thing applies to you and me. If we change our environments, then we can grow much more than when we're surrounded by the wrong people.

SUMMARY

Sleeping your way through life is comfortable, but it doesn't work well. Or, well, I suppose it actually does, which is the very kernel of this problem. Shutting your eyes to real life does work.

But is it the best life you can experience?

No. There is always more to see and do: more things to experience and great things to achieve if you don't just wander along. But this demands that we actively think about our situation and sort out how we want to live.

It's not a failure to live all your life in Laterville. But think about it: if you could drive a (fill in your dream car) instead of your ten-year-old (fill in what you have in your garage right now), wouldn't you like that?

If you'd rather spend your winter vacation with your family in (fill in your dream holiday) instead of staying at home with Auntie G—wouldn't you like that?

If you could sleep well at night instead of waking up virtually every night worrying that your marriage might be falling apart—what would you choose?

If you could avoid that sinking feeling every month when the bills arrive, and instead could be blown over by the wonderful thought that you can put some money into the kids' college funds this month—wouldn't that be great?

If, instead of looking away when a homeless man asks for a few dollars, you could donate monthly to a shelter—wouldn't that feel better?

Even if you live a perfectly okay life today and nobody in your family is suffering—what would it be like to explore your real potential?

(Not) Working Smarter

One of the big problems in Laterville is that a lot of people there live with the delusion that there is an endless amount of time. The problem: there isn't. Time is the most limited resource you have. It's the only resource that can never be replaced. Nobody can get more time. Nobody. Let's look at the effects of wasting your time.

We often assume that success involves working harder. Much harder. Harder than anyone else, in fact.

Sure, it's hard to become phenomenally successful by being completely lazy. Very few success stories have been written by sitting on the sofa and scratching your head. Laziness is hardly the key. But the solution? Is it really to work harder than everybody else?

Hmm. There's nothing wrong with working hard, but I am convinced that you know lots and lots of people who work extremely hard—you might even be one of them—but they don't get anywhere. They just stay where they are, treading water, doing the same job year after year. They've found their spot in life and now they devote all their energy to it. And that's perfectly alright. But as I wrote in the introduction to this book, I assume that you're reading this because you want to grow and move forward.

It's about working smarter.

The key is what you do with your time. It's almost guaranteed, if you handled your time better you could be enormously more productive than you currently are. Time is the golden variable that you need to learn to master.

THE MOST IMPORTANT FACTOR FOR SUCCESS: STOP SQUANDERING YOUR TIME

There have been so many studies on our efficiency that we're all sick and tired of hearing about them. We don't need yet another scientific report to tell us what we already feel with our whole body: most of the time we are not efficient.

But success is fundamentally about using your time to do exactly the right thing. Because when that time ends . . . there is no more time.

My advice is: don't squander your time!

Nowadays, I am incredibly careful about how I spend a day. With whom and why. My mailbox is forever full. The telephone rings; social media sometimes boils over; all my channels of communication are filled with demands on my time.

There are studies and statistics that say that really successful people say no to virtually everything. Interesting, isn't it? Warren Buffett, one of the richest men in history, evidently says no to 99 percent of the opportunities he is offered.

THE EASIEST WAY TO LOSE FOCUS

You open your web browser to check something quickly, a little detail connected with a job you're working on right now. Unfortunately, your home page is some news website, and it is amazing at concocting snappy headlines. You get ensnared in a fascinating article about Kim Kardashian's backside, something that, naturally, *has* to be read immediately. This links to another article, one about her sister's new Mercedes. This tempts you to look at cars online. Soon, you know all about the latest, fabulously expensive Mercedes. This reminds you that you need to take your own fabulously inexpensive car in for an oil change. But where's the best place to go?

You start looking at different mechanics nearby to see if you can reserve a time online, which means checking your calendar and realizing that you probably can't get the oil change done during work hours because you have so incredibly much that you have to get done. This reminds you of a deadline that is threateningly close. Now your thoughts are back on your work, but not at all on the task you were originally working on.

And as if by magic, you've wasted half an hour of your day on . . . nothing. If you're the average person, you will probably feel a bit sheepish at this point. You might even feel a bit guilty. You don't get paid to read up on the Kardashians. But this is how our brains work, and some of us have chosen to take advantage of that.

You don't need to take my word for it. Read the work of Swedish doctor and brain researcher Katarina Gospic. She knows about these things.

A lot of our time is spent surfing the internet, but that is far from the only thing that steals time from what you should be focusing on. Below is a list of possible time thieves in your life, which will use up altogether too many of your (approximately) seven hundred thousand hours here on planet Earth:

- all social media—no exceptions
- everything on TV, on every channel day and night—including the news (especially the news)

- video games, computer games, phone games, online casinos, and online poker
- commuting—traveling, i.e., not the destination
- bad planning, your own or somebody else's
- partying too late the night before
- sleeping too long the day after
- only reading for pleasure
- drinking coffee and chatting with your colleagues instead
  of working
- virtually every meeting you are going to participate in—
  ever
- sitting in your yard all summer, drinking beer and complaining about the government

There is nothing wrong with any of the "activities" in the list above. But if you want to achieve something specific in life, then these activities are not going to get you there.

However you define success—inner harmony, a stress-free existence, economic independence, a strong body, better health, a loving relationship, wonderful children, a brilliant career, a spiritual experience, saving enough money so that your children won't have to take a loans out for college, being debt free—these things aren't going to get you there.

SO WE DON'T GET TO HAVE ANY FREE TIME?

As you've seen, a lot of what I consider time thieves are actually forms of entertainment. TV shows, listening to music, reading books, surfing the internet. We need to allow ourselves recreation and entertainment. We need to rest and do things that are just for fun. But when you lack a deeper meaning in your day-to-day life, you often distract yourself with simple, short-term entertainment. Unfortunately, such pleasures can leave a bitter aftertaste. The challenge is to amuse yourself "just enough"—i.e., take time to rest and have fun, but don't let these things mindlessly consume your life.

There is evidence that we truly do need to take breaks, get an energy boost, or rest awhile. But resting is, as I see it, a way of finding the strength to go further in the direction you want to go. Rest is not a goal in itself.

This is a critical insight.

REST IS A MEANS—NOT A GOAL

Neither our bodies nor our brains function at their best when at rest. Nature never intended us to sit on a sofa and stare at a screen, no matter what may be on it.

Nature designed us for activity! Especially physical activity. If you are physically active, you function better mentally. There's no doubt that the physical and the mental are connected. Of all the successful people I've met, the vast majority have been physically active. They go to the gym, they run, play tennis, go skiing, and do all sorts of other things. Body and mind undoubtedly belong together. Don't you believe me? Read *The* Real *Happy Pill* by Dr. Anders Hansen.

If you want to achieve something that is important to you—build your own company, train your body, educate yourself for your dream job, make a career, find your dream house, renovate a summer cottage or that vintage car you've always dreamed about, make a fortune, or get your children into the right schools—then you have to take action first. Make a list of what needs to be done, and work your way through it.

Once you've started and are working toward your dream, you can take a bit of time off. I'm definitely a fan of treating oneself. But like in every job, you don't get paid if you don't do the work.

Accomplishment first, reward afterward.

Do the job first, then rest.

Could it be simpler?

The frustrating truth is that it is that simple. And yet we don't always manage to do it.

DO YOU GET PAID BEFORE OR AFTER THE PERFORMANCE?

When I hold certain types of workshops, I ask the group what they would pick if they could choose between two alternatives:

1. To be paid on January 1 (in advance) and then work for the whole year
2. To get paid on December 31 the same year, that is, in arrears, or after the work is done

Naturally, everybody answers January 1. We don't like waiting. The problem is, of course, once I've been paid I don't really want to do the job. What happens then?

Imagine a one-hundred-meter sprinter who starts a world-championship sprint with a victory party. She's carried into the arena on a throne, wrapped in her country's flag—before the final race. The crowd cheers! She's lifted up on the podium and receives her gold medal. The sponsorship contracts are waiting in her hotel room. When she steps down from the platform, she puts on her running shoes and stretches. She lines up with her nine most fearsome competitors from the whole world. They glare at her. Now there is just one tiny detail left—to actually win the race.

You might be thinking, *What an idiotic example!*

Are you sure about that?

WHEN YOU REST FIRST

Imagine that you run a little business with a handful of employees. They arrive at work at eight o'clock in the morning, and the first thing they do is drink coffee and chat for fifteen minutes. Then half of them go out for a smoke. Then it's time for lunch, followed by a coffee break. Then they need another smoke break, right? After that, they make some private phone calls, check out some vacation cottages on the internet, check up on the sports results, and wander around in the building for a total of half an hour hunting for a missing stapler.

You observe this bizarre scene with a mixture of fascination and horror. At half past four, when you ask them what they've been doing, since they certainly haven't done a bit of work all day, they answer:

It's no problem! We just like to get paid first. We're going to work really hard from 11 P.M. to 5 A.M.

The psychology is exactly the same as for the hundred-meter sprinter. It looks crazy when you think about it.

A Really Stupid Example

January begins with everybody taking a full holiday for five or six weeks. Then they combine all the rest of the free days (all the weekends, holidays, and a bundle of sick days). In Sweden, we end up with something like 135 days per person. If you—the employer—aren't already having a breakdown due to the stress, you'll welcome your employees to work sometime in May—135 days into the year.

The same psychology again, but on a larger scale. And when this interesting group of employees eventually comes to work, they'll have to have coffee and lunch first, of course. Because they want to do the fun stuff first.

Why Not Take It to the Extreme While We're at It?

Let's assume that you live to be 80. We won't count the first twenty years, because you were in school. But once you start at your job when you are 20, you'll immediately ask for and take those 135 free days per year, up until you plan to stop working at age 67. That means . . . that you don't need to physically present yourself at your workplace for another 6,345 days, i.e., when you are 37.4 years old. Unfortunately, now you're in for a serious amount of work and no breaks whatsoever. Just work until the very end.

I know. Nobody does that.

That's an extreme example of trying to get your reward first. You can't build a society on that mentality, but nevertheless we both know that many people find it hard to do the work because they're looking for quick rewards.

So when do you need to put your boots on and get the work done? That's the question we all have to ask ourselves. It's better to wait for the reward than to enjoy it in advance.

SUMMARY

How much time do you waste? You can't re-create time. When it's gone, it's gone. Time is your most limited resource. Every time you use an hour on the wrong thing, you're squandering your most valuable resource.

People who learn to handle time so that time itself works for, instead of against them, are going to be successful. Regardless of how they choose to define success.

But a person who never has control of his time is never going to be fully successful. That person is going to meet setback . . . after setback . . . after setback . . .

Dare to Notice What Doesn't Work

In order to avoid setbacks, we need to take a look at what doesn't work—the small warning signals that I touched on very briefly in chapter 2. If you notice them in time, they might only indicate slight bumps on the journey to success, little setbacks rather than big ones. If you wait to address them, the problems can grow until they're too large to solve.

If you consider your situation (for the moment it's irrelevant whether you live in Winnerville or Laterville) and you notice something is off, that might be a warning sign.

And there are a lot of them, once we start looking.

For example, let's think about your job. If it's Sunday afternoon and you start to feel irritated, tired, or just sick, it says something about your attitude toward your job. You might not hate your job, but these bodily reactions signal that something is wrong. According to international studies, most serious heart attacks in the West happen in the mornings. Mondays are also the worst day. The second most common is evidently Sunday evenings. Why is that?

Is it because you're actually working in a poisonous and aggressive environment? Or is your boss a bastard? You might say that there aren't any other job openings available, and while that might be true, it still won't help your physical and mental health. It might only make the matter worse.

Your work environment is just one of the areas we need to take a good look at.

If you run your own business, do you accept that your profits have gone down by 30 percent, or do you pretend that everything is just great?

If you don't feel well physically, have you done the work to discover why?

Relationships are particularly difficult.

Some people make excuses for a dysfunctional marriage. They don't want to see their partner's negative behavior in the light of day. They shut their eyes to how their teenagers speak to them. They have a good friend who's in the process of wrecking her own life, but they keep quiet because they convince themselves it's only a phase.

They mean well, but sometimes it all goes very wrong. And then you have to do something instead of continuing to live in denial.

HOW DO SUCCESSFUL PEOPLE DO IT?

Few individuals on this planet are more closely scrutinized than successful people. Shelves have been filled with books about entrepreneurs, athletes, best-selling writers, top bosses, investors, spiritual leaders, and anyone else who has achieved some sort of success. At the end of this book, there's a list of books you can read to find even more inspiration.

One thing is clear: these people encounter just as many problems and obstacles as you and I do. More, perhaps, because they very rarely sit still. The difference is that they don't deny what is happening around them. They don't shut their eyes and ignore trouble— regardless of whether it's a major problem or a little inconvenience.

Keeping track of obstacles is one of the things that made these people successful. Instead of pretending that a problem will soon pass, they start by trying to understand it, and then they work on solving it. And it doesn't make any difference how challenging or exhausting it is; they do it anyway.

The advantage of this attitude and behavior is obvious: by acting early when something is going off the rails, you can reduce considerably the negative consequences of the problem.

BEWARE OF YOUR OWN DEFENSE MECHANISMS

You'll remember the warning signals I mentioned earlier—small things that indicate that something isn't quite right. Your teenager comes home late again. Weird messages in your work inbox. A strange comment from a neighbor or friend. Somebody you care about smells of alcohol and it isn't even noon.

All too often we choose to pretend to be stupid or blind and ignore everything. We sweep all those unpleasant signs under the rug. This can be an effect of the defense mechanisms that our psyche uses to protect us.

All people have defense mechanisms when the pressure is too overwhelming. This often happens automatically. Defense mechanisms can be functional and, to an extent, beneficial, but there are also some tendencies that are unhelpful.

Functional defense mechanisms give us continued access to emotions and impulses. Sometimes, however, emotions and ideas and the consequences of our own actions completely pass us by. This can lead to serious problems if we're not attentive.

Different people use different types of self-protective mechanisms and may have several to choose from or only a handful. Relying on the same defense mechanisms, regardless of the situation, is not functional.

Repression quite often means self-deception. You try to repress unpleasant experiences from your conscious thoughts. However, you may find that you still feel anxious and worried even as you've made yourself ignore or forget the real reason behind your worry.

Intellectualization or *disassociation* happens when you observe a threat without involving your emotions. That way, you avoid worry and discomfort.

Rationalization involves attempting to justify an action or inaction as appropriate regardless of whether it actually was. Few people like to admit to failure, so they often respond by rationalizing and blaming the failure on external circumstances that they can't control. This can also often manifest as attempting to justify irrational behaviors.

Projection means that you unconsciously shift feelings and qualities onto others. You don't want to take the blame for what has happened, so you find other scapegoats. This also happens on a collective level and can be used by various types of leaders to demonize their opponents, for example. History is full of shocking examples.

Displacement occurs when your own worry, or perhaps anger, is transferred from the real cause to somebody else who gets the blame. Displacement is reminiscent of projection, but whereas projection is unconscious, here the person is (in a rather obscure way) aware of the process.

Humor can also be a defense mechanism. It helps reduce anxiety to be able to laugh in stressful situations. Thanks to the release of hormones, we feel physically and mentally better when we laugh, even though it still doesn't solve the actual problem.

Denial means that you reject the reality of the risks in your surroundings. You simply shut your eyes to a situation that is fully visible right in front of you. The everyday term for this phenomenon is "ostrich behavior."

WHAT DEFENSE MECHANISMS DO YOU USE?

Confronting things that don't work often means that you need to do something uncomfortable. You might need to build up your self-discipline; confront somebody who doesn't like you or whom you don't like; accept that there are going to be people who aren't going to like you or what you do; ask for something you need from somebody who has it; or demand respect instead of being trampled in a relationship.

But since you're an ordinary person, the last defense mechanism on the list, *denial,* is going to prevent you from acknowledging the truth. It's going to tell you that there isn't really a problem. And you'll do nothing to fix the situation, because it's not a problem. So let's take a look at the effects of denial.

SO WHAT DOES DENIAL LOOK LIKE?

You'll probably recognize most of the responses on this list, since you've heard and said them a thousand times:

- Teenagers these days are impossible to control.
- That has nothing to do with me.
- I mind my own business, and you should do the same.
- Don't rock the boat.
- That's how it should be; leave it alone.
- Everybody has credit-card debt.
- That's never going to happen to me.
- If I say anything, I might end up in trouble.
- In California, marijuana is legal.

- Meh—it's just a phase she's going through.
- I can't sleep without a glass of red wine.
- It's impossible to do everything in normal working hours.
- Keep quiet, and it will blow over.
- He said he would pay me back.

Sometimes, we make up reasons why something didn't work, instead of admitting that the situation wouldn't even have happened if we'd dealt with the warning signs in time. Being proactive when something starts going wrong is always better than "wait and see."

You don't need to feel like a failure if you've done this, because everyone else has, too. But you do need to change the way you handle certain situations so that you can avoid unnecessary setbacks. It's cheaper, simpler, and involves less conflict. You'll be a great deal more satisfied with yourself if you confront things as soon as you realize that something is off.

Success here would be to calmly observe a situation without making light of it or seeing it as worse than it is. Just evaluate what's happening and think of it as an opportunity to learn something.

In the business world, some companies are led by people who, instead of making the annual returns look better for the board of directors, actually find out why the sales figures for their biggest product have gone down the drain. They really do want to know why customer satisfaction has tanked. They're always asking which advertising campaigns are performing the best, and they're prepared to take a hard look at rising costs.

They approach things rationally and logically, not hiding or explaining away what happened. And that's totally different than searching for scapegoats.

DENIAL IN EVERYDAY LIFE

In 2019, an American study showed—brace yourself—that 75 percent of all employees hate their jobs. Do you have your dream job? If you do, then I want to congratulate you.

But if you don't have your dream job, what are you currently doing to get it? Or are you living in denial? Are you one of those people who go around singing the praises of your own job and praise your employer every time you get the chance? And if you are, is that genuine, or are you trying to ignore the fact that you would rather do something completely different?

Workaholics often live a lie. An extremely packed calendar doesn't work out well for anyone in the long term. But this gang often justifies it by saying that they earn loads of money, that the company demands it of them, that everybody else works just as hard, or whatever—anything so long as they don't have to question their own lifestyle.

Getting out of denial is tough. If it was simple, they'd have done it long ago.

DENIAL IS BASED ON FEAR

Often, denial is about the fear that something else could be much worse. If we act, perhaps everything will crash down around us. So it would be better to pretend there is nothing wrong.

While I wrote this book, I interviewed some psychologists who work in clinical psychology. Several of them said that they had clients who were masters at denying reality. Even if there was clear evidence that their partner was having an affair, they refused to confront the partner. They didn't want to accept the fact that the relationship was over. It was simply too much to contemplate.

Think about your own life. What situations are you reluctant to deal with? Are there examples on the list below that frighten you?

- Your boss always leaves work early but is happy to dump lots of last-minute projects on your desk.
- You have a business partner who doesn't seem to be really committed to the business.
- Your monthly bills are starting to add up to more than your salary.
- Your teenager smokes or uses drugs.
- Your aging parents need to be looked after.
- It hurts every time you pee.
- Your partner has started to withdraw and has become more condescending toward you recently.
- You never have time for things that you would like to have time for.

YOU DON'T NEED TO MOVE HEAVEN AND EARTH TO SOLVE THE PROBLEM

Some things are easy to deal with; others, not so much. But remember that the situations you've ignored up to this point don't necessarily need a radical solution. If you have problems at work, perhaps you don't need to change jobs. Sometimes it's a question of addressing a particular issue with the right person. If there are problems in your relationships at home, talking them out is often a big step in the right direction.

My point is that if you deal with these types of situations as soon as you see them, and *don't wait* for them to disappear of their own accord, then dramatic measures are rarely needed. Most of the time, ordinary, simple methods are perfectly adequate.

But it starts by accepting that some situations aren't working. See them for what they are. And then act.

I'll say that again.

Act.

ACT NOW, NOT LATER

Make a concrete list of things that you have ignored/denied up until now. Write down three things you know need to be dealt with, but that you've chosen not to pay attention to.

Pick the simplest. (It's better to start with something small, like finally touching up that scuff on the living room wall, than with something big, like asking your thirty-six-year-old son to finally move out.)

Then write down three actions for each problem that will help correct the situation.

I asked my old friend Stefan, from the far north of Sweden, to help me with examples. He definitely tends to put things off. He's a great guy, competent and ambitious, but he has a pathological pattern of waiting things out when something isn't working right. This is what he wrote:

What I Tend to Ignore

My boss has started to hover around my desk and ask when I'm going to finish one of the projects I'm working on. I know this is because I virtually never make my deadlines. It's always been like that, and I hate talking about it. That's just how I am.

What I Need to Do to Deal with the Problem

1. I need to talk to my boss. I need to admit that I'm aware of the problem, but that I've been avoiding it for years.

2. After that, I need to ask her to help me keep to my deadline by taking a few things off my plate so I can focus undisturbed on the project. I'm easily distracted by everything else that happens and often lose track of big goals in favor of smaller tasks.

3. Then I need to talk with somebody who is good at meeting deadlines and ask if he or she can show me how to approach the projects.

These are all things that won't get anybody fired. And if Stefan follows his extremely simple plan, he'll avoid a lot of headaches and anxiety. The challenge here is Stefan's Yellow behavior. He finds it hard to stick to a plan, regardless of how good it is.

Now it's your turn! Be honest with yourself. There's no point in trying to fool yourself. The only person who suffers from that is you.

What I Tend to Deny

What I Need to Do to Deal with the Problem

1. _____

2. _____

3. _____

It doesn't have to be any more complicated than that. Make sure that you really define the problem and that the steps you list actually solve the problem in question. Then make sure you carry out the first step on the list. Write it down in your calendar. Right now. I promise you that you're going to feel relieved, satisfied, happy, and proud of yourself when you've done what you need to do. Then deal with number 2, and once that's done, move on to number 3.

Break the bad habit of letting denial be a part of your everyday life. Choose to act, and then just do it. Once you've created the habit of action, possibilities that you can't even imagine will open up for you. That's a promise.

I had to pep Stefan up a couple of times before he found the courage to go to his boss, clutching the sheet of paper. Instead of saying what he came to say, he simply handed the sheet of paper to his boss. She read through it all carefully, got up, and gave him a big hug. She was happy to not have to raise the problem herself with Stefan. She congratulated him on his self-awareness. Together, they solved the problem one step at a time. Of course, Stefan still sometimes procrastinates on difficult tasks, but not to the same extent as before.

SUMMARY

We all have things we know we need to do, but we hide behind various rational and irrational reasons for avoiding them. Sometimes, they're ordinary defense mechanisms. By learning to recognize the type of defense mechanisms we use, even very difficult things can become much easier.

You can train yourself to see warning signals. A simple method is to have your eyes open for changes in people's behaviors. It doesn't necessarily signal the end of the world, but when somebody changes his or her normal behavior, it might be a good idea to take a closer look.

If it turns out to be a false alarm—so much the better! Now you've saved yourself many sleepless nights!

In order to solve the problem, you often have to do something you're not accustomed to doing, which in turn means that you need to be willing to leave your comfort zone.

Leaving Your Comfort Zone

I just mentioned that behind denial there is often some sort of fear. Fear governs us more than we're aware of. Oftentimes, the greatest setbacks are those we've imagined inside our heads, typically because we are afraid of something.

Fear can paralyze us. It can create a kind of passivity that can't be broken. Fear is dreadful, yet we all have fears. Most things outside our comfort zones make us uncertain, worried, and even afraid. What's interesting is that all of us have different-sized comfort zones. They are completely unique to the individual.

A while ago, I met Jeanette, who has been a security guard and bodyguard in extremely risky environments for more than twenty-five years. She has no problem stepping straight into potentially lethal situations in the middle of the night with who-knew-what kind of terrifying people hiding in the shadows. She has been, in countless times doing her job, threatened by every imaginable type of weapon. Not a pleasant work environment. It would scare most of us to death.

But Jeanette just shrugged her shoulders at that kind of fear. Just another day at the office. So she must not have been scared of anything, right?

In personal situations, however, she was afraid of saying what was on her mind. It was frightening to challenge people in her immediate vicinity, people she liked and met every day. But never wanting to leave your comfort zone, or only doing so with extreme reluctance, is limiting. The only way to grow or develop is to step outside it.

What about you? I'm sure that you've heard this before, so I won't elaborate too much. But in order to avoid unpleasantness, many people choose to stay in their comfort zones. It feels better there. Safer. Fewer risks. But at the same time, there's an almost total lack of development. It's a permanent move to Laterville.

And Laterville is where dreams die.

IS PESSIMISM ALWAYS BAD?

Mark Twain is reported to have said, "I am an old man and have known a great many troubles, but most of them have never happened."

If you aren't much of an optimist, then it sounds crazy to hear somebody chirp out, *Think positively!*

A few years ago, psychologist Mattias Lundberg and comedian Jan Bylund wrote an entertaining and illustrative book called *The Happy Pessimist*. To very briefly summarize, the authors have a thesis that for certain people it's actually better to think negatively, because that ensures that they will never be disappointed by the results. Even though that's not my personal attitude, I respect the fact that there are some people who think like that. The delightful thing about us humans is that not everything works for everybody.

CAN WE REALLY PROTECT OURSELVES
FROM EVERYTHING?

There's a strange attitude in society today that seems to prioritize avoiding potentially messy or troublesome situations above all else. You can't take risks, no matter the context. I touched on this earlier, and it's certainly no fun to experience fear. That's why many people protect their children from everything bad. Of course, I don't mean that we should subject our children to unnecessary risks, but to protect them from absolutely everything is simply not possible.

I don't mean to downplay the struggles of those who have experienced true suffering in life. But the expression "What doesn't kill you, makes you stronger" does indeed have some truth to it.

You remember the long list of my own setbacks in chapter 7. Besides the simple fact that, in retrospect, I couldn't have done much about many of the incidents on the list, they've also given me something. I have a certain sense of strength and protection against future setbacks that life might throw at me.

Trying to eliminate all potential future threats just doesn't work.

As a child, when I stood on the lowest diving board at the swimming pool and was about to jump a whole three feet, I was terrified. Why, I don't really know.

You can never get rid of fear. You've been in situations when you were genuinely afraid. And a well-meaning person promised you that there was nothing to be afraid of. Right? The problem is, there is. There are lots and lots of things to worry about, to be afraid of. And those things are always going to be there.

WHAT AM I AFRAID OF?

Personally, I always observe myself carefully when I realize I'm hesitating in the face of things that shouldn't be very complicated. These can be minor things, like making a particular phone call, or discussing something at home that might involve potential conflict, or spending money on a consultant I'm not sure of. When I feel reluctance about something, it's often because there's a difficulty somewhere, and it isn't always easy to see what that is.

None of these fears are particularly serious. Just like on the personal-setback ranking in chapter 7, you need to put things in perspective. Work-related things I feel nervous about are hardly deadly.

But fear, pure and simple? Well, I'm afraid . . .

> . . . that something will happen to my children: that they
> will get sick, lose their jobs, lose their faith in the future,
> or have their hearts broken by some bastard;
> . . . that something terrible will happen to my sister, despite
> her rock-solid positive view of the universe;
> . . . that I will get sick or too stressed or just such a pain
> to those around me, and my wife will leave me, and so
> on;
> . . . that I will never be able to finish another manuscript;
> . . . that my published books will never reach any readers;
> . . . that the app and the web courses I've produced will be
> gigantic wastes of time and money;
> . . . that I will be suddenly gripped by stage fright and
> never be able to give a lecture again;
> . . . that I will lose faith in what I do and never want to leave
> my house again;
> . . . that I've wasted half my adult life on the wrong things;

. . . that all of humanity will die out during my children's lifetimes.

These are just off the top of my head. Why ever get out of bed again?

On the other hand . . . most of the things on this list are totally outside my control. But the fear is real nevertheless. So I try to stay realistic and keep moving forward.

Even though he's in great health for his eighty-seven years, my beloved father is still getting older.

Even though I can't control whether U.S. readers are going to love or hate my book, I still need to send it out and let the market take care of the process.

Even though three hundred Swedes died in traffic accidents last year, I'm still going to drive my car.

There is nothing to fear but fear itself.

But the feeling of being afraid is there, regardless of how illogical it is. Everyone experiences that now and then. All you can do is accept that bad things *can* happen. The risk is there, but we can't let this fact paralyze us.

It's possible to learn how to handle your fear. And it's almost ridiculously simple.

FEEL THE FEAR, AND DO IT ANYWAY

All you need to do when you are faced with a situation that frightens you is to identify the fear, accept that it is there—and do what you need to do anyway.

Perhaps the best book in history about dealing with fear is *Feel the Fear . . . and Do It Anyway* by Dr. Susan Jeffers. It became a monumental best seller many years ago, thanks to its incredibly simple message: even if you're afraid of something, the fear isn't going to disappear until you've learned to handle it. Jeffers says that fear is always going to be with us, and that sometimes you need to deal with it head-on.

I read the book some years ago, and I can't express how much it has helped me. It helped me out of a very destructive relationship. Now I very rarely back away from conflict, and that's largely due to my experience in that relationship.

After I read Jeffers's advice and prepared myself well, I took the bull by the horns and said exactly what I thought: "This isn't working. What you do to me is not acceptable. It's going to stop, and it stops here." After some very intense moments, I was suddenly free. And stronger than ever before. I felt the fear and did it anyway.

FACTS ARE ONE THING; RELATIONSHIPS, A COMPLETELY DIFFERENT STORY

Do you want to live your life on your own conditions or on somebody else's? One of the challenges when you want to grow as a person— whether it be building your self-confidence, getting into shape, earning more money, or building a company—is that the people around you may not like this change. Very often, people feel threatened and start to oppose you.

This is problematic. When people around you don't support your growth, then you must choose: the relationship or your dream.

This kind of obstacle is extremely frustrating and hard to understand. Why would a person who insists that he or she loves you stop you from achieving your personal goals? This is often related to how hard change can be. But it might also be jealousy. Or simply a threat to the person's status within the family.

A man I met at a dinner many years ago said that he left his wife because she'd gone and gotten a better education than he had. I was flabbergasted and wondered what he was talking about. Remarkably, he thought that it was completely natural to specifically look for a woman who was less educated than he was. It was his task to support the family, and he was the alpha male in the family. If she was suddenly more educated, she could potentially get a better job than him, and he found the idea totally impossible to accept. What can you even say to that?

And that might be our greatest fear of all—to be forced to deal with these painful situations.

WHAT ARE YOU AFRAID OF?

Put the book down for a moment. Think about what limits you. What makes you hesitate and even refrain from doing something that you hope could lead to good things?

Take a pen and paper. Write down three things you feel fear, worry, or unease about, but that you know that you should confront. It doesn't have to be shipping off to a war zone. Or putting the family's life savings in a high-risk investment fund. It can be something as simple as going across to your neighbor and asking him to stop smoking on his balcony because the smoke goes straight into your bedroom.

Write down your three points now.

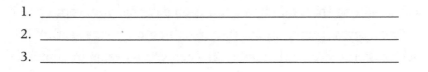

1. _____

2. _____

3. _____

Your list could include things like this:

1. Asking your boss for a raise
2. Asking your spouse to spend more time at home
3. Starting that fun project in your free time that you've been thinking of for a while

When you think about starting that project, perhaps you mainly feel excitement, but at the same time you feel daunted thinking about all the extra work it will entail. And the stress that might follow. And what your partner is going to say about it.

When you think about asking your spouse to spend as much time with the kids as he or she does with coworkers, perhaps your pulse races a bit.

If your boss is the tough type, perhaps you'll get stressed even thinking about asking for a raise.

Sort the list from the easiest to the hardest. Perhaps your list would look like this instead:

1. Starting that fun project in your free time that you've been thinking of for a while
2. Asking your spouse to spend more time at home
3. Asking your boss for a raise

You can now see that the least scary thing is to start that fun project. You can now get right to it, even though you feel some butterflies in your stomach.

Because this is what happens: by doing what feels the least uncomfortable, and succeeding in that, you build up your strength. Your fear tolerance becomes higher. Just like at the gym, you don't start squatting three hundred pounds on day one, you work up to it.

Once you've accomplished the first thing on your list it, will be much easier to deal with number 2. Then you move on to number 3.

Does that sound simple? That's what's so brilliant about it. It's so simple, it almost feels unreal. Simple if you *do* it, that is.

By not pushing against your fears, you're depriving yourself of a future that could be magnificent. You lose the possibility to really live the life you've imagined.

Do you want to govern your fear, or do you want the fear to govern you? Only you can answer that.

Fear and the Four Colors

Not everyone is afraid of the same things or feels discomfort about them. Of course, a lot depends on what you experienced as you grew up and what you've been through in the past. Yet there are certain patterns that can be worth pointing out. Patterns linked to our basic behaviors can teach us something. And even though the four colors in the DISC model are primarily focused on communication, we can find some interesting clues here.

AFRAID THE RED WAY

If you're mainly a Red, then your greatest fear is losing control. You want to have control, and losing it can be really frightening for you. You want to have control of the situation and what others do or don't do.

It's perfectly alright to feel that way, but you need to think about how you're going to handle it. The person with a dominant red streak prefers to make all the decisions and steer others. The problem is that this doesn't always work. If you're the boss or the head of the family, then it might be simpler. But your need to always feel like the alpha can be a serious limitation.

My recommendation is that you accept that the world is complex, and you can't have control over everything, no matter how hard you work.

The Solution

Hand over some of the responsibility and control to others. See how it goes. Give a helping hand if necessary, but learn that things can happen without you. When you become accustomed to this way of behaving, you're going to feel stress release its grip on you. This is how a Red person can step outside his or her comfort zone.

It's not a sign of defeat to give up control. On the contrary, it's a strength that is gradually going to improve your efficiency and results. If you want to go really far, you need to learn to accept and use the energy of those around you. And accept that you don't have all the answers. Nobody does.

UNPLEASANT FOR A YELLOW

Yellow behavior includes a very deep-seated fear: losing your prestige and sinking in status. Yellows are very sensitive to what people around them think of them. Being in an elevated position suits a Yellow very well. Yellows really love to be in the limelight. And the risk of descending to the same level as the rest of us simply scares them.

You might not admit that even to yourself, but, with sufficient self-awareness, you know it's true. If you've always been the one people come to and ask questions about X thing, then you'll find it very painful if somebody else outcompetes you. It will go right to your heart, and you might find yourself completely paralyzed.

Relying on a gut feeling is very natural for a Yellow, but it won't help you. You need to accustom yourself to not being the center of attention at every meeting.

The Solution

Trust that everyone else is not going to forget you just because you're not in the limelight every second. You're already an interesting person—you can adopt a more laid-back position. When you realize that there's a lot to learn from listening to others, you'll feel more comfortable biding your time a little. This is the Yellows' way of stepping beyond their comfort zones.

A person who listens and lets others into the fold is going to be extremely popular with the rest of the group. You're going to feel their appreciation.

GREEN ANXIETY IN EVERYDAY LIFE

Perhaps you're primarily a Green, and it's perfectly obvious—both to you and to others—that you're afraid of conflict. You don't just feel uneasy when people raise their voices and make a bit of noise, even a dirty look or ambiguous comments; irony in general, and sarcasm in particular, can unnerve you.

You want to be a friend to all, but since that isn't really possible, you struggle to protect yourself from a merciless world. You try to be gentle, friendly, and always behave in a nonthreatening way. The problem is that many people aren't going to understand where you stand on certain issues. Which can be exactly what leads to raised voices and dirty looks.

You need to find a new approach here, because it's not helpful to go around being terrified of what might happen in the next meeting.

The Solution

You need to become a little clearer with your true opinions. Dare to express a distinct point of view and see what happens. Some people are going to agree with you; others are going to disagree. But you can improve your ability to listen to the opinions of other people without taking them personally. Remind yourself that people don't think about you as you might believe. Most people think more about themselves than anything else, which makes the risk of conflict rather small. If you, as a Green, really push and go outside your comfort zone, you're going to discover that it isn't so dangerous after all.

Try it on a small scale. Notice what it feels like. Realize that nothing terrible happened. And move on. For your own sake, you ought to stand up for yourself and say what you think, instead of forcing others to find out afterward. That, my friend, is in fact often the issue behind these conflicts. The clearer you are early on in a process, the less bickering there will be later on.

FEAR FOR THE BLUES

Even though you Blues are task-oriented, there's something that really frightens you: making a fool of yourself. Supplying the wrong information, incorrect data, or coming to unsound conclusions— terrible! Everyday life contains unlimited possibilities to make a fool of yourself and have your mistakes revealed to one and all. But this fear limits the chances for those around you to see you for the true professional you are.

Nobody thinks that you're infallible. There are no perfect people, even though there are many who try to be. And Blues are the ones who try the hardest. Your nose for perfection might sometimes be an advantage, but the only way to entirely avoid mistakes is to lock the door from the inside and throw away the key.

You need to find a more logical method of attack. That's how the real professionals work.

The Solution

Let go of this need to appear perfect and the fear of making a fool of yourself. Accept that you are an ordinary living human being who, like all of us, is sometimes going to be wrong. It is not going to kill you. That's what it feels like to leave your comfort zone.

I am not suggesting that you start being careless. That doesn't do any of us any good. But you can let go of some tasks sooner than you normally do. When you think you've achieved 90 percent, you'll still have gone much further than other people would have. Be satisfied with your achievement (unless you're a brain surgeon; then please hold out for 100 percent). Accept that you've done your part, and move on. If—and it's highly unlikely—somebody should find some mistakes, don't see it as a defeat but as a good opportunity to learn new things. Because you like to improve your skills, right?

SUMMARY

Being afraid is completely natural, and nobody totally escapes this. Even the most successful people you can imagine have a particular comfort zone. Only psychopaths and narcissists never experience fear or stress. The only way to get around this for the rest of us is to push directly against the fear—and just do it anyway.

Even though the fear is real, we sometimes tend to exaggerate it.

Don't do that. Don't picture worst-case scenarios in your mind. But don't underplay anything, either.

Once we act despite the fear, we often discover that the feeling was exaggerated.

Look at what you are afraid of. It's okay; it only makes you human. But act on what you see. Start with smaller things to build up your confidence. That will strengthen you for bigger tasks.

Okay. Now it's time to look at a serious setback and see how to tackle it piece by piece.

The Harry Case, or How to End Up in a Ditch

A man who is definitely past his prime—let's call him Harry—is fed up with his beer belly and his poor health. His eyesight is not what it was, and he doesn't feel particularly strong. Over the last twenty years, he established bad habits like eating too much junk food and snacks, and drinking too much beer and "diet" soda (thinking it's not unhealthy). He hates walking for more than a short distance, he takes his car everywhere, and hasn't seen the inside of a gym for fifteen years. He persuades himself that he has some sort of innate basic fitness because he played football in high school.

We don't know anything about Harry's colors or driving forces, but we do know Harry sits in front of the TV in the evening with his hand in a bag of peanuts, watching meaningless reality series. His favorite shows are the ones with dysfunctional characters, since they make Harry think that his own life isn't so bad after all.

He might end the evening with the late-night news and all the depressing updates it contains.

He fills his mind with negative thoughts and then goes up to bed. Of course, he sleeps badly and finds it hard to get up when the alarm clock rings at six thirty. He feels more dead than alive at work until lunchtime, which means he doesn't get much done. His body aches and he can't concentrate.

Between you and me, it doesn't look good for Harry.

But something suddenly causes him to wake up. It might be a friend who died young, an old flame who has gotten back in touch, a comment from one of the kids, who is genuinely worried about him. It doesn't matter what sparked the change, but now things are going to happen. He is going to be a new man!

And that's great. Sometimes you need that aha moment to say, *That's enough! I don't want to live like this anymore!*

He gets a gym membership, buys some new workout clothes, pumps up the bike tires, and throws away all the junk food he has in the pantry. He promises to go to bed by 10 P.M. every evening so that he can go for a run at 5 A.M. the next morning. He solemnly swears to his wife that things are about to change.

HOW YOU START A HEALTH JOURNEY

Harry starts a health plan that would make the producers of *The Biggest Loser* green with envy. From now on, he is going to bike to work. He will visit the gym six days a week. He is going to steam with sweat. No TV and peanuts or beer in the evenings.

Two months have passed with six days a week in the gym—we will assume that our friend Harry actually does work out at the gym (obviously not everyone does)—and now he has aching muscles he didn't even know existed. He pulled at least three muscles, because the first thing he did was put too much strain on his body. He's beginning to worry that he's done serious damage. He's already fed up with a diet of boiled cod and broccoli. When he bikes to work, it rains three days in a row. His butt is sore, and he has aches and pains all over.

Every time he steps on the scale, he's worried. Nothing has changed. His jacket is still as tight as before.

Sometimes he forgets to pack his gym bag, and he finds it hard not having cream in his coffee after lunch. He's had cream in his coffee for at least twenty years, after all, and is well aware that it is not exactly beneficial for his weight.

Then there is a happy hour at work.

Everybody nags Harry: Can't he just take it easy? There are several couch potatoes in this gang: Roger and Freddie, for example, are even worse off than Harry. At least one of them will have serious heart problems soon.

And Harry resorts to a tactical defense mechanism called rationalization. He really does deserve a couple of beers and some fries, since he leads such a healthy lifestyle these days. For God's sake, it's possible to live a good life without having to exist solely on kale! So he goes *all in* this Friday night—beer, whiskey, and every kind of snack you can imagine—and wakes up the next morning with a hefty hangover, a headache that eclipses the sun, and a stomach that is desperate for a really oily pizza with extra cheese. After a party like this, his body is screaming for liquid and fat.

NOW HERE'S A REAL SETBACK

Is all hope lost? Or was that just a little relapse?

Well, it depends. Mainly on Harry, of course, but also on those around him. There is a risk that this might happen:

All the good habits are abruptly broken after an evening out with his workmates. If you've cheated once, then you can cheat again. Besides, Harry's wife doesn't really like how Harry goes to bed earlier and earlier. She misses his company in front of the TV in the evenings. And when she takes an extra cinnamon bun, his good eating habits make her feel bad. So he starts listening to her when she encourages him to ease up on the restrictions a bit.

And the fact is that after another couple of months of intensive training, he starts to hesitate: Why is he actually doing this? What was he thinking when he first started? Was he really in such bad shape? His goal seems to be more distant than ever. He's not going to lose thirty-five pounds in the immediate future.

Bit by bit, Harry goes back to his earlier life and soon makes up for everything he missed during his health kick.

Six months after his aha moment he weighs even more than he did before. And he feels even more tired than ever. His body is screaming after all this mistreatment, but that isn't the real problem.

Now he feels like a failure, too. And he's in a worse place mentally than he was before he started.

He had such high hopes and did so much right. So how did it go so wrong?

THE SETBACK BROKEN DOWN IN EIGHT PIECES

Why did it go so totally wrong for Harry? Why did he end up in a ditch despite the fact that he had both the desire and the commitment?

If you knew why Harry failed, what conclusions do you think you would draw? Would you be able to make use of that insight in your own life?

How fantastic it would be if you could be certain that you would succeed at whatever you set out to achieve.

I pulled a muscle. Became allergic to kale. My shoes were no good. The gym was too far away. I had too much to do at work. Beer just tastes too good. Those are just meaningless excuses. You know that. I know that. And I bet that that Harry knows it, too. You either have results or you have excuses. You can't have both of them at the same time. And very rarely is there just one single cause for failure.

Harry's problem can be listed in eight points:

1. He didn't know *why* he was doing all of this.
2. His goal was far too *vague* and *fuzzy*.
3. He took on *far too much* at the same time.
4. The results were initially *invisible*.
5. He lacked *persistence*.
6. He underestimated the difficulty of *breaking old habits*.
7. He *surrounded* himself with the wrong people.
8. He drifted . . .

Let's have a look at each separate point.

1. He Didn't Know Why He Was Doing All of This

If there isn't a clear, sensible reason to change a particular aspect of your life, then it isn't going to work. Why suffer through nights of salads and mornings of running if there's no rational explanation?

Harry wanted to get into better shape. That was a good idea, of course. But why did he want to do that? Was it for fun? Did he want to impress somebody? Did he simply feel bad when he looked at himself in the mirror? If he knew exactly which *problem* he wanted to solve, it would have been much simpler. You need a more specific motivation than simply thinking *Now's the time!*

The answer to the question *why* identifies the specific problem. We don't take an aspirin if we don't have a headache. If there isn't an identified and accepted problem, there's no need for a solution.

If Harry had identified that he couldn't go on long hikes with his best friend like he used to, perhaps he would have been motivated to stick with his health regimen. Without those hikes, he rarely saw his buddy.

If he knew that it was starting to be hard to make it through a regular workday because his body was so sore and stiff, he might have had a proper reason. If you can't do your work well, you risk being criticized, demoted, or perhaps even laid off the next time the company reorganizes. Serious concerns.

If he genuinely missed his sex life with his wife because he was often too tired to even think about it, perhaps something would have made him stick with the exercise program. Is that a problem or not? Hard to say.

Perhaps if his *why* had been admitting to himself that he wanted to impress that new pretty woman in the department, things would have gone better. I just made up Harry, so I can't be entirely certain. Sometimes it isn't a problem that needs to be solved, but a possibility that could be opened up. But there are worse reasons to get into better physical shape.

None of his goals will succeed until Harry has established the real reason why he needs to get into better physical shape. That is what keeps him going. That's what provides the basis for all motivation, that subtle and—admittedly—elusive ingredient. It's what really drives him forward, even when the going gets tough. It's what gets him out of bed in the mornings when it's raining, that helps him to say no, thank you to a piece of cream cake (even though cream cake is the best). It makes him sweat on the step machine, instead of bingeing peanuts.

A Hair-Raising Example of Denial

A few years ago, American researchers carried out a so-called screening study. They wanted to find out more about people who were at higher risk for a specific type of cancer. They placed ads designed to appeal to the demographic in the risk zone and offered them a free screening test. Thousands responded. Some of them turned out to be predisposed to this form of cancer. Then one thousand of these people were offered free advice about their lifestyles to minimize the risk associated with this cancer.

How many of them dropped out of the program, and how many stuck with it?

Of the *one thousand* people who voluntarily contacted the study—i.e., acted on their own initiative—*nobody* accepted the free advice.

Think about that for a moment.

The number of people who wanted to avoid dying of cancer: zero.

Even though they now *knew* that they were at a higher risk of becoming seriously ill, nobody wanted help. How could that even be possible?

It is easy to laugh at this depressing example, and think, *What a bunch of idiots!* But before we do that, are we certain that we would make a more rational decision if we were in the same position?

It's hard to change yourself. It requires a very strong reason, a purpose, a cause—a powerful *why*—for a person to deny him- or herself obvious pleasure in favor of a long-term reward.

2. His Goal Was Far Too Vague and Fuzzy

I need to get in better shape. Can you get much vaguer than that? Even though it sounds like a brilliant goal, Harry needs to ask himself this question: What does that mean? *Get in better shape?* What sort of shape are we talking about?

If you and I were to try to picture somebody who's in good shape, would we see the same image? I know what I would see in my mind's eye, but is that what you would envision? And what does Harry think of?

Perhaps he has a vague idea of a (twenty-year-younger) fitness guy in fancy shorts with the flattest stomach you can imagine. Perhaps it's somebody with enormous biceps. Maybe all of this, or none of it. The risk is that his mental image of what he wants to look and feel like doesn't exist at all. It could be a vague desire that things should be different. All Harry knows is that he's unfit, and that's *not* what he wants to be.

But where does he *want* to be? Without a more concrete goal, there will be no results.

Some People Completely Lack Goals

And perhaps that's the main problem. The majority of us have virtually no goals.

For years, I've wondered why so many people are resistant to setting goals. And I have an idea why that is.

To know who won the football game, we need to keep track of the points. And if somebody wins . . . then it means . . . that somebody else loses. That, I think, is where people get nervous.

Nobody Wants to Lose

We don't all have a need to win. But nobody wants to end up last. Nobody wants to hear that they failed. And if it feels so bad to lose, then it's actually better not to know. The resulting logic is:

If I don't set any goals, then I can't fail to reach them. If I don't have any goals, then nobody can judge me by them. Not me nor my colleagues nor my boss. On the surface, everything is going to look fine no matter what, right?

The problem isn't that you aim too high and miss. The problem is that you (to avoid leaving your comfort zone) aim too low . . . and hit the target. Then you stay there. You're satisfied with something mediocre, because you at least got what you aimed for. And who can argue with that?

What Do the Experts Say About Taking Risks?

Our brains aren't designed to make us feel good. They're designed to do everything necessary for us to survive, regardless of how bad it makes us feel. Our brains would prefer that we survive, even in total misery, rather than risk that we die happy.

What's the consequence of that impulse? Don't take any unnecessary risks.

Setting tough goals is a way of taking a risk. You can fail. Horribly. Once upon a time, failure meant a threat to your life. If you took a wrong step in the jungle, a tiger could eat you. If you lost your bearskin during the winter, you might freeze to death. If you stay where you are and keep your head down, then you're going to survive. Don't challenge anybody, don't stick out. Don't be different. You won't be kicked out of the group, which could be deadly. Your brain is going to try to resist all such ideas.

Think about it: When you set a really challenging goal and achieve it, what do the people around you say? A few, the people who really care about you, are going to be pleased for you. Those closest to you. Your mother and a handful of others, perhaps. But make no mistake about it, most people won't be pleased by your success.

The majority probably won't care at all. They couldn't care less. But many people around you will be surprisingly pleased if you fail.

That's the sad truth. It means that their own efforts don't look so bad.

Why Lottery Winners Go Bankrupt

Nowadays, we don't risk our lives in the same way. Nobody is going to bar you from the tribe to die in the wilderness, but social exclusion is still a risk. It's a basic need to feel socially accepted. Being rejected by the group is a uniquely painful experience for any person.

There have been studies in the United States in which million-dollar lottery winners were interviewed. A lot of them became depressed after they won the money. If you live in a particular socioeconomic class and suddenly you find yourself sitting on a pile of money, then you're undoubtedly going to stick out from the group. And nobody is going to love you for it. Quite the opposite: a lot of people are going to resent you. Some are going to hate you. You don't fit in anymore, because you have a new car and nobody else has one.

Nor can you just get up and move into a so-called affluent area, because everyone there will know instinctively that you haven't earned the money yourself. They know that it's just a lottery win. You don't fit in there, either.

So where do you fit in?

Perhaps it is easiest to just spend all the money quickly so the problem disappears. This presumably happens unconsciously.

Indeed, it is more common for lottery winners in America to declare bankruptcy than it is for ordinary Americans. Approximately a third of all lottery millionaires (according to the National Endowment for Financial Education) go bankrupt within three to five years. Before you think, *That's because they haven't learned how to look after their money*—I agree that can be one reason, but lottery winners' brains can mess things up for them. The mind quickly reverts to its earlier situation: being broke. That has become a sort of default position.

The best salesperson is praised by the management at all the sales meetings. But all the other salespeople say rude things about her behind her back. The person who has the nicest house on the street gets smiles from his neighbors. But that person is probably not invited to many spontaneous backyard BBQs. The person with the fanciest car might be suspected of shady business activities. There might be something not right there. Illegal gambling on the internet? Narcotics, perhaps?

Besides, this doesn't have anything to do with money; it's about what you make of yourself. If you win the lottery—which is extremely unlikely—and suddenly have millions of dollars, then you'd better become a millionaire mentally, too, and fast.

With the wrong mindset you'll soon be back where you started. Subconsciously or otherwise.

Unspecific Goals Rarely Lead Anywhere

Let's say you want a higher salary. The annual salary discussions are coming up soon, and you hope to get a share of the pie this time. You go in to your boss's office and tell her about your desire to get a salary increase.

Sure, says your boss. *You can have ten dollars more a month.*

Are you satisfied now? No.

So you try again.

Okay, let's talk about it, she says. *How much more?*

If you start stammering and can't answer, this is not going to go very far. And you should not ask her how much she's willing to give you. The risk is that she will answer, *Nothing.*

Conclusion: goals need to be so clear that people can understand them.

3. He Took On Far Too Much at the Same Time

How do you write a book? Answer: One word at a time.

How do you walk coast to coast? Answer: One step at a time.

How do you build stronger muscles? Answer: One push-up at a time.

How do you eat an elephant? Answer: One bite at a time.

How do you acquire better eating habits? Answer: Start by drinking an extra glass of water.

The problem is that these things take time. But bad habits have been built up over the years, and you won't be able to get rid of them in just a few weeks. You need to accept this simple fact. Harry started doing everything at the same time. Working out, eating better, not drinking alcohol, getting up early, and going to bed early. The complete opposite of his previous lifestyle and daily rhythm.

If Harry hasn't taken care of himself for years, it's going to take time to remedy that. But regardless, he can't do everything at once. That is an unreasonable demand. And if it doesn't work, he'll soon meet new setbacks. Failing with a workout routine, or with a diet, or with sleeping habits, or with a active lifestyle, or whatever it happens to be is discouraging. This is only going to add fuel to his this-isn't-working bonfire.

There are inspiring public speakers who say that you should aim high! *The sky is the limit! You can do whatever you want!*

Absolutely. You should dream big. Then these same big thinkers say that you should repeat to yourself your (typically) unrealistic goals as often as you possibly can.

- I'll be ready for Mr. Universe next year!
- I'll be the CEO!
- I'll spend all my time with my children!
- I'll visit ten countries in the next three years!
- I won't work a single hour of overtime next year!
- I'll be financially independent in two years!
- I'll live in a country mansion by a lake!

All of those are excellent and honorable goals, but the risk is that it's too much to bite off in one go.

Let's take the question of money, because it's so easy to do the math.

I shall be 100 percent debt-free next year!

Great! But if you have just taken out a $350,000 mortgage on your house, have no savings in the bank, but still have an ordinary salary, then it isn't realistic. What would be realistic, would be to say to yourself, *This year, I am going to pay an extra 10 percent over my required payments toward my mortgage.* (Don't bother working out how many years it will take; that isn't the point here.)

The following year, perhaps you pay an additional 12 percent off. And after that 15 percent more. Suddenly it becomes manageable.

Harry needed to have a much more detailed, gradual plan to be successful. He needed to start on a smaller, more manageable scale. Instead he ended up creating even more painful obstacles.

4. The Results Were Initially Invisible

The worst part about setting goals and starting to work toward them is that, at first, you will hardly see any results at all. What Harry had forgotten was that it had taken him perhaps twenty years of neglect to get where he was.

Question: How do you put on thirty extra pounds?

Answer: By one bad decision at a time.

It would be much simpler if after the first mouthful, you immediately put on thirty pounds and started having heart problems.

If you wolfed down a bag of potato chips and immediately found that your pants were four sizes too small . . . how many more bags of chips would you have that week?

But the process doesn't work like that. It's slow, long, and drawn out, and the pounds sneak up on you without much fuss.

The crazy thing is that it works the same way in the opposite direction.

If you change your diet, you can't expect those thirty pounds to disappear by the next weekend.

The same applies to smoking. If, after smoking your first cigarette, you suddenly had a terrible hacking cough and woke up the next morning connected to a ventilator, with graying skin and feet you can hardly feel because of poor circulation, then you'd understand immediately how bad smoking can be.

And when you stop smoking, it takes up to a year before you notice what your food actually tastes like. Yes, that's right. If you're a smoker and you think you know what food tastes like, then you have a surprise in store. When you finally stub out your last cigarette, it will take six to twelve months for the poison to leave your body.

If you run on autopilot at work too long, perhaps your new boss will finally notice and nominate you to be the next in line to try out those nice unemployment benefits. It won't happen the first week, but after a month or so of being lazy, someone will notice.

This is how the world works. Even if your actions don't result in any visible effects at first, they will in the end. And, yes, sometimes this planet is an unfair place to live.

The same thing happens in a relationship. If you have an argument—when you refuse to admit that you're wrong, you make a scene, rush out of the room, and slam the door behind you—and come home from work the next day and find signed divorce documents waiting for you, then you would immediately know that you were out of line. But it might have taken twenty years to build up to that scenario.

Think about what happens when you plant a seed. Some seeds will start to germinate in a few days, others will take months. There is a Chinese tree with seeds that can take up to five years to start germinating. And you have to tend it, water it, and add nutrients, even if you don't see any immediate results. If you stop tending your completely invisible seed, well, it will die down there in the soil.

Harry gave up because nothing happened right away. The results were invisible.

The Richest Man in Babylon

Here I'm going to condense a whole book into four sentences.

In the book *The Richest Man in Babylon,* by George Clason, we learn that the path to becoming rich is so simple that the majority of people miss it. All you need to do is put aside 10 percent of your net income every month. The fact is that rich people save first and consume afterward, while less financially successful persons consume first and then save what might be left over. Then it's simply a question of mathematics and time that determines when you'll consider yourself to be rich.

Simple, right?

I once went to a financial freedom seminar. A money guru stood on the stage like a glowing ball of energy, and his first promise to us was this: *Everybody here is going to double their income.*

A murmur passed through the lecture hall. Each and every one of us leaned forward. He definitely had our attention.

Then he said, *The question is: How long is it going to take?*

What a disappointment.

As usual, we wanted a quick fix. Sure, sometimes somebody might achieve "overnight success," and, sure, people do make a huge amount on the stock market. But if you plan your future on those odds, then you'll almost certainly die destitute.

You don't expect your children to turn into adults in a single day. You don't say to your six-month-old daughter, "Now you need to pull yourself together and start walking on your own. This is taking forever. And why are you still crawling around?"

You would never shout at a tree to make it grow quicker. It is going to take thirty to fifty years to reach maturity. The same applies to physical training, your career, building relationships, or creating a profitable business.

If you have a conflict with someone and that person finally apologizes for what they have done, that's good. But it's going to take some time before you fully trust him again.

At first you won't see any changes in your relationship. Building trust definitely takes longer than apologizing. It can take years.

Even if the results aren't immediate, we sometimes need to trust that we're going in the right direction. If you've set a good goal and identified the right steps to take, then you're doing it correctly. Have faith in the fact that you're on the right track. But accept the reality of the world we live in.

5. He Lacked Persistence

The next problem in Harry's case was his persistence. Or rather, his habit of instant gratification.

Now, Harry is not unique in the least. We want what we want, and we want it now. Waiting is not something for modern man. Harry gave up because, despite his considerable efforts, the mirror showed no proof that he was on the right path. Despite his weight lifting, his muscles hadn't gotten bigger. Despite his morning runs, his beer belly hadn't disappeared.

This isn't a book about the best way to get into good physical shape, but what we do know is that your body, which is governed by your brain's striving to survive, is going to resist change. Your body is not going to let go of fat just like that, because that is valuable energy it has been carefully storing for years.

Remember, your brain couldn't care less what you look like on the beach. It only cares about one thing: that you survive.

That makes it easier to build muscle. And, paradoxically, the more muscle you have, the easier it is to burn fat.

But how do you keep going when you don't see results?

Imagine a tasty slice of hot juicy apple pie made from fresh apples. The pie is still warm from the oven, steaming and golden brown with a crunch of caramelized sugar on the outside. Every mouthful melts on your tongue. And it's topped with a magical vanilla ice cream. Perfect. It's a flavor orgasm.

Now imagine a glass of water.

What do you get here?

Nothing. Absolutely nothing.

We'll go through it again: apple pie = heavenly delight.

Water = nothing.

For the first year at least. Perhaps even for the first three years. After that, the glass of water will win by a mile. And after twenty years of apple pie, your regret will be deeper than the Mariana Trench.

This is one of our great challenges. The right choice—the water—gives no immediate gratification. The incorrect (over the years) choice—apple pie with vanilla ice cream—gives an instant payoff.

Harry was wandering through a minefield of temptations every day. Ads for easy pleasures are everywhere. Food, sweets, drinks, TV, apps, games—all sorts of things that give us short-term enjoyment at the cost of the long term. The world happens to be full of temptations.

Here we have a problem.

Life has two types of hardships: either we live with the restrictions of discipline or we suffer under the pressure of regret. Discipline, however, is light compared with the burden of regret.

Short-term pleasure often leads to long-term pain.

But short-term pain often leads to long-term pleasure. Patience, durability, persistence, determination, stubbornness, obsession. Or a passion for change?

6. He Underestimated the Difficulty of Breaking Old Habits

We've all made this mistake, particularly when it comes to our health. Change is going to happen now! But bad habits that have taken years to build up won't disappear that easily.

The old line *I've had a drink every day for forty years, but I haven't made a habit of it* is, of course, amusing, but there's a treacherous psychological truth here. We are always going to stop/start in the future. That sounds logical, because in the future we're going to be delightful people with perfect self-control. We fool ourselves that we can stop bad habits whenever we want. And start with the good things. Later.

But this is where our brain plays a major trick on us. Change can be a threat to our survival, so we don't have any built-in support system. Which means that we have to summon almost inhuman will-power to do what's necessary.

Your Active Choices Govern Your Results

Of course, there are people out there with wills of steel. The people who can just decide and then go and do something. I've met some of them, and they are nothing but impressive. So there are exceptions, and perhaps you're one of them. But those are exceptions.

Habits are about choices—the choices you make, things you choose to do or not to do.

Everyone can choose. All the time. If Harry's choice for the last fifteen years has been to hit "snooze" three times then fall out of bed, flop into his car, and buy a cinnamon bun and a huge caffe latte with extra everything on the way to work, then we know just how diffi-cult it will be to jump out of bed at five o'clock to put on his running shoes and run for half an hour before he's even eaten. And then to celebrate his run with three boiled egg whites and a glass of water. That, too, demands an active choice.

To spell it out: the solution to Harry's problem is still to do it right. But the path to creating the new habit is not straightforward. Say that Harry was sitting at a restaurant because that particular day he forgot the lunch he packed. The kale-and-sweet-potato salad is still at home, in the hall. Now he's sitting with a menu in front of him. There's good food on the menu, but there is also not-so-good food on it. Because a menu is just one long list of possible choices.

Perhaps he will choose the salad. If he does that, then it's okay. But if he chooses the hamburger with fries? *One hamburger doesn't make any difference,* thinks Harry, and he chooses the hamburger.

But how did he end up so unhappy with his health?

Answer: One hamburger at a time.

As I mentioned earlier: he didn't put on thirty-five pounds after the first hamburger. It probably took a couple of thousand hamburgers to get him to where a daily salad would never have taken him.

He can also choose to fool himself. If he takes the hamburger and fries, that just means ninety minutes on his exercise bike tonight. So he *could* actually order the hamburger. But speaking of choices . . . tonight, perhaps, he skips the exercise bike and chooses to catch up on the TV show he has missed, and now watches three episodes in a sitting.

That sort of choice is not going to help his plan to get in good shape.

If he and his wife usually end every evening in front of the TV with something tasty and a couple of shows on Netflix, then it's going to require an enormous effort to skip that and simply go to bed. And do that without staring at his cell phone for an hour, too, because that effectively sabotages his night's sleep. Google it!

Harry's wife is still going to want to have him on the sofa, otherwise she'll be on her own in front of the TV. That's *her* choice. *Her* habit.

Good habits can be difficult to build, but they are easy to live with.

Bad habits are easy to create, but difficult to live with.

What Is a Bad Habit?

A bad habit is something you do that goes against your larger goals in life. This is important, because it means that whether a habit is bad or good depends entirely on the person.

If you drink energy drinks by the bucketful, but your goal is to be best at *Fortnite*, then it doesn't make any difference. If, on the other hand, your goal is to be slim, then the energy drinks are not going to help you.

If you usually work late in the evenings, that's a good habit if your goal is to boost your career and move up in the company. But if your goal is to spend more time with your kids, then overtime is a coup de grâce.

If your goal is to save enough money for a down payment on a house, then it's a good idea to put aside some money every month. If you regularly empty your bank account thanks to your shopping habit, then there won't be any house. But that won't make any difference if your goal is to build muscle.

Your Goal Is the Deciding Factor

You need to focus on your goal. Any habit that prevents you from reaching your goal is a bad habit.

Example: Your goal is to fit into your wedding suit on May 1, 2022. You should go downstairs and pedal away on your exercise bike for sixty minutes every morning before you eat breakfast. Which means that watching yet another episode of The Big Bang Theory at eleven o'clock the night before is a very bad habit. Why? You don't put on weight from watching TV. That's true, of course. But if you stay up too late in the evening, then you're not going to manage to climb out of bed in the morning.

Here's another example: You want to become the boss of your department within the year. You should focus on your primary work responsibilities and attend all the leadership courses you can find. Also, during the year you intend to read at least ten books about leadership. What does this mean? That whenever you waste time on the wrong things during work hours or listen to podcasts on other subjects—regardless of how fascinating they are—instead of reading those books, it's a bad habit.

Or another: You've made it clear to your family that you need to stop wasting money because it's difficult to cover all your expenses. You and your partner are completely agreed about this (but perhaps not your teenagers). It's essential that you pay down your debts faster rather than continue to spend at the same pace. When your partner signs up for an upgraded cell phone account or even more TV channels . . . and you, also stuck in your old ways, don't protest, then your behavior is an extremely bad habit. You need to establish another way of reacting.

This isn't easy, but even small things are important if you want to start a new life.

7. He Surrounded Himself with the Wrong People

Everybody loves a winner!

That's bullshit. Everybody definitely doesn't love a winner.

Some will love him or her, sure, but many more will want that person to fall from the pedestal, never to be seen again! In her book, brain researcher Dr. Katarina Gospic describes this phenomenon perfectly.

Again, it's about survival. But survival forty thousand years ago was, as I mentioned earlier, something different from what it is today. If we wanted to survive, it could be valuable to spread distrust of the strongest member in the group. It could potentially strengthen our own status. If, for example, a popular person falls into disgrace, the collective is often quite ready to drag the former hero through the mud.

Why?

Well, if we diminish the person we previously worshipped, then we can shine a bit more. Perhaps we might become the star ourselves? The more we shine in relation to others in our social setting, the more we increase our chance of survival.

"That's why we like it when stars fall," writes Gospic.

We feel smug when things go poorly for somebody else. The most extreme form of this eternal competition and comparison is extremely unpleasant.

With weak self-esteem, you risk being tempted to diminish

somebody else to make yourself seem bigger. It feels good, and it does actually work. For a while. Then the novelty fades, and you need to think up new nasty things to make yourself feel superior.

I don't really know what the solution to this pattern is, except that the more self-esteem you have, the less the rivalry between individuals. So, in simple terms, we need to build up everybody's self-confidence so that they don't feel threatened. The path to get there might be a difficult one.

The people around you aren't necessarily on your side. Some of your seemingly strongest supporters dream of kicking you down again.

So you need to surround yourself with the right people. Before you rely on your gut feeling and start thinking that there aren't any "wrong people," I want you to hear me out. Okay?

To Succeed, You Need to Surround Yourself with the Right People
The wrong people will pull you down quicker than the right people will be able to lift you up.

If you've found an important *why;* if you've succeeded in formulating a clear and exciting goal; if you've prepared a plan and broken everything down into manageable steps; if you've learned what persistence means; and if you're in the process of building new, better habits that will take you to your goal—people are still going to tell you that you are doing everything totally wrong.

Unhelpful people immediately compare themselves with you. If you do something that is a bit too good and a bit too ambitious, they'll appear less successful. It's best for another person's self-image to persuade you to abstain.

But Who Are the Wrong People?
Living in a context where you're surrounded by the wrong people can be so toxic that you won't be able to achieve anything at all.

Envy, jealousy, laziness, comfort, ignorance, unwillingness to listen, their own failures . . .

You remember what it was like in Laterville. That's where these people mainly live, the people who don't see success as something important and worth striving for. They would rather watch soap operas and laugh at some fictional characters than go to a symposium and be inspired by new ideas and ways of thinking. The wrong people are the type of friends who only see risks in every opportunity and immediately ask you to sit down and stop rocking the boat.

The wrong people are those who are perennially negative and look for faults in others.

The wrong people live for drama.

The wrong people are like shadows that disappear as soon as the sun stops shining on you.

But the wrong people are also those who effusively praise everything you do and never, ever give you any constructive feedback. That is also a form of deception.

The wrong people are those who regularly say one thing but do another.

The wrong people stubbornly maintain that you need at least a PhD if you're going to accomplish anything at all. The wrong people confuse education with intelligence. It's perfectly possible to have a shiny college degree (or several) and still be a blockhead.

The wrong people talk about you behind your back. Listen to what they say about your shared acquaintances. If they talk badly about your other friends in front of you, then you can be pretty sure they're doing the same thing to you with someone else.

The wrong people pay lip service. They do the right thing only when somebody is watching. But wrong is wrong, even if nobody sees you. Just like right is right even if nobody sees. Right is right even if nobody does it. And wrong is wrong even if everyone does it.

They're going to drag you down and poison your air quicker than one can say schadenfreude.

Was Harry Surrounded by the Right People?

What support did Harry have from those around him? Did his family support him? His wife was hardly going to say that it would be better if he stayed in bad shape. She would certainly have said that getting into good shape sounded like a great idea. But then what?

If she still wants to drink wine and eat sweets in front of the TV in the evening—what are his chances of breaking this habit? If she mentions that his alarm clock, which rings at five o'clock every morning, disturbs her because *she,* of course, isn't going to get up at that ungodly hour of the day—what will that do to his motivation to crawl out of bed? If she complains that he leaves sweaty clothes lying around, or insinuates that, wow, there are certainly lots of women who go to his gym—how is that going to affect his desire to work out?

What about Harry's friends at work? That gang that still drinks gallons of beer every Friday and Saturday night as if their lives depend on it, who smoke and eat a pizza for lunch—what kind of support is he getting from them? After all, they're going to be frustrated if he—against all odds—succeeds with his ambitions to get into shape. Many of them simply want him to fail. If he succeeds, they'll be forced to see themselves in a completely new—worse—light. So what do they do? They pull him down.

Come on, Harry, man, just one beer. You're no fun.

Surrounding yourself with wrong people is like breathing poisoned air. It only leads to new setbacks.

8. He Drifted . . .

The most subtle difficulty that Harry found himself in, in this series of blunders, was that he simply drifted away from his path. He probably wasn't even aware of the fact that he gradually fell off the wagon. For various reasons, he lost his focus, started easing up on his good intentions, didn't get up at the crack of dawn, started taking a bit of cream in his coffee again, ate fistfuls of peanuts here and there, and so on. Bit by bit, he stepped off the straight and narrow and fell back into his usual behavior.

Sometimes everything is just how it should be. You know why you decided to do a certain task. You've set a sensible goal. The plan is realistic and sound. All the right components are there. You're aware of your bad habits and have actively started to exchange them for new, better habits, in terms of your health, career, relationships, money, home, or whatever. The negative heckler types among your circle of friends have been exchanged for enthusiastic supporters.

And nevertheless . . . you wake up a year later in a completely different place than you'd intended. Oops, how did that happen?

This can happen for a lot of reasons, but based on my own experiences, somewhere along the path you might encounter a distraction that puts you off your intended course.

It can be the tiniest thing that steals your focus—a meeting, a trip, a friend, new demands on your time, some other problem, a conflict at home, a crisis in your immediate vicinity. Or nothing special at all.

You don't even notice it. It just happens. Your focus slips away.

And everything returns to what it was like before.

There is a well-known trick—you might have seen it before—but when you interlock your fingers together (i.e., interlace your fingers as in prayer), either your left or your right thumb comes out on top. That's how your hands settle, and that's what feels right. If you now open your hands and adjust your grip so that the other thumb ends up on top—how does that feel?

Test it yourself.

You'll discover that it feels weird. *Wrong*. It isn't really you.

Now go back to the "right" grip.

What do you notice now? Oh, much better!

Precisely. It's more comfortable like this.

And herein lies the danger. For various reasons we tend to strive for comfort. And we don't even notice when our ancient instincts pull us back to the old, established ways. It just happens.

There are several ways to avoid this, but it can be really tricky. It's so unbelievably subtle. First of all, you need to see it. Then you can think up a solution.

The reason Harry fell back into his usual pattern was probably a combination of several factors, but it ended the same way. One of the major issues was that he simply drifted off . . . to Laterville.

SUMMARY

It's obviously impossible for me to know how many of these obstacles you recognize in yourself. Perhaps you've tried something similar to what Harry did, and actually succeeded. Or you got further than him, and yet still ended up on the rocks. But what I want to emphasize is that it isn't just one thing that prevents us from reaching our goals. It's several factors that work together, and that's why it's deceptive when you try to understand what went wrong.

It's simplistic to bring out the usual list of defense mechanisms and rationalizations.

- It was Steven's fault for not supporting me.
- It was that sprain in my right ankle that did it.
- If it hadn't been for all that overtime I had to do last fall, it would have worked out.

It's rarely that simple.

The fictive Harry didn't lack the willpower to come to terms with his life. He understood that a change was necessary. What he lacked was insight about how difficult it is to change yourself.

It's about starting in the right place. Starting with *why*. That's where you need to begin to avoid being pulled down into a swamp of poor self-confidence, disappointment, and, in the worst case, self-pity.

Ten years ago, the American author, lecturer, and philosopher Simon Sinek made a name for himself across the world with his book *Start with Why*. He was later accused of simply repackaging old information. But I think that completely misses the point. It makes no difference whatsoever if we've already been told what we need to do in order to change. If we don't do it, if we haven't done it, then we need to hear it again. And again.

But Simon Sinek was completely right. Important change rarely occurs without having a really good reason behind it. Without a powerful reason, it simply won't happen.

Now it's time for you to take in that message and find your *why*.

Adapt or Go (Extinct)

If you really want to avoid setbacks and obstacles in your life, you will have to accept change. Before we deal with concrete solutions, I want you to get accustomed to the idea that if you want new or different results, you are going to have to change some aspect of your approach.

Things weren't always better back in the day; a lot of things were simpler. The measure of success wasn't complicated. Work hard, play by the rules of the game, keep your head down, don't ask too many questions, follow the leader, and become the expert nobody can survive without. Stay where you are.

But the building blocks of success have changed: work hard, break all the rules, keep your chin up because optimists always win. Question everything. You can lead yourself. Take initiative.

What's the measure of success?

Interesting question. These days, nothing is certain anymore. Nevertheless, expectations are higher than ever. When I asked an old acquaintance, in the middle of her career, for her opinion, she explained that she works as hard as she can, while at the same time doing all she can *to look as if she's hardly working at all*. Sure, she asks questions, but she doesn't really expect anybody to have any answers.

We can't influence most of what happens around us. That doesn't, of course, prevent us from being shocked by misery, injustice, or violence. But sometimes you don't have any choice. You're simply obliged to accept that the world looks the way it does. And adapt to that reality. That's part of taking responsibility. Observe what's happening around you, but don't get stuck in it.

There are different theories about what creates success. They range from the idea that you need ten thousand hours to master something, to the thought that you simply need to work harder than everybody else. Maybe it's the ability to think positively or the ability to control your emotions.

All of that is probably important, and I wouldn't disregard any of these skills, but as I've said earlier, I suspect that people have varying abilities to handle setbacks when they arise.

Which brings to mind an interesting theory.

The ability to adapt.

Everything changes all the time. Darwin talked about natural selection, or as he also expressed it: survival of the fittest.

A lot of people have interpreted Darwin as meaning that the strongest survive, but that isn't quite correct. It's about the ability to survive in your particular environment. There were bacteria back in the days of the dinosaurs. They adapted; the dinosaurs did not. Bacteria have even adapted to our very best antibiotics; they seem to have an ability to mutate and adapt endlessly.

And a lot of really successful people have the same ability. They can see the same situation that everyone else sees, but nevertheless respond in a completely different way than everyone else. That's an example of adaptation.

There are so many examples of companies and organizations that refused to adapt and are now extinct, that it's pointless to list them all. So I'm not going to even mention Kodak.

In modern times, there are lots of examples of the exact opposite: companies that actually have adapted—and survived. And not just survived, but prospered more than ever.

I was astonished when I heard that Netflix began its business by mailing DVDs to people's mailboxes. Then they saw what was happening in the tech world, did their homework, and adapted. I think you could call Netflix a fairly successful company.

What does it look like for you and me? Have we chosen to adapt? It's an active choice. When was the last time you had to adapt to a situation that was the last thing you wanted?

Every time you move to a new "environment" you need to adapt. All of us have moved environments, and we need to learn to adapt to new situations. We have the ability. But how do we use it?

ACCEPT THAT THIS IS HOW THINGS WORK

There is an enormous difference between accepting the possibility of something and living in fear of it. We could suddenly find ourselves at war. We are privileged to live in a part of the world where that hasn't been the case for many years, but it's still a possibility. But despite knowing this to be true, most of you haven't gone out in the last fifty years and built a bomb shelter in your yard or sat up at night keeping a lookout for airplanes.

If you mess things up at work and risk hearing some sharp words from your boss, you know that the risk of being reprimanded decreases when you do better work. So you do the best you can, deliver the best you're capable of—but you don't sit there and worry about the possibility that your boss might be in a bad mood that might result in you bearing the brunt of her annoyance.

You do the best you can, then you move on. You adapt as best you can. When the time comes, you'll find out whether it worked or not. If it didn't work, then you need to adapt further. And move on. But you always need to look at the results and let them determine whether you're on the right path or not.

Because results do not lie.

If you've lost your keys in the dark, it doesn't matter how long you look for them. However much you crawl around in the gravel, you won't find them. More of the same doesn't work.

If you want to win over a client from your most successful competitor but the client isn't impressed by your proposal, then you'll have to try something else. More of the same doesn't work.

If you want to lose weight, and your morning walks don't have any effect, then you need to try something else in your exercise and training routine. More of the same doesn't work.

If your children refuse to do their chores, then you'll have to seriously think again whether your chore chart with stickers is really motivating them. Try new methods. More of the same isn't going to work.

It's always a bit of risk to use yourself as an example, but I'll stick my neck out again. As I've said before, I wrote for twenty years without being published. So the question is: Is that really a success story? Well, it depends on how you look at it. I wrote a bloody horror manuscript in 1991 and sent it out as soon as I finished it. No revision, no editing, nothing. I was surprised and a bit offended that nobody wanted to publish the masterpiece. If I'd continued to do the same thing, I still wouldn't have had any books published. But I changed my strategy, changed my style, content, genre, got some help, and practiced lots of different skills. And now you're holding my tenth book in your hand.

WHAT ADAPTATION IS REQUIRED TO WRITE A BOOK?

Writing a book is a surprisingly good metaphor. It's a difficult project. You have to put in at least one thousand hours per book and do it without being paid. And that demands an almost inhuman degree of adaptation.

Deciding to write a book that might take six months of work without knowing if you're even going to get it published . . . that's a crazy project. No reasonably normal person should take it on.

Authors who have sold millions of books have no guarantees of anything. Nobody knows whether the next book is going to take off. Not the author, not the editor or publisher, not the marketing people, not the readers. Nobody knows.

Writing a book gives you no guarantees. The entire work is a gamble, pure and simple. And yet there are thousands of crazy people like me who just can't stop themselves.

For all of us, it starts with a *why*. Writers *want* something. We don't all want the same thing, but we want *something*.

HOW A BOOK ACTUALLY COMES INTO BEING

First you have to have an idea. Then you need to develop that idea and try to write it down so that it becomes comprehensible, at least to you. If you can convince others that the idea is going to work, even better.

Then you'll have to set aside sufficient time (one thousand hours is probably not enough) so you can work on the project. On top of all the normal things you must always do. Most authors have a day job, too.

Then you start writing.

And then you should keep on writing. And you don't know if you'll get anything for doing it.

This demands enormous adaptation while at the same time you make sure that the rest of your life is functioning properly.

ADAPTATION IS THE KEY

Once you get started, you need to keep up the pace so that your self-confidence doesn't have time to completely erode. More than once, you're going to question your own ability. If you aren't accustomed to working with mental brakes demanding that you stop every second, then you'll be forced to adapt to this new frame of mind. And when you've eventually written the whole book, it will be time to rewrite it. Everyone has a different process, and only a handful of rare people can hand over the first version of the manuscript to their publisher and say, *Here you go. It's finished now.*

No, no, no. Even the best authors are obliged to rework their manuscripts many, many times.

Then your manuscript can be sent to a publishing house, which, hopefully, will accept it. I don't know what percentage of books sent to publishers are accepted, but it's some depressingly small fraction of a fraction of 1 percent.

The publishing house will then want to make more edits and changes. Now we're really talking about having to adapt. However good you think your book is, they'll want to change it. And all you can do is hang on. All my books have been revised several times, even well after the point when I considered them to be perfect! But in every case, they've become a great deal better once the professionals have had their say. You just have to get used to it.

Then it starts again.

A new round of editing. One, two, three, four, five times.

And still none of the people involved really know whether there is a guaranteed market for your book. In the 1980s, people said that you just had to "accept the situation." I heard that so often that I started to detest the phrase.

So instead I say, adapt. That's how it works.

AM I JUST TRYING TO GET RID OF FUTURE COMPETITION?

Absolutely not. If you have a good idea—then go ahead! Go for it! You can write a book, too. That's what I did, and it's been a fantastic experience. But my point is this: trying to do everything right away is not going to work. You need to accept that it's an enormous project that you have to approach step-by-step. What you can do is sit down and sketch out your idea. Then start jotting down whatever comes into your head. And while you're on this journey, you'll discover loads of things you didn't have a clue about. As you learn, you'll have no choice but to adapt.

Now imagine that along with your book project, which still requires a thousand hours of your life, you're going to be taking a leadership course, and you'll be putting in a few extra hours at work to ensure your career stays on track, and that you're also going to transform your body from head to toe. All at the same time.

No, no, no.

Remember Harry. He tried to do everything at once. Working out at the gym and trail running. Changing his daily schedule. Overhauling his diet. Giving up alcohol.

It's too much. Think of this as another form of adaptation. You need to adapt your life to move the focus from many different things to pursuing a single important dream, whatever it may be.

Time is the limiting factor you need to consider. Everything that is worth doing is going to take time. There are no shortcuts.

But use your time well. Make it your friend. It isn't too late.

Henry Ford started the Ford Motor Company when he was forty-six years old. The rest is history.

Small steps are the way forward. You don't need to turn your whole life upside down. You don't need to revolutionize the world. You can get where you want to go with very small changes. But how?

How Do Your Colors Affect Your Ability to Adapt?

Your color(s) definitely influence your ability to adapt successfully. To understand how your behavior is affected, you first need to understand the strengths and, even more importantly, the weaknesses of your profile. All behavioral profiles have their strengths and weaknesses. The strengths are, of course, more fun to talk about, and they'll get you started on your way. But not all the way. Later on in this book, I discuss how we can't become successful by building only on our strengths. We also need to be aware of our weaknesses, and that's where the most adaptation is required.

Let's turn it all around. How does each color need to adapt in order to achieve success and reduce unnecessary friction around them?

THE STRENGTHS AND WEAKNESSES OF RED BEHAVIOR

Red individuals might not love change, but they accept it and push through as long as the change leads to results. They are fast movers. Thought and action are almost the same thing. They'll move forward efficiently and rapidly, however tough it looks. They're goal-oriented and really do love to win. They're often competitive people.

Another one of their obvious advantages is that they're task-oriented. Why is that helpful? Well, they often manage to put their own feelings to the side in tough situations. They look at the actual issue and try to find a solution to the problem in front of them. The fact that they're not primarily relationship-oriented makes it simpler for them to appraise a person's virtues, instead of only considering (like many people do) who they are as individuals.

All of this is positive. It's best for the Reds to continue down this road. But these strengths have a flip side, too, and there are failings in Red behavior.

The greatest problem is also their greatest strength. The tireless Red drive is a headache for many of the people around them. They're seen as aggressive because they'll look virtually anybody in the eye and aren't afraid of raising their voices if they want to get their own way. As a result, Reds can step on people's toes and make enemies. They might not always care about that—they're not relationship-oriented, after all—but it does become a problem when they need help.

In the heat of the battle, Reds often forget that they can never achieve their goals entirely on their own. Nobody can succeed by themselves. The only way to achieve real and long-term success is to adapt to your surroundings.

How Reds Should Adapt

Reds need to be sensible and slow down the pace a bit. They need to actively avoid behaving too dominantly and authoritatively toward those around them. Since nobody likes to feel controlled, the Reds can learn to back away a little and let go of some things. But, as we've seen before, this is one of the things that the Reds hate most: losing control.

But this is an extremely important adaptation for them to make.

If you have mainly red in your behavioral profile, you don't have to let people walk over you or stop being committed to your work. But you do need to let others have a say. You can't succeed entirely on your own, however much you would like to.

You also need to show that you care about others. Simply asking questions and finding out how people feel is greatly appreciated by almost everyone. Except other Reds, since they think that you've just wasted several valuable seconds on nothing.

You should also be aware that your feeling of urgency sometimes creates a situation we call "fast and wrong." Accept the fact that speed is not everything. That's one of the most important changes you need to focus on: slow down and reflect a bit more.

THE STRENGTHS AND WEAKNESSES OF YELLOW BEHAVIOR

Yellows love change. They're bored with anything they've already done three times. Time to think up something new! The result doesn't matter, because change itself is fun! Does this mean that Yellows are the best at adapting?

There isn't really an answer to that question. Yellows are good at seeing possibilities, at finding new paths, at thinking outside the box. They're rarely limited by tradition or convention. They don't think that things were better before. Rather, their focus lies somewhere far in the future.

They're also graced with creativity. They answer questions that nobody has ever asked and solve problems that nobody has considered. Through their incredible imagination, they have the capability to see the invisible. And they can also explain what they mean in a way that others will appreciate and enjoy. Yellows often speak in metaphors. The pictures and worlds they conjure are amazing, which means that you're excited and want to join them in creating something brilliant.

The flip side of this is that a lot of people perceive exactly the same qualities as dreamlike and frivolous. They talk too much, and when they open their mouths, they haven't thought through what they're going to say. Long soliloquies of unprocessed thoughts pour out of their mouths. Since Yellows often smile, laugh, and joke about everything and everyone, they're not taken seriously. Their tendency to avoid details often leads to an enormous mess. Because they can't keep track of their own work and find it hard to be punctual, they can cause problems both for themselves and for those around them.

Yellows need to realize that they are far too focused on themselves. Their ability to continually place themselves in the center of everything can really get on people's nerves.

How Yellows Should Adapt

What you, as a Yellow, need to do is to sit down and exhale slowly. Put your cell phone down, and put on your thinking cap. Look around you and notice the fact that there are lots and lots of other people in the world.

If you're the only person talking, then you'll only hear things you already know. But, regrettably, that won't lead to any development or growth. Your tendency to put yourself first is not appreciated by other people. You definitely need to tone things down a bit. You don't have to start wearing gray clothes or take a vow of silence, but you do need to work on your ability to listen. You need to do this very intentionally, because you don't focus on what others say.

You should also realize that however incredible it may seem, other people also have ideas that you'd be smart to consider.

Finally, perhaps the greatest change you need to implement is to start focusing on facts and details. Right now you're far too broad in your assumptions, and you need to make the effort to acquire a more thorough understanding of the situation and the details involved.

THE STRENGTHS AND WEAKNESSES OF GREEN BEHAVIOR

Greens are often allergic to change. Especially rapid ones. That kind of change is decidedly unpopular. Even if it may lead to results. Greens can find it extremely difficult to adapt in general.

It's not all doom and gloom, however. Green behavior usually includes a friendly and accommodating attitude to most things, as well as to most of the people the Green meets. Like the Yellows, they are relationship-oriented, and they'll often go out of their way to accommodate and agree with those around them. They're generous to others and are actually the best listeners of all four colors. Their genuine interest in their fellow human beings is also reflected in their behavior.

On the whole, Green people are also reliable. They try to do what they've promised, and in general they behave fairly considerately toward their fellow human beings. They don't forget to ask how you're doing, and if things aren't going well, they'll take your suffering to heart.

The flip side of this Green behavior—and what you as a Green need to be aware of—is this aversion to change. Since Greens are governed by emotions more than by rational motivations, it can be particularly difficult for them to adapt.

This can sometimes lead to others perceiving Greens as stubborn. Even if the proof is there in front of you, you're not going to want to change.

Another weakness is your inability to handle conflict. There aren't many people I've met who enjoy conflict, although some probably do, but Greens avoid conflict to an absurd degree.

Greens tend to agree rather than oppose, no matter the situation. If somebody says "Let's go right," the Green will say yes. If someone else says "No, let's go left," then the Green will say yes again. It's easy to see how that's going to go wrong.

How Greens Should Adapt

If you have a lot of green in your profile, then you probably already know what you need to do in order to adapt to those around you. It's just that you don't want to do it, right? Sometimes you wish that the world worked differently and that you didn't have to continually change yourself.

Try it on a smaller scale. Make some small adjustments, a little bit at a time, and see how you feel. Don't think like a Red or a Yellow, who love to make big, dramatic changes. No. Baby steps. Then you'll feel more in control of the process.

If you always plan your work projects the same way every time, or work with exactly the same coworkers all the time, try changing something in that well-worn methodology. There's a good chance that you'll discover things you like.

Since you're aware of the fact that you can be fairly passive, you should—for your own sake—challenge yourself by climbing out of your comfort zone.

THE STRENGTHS AND WEAKNESSES
OF BLUE BEHAVIOR

Blue people don't have any issue with change, but the change must be based on logic and designed to improve results. The best changes are ones that are backed by comprehensive studies and a clear understanding of the problem being addressed. If there isn't a problem, then there's no need for a solution.

Other people might have a gut feeling that it's time for a change, but Blues will see that as frivolous. Feelings are not a necessity and should not be part of decision-making. We're talking about facts and concrete information. It's a bit of a paradox, but Blues are actually extremely likely to follow new rules and regulations, i.e., to adapt, but only if they understand and accept their utility.

They'd be happy to put together the new guidelines themselves, and they'll follow them to the letter.

The flip side of this is obvious. In situations where their high standards aren't being met, Blue people will block everything and will refuse to play along. They stop listening and continue to do things as usual, following the same familiar path. Whether this path is right or wrong is of less importance. It's the proper route, so they'll follow it off a cliff if they have to.

Unfortunately, people around them will react rather negatively to this. Blues need to learn that they're dependent upon others and that if they see only risks and problems, they will repel certain people. It's not possible to work entirely on your own, isolated from other people. Blues are sometimes obliged to adapt their speed to that of the majority.

How Blues Should Adapt

To adapt to new circumstances and conditions, you need to be well informed. Okay, we get it. But you should remember that a dozen trains have left the station while you've been weighing the merits of sixteen different alternatives. You should, of course, gather information and look for the best options, but you also need to realize that this can go too far. When the people around you tell you to stop digging, then you know it's time to stop digging.

Write down exactly what you need to know. But don't make the list too long. And promise yourself that you will jump into action when the facts are there in front of you. Distance yourself from that sometimes paralyzing passivity you experience that says you should sleep on it one more night, think a little longer. No, no. You need to get your boots on and make some decisions.

Why not work with some Reds and Yellows? You could complement their energy with your focus on detail and create a really winning team.

SUMMARY

If you want to change and adapt, it's a good idea to know exactly where to begin. The greater your self-awareness, the better you will know where you stand—and the greater the likelihood that you really will manage to make the necessary adaptations on your path to success.

Now it's time to move on. Toward the bright future. Are you going to come along?

PART II

Creating Lifelong Success, or How to Win Every Time

. . . .

The Three Coworkers

Let me introduce you to Lena, Karin, and Mari. These three women are friends who've known one another quite a long time. They work at the same firm and are in their forties. They've perhaps become rather settled in their ways. But one of them, Lena, by chance, puts together a plan to shake things up and find greater success. Keep an eye on her as you keep reading.

THE FIRST MONTH

Lena has worked at the same company for several years, and she thinks things are beginning to stagnate a bit. She works in sales and is quite a good salesperson. She's been given a ticket to one of those inspirational seminars that's being hosted in town. Karin and Mari will also go to that event.

Have you ever been to this sort of seminar? Lecturers and inspirational self-help coaches try to convince the public that they should aim high and build a brilliant future. They might focus on health or education or leadership or personal development.

A bright, sunshiny person will tell you that if you only do this or that, then your whole life is going to change. Your world will be transformed in ninety days. Except that after ninety days, nothing's happened. So you and I dismiss those stupid ideas, because we must have missed whatever magical thing would have changed our lives.

During the seminar, the three friends all have slightly different reactions to what they're hearing.

Lena feels positive and tries to actively absorb what she hears. She feels she might as well try to learn what she can from the speaker while she's here.

Karin makes some sporadic notes but mainly just listens, because she thinks rather highly of her own memory. She thinks the speaker says a lot of sensible things, but nothing so revolutionary that she couldn't have figured it out by herself.

Mari, on the other hand, doesn't listen at all. She mainly just occupies herself with her cell phone. She doesn't even know why she agreed to go.

How will these different attitudes and reactions affect the friends?

Lena

Lena is influenced by some of the advice from the seminar, and starts to implement it bit by bit. One of the things she does is to start reading inspirational books instead of just watching TV. For half an hour every day, she reads an interesting book and gets new ideas about how she can improve in her career.

She also listened to the health advice she heard during the seminar. She's not in bad shape, but she has put on a few extra pounds that she doesn't really want. So now she starts biking to work on the days when it isn't raining. It's only a few miles, and it gives her some much-needed exercise without taking up too much extra time.

The sales office is on the fifth floor, and instead of using the elevator, she now walks up the stairs. On the food front, she makes just one little adjustment. Instead of coffee and a couple of sandwiches with cheese, she starts making scrambled eggs for breakfast. Not a big deal.

As for her relationship with her partner, she decides that they'll go out on a date every week. They'll go to a restaurant and leave their phones at home. That's all she decides to do differently.

All of this gives Lena so much extra energy that she starts making some extra sales calls every week. She has three more conversations a day than she did before. She goes from ten calls to thirteen calls. Not a huge change.

What do you think of Lena's plan? Does it feel insurmountable? Would you be able to eat a more nutritious breakfast, take your bike to work and climb the stairs, do just a little bit more at work, and devote a couple of hours of "quality time" to your partner every week? Perhaps you could listen to audiobooks while you eat breakfast.

We're not talking about gigantic leaps here. Just small, simple things that you and I could manage if we decided to do them.

Karin

Karin goes on exactly the same as usual after the seminar. She has a vague conversation with her husband about how they ought to take a trip somewhere together and work on their relationship (something one of the lecturers talked about), but they don't decide on anything. They talk about whether they should renew their gym memberships. Nothing else happens. But Karin feels quite satisfied. She doesn't see any real problems with her life.

Mari

Mari . . . hadn't really heard any of what was said that day at the seminar. But she, too, is going to change some of her behavior. We can speculate as to why, but she makes some unfortunate choices every day. She used to go to the gym fairly regularly, but now she's had a busy few weeks at work, so she misses a few workouts.

She takes a handful of toffees from the receptionist's bowl before lunch and another when she goes home. You need something sweet when your blood sugar gets low. Unfortunately, sugar makes you tired, and that affects her job. She starts to make *fewer* sales calls. Instead of an additional three calls, she now makes three fewer than before. She's now down to seven phone calls a day. She busies herself with other, more important activities at the office. She spends some time looking to update her fall wardrobe with a little online shopping. It works. Orders are still coming in at a fair rate, and nobody's fired.

With the sun setting earlier, it's nice to have a glass of wine now and then. Sometimes with dinner on Wednesday, Friday, and Saturday. Not to mention the bottle of wine that stays on the table all Saturday night. She doesn't really know how much wine she and her husband actually drink. But the neighbors haven't complained.

THE SIXTH MONTH

What's interesting is that if you check in on the three friends after six months, you won't notice much difference. Lena, Karin, and Mari are all doing fine.

Lena wonders sometimes. She started to try to improve her life, but she doesn't see any results. So what's the point? Why do all that work? She perseveres, however, and continues to read interesting and inspiring books to help her grow and develop. She sticks to her plan at work, and makes sure she keeps her bike ready to go.

Karin is hardly aware of what's going on. Everything just continues as usual.

Mari might not love her life, but nothing's really changed.

THE TWENTY-FOURTH MONTH

We move farther on in time.

After two years, quite a lot has happened. Let's start with Lena.

Lena

Lena is now very successful. As a result of her daily exercise and her changed diet, she lost ten pounds. That's given her more energy and she started going to work out at the gym. The fact is that Lena, now forty-three years old, has never felt stronger.

She reads at least thirty minutes every day. Which means that she's plowed through more than two hundred books about marketing, leadership, communication, and personal development. She's encountered lots of new ideas, many of which she's tried in her life.

Her more active work has made her Salesperson of the Year, and her performance-based salary has more than doubled. Thanks to the quality time she and her partner now spend together, their relationship has never been better. Life is wonderful. Her CEO mentioned the possibility that she might be able to take over the entire sales department next year when Sarah moves on to another job.

Karin

Karin has continued to go on doing what she's always done. She's generally slightly dissatisfied with life. She thinks it's stressful, she hardly has time to do everything she needs to, her children are dissatisfied, and her husband is his usual self. She's in exactly the same place she was two years earlier, just a bit more bitter than before. She feels uncommitted, frustrated, and blames the whole thing on the government.

Mari

Mari . . . has gone in another direction.

She eats too much at every meal. For a long time nothing happened. But now her clothes don't seem to fit. She can't understand it. She hasn't done anything different, has she?

What Mari doesn't notice is that those big meals make her rather drowsy in the evenings. She doesn't sleep so well either. And waking up in the morning feeling tired makes Mari grumpy.

After a few months, her grumpiness and her tiredness make themselves felt at work. The number of sales contacts she makes every day falls even lower. Her boss wonders what's wrong, which makes Mari completely furious. Now she has a bad relationship with her boss, too.

Mari is often grumpy, tired, and stressed. So when she comes home she treats herself to something tasty as a consolation. Her energy level goes down. When her husband wants her to join him and go out to walk the dog in the evening, she starts to say no. She's too tired. Her husband misses that time with his wife but hasn't really suspected that anything is wrong. But there are other things she doesn't feel like doing anymore. The less they do together, the worse things are between them. The less she does, the more tired, sluggish, and grumpy she becomes.

Mari doesn't like what she sees in the mirror. This hurts her self-confidence even more, and she starts to feel more and more unattractive. Her romantic side is put on hold.

What Mari doesn't realize is that her way of withdrawing makes her husband feel that there's something wrong with him. To avoid being intimate with her husband—she simply hasn't the energy right now—she stays up late and watches meaningless TV shows. Her husband becomes more and more worried. Doesn't she love him anymore?

He becomes more demanding, which makes Mari withdraw even

more. She isolates herself. Her husband starts to protect his own feel-ings. Instead of trying to get his wife to do things with him, he starts going out more often with the guys.

Mari sees that he gets dressed up on the weekends and disappears to the pub. She's never been jealous, but now she wonders if some-thing is wrong. It's obvious that her husband has something going on. Mari stays at home and eats more, drinks more, and falls into self-pity.

She doesn't connect any of this to the small choices she started making two years earlier. Instead, she starts thinking about her hus-band. And soon her entire relationship is in danger.

SUMMARY

This is a modern version of the old fairy tale of the hare and the tor-toise. Somewhere along the way, we as a society have forgotten the value of hard work—the work ethic—and staying power, and that rewards come to the person who has the patience to wait for them. A lot of people seem to think that the world owes them something. That they have a right to this or that. But it doesn't work like that. You do owe it to yourself to make the best of the life you have.

When a person makes some small positive choices, there will be results. It might take a while, but eventually the reward will come.

When the same person, however, makes some small negative choices, this will often lead to bad consequences. This, too, might take some time.

But, and this is just as important, if you don't make any choices at all and instead simply drift along in life, you'll actually be halting your own growth. This will eventually catch up with you, and you'll start slipping backward. This applies to most of us. We haven't even thought about the choices we've made. We just exist.

But by being a little observant, it's possible to change things completely. All you need to do is see your own power in the situation.

If you could choose, which of the following alternatives would you vote for?

1. You choose your own goals and decide how you'll get there.
2. Other people tell you where you should be, what you should do, and when it should happen.

The choice should be obvious. To see how little changes can have a big impact, we're going to follow Lena through the next four chapters of the book.

How *Not* to Achieve Success

So, how do you achieve success? There are many descriptions of what the path looks like. Successful people have some shared characteristics. This isn't about who they are or how they think or how they function. It's about what they do. Success comes from what you do, nothing else.

We've often been told that to get anywhere in life you need to do some combination of the following things:

Work hard.
Be passionate.
Focus on your own strengths.
Practice makes perfect.
Never give up.
Never be satisfied.
Be grateful.

Parents, bosses, performance gurus, and a whole crowd of other people say these kinds of things. Do all that, and joy and affluence will follow. And, sure, it's good advice. It's a hell of a lot better to follow such a plan than to just loll around and hope for a winning lottery ticket.

But we need to ask ourselves this question: Is it good advice, is it *useful* advice? Working hard, for example, sounds like obvious good advice, right? But what if you work really hard . . . at the wrong things? Then where do you end up? Sure, you might make it partway to meeting your goals. But I'm absolutely certain that you know lots of people who work hard, really hard, without getting anywhere at all.

You should be passionate. I think so, too. I like working on stuff that I feel passionate about. But sometimes, on mornings when I get out of bed at three o'clock to get a taxi to the airport to fly to God-knows-where, I feel a shockingly small amount of passion. Mainly irritation, to be honest. I am, however, obliged to do the job anyway.

How about focusing on your strengths? What sort of advice is that? Certain people in my type of work are of the opinion that the easiest way to achieve success is to build on your natural strengths. There are even tools that will measure what your greatest strengths are. And it does sound like a good idea. Why slave away at something that doesn't come at all naturally? Why make everything harder than it has to be?

But think about if for a moment: if you build your life on your innate strengths, it will be a tough battle. You've presumably had the same strengths since you were twelve years old. Which means that at age forty-three you should still be building on what you were good at when you were twelve. I'm not buying that. We need to develop new skills.

And "never be satisfied" is absolutely the worst piece of advice of all. I must have said it myself at least a thousand times. Nowadays, I bite my tongue when I'm about to mutter a similar cliché.

It is okay to be happy, but you should never be satisfied. Then you just end up fat and happy.

It wasn't so long ago that I told my wife over a cup of coffee that

I'd received the highest rating of any lecturer in the past ten years in a certain public forum. A big deal for sure. But, I said, and hid my face behind the cup, it doesn't feel like anything special. I should have been able to get an even better rating.

It's been so drilled into me that I should "never be satisfied" that it's become absurd. In my case, I've developed a kind of distorted perfectionism that probably irritates everyone around me. For the first fifty years of my life on this planet, I've basically never been satisfied with anything I've achieved at all.

Think about it. If you never get to be satisfied, happy, and genuinely pleased with what you have achieved—what the hell is the point of it all?

During my career as a management consultant and leadership coach, I have met many incredibly successful people. Some of them have been superb top performers. And they have been extremely satisfied, happy, and proud of their successes.

They still want to improve their results, work so that their clients are even more satisfied, or reach even further and create more success. But they are also satisfied with what they've achieved. That sort of peak performance gives many people positive energy, rather than terrible performance anxiety.

There's no doubt but that the attitude of never being satisfied has damaged me personally, and many others like me, and turned us into dissatisfied ghosts hunting for better, better, better and more, more, more.

So skip the whole idea of not being satisfied.

Success, performing, getting somewhere—however you want to define it—should be pleasurable. You should celebrate, be joyous and really satisfied.

Then you can create new goals and paint new visions and all of that. But we should never forget to celebrate what we've achieved.

MY OWN SEARCH FOR SUCCESS

Obviously I've been there, too—searching for the path to success. I've read loads of books (we're talking hundreds of books) about how to become successful. In addition, I've spent a small fortune on various types of lectures and seminars, and I've listened to I-don't-know-how-many hours of YouTube videos, inspiring audiocassettes, and (later on) CDs. Probably thousands of hours.

And I really did follow the recipe that everyone—with just a few exceptions—talked about. I worked hard. I searched for and indeed found my passion. Worked with visualizations and affirmations, took Neuro Linguistic Programming tests, and practiced, practiced, practiced. I focused on my strengths until I saw that they were not enough.

And you know what? It worked. A sort of career materialized. Bit by bit I built up a reputation as somebody who got things done. I earned a bit of money and led people forward. For many years, things went along very nicely, in fact. I thought that I had found my place in life.

But then . . . things stopped happening. Everything slowed down, and I suddenly found myself in some sort of mental quicksand. It was as if I'd landed on a plateau with no way off. For years, everything stood still, I was treading water and realized that, if anything, I was moving . . . backward. I was still working hard, sacrificing evenings and weekends—but not getting anywhere. And all of a sudden I found myself far from my own vision. It was painfully frustrating.

Of course, I realized that I'd achieved certain successes—mainly with regard to my career—but I didn't really know why that was. For some reason, I wasn't as disciplined as I should be. Really, I wasn't the best at anything. Nor did I think that I contributed enough to the business. My own values and my own work ethic meant that I was completely smothering myself.

It took me several years to discover that what had gotten me on track—working hard, being passionate, focusing on my strengths, practicing, not giving up, never, ever being satisfied but only grateful—wasn't enough in the longer term.

GETTING STUCK ON A PLATEAU AND NOT GETTING ANYWHERE

I'll be candid and admit that at that time, I simply felt dissatisfied. I slept poorly, nothing was fun, and I was stressed morning to night. *Despite the fact that I was still performing well!*

What I didn't understand until much later was that the old advice was about individual success and short-term results. It meant that I was in the game, absolutely. And it kept me in the game. But it didn't match the potential I knew I had.

I worried that I didn't have a clue how to achieve success and feel good at the same time. I realized that long-term success demanded that I also think in the long term.

When I actively shifted my focus to what we're going to talk about in the next chapter, a whole tangle of knotty problems began to unravel. I, of course, still have a ways to go, since I came to these realizations so late in life.

One of the biggest issues is that when you're not seeing the results you hope for, you tend to start to let go. And you start sliding backward. Which is exactly what ended up happening to me. It felt as if I were on my way back to the same point I'd started from.

The crazy insight was that I didn't even know the definition of "success." The only thing I knew was that I wanted to feel smart and that I wanted others to see me as somebody who mattered. But that was so vague that it didn't help in the slightest.

So I was obliged to start thinking about what we're going to talk about: What is success?

SUMMARY

Not every method works for everyone. What makes one individual successful is not necessarily the same as what makes his or her friend successful. Sometimes you need to sit down and think about what works best for you yourself. However, there are certain things that are universal. And one of the most important is to know how you personally define success. And why it is so important that you be successful.

You need to devote time to thinking through what you want. You can't just listen to what others say or want for themselves. This is a part of your own responsibility toward yourself. Think actively, try something, but if it doesn't work out, change your strategy. Try something else. Don't just keep on treading water. If you end up on a plateau and feel like you're stuck, then it is time to look up. And pick a new direction.

But first, decide what success means to you.

How Do I Know If I'm Successful?

Let's leave the difficult world of adversity behind us for a moment and look ahead. Let's talk about success instead. Because the more success you have, the better equipped you will be to meet obstacles when they arise.

There are endless ways to define success, and some of them are—to be honest—rather convoluted and over the top. If we use Microsoft Word's thesaurus to help us and look at a few synonyms for the word "success," we'll see: *achievement, accomplishment, victory, triumph, realization, attainment.*

That's not bad, is it? Except for the fact that we still have no idea what success really means.

WATCH OUT FOR SNOBBERY!

There are people who like to put others in a box. The best example of this is when you're at a dinner and are asked, *What do you do for work?* And depending on how you answer, it can go well—or really badly. And the result depends, of course, on the questioner's opinion of whether you've chosen the right career path.

Not long ago, I was at a wedding party. One man at my table must have been asked that question at least five times during the evening. *What do you work with?* He answered, *I work with something I really love.* None of the questioners reacted exactly positively, despite the man's fluent and appealing description of his profession. Upon hearing his answer, most people tried to get out of the conversation as quickly as they could. (He sold cars, which has never ranked particularly high on the "approved careers list." Which is strange, since most of us buy cars.)

As an example of the opposite behavior, we can take a mother who doesn't care the slightest about what her children achieve in life and loves them unconditionally no matter what. Unfortunately, most people aren't that mother. Instead, lots of people make a direct link between our jobs and how much of their time and attention we deserve. My theory is that this is why we care so much about our jobs and our careers. We need this social acceptance to actually feel successful.

Most likely, our obsession with material things comes from the same motivation. We don't really need the things we acquire, but we do sometimes need something to display to others. To put on a show. A fancy car, a luxurious house, the latest cell phone, the snazzy running shoes. It's no coincidence that the logo is on the outside of those shoes. It wouldn't be much use on the inside. So the next time you see somebody driving around in a Ferrari, don't assume that he's a greedy jerk. Think instead that there is somebody who needs a lot of confirmation and love from those around him.

But there is also an interesting connection to our current times. If you listen to prevailing wisdom, you'll often hear that you can become, and do, whatever you want. Anybody can be successful if they work hard enough. We look at successful people such as Bill

Gates and think that it would be really great to be as rich as him. He never even graduated from university. All you need is an idea, a lot of energy, and possibly a garage.

ENVY CAN BE A DRIVING FORCE

Let's be honest. Envy is an important driving force. Even if it doesn't look pretty, it should be quite clear to us that our presumably egalitarian society has cultivated quite a lot of envy. Think about it: If we can all be whatever we want to be and achieve massive success, then it becomes a problem when some of us do and others don't. So we start comparing ourselves with each other.

Strangely enough, we're not, however, envious of Bill Gates. Not really. He's a fabulously rich nerd with so many billions in the bank that the numbers are hard to fathom. You simply can't compare yourself with him. Or why not the king of Sweden? He is also fabulously rich and lives in a very large mansion, but he talks in a rather weird way and, on the whole, is impossible to relate to.

No, the people we compare ourselves with are those who are closer to us. Who are they? They're the people who remind us of ourselves in terms of background, education, sex, and age. And that's why you should never go to a high school reunion.

In today's society we tend to look similar. We wear the same type of clothes, most of us can afford the same gadgets and gizmos to fill our pockets. Most of the people you interact with do, despite everything, have a job. So we look alike on the surface, and yet we aren't really alike. Social equality often hides deep inequality below the surface.

"Self-help" books (even though I don't like that term) are probably partly to blame for this.

If you look at the bookshelves, there are lots of subcategories, but basically there are two kinds of books. Either they say, *You can do it! Everything is possible!* . . .

. . . or there are books about your poor self-esteem, i.e., how you see yourself. And if we're totally honest, the day we stop comparing ourselves to others, our self-esteem will shoot through the roof.

YOU ARE SUCCESSFUL FOR YOUR OWN SAKE

Do what is important to you, and do it for your own sake. Not just so you can show off to others and say, *Look what I did!* Because the moment you do it, you'll be judged and often found wanting. And the people who remind you of yourself will detest your success.

The closer they are to you, the more they are going to dislike you. If they have a similar job, education, and attitude, they are going to be even more irritated by your success. Think about that.

Your biggest fan is somebody you don't know. But your greatest hater is probably somebody you know. Sorry, but that's my experience.

MAKING YOUR WAY UNDER YOUR OWN STEAM

Today, we live in a society that values the right and possibility of achievement for everyone. Personally, I couldn't care less about your background, the color of your skin, or what your last name is. In theory, if you do the right things, then you'll make progress in life regardless of who you are. As we know, the reality of life is far more complex, and inequality and discrimination are undeniable aspects of our society. But it is also undeniable that we enjoy far more social mobility and opportunity than in previous centuries: if you key in the correct combination, the lock will open regardless of what sort of haircut you have or where you live.

And that, in broad terms, defines a meritocracy. You make your way in life on your own merits, not based on what your grandfather did or didn't accomplish. If you work hard, then you deserve to be at the top.

The problem with that picture, however, is that it implies the opposite: if you sit at home and laze about, then you can't blame anyone if you end up at the bottom.

In other words: we are all responsible for our own success.

At one time in the world, the responsibility for our lives rested with God or equivalent higher powers in the form of fate or the universe or the sun, or something else that you couldn't understand. Later on, in some cases, the state took care of us, but nowadays a great deal lies in our own hands.

You're responsible for your own success; it follows that you are also responsible for your own failure if you choose to squander your resources. That's tough. I find it hard to accept. But, nevertheless, it's hard to ignore.

A wise philosopher has said that a society is defined by its ability to take care of the weakest, and that is an important idea. We should never forget it. I believe that society, the state, the government, and other organizations are definitely necessary to ensure that nobody suffers unaided due to a rotten economy, unemployment, physical or mental unhealth, and so on. That is one of the reasons I don't have any objections to paying taxes.

Self-help books and inspirational lectures can be useful here. They can help us envision success, however each and every one of us chooses to define it. How do we define success? And who should have it?

Everybody, if you ask me. Since everyone has a different definition of success, resources will not run out.

WHEN WE CAN ONLY RELY ON OURSELVES

The psychologist Alfred Adler believed that winners and losers can only exist if we accept that life is just one long competition. If we stop competing, then in the end there will only be winners—or losers. The only person you need to compete against is yourself. The person I am today can compete against the person I was yesterday. The person I am tomorrow can compare himself with the person I am today.

With this perspective we can avoid so much stress, and our self-esteem will be strengthened. We can focus on our own development, our own success, our own place in society without having to keep track of what everyone else is doing. Does that sound appealing?

There are ample opportunities for success—if we choose to make use of them.

YOU DECIDE YOURSELF WHAT SUCCESS MEANS FOR YOU

Success is something that each and every one of us needs to define ourselves. We first have to be bold enough to distance ourselves from what everybody else says and create a personal definition of success.

For me, success is *achieving a goal that is worth achieving, while at the same time becoming something worth becoming*. But this is *my* definition. You don't need to agree with my definition, since success is more of a feeling than a result.

We've all heard of extremely successful people who suffer from the deepest inner despair imaginable. Enormous achievements, piles of money in the bank, respect and admiration the world over. But inside themselves, they may be deeply unhappy. A lot of this is because we can't stop comparing ourselves with each other. And there is always somebody who's done it even better. So forget that idea, and concentrate on your own success. That will get you a long way.

To get you started, I want to give you some ideas for your own thinking process. Here are some suggestions to think about. Could these be ways that you personally define success?

HAPPINESS = SUCCESS?

Does that sound good? People are happy when they have everything they want. What more can anyone possibly ask for? It must have been simpler to get what you wanted years ago when there wasn't so much to get. Nowadays—and now we're back to where we were a moment ago—everyone else has more than I have. That's why I'm unhappy.

Researchers exploring the concept of happiness have found three factors that seem to attract extra joy and happiness: money, marriage, and children. If we're well off in those three areas, then we're going to feel successful.

Many people—though not all—would say that happiness means having so much money that you can do whatever you want. Maybe even having so much money that you can afford to be honest with anyone you want. Or "fuck-off money," as it's colloquially termed.

MONEY = HAPPINESS?

Money is hardly the same thing as success or happiness. No, money can't buy you happiness. Poverty, on the other hand, can't buy you anything at all. So next winter try to explain to someone sleeping in the park that money really only creates problems.

But then what's the answer? Does money actually make you *un-*happy? I heard that endlessly when I was growing up. Money doesn't make anybody happy. There was, however, no concrete proof offered to support this statement. So it's probably something we just reiterate because we're used to hearing it. Previous generations often had very different ideas about money.

What's funny is that there's research that supports the idea that money actually does make us happy. If you don't have anything, then you become happier by gaining money. But that only applies to a certain degree. Having billions doesn't seem to be the happiness guarantee you might think it would be. Perhaps such wealth simply means that you have more to lose.

In a study carried out at Harvard University, researchers found that the happiest Americans earned about $75,000 a year. Above or below that amount people weren't anywhere near as happy. More money doesn't mean happier people. But neither does less.

GETTING MARRIED = HAPPINESS?

Marriage makes people happy. Otherwise they wouldn't get married. And married people are, statistically speaking, happier than unmarried ones. Even though married people are happier than unmarried ones, their level of happiness doesn't remain constant for the rest of their lives. The greatest happiness is enjoyed the years before and directly after the actual marriage ceremony. Then it evens out, and it's not until fifteen years later that the (un)happiness is back on the same level as before. But fifteen good years isn't bad at all.

Oddly, another thing that clocks in at the same level on the happiness-intensity index is . . . divorce. How can that be? Simple: some people have gone and married the wrong person, and they immediately become happier once they've ditched the partner in question.

According to several studies with similar findings, the happiest marriages are those in which you can say that your partner is your best friend. Those marriages seem to be the ones that last longest and make people feel their best. Not a bad definition of success. And then you probably have more than fifteen years to look forward to.

ARE CHILDREN THE KEY TO HAPPINESS?

So what about children? Don't we take it for granted that kids make you happy? There's nothing that can make a person happier than a child, right?

Regrettably, it's not that simple, not at all. Available studies reveal the unfortunate truth that couples *without* children are a great deal happier than couples *with* children. Especially when the children are still living at home. Not to mention couples with small children. They are rarely completely happy.

In a study of one thousand American housewives who reported on their levels of happiness and unhappiness over a long period of time, the following factors were compared: socializing with friends, eating, going shopping, keeping the house nice and clean, or being with their children. While socializing with friends ranked very high on the happiness scale, socializing with your children rated the same level of happiness as cleaning the toilet. It was more fun to go shopping. This particular research study was carried out by a Nobel laureate, so there must be something there.

Of course, this doesn't apply to your kids. Or to mine. And there are, naturally, lots of parameters to take into consideration. For instance, the happiness connected with raising kids varies in different parts of the world.

NOW IT'S YOUR TURN. WHAT IS HAPPINESS FOR YOU?

What would make you really satisfied? Peace of mind? Being able to work your absolute dream job? A house in the Maldives? A billion in the bank? Staying in good health? Married life? The courage to aim for higher goals? Achieving something you've always longed to do? Growing and developing? Daring to face your fears?

A lot of people who are asked what they would do if they were economically independent answer with different variations of . . . nothing. That is, they'd take an unlimited number of sabbaticals or just lie on the sofa at home and take it easy, play video games, or something else on the same theme. But we know that none of those things are going to make most people particularly happy.

Let's leave the happiness research for a while.

You need to have a long think about what happiness looks like for you.

SOME TIPS FOR DEFINING YOUR OWN SUCCESS

Let's be serious. Think about what you're doing and where you are when you *don't want to be somewhere else*. When you're in the right place and do exactly the things you'd like to be doing.

Where are you? What are you doing?

The answer could be, of course, that you're lying in bed and watching a Netflix marathon and that you've never felt better. Absolutely. The only problem is that it's slightly difficult to support yourself that way. (I don't want to ruin the party, but realism is a necessary element here.) Unless your job is to write about TV shows and you can work from home, of course. Then that might be the right thing for you.

But it's probably something else.

If success for you is having $5 million in a savings account, then I think you should go out and look for ways to get hold of such an amount. But if success for you is to put aside a little bit every month, that's just as good. You deserve success as long as you achieve it without hurting others.

WHAT KIND OF TIME FRAME?

Winning the next competition or clinching a big business deal is a short-term goal. That was one of the traps I set for myself many years ago: I didn't think in the long term.

Achieving economic independence for the rest of your life is, for most of us, probably a long-term goal.

But success basically demands continual work. You don't *own* success, but you do *rent* it. And the rent is due every day. Ask any successful person. The second you lean back and declare, *I've arrived,* then the decline will start. So make sure that doesn't affect you too soon in life.

SUMMARY

Define your own picture of success. Decide whether you are looking for a feeling or a visible result.

If it's a feeling, what is that feeling? Happiness? Security? Joy? Energy? Freedom? Influence? Responsibility? Calm? The feeling of doing good? Helping others? To feel you are important? To have power?

Is your vision of success linked to a specific result?

Is it about your physical health? About how you feel mentally? Is it an economic goal? A career goal? Something material? Do you want to work at a nonprofit? How?

I can't say how you should feel or what you should think about these things. All I can tell you is that my definition of success is not the same as yours. But that's okay. What is important is that you know what *you* would describe as success.

And in the end, this is about the simple, but so intangible *feeling good*.

So: *When* do you feel good? *Where* are you then? *What* are you doing? What are you doing when you *no longer wish you were somewhere else*? And *how* can you stay there for as long as possible?

Make Your Own List of Successes

In the first half of this book, you made a list of setbacks to help give you a sense of the obstacles you've already encountered in your life. We considered whether the things on this list were really setbacks and what you might have learned from those experiences.

I'm not one to spend a lot of time thinking about the past. It often just opens up old wounds. But there is one other thing we need to take a closer look at—all your previous successes. Because there are definitely a lot of them, even though it might not feel like that.

You have lots of successes in your track record. You might not think about them, but there's an important benefit to listing the things you've been successful at.

Here come those brain researchers again. They say that we're programmed to focus on the negative. We can't help it. But we can balance things out by reminding ourselves about the things that are worth celebrating.

Perhaps you're one of those people who celebrates every little success, but if you're like most people I know, then you'll tend to remember mistakes more clearly than victories. Strong feelings stay with you longer, and failure is associated with stronger emotions than winning is.

The truth is that the majority of us have a lot more successes than defeats in our lives, but if you ask around, it sounds like the opposite. That's a pity. But we're going to fix that.

You don't have to shout from the hilltops that you're a fantastically successful person. But you are going to put together your very own list of triumphs.

Many years ago, I attended a class where the consultant told us to write down—in no particular order—at least thirty successes.

Most of the participants could do this fairly easily, but I suffered a sort of mental block. I couldn't think of anything. Everything I could remember sounded boastful and arrogant. Who wants to look conceited? Then the woman leaned over toward me and said, *Thomas, how did you get here?*

By car, I answered miserably.

Well, then, you passed your driving test, she said, and pointed at the sheet of paper. She had a point. Passing your driving test is actually quite difficult. And that's where the idea for this activity was born. I found that I needed different types of inspiration depending on the situation, so I sorted the successes into slightly different subheadings.

As an example, you can write down small successes you might not even think of as successes. Things like the fact that you haven't been late to work or school a single time in two years.

THE AUTHOR'S OWN LIST

I've done this exercise myself. Years ago, I just jotted everything down on a piece of paper, but nowadays I've sorted the details a little.

My list of successes would look like this:

Successes	Personal	Work-Related
Small	I passed my driving test after only four lessons when I was eighteen.	After fourteen years working in one branch, I stepped out of my comfort zone and switched jobs completely.
Medium	I live in a lovely house in the countryside.	I control my own time 100 percent. I didn't give up my writing even after twenty years of refusals.
Big	I succeeded in persuading a wonderful woman to marry me.	Together with my wife, I run a successful business that shares my message of understanding and better communication.
Fantastic	These days, I care very little about what people think of me.	My books are available in more than 100 countries all over the world and in more than 40 languages.

I write down new things as soon as I think of them. But I also read through the list now and then. Especially when I'm working on something tricky or intimidating and I notice that my self-confidence is shaky.

If I'm going to pitch a big project with lots of zeros in the price tag, then I might pick up the list of work-related successes. Sometimes I look back at my entries over ten years to give myself a little boost. I just looked over that list. It has more than twelve hundred successes. They aren't all fantastic and life-changing, but some certainly are. And there are always more than I think there are.

I'm always surprised when I realize how quickly I forget the good things. Like everyone else, I find it easier to remember the bad things. I don't fight that tendency. I still haven't found a way to actively forget things, but I balance the negative things with my list of successes. And I can attest to the fact that it is incredibly helpful if you want to keep your focus on the future.

WHAT SHOULD YOUR LIST INCLUDE?

Anything at all! Include everything you can remember that was positive. Don't stop writing until you have one hundred things to include on it. Keep it nearby—in your desk drawer, perhaps. Add to it regularly. Every time you do something well, put it on the list.

Why not? Forget the excuses about feeling stupid or not having enough time. I'm not asking you to put the list on a billboard or plaster it on the side of a bus. You can, but you don't have to tell all your friends what you've written on the list. Write it for your own sake. It will make you more confident and remind you that you're actually fairly successful already.

So list all your classes, certificates, exams, driver's licenses, your children, having a good job, raises you've received, that you feel good, that you go to the gym every week. Perhaps you're a good boss, or you have a fantastic partner, or you can sing every line of "Bohemian Rhapsody," or you managed to fix your first car, or you renovated your kitchen all by yourself without using the curtains to hide any missing window trim.

One hundred things.

Do you accept the challenge?

Of course you do. Get to work. Just do it.

SUMMARY

Negative experiences linger in our memories. One way of balancing them is to keep track of the positive things. So start your own list of successes today!

Just like when you watch the news on TV and notice that most of it is terrible, you'll be negatively affected if you don't seek out the positives. I'm not encouraging you to be naïve and pretend that everything is perfect when a genuine crisis is at hand. But all of us need a measure of balance.

Now we're going to look at what you can do to have a lot more things to add to your list.

Harry, Part Two: The Solution

I'm sure you remember Harry from earlier in the book. The guy who wanted to get into better shape. He started going to the gym, running in the mornings, dieting, changed his daily routine, stopped drinking beer, and so on. But it didn't work. After six months, he gave up the project and felt worse than before. Despite all his good intentions, ambitious plans, and genuine desire to change, he didn't reach his goal. He looked for success but got lost on the way.

Why? Let's quite briefly recall what went wrong:

1. He didn't know *why* he was doing all of this.
2. His goal was far too *vague* and *fuzzy*.
3. He took on *far too much* at the same time.
4. The results were initially *invisible*.
5. He lacked *persistence*.
6. He underestimated the difficulty of *breaking old habits*.
7. He *surrounded* himself with the wrong people.
8. He drifted.

As I mentioned earlier, it's rarely any one thing that causes us to mess up. It's far too easy to point at only one thing as the villainous cause of failure, but that also means we risk missing the real problem. And there is almost always more than one.

It was the bad weather. Or there just wasn't enough time. Perhaps it was too boring? Or maybe it was everything, *plus* a few other things?

If you wanted to help coach Harry so that he learns something from this experience, what would you say? We'll simply look at the difficulties one at a time and see what solutions we can find.

1. HE DIDN'T KNOW WHY HE WAS DOING ALL OF THIS

Would Harry have felt successful if he'd managed to get in shape? If he had a conversation with his doctor, who explained he was shortening his life by at least twenty years through his unhealthy lifestyle, would that have been enough to get him to continue with his ambitious program? We can only speculate here. If his wife had said that she dreamed about the man he was twenty years earlier—appealing to his ego—would that have kept him on track? Well, maybe.

On several occasions in this book, we've touched on how important it is to know your own motivation. So how can you find your *why*?

Decide What Needs to Be Fixed

The simplest way to find a *why* is to identify the problem you want to solve. The challenge, however, is not to get stuck on the solution too quickly, because it might be a cul-de-sac. Sometimes you simply need to step back and see the bigger picture. Going to the gym—that's one solution. But *what* exactly does it solve? Being overweight? Not having enough muscle? General stiffness in your body? Rheumatism? Social isolation? Boredom?

Regardless of how boring it might seem, you can put together a short list of things that aren't working in your life. Here are some examples:

> *I don't get home in time to put my young children to bed.*
> *My mother is sad because I don't get in touch often enough.*
> *I feel stressed as soon as I arrive at work.*
> *My partner and I argue about money every week.*
> *The new car turned out to be way too expensive, and now I can't sell it without looking like an idiot.*
> *I find it hard to go up the stairs because I've put on so much weight.*
> *I have a good job, great kids, a good relationship with my partner, but I'm still not happy.*
> *I have a good job, but it feels as if I should do more for others.*
> *I'm envious of some of my acquaintances for their career success, and that makes me feel a bit ashamed.*
> *I don't have time to read, which is my favorite hobby.*
> *It is difficult to stop using my cell phone at night, and that makes me sleep badly. I scroll back and forth between different social media pages, and when it's time to sleep I feel wired instead of relaxed.*

One of my clients recalled how her husband noticed that she was happy whenever she went to take their dogs out on a walk, but usually irritated or almost angry when she came back. He tried to understand what was happening: if the dogs had misbehaved, if the weather was bad, and so on. Until he realized that she got angry when she walked past the house next door, which was the last house she passed on her way home. His mother lived in that house, and for several decades they'd had a long, unresolved conflict. The man mentioned this to his wife, and she agreed that his mother's house reminded her of this unpleasant conflict.

Now he knew what the problem was. The conflict with his mother. Short-term solution: walk the dogs on a different route. Long-term solution: raise the problem with his mother and try to find a resolution.

What Problems Are You Struggling With?

What does your problem look like? When do you feel irritated, dissatisfied, exhausted, angry, or generally stressed?

If you know what the problem is, then you also know what you want to achieve. My best tip is to start with something that is feasible. Not because you're going to work miracles by fixing small things, but because it's hard to change yourself and your habits, so you shouldn't go for a total transformation right off the bat.

We can use Harry as a reference here. Let's say that you, too, want to make healthier choices in terms of nutrition, exercise, sleeping, and alcohol habits.

That sounds great, but *why*?

It isn't enough to say, *Well, it's a good idea to live healthily*. Everyone knows that. But we still don't do it. *Why* is it important? What's the *real reason*?

Why do *you* want to be healthier?

Do you not have the energy to play with your kids? Do you sleep badly because you have too much coffee or alcohol before bed? Does the thought of being on the beach in a swimsuit make you panic?

What exactly is the problem you want to solve? It needs to be specific, and the more honest you are with yourself, the stronger your motivation will be.

The Problem with Being out of Money

If we take one of the earlier examples and look for the all-important *why*, it might sound like this:

My partner and I argue about money every week.

What do those arguments lead to? Maybe they make you stressed, or you're in a bad mood, your partner is angry, the kids are frightened, and the whole house is seething with bad vibes. Is that a good enough reason to deal with your finances? Or would you rather bury your head in the sand?

Imagine that you've lived paycheck to paycheck all of your adult life. You haven't given much thought to all this talk about finances and saving. In fact, it's never been a problem. You have had a job, a decent salary, you have been able to support your family in a reasonable way; you and/or they have been able to travel and see the world. Your salary is enough to pay the mortgage for your house, and you're content. But somewhere in your forties you start thinking and look at how much you've set aside after all these years of working life.

The risk is that the balance in your savings account is . . . frighteningly small—if it has anything in it at all. In fact, you're in good company. A lot of people run into problems if a month's salary payment or a pension payment doesn't arrive. Two months' salary? Not at all good. Three? Panic in your wallet.

But why should you save? It's a good idea to connect the behavior to a specific problem you want to solve.

The stress every month when the bills have to be paid. Your partner's wish for vacations that are far too expensive. The size of your shared bank loan. Or maybe your neighbor's new, very expensive car. As I've said, envy is also a driving force.

But it isn't just about health or economy. It could easily be about your career.

Why Not Aim to Get That Fancy Corner Office?

You can take a big step forward in your career if you make an extraordinary effort and work extremely hard for three years. You'll have the chance to be promoted, get a higher salary, greater freedom, power, the possibility to have influence, and so on. But you notice that your boss looks rather worn out. Perhaps you ought to see her example as something of a warning? Better to stay under the radar and avoid too much responsibility. After all, a splashy career isn't right for everybody. And there is no rush, right? You're still young!

There are many misunderstandings here as well. It's not unusual for me to hear the comment, *If only I had a better position and a better salary, then I'd really show them what I'm capable of and put in a lot more effort at work.*

In the real world, unfortunately, it works exactly the opposite. First you do a really good job in your current position, then you might be considered for promotion. And what if this promotion is three years away? Why slave away for something that *might never happen*?

And here we are again: What is your *why*?

Why do you want to make a career?

What would this career give you when all is said and done? Not give to the people around you, but to you yourself. What would you gain from achieving a particular goal?

Some people might answer, *I need a higher salary so that I can take better care of my family.* That's a good and unselfish reason. But it's not enough. You need to dig down to what it would mean to *you* to be able to take care of your family. Your personal gain.

Would your life be magically stress free? Would you have immense personal satisfaction? Would you look like a hero to your immediate family and other relatives? It all boils down to figuring out what makes you feel good; there's your answer. Because in the end, that's what all of us want.

To feel good.

Lena Knew Exactly Why She Did It

At the beginning of this part of the book, we talked about Lena, who had gone to a conference and decided to make something of her life. Of the three friends, she was the one who managed to change her life, so let's look at how she went about it.

When Lena, at home with her partner, Catherine, raised the subject of changing her approach to health, education, and career, they jointly agreed that they had nothing to lose. They lived a good life with steady jobs (and salaries). But they realized that there was the potential for more. So why not try to make some changes based on what Lena just learned at the conference? Catherine saw it as a challenge and gave Lena all the encouragement she could.

What was Lena's *why*?

She had realized her potential was greater than the life she was living. So why not give it a try? She'd gotten the inspiration to push her limits in a way she hadn't done for many years. She discovered that she had become stranded on a sort of plateau in life without ever noticing that her life had stagnated. Her problem was simple. She was bored with her usual work. Everything was fine, but it gave her no energy. And she was frustrated with her health and weight.

Since she was a person who didn't like standing still, she decided to try something new. That became her *why*. And that motivated her.

2. HIS GOAL WAS FAR TOO VAGUE AND FUZZY

Let's say that Harry has figured out what his *why* is. He knows why he wants to start this new healthy lifestyle. So what should his goal be? He needs to have a direction.

Direction is far more important than speed. Many people are on their way nowhere . . . in a hurry. If they'd identified where they were going, then they might have actually gotten where they wanted to go instead of ending up in a ditch.

Just like before, there are different ways of thinking about and creating goals. Goals are a bit like diets: Not everything works for everyone. But every diet works for somebody.

You Shouldn't Have Too Many Goals at the Same Time

In order to avoid setbacks, and create success, you need to take the risk of setting a defined goal. And preferably a fairly tough one. Even though there's a risk that you won't manage to reach it and will be discouraged, you're going to be on the right path.

I've seen sales organizations that set ten, fifteen, or as many as twenty different goals for their salespeople. Activity goals in the form of the number of conversations, number of meetings, number of follow-up calls. But also pure sales goals. If you have twenty-five products and need to meet the goals for each of them . . . well . . .

Hopeless. Nobody can focus on so many things at the same time.

One goal at a time. That's the best method. You can have several goals, but if you aren't used to setting concrete goals and achieving them, I still recommend one at a time.

Financial goals. *That means money.*

Relationship goals. *Family and everyone else.*

Health goals. *Eat nourishing food or meditate.*

Training goals. *Build up your strength.*

Material goals. *Things, cars, houses.*

Career goals. *Be the best in your field, or start your own business.*

Experience goals. *Travel. See new places.*

Ego goals. *Your own personal development.*

Competence goals. *Learn new things.*

Spiritual goals. *Could be anything.*

Does all that make you have a heart attack? It can be hard enough to start drinking water with your meals instead of diet soda. Take all of this with a bit of positive thinking—*you can do it*—and *hallelujah*.

Write this down: Decide what is your most important goal—singular. Write it down on a piece of paper. But just one thing to start with. One.

It doesn't need to be a work-related goal. It doesn't have to be terribly ambitious. But you need to understand the goal and you need to be able to measure it.

Let's say that you aren't satisfied with your weight. You think that you weigh fifteen pounds too much. A reasonable goal would be to lose fifteen pounds.

But that isn't the best option. It's going to make you focus on losing weight, not on maintaining a certain goal, and you will end up creating problems for yourself that you don't need. Instead try setting a goal such as: by _____ month this year, I am going to weigh _____. You want a goal weight, not just weight loss. Just focusing on the weight loss instead of your goal weight can create a block in your thinking. It's easy to start chasing the weight loss itself, instead of focusing on the goal.

This is the only goal you set.

Avoid *simultaneously* starting a German course and learning at least a thousand words in three months. Nor should you renovate your house or have the goal of finishing the new veranda *before* the Fourth of July.

If you also have an economic goal, I would recommend that you wait on that, too. You can start working toward your first million when you've hit your goal weight. Otherwise, there will be too much to keep track of.

If you concentrate on making your goal weight, then you can keep your mental focus there, which increases the likelihood of reaching your goal. And it's important that you *do* reach the goal, because you need that success. It gives you the energy and self-confidence to take you to the next item on your list.

One thing at a time. That's the solution.

Be Specific When You Set Your Goals

Harry wasn't specific. He just wanted to get into better shape. That's why he didn't get anywhere. I'm sure that after two months of training and dieting, he was in better shape than before he started. But was it good-enough shape?

Say that you want a higher salary. Your annual salary discussion is coming up, and you hope to get a bigger slice of the pie this year. You go into your boss's office and tell her you want a higher salary.

Sure, says your boss. *You can have ten dollars more a month.*

Are you satisfied now? No.

So you try again.

Okay, we can talk about it, she says. *How much more?*

If you start stammering and can't answer, then nothing is going to come of it. And you shouldn't ask her how much she's prepared to give you. She might answer: *Nothing.*

What you need to say is: *I want another $250 a month.*

Then the negotiation can go from there, but that's a whole different topic.

If we apply all this to Harry's situation, we could say that what he should have decided was that by the last day of the year, he would weigh ____ pounds and have a body-fat ratio of 15 percent. That concrete goal would have had a much better chance of working.

How Did Lena Create Her Goal?

For Lena, it started as something fun. But as she began to see results—weight loss, insights after reading interesting books, and objectively better sales—the entire process became more exciting. It wasn't until she had experienced the changes that Lena actually set her own goals for what she wanted to achieve. I personally would have done it differently, but as I've pointed out many times—the process is not identical for everyone. Once she and her partner formulated clear goals, things really started to change.

The goals she set up were very concrete:

- Read for 30 minutes every day.
- Cycle to work every day unless it is raining or snowing.
- Take the stairs 100 percent of the time.
- Make three extra sales calls every day.

You can't be more concrete than that. Yes, it's more than one goal, but it worked for her. You need to find your own way.

3. HE TOOK ON FAR TOO MUCH AT THE SAME TIME

Harry did everything at once. This is another problem that is more likely to lead to setbacks rather than success. He changed his diet and drinking habits, added a lot of gym time and intensive training, and changed his daily routine. It was a total makeover. Great ambitions. But it didn't last. That's an important lesson to learn. You need to limit yourself so you can go the distance.

This isn't a book about fitness and health, but Lena had a completely different tactic. Let's compare what she did on the health front.

She Took Completely Manageable Steps

Lena didn't ask the impossible of herself. Even though she'd gone to the gym now and then, after a crazy time at work, she had gotten out of shape. She had gained about fifteen pounds over several years.

However, she only did three things to solve the problem:

- She changed her breakfast from rather unhealthy to healthy.
- She biked to work whenever possible and took the stairs up to the fifth floor year-round.
- She also drank more water throughout the day.

And that was it. No super program with nineteen steps. No weird diets. No gluten-free or juice-only or put-butter-in-your-coffee strangeness. No kick-start, no Weight Watchers or *Biggest Loser*. No gym routines with five hundred exotic exercises for a flatter stomach. Just simple things she knew she could manage.

The solution was very simple: since Lena's partner did the grocery shopping ninety-eight out of ninety-nine times, she was instructed to buy the healthier breakfast foods Lena had committed to.

Step 2 was about biking to work when it didn't rain or snow.

Since Lena already had a bicycle and knew how to ride, all she had to do was pump up the tires and get the bike ready to go in the evening. She had to get some sensible clothes, but since Lena was an adult, she didn't fuss a lot about having to buy the absolutely best (most expensive) windbreaker or a pair of multifunctional bike shoes.

The third step she took was to drink more water. She used to drink a lot of coffee and some fizzy drinks now and then. But now it was going to be just water. She did find that it was difficult to remember to drink enough water, so she set an alarm on her phone to ring once an hour between eight in the morning and eight in the evening. Each time it buzzed, she drank a glass of water.

The Result?

What happened when she made these small changes? Answer: Lena lost a little weight, just over fifteen pounds. Her health improved. She built stronger muscles. Slept better. Had more energy. She was happier, which affected her work and home life. She could do more in a day.

Would it work as well for you or me? We don't know until we try.

Those little activities gave her the energy to do other things, too. She started reading for half an hour every day.

Every week, she and Catherine went to a restaurant and left their cell phones at home.

Anybody could do these things. According to Lena herself, setting these goals was one of the most important decisions she made. She was pleased that she hadn't tried to also add three days at the gym, enroll in two online courses, and cut out television at the same time.

Don't Start Doing Too Much at Once

Start with a few things. Not everything at once. You can't imagine what this will mean for your motivation and self-confidence. Every time you succeed at something, you'll get new motivation to tackle the next thing, and then the next after that. And the next.

Lena's attitude to her work was the same as with her health.

She decided to make three extra sales calls every day. She went from ten calls to thirteen calls. A 30 percent increase might sound like quite a lot, but we're still only talking about *three* calls. Total time for this—less than thirty minutes a day. After two years, her sales increased by more than 200 percent.

To keep her motivation up, she read inspiring books about subjects like marketing, social competence, and communication. Even though she certainly didn't follow all the advice in all the books, she did learn something from every book. That's how it works.

Getting the Job Done

This is how you start: Look at your most important goal, the one you decided to focus on in the previous chapter. Write down this clear, specific goal at the top of a sheet of paper. Then make a list with twenty to-do points, activities that will bring you closer to that particular goal.

Your list might look something like this:

My overall goal in area X (Perhaps: To get my first management position in the next two years)	
Task 1—to achieve my goal	Let the HR department know about my interest in management opportunities.
Task 2	Read ten books about leadership.
Task 3	List my greatest models as leaders.
Task 4	Start acting like a leader now.
Task 5	Go to at least four lectures on leadership.
Task 6	Schedule time to attend a leadership training course.
Task 7	Find a mentor who can show me how management works in real life.
Etc.	Etc.

The first five things will be easy to come up with.

The next five will take a little longer and a bit more thought.

The last ten might be a problem. When you get to number fifteen, you might have a headache. But don't give up until you've come up with twenty steps. Make yourself do it. Then take a little break.

When you're ready—look at your list again. And ask yourself:

Which of all these points will get you to your goal the fastest? If you could only do *one single thing,* which would it be?

When you look at the list, this item will jump out at you. It's going to be obvious what it is. Underline it. Red pen. Three lines.

Now, if you could do one more thing to reach your goal, what would the *second* most important activity be? It's just as likely that this will also be completely obvious.

A final time: What is the *third* most important thing that would help you achieve your goal?

That's it! Now you've got it.

Now you have your *three most important priorities* clearly listed.

Your list might look like this:

My overall career goal: To get my first management position in the next two years	
Task 1	Explain to my boss that this is my new ambition.
Task 2	Attend an in-house leadership course.
Task 3	Identify my strengths and weaknesses in that area.

Write down the goal plus these three activities on a new sheet of paper. Throw the old piece of paper in the trash. Forget all the other steps for the time being. You're never going to do an additional seventeen things. I mean that. Throw it away. This is one of the most important things to do to achieve success. Remember Harry. Don't bite off too much at once.

Your Final List

Now start working on the three most important activities. But only those. These three activities are what you need to really concentrate on. Everything else is unimportant by comparison.

When those three things have been accomplished—add three new activities to a new list. You're going to realize that the first list wasn't quite the solution you thought it was. With your new knowledge and more experience, you now realize that you need to try some other methods. This is also a good example of adaptation.

4. THE RESULTS WERE INITIALLY INVISIBLE

Even very small decisions can, over time, lead to incredible consequences. Both good decisions and bad decisions lead to results in some form. But those results won't always be apparent right away. Time makes everything clearer, whether it be positive or negative.

If you make a bad choice, it will be noticeable in the end. The good news is that if you make a good choice, that will also be noticeable—in the end.

On top of all the other setbacks, Harry saw no results from all his efforts. He could have accepted that results take time and stuck to his plan nevertheless. He started a diet, he did his workouts, he denied himself every imaginable form of pleasure and fleeting happiness, but he still thought that nothing happened. After six months, he was still overweight. In fact, he *put on* weight at first, as often happens. He was sore from all his effort at the gym, he was bored, and he missed the little pleasures he was denying himself.

He needed to accept that you can't lose more than a pound or two a week. Besides, when you go to the gym, you build muscle, which weighs more than fat. We know that. It means that losing weight goes even slower.

But we can look at other examples besides health and fitness. It works in the same way with your finances. It can take a really long time to see results.

What Was the Difference Between Harry and Lena?

This is what's so interesting. The small actions that Lena took gave her fantastic results—in the long term. There wasn't much to see at first. She wrote down her initial (minimal!) progress in a journal. But since she had nothing to lose, she carried on. In two years, she hardly recognized herself anymore. When she bumped into old friends, they were astonished at the change. She was told she looked five years younger than she did two years earlier. If nothing else, that was good for her ego.

How Did Lena Stick to It?

When I told Lena's story earlier, I took a couple of shortcuts. The big difference is that in real life she had serious doubts about herself in the beginning. She knew she was good at her job, and she knew that she was appreciated both as a colleague and as a good mother and wife. But she didn't believe in her own ability to change herself. She thought that the ability to change was out of her reach.

Lena had heard all those inspiring stories about the dyslexic who had written ten books; about the orphan who'd started the world's biggest company in the X area; about the entrepreneur who'd gone into bankruptcy time after time but never given up; about the boy with no arms who now competes in the Olympics. She'd read books full of such glowing stories and she heard even more when she attended that first conference with her friends.

Successes That Irritate

In all honesty, these examples tended to irritate her more than anything else. How could those damned motivational speakers compare
her with these superstars? She was just a completely ordinary woman
and employee; what possibility was there for her? She couldn't see
that these people had once also been just as ordinary as her.

Lena was certain that she wasn't well educated enough to get
anywhere. And more school wouldn't help her, anyway, because
she probably wasn't smart enough. Besides, with two children and
a partner who demanded a lot of her when she was home, she didn't
have time. And as if that wasn't enough, she thought she was too old
to change anything. She had, after all, just celebrated her birthday—
forty years old. In her mind, she was already past her prime.

It was not until Lena bumped into an old friend, a woman from her
high school, that the scales started to fall from her eyes. Her friend
had taken some courses in programming without really knowing
where it might lead. Then she'd practiced her skills. When a better,
and better-paid, job turned up, she applied—and got it. Two years
later, she started her own business and now had fifty employees. She'd
just received an award for Woman Entrepreneur of the Year.

This friend was, to be honest, not especially smart. How was she
so successful? Lena wasn't envious. She realized that her friend had
worked hard to get where she was. But she couldn't understand how
it had even been possible.

And then she realized the truth: it's about choosing to believe that
you can do it, and then starting.

And that was exactly what she did.

She changed her diet, her exercise routines, and her client marketing strategy at work.

Lena doesn't have her own business, but she is the boss of her former boss. She runs the most profitable division in her international group, and she already has the highest rating from her staff of all the divisions across the world.

How long did it take for her to go from a good but rather disillusioned salesperson to her current success?

Seven years.

Be patient, which isn't always easy.

5. HE LACKED PERSISTENCE

A lack of "staying power" is often the difference between those who stick to something even when results are slow to appear and those who give up. Our warrior gentleman Harry had the best intentions but met with so many difficulties that he finally gave up.

But others manage to do what Harry failed at. Why is that? It might mean that there wasn't really anything wrong with the plan. Was there something wrong with Harry? History is full of examples of people who climbed up out of ditches so deep they seemed bottomless. Edison and his ten-thousand-light-bulb experiment, and J. K. Rowling, who hardly had food on the table and was met with rejection after rejection before a publisher accepted *Harry Potter*—to name just two.

What did they have that Harry lacked?

Answer: endurance. Lots of it.

Do you have limited endurance? Then don't write a book. Or: write a book. Perhaps you'll surprise yourself and show more endurance than you ever thought you had.

Earlier, I listed some things to keep in mind if you, for example, want to write a book. All (published) authors presumably have a lot of persistence. How do I know? Because it seems to take half an eternity to get from idea to finished product.

It doesn't matter how good the book is in the end, or if you like it. You need determination and persistence to write even a bad book. The simple fact that a book is published by one of the large publishing houses is enough to affirm that a great deal of effort has gone into it.

We authors remind ourselves all the time why we write. And if this *why* is sufficiently strong, it's a bit easier to keep on going. But even with a strong *why*, you need a sort of stubbornness that is sometimes hard to describe in words.

Allow me to use myself as an example.

My File of Fuck-Off Letters

That's right. A whole file full of letters from various publishers who politely, but with upsetting clarity, said no thank you to my manuscripts.

It's over there on the bookshelf by the window. Filled to the rim.

Year after year, sitting and working away, putting in a thousand hours a year on this weird hobby without having the slightest indication that it would ever lead to anything—that's what some people would call madness. I call it determination, perseverance, an immunity to setbacks that is somewhat hard to explain. A degree of defiance and perhaps a measure of pigheadedness.

For me, it did work out in the end. After pestering the publishing industry for twenty years or so, I finally made it through the eye of the needle.

But How Do You Develop Perseverance?

My experience is that perseverance lies in accepting the situation as you encounter it. Understand the fact that you're going to meet with setbacks on the way to success.

For me, it's been helpful to break things down into small parts. Then they aren't such a pain to deal with.

Let's say that you want to do some push-ups. You start with five at a time.

Five? you might be thinking now. *That is not many!*

No, but after a while you can do another five. After a while you can do ten more. After a while you can do another ten.

Now you've done thirty push-ups.

How did you go from five to thirty? It's a miracle.

Breaking down what needs to be done into manageable parts is the key to developing perseverance and not giving up too early. Even if you have an outstanding vision and a detailed plan, you still have to look at the next step and start there.

When it came to writing, I accepted that I could only influence one thing—the quality of the manuscripts I wrote. Everything else was beyond my control. How a manuscript was received, whether the timing was right for the idea I was working on, whether the market needed a male detective-story writer just then—I put all of that to the side.

For me, staying power implies continually reminding yourself of your *why*. It's about keeping your final goal in mind while accepting that you check off partial goal after partial goal on the way there.

Look back at what you've done. Look at everything you've survived in life up to today. Go back to your list of setbacks and your list of successes. You've gone through so much. Praise yourself for it. If you've managed all of that, then you're going to handle a whole lot more. Believe me. You've got it in you, if only you trust yourself.

You simply have to take one more step. And one more. And one more.

Did Lena Have Staying Power?

As we touched on in the previous chapter, Lena had a certain degree of staying power. On the other hand, why didn't she use it until she was in her forties?

This is where Laterville comes into play. Life simply chugged along. The idea of doing something more simply hadn't occurred to her before. She had no *why*. She hadn't made any goals. There was no plan. But once she had these things, it was easy for her to start and to continue along the path she'd plotted out for herself—even though the results were slow in coming. And then a fortunate personality feature appeared: perseverance. Her desire to succeed was apparent in the way she endured even when the results didn't come quickly.

She Made Sure She Had Staying Power

The real boost came when she bumped into that old school friend who'd enjoyed so much success, despite Lena's assumption that the woman wasn't particularly smart. However sad it may sound, a bit of envy isn't bad as a driving force. And that is what made Lena kick into gear. She added more things to her schedule at work, for example. She took on more work tasks, offered her time to her bosses, and did everything she could so that everybody would see that she was ready for more responsibility. The old school friend gave her the motivation to stick with it. Lena wanted to prove that she could be just as successful, which helped her to persevere.

6. HE UNDERESTIMATED THE DIFFICULTY OF BREAKING OLD HABITS

Harry wasn't aware of his own habits. Habits are one of the most important keys to change. You can easily become more aware of your own habits by being observant of your daily behavior. Take time to consider what's a habit and what's an active decision. There's a great deal of research on this, and I strongly recommend that you look at the Further Reading list at the end of this book to find out more.

Depending on which researcher you ask, between 45 percent and 50 percent of everything you do is a habit, be it good or bad. What clothes you put on in the morning, how you drink your coffee, how you drive your car to work, how you start your workday, how you choose which lunch restaurant to go to, how you behave when you see a pile of oven-warm cinnamon buns, how you start your workout at the gym, which TV shows you watch.

But regardless of the exact percentage, an awful lot of what we do is simply because we are on autopilot.

What Is a Bad Habit?

As we said in the first part of the book, a bad habit is anything you do that works against your goals.

If, like Harry, you want to get in shape, then desserts are bad habits. Drinking beer with your meals is a bad habit. Slouching in front of the TV on the couch for hours, instead of pedaling on your exercise bike, is a bad habit.

Always taking your work home with you in the evenings is a bad habit if your family is the priority. It doesn't make any difference if you think you need to finish up some work; if your family is the focus, then overtime is a bad habit. Full stop.

Buying things you don't need, without even thinking about it, is a bad habit. Especially if you have a specific savings target.

How Is a Bad Habit Created?

The solution to bad habits is in fact relatively simple, but it isn't easy. The first thing you need to do to break a bad habit is to realize and accept that that's what it is—a bad habit. Exactly like when you drive home in the evening and really should do an errand on your way back, but before you know it you're already home. Your subconscious steers you home while you're thinking about something else.

If we look at Charles Duhigg's method in his book *The Power of Habit*, we'll find some interesting things. For a habit to become established, three things need to happen—regardless of whether the habit is good or bad:

1. The habit needs a *cue* of some sort. A trigger. Something that sets off the impulse to act in a particular way.
2. Then it needs a *routine* type of action. Something that you do similarly every time. A habit is the repetition of a particular action.
3. And finally comes the *reward*. Something that stimulates you to perform that action again.
4. But, and this is where the danger lies: once this pattern has been repeated a number of times, the habit is established. Then the whole thing gets flipped. You're going to feel a craving for that reward, and go straight to the second point without needing any cue. That is how habits are created.

So how does this work in real life? If you're in the habit of stopping at Starbucks on your way to the office and buying a triple latte with extra everything—for six dollars and 350 calories—but would like to break the habit: Recognize that it is a bad habit. And then choose another route to the office.

When you see the coffee shop—that's the *cue*—where you usually buy this coffee derivative, your autopilot clicks on and you go in and buy your coffee; that's the *routine* type of action. The *reward*, the third step, is when you drink the coffee. It's extremely tasty. You get a dopamine boost and experience short-term satisfaction and happiness.

But after a while, you'll start thinking about that delicious latte with all the toppings, even when you're not driving to work. Now you have a craving, a strong desire for that particular coffee. This is when you leave your desk and nip down to the shop of your own free will. The coffee will still be very tasty. But perhaps not what you need to be guzzling if your goal is to reduce your calorie intake. Or save money, for that matter. A latte every day during a whole year is—$2,190. Or 127,750 calories.

How Do You Break a Bad Habit?

If you look over the three-point activity list you made to help you lose weight, and you don't find any triple lattes with extra every-thing on them mentioned, then you already know this will not help you meet your goal. If you're sufficiently self-aware, you'll notice that this is an unhelpful routine even before you create a habit.

But you can also use the same approach if you've already estab-lished this bad habit. The best thing to do is simply to avoid that particular shop. Before you think, *But there are other coffee shops on my route,* remember that it's going to take a while to establish the same habit in a new place. And now you're aware of it. You won't fall into the trap again.

What About Harry? What Should He Have Done?

If Harry, for example, had always had a beer with his dinner at home, then the first thing he needed to do was to recognize that habit. Then he would have had to work out a solution. It would, of course, have been simplest to stop buying beer to have at the house. That sounds so simple that it's almost silly, but it does make it more difficult to drink beer. Or he could put a note on the fridge door with the mes-sage: NO BEER TODAY! He might have realized that what he really craved was a cold drink with bubbles in it. Perhaps some seltzer would have done the trick.

What Lena Did About Her Habits

Lena, too, had trouble establishing her exercise routines since she hadn't exercised that much in recent years. She noticed that it was a problem if she didn't have her gym bag ready and in the right place. She needed a change of clothes and toiletries so she could shower once she arrived at work. It was easy to think of excuses and skip the bike ride. Instead, she started packing her bag the night before and putting it by the front door. When she got into that routine, she created a new habit, which meant that she didn't have to make any active decisions in the morning. If the socks and towels weren't already packed, there was a risk that she'd actively make the wrong decisions during that stressful half hour early in the morning. It's better to establish the habit of packing everything the previous evening. (I know people who even take their gym bag out to their car the night before, since they know that they otherwise might "forget" the bag in the morning. That's insightful.)

Bad Habits Exist in All Areas

Habits can also appear in your relationships with other people. Every time Göran opens his mouth, you prepare to start contradicting him, regardless of what he says. You do it automatically. Or when Sara says something, you're going to agree. Of course, this can be about prejudices concerning different individuals, but a habit is a habit, and your autopilot kicks in faster than you can even get a sentence out.

Observe your habits and write them down. For the ones that you're not satisfied with, also write down an alternative behavior.

For example, it's your custom that every day at 3:00 P.M. you go down to the cafeteria and have a coffee and cake. While you do this, you exchange a bit of gossip with your colleagues. No problem; that might be something you enjoy. If you want to avoid having all that extra sugar, though, set your alarm to 2:55 P.M. and go across to your coworker's desk and start gossiping a bit with him or her.

A Concrete Plan to Break Your Bad Habits

This is what you can do:

To help you achieve your goal, write down the negative effect of the habit, for example: it prevents you from keeping your food budget in check and saving money every month.

If you tend to waste money at restaurants and bars with your friends, next time take your car. You'll save lots of money because you'll have to drink less (and save the cab fare) and you'll wake up well rested the next morning.

To break a bad habit, you need to accept it. Then you need to write it down and clearly write down an alternative behavior or habit you'd like to replace it with. Like I said, simple, but not easy.

My bad habit is . . . (Write down anything that prevents you from reaching your goal, whatever it might be.)	An alternative behavior would be . . . (Write down what you can do instead.)
I always do the grocery shopping spontaneously without knowing what I really need.	I have a list in a prominent position in the kitchen, on which I regularly write down what I need to get at the store. I never put anything in the grocery cart that isn't on my list, no matter what the kids might be begging for that day.

Good Habits—and Bad Ones

When considering a habit, which ones should be considered bad?

Sitting with your cell phone in your hand while you're having dinner might not be a good habit, but if it doesn't affect much, then perhaps it isn't really a bad habit, either. It depends on whether you should be doing something else instead.

If, before every marathon study session you usually play video games for exactly thirty minutes, that's probably not a problem. It could be your way of getting ready. But if, on the other hand, that half an hour becomes three hours every time, then it's a bad habit that could poorly affect your test scores and stop you from starting a promising career.

Just like with everything else, everything does not work for everybody. That's why you need to take a good look at yourself and decide: What is an honest evaluation of your particular case?

To break a bad habit you need to make an active decision. It takes time to establish a new habit. You just have to accept that.

Make it a habit (ha ha) to observe your own behavior. Spend a few minutes every day thinking back over everything you've done. How much did you do as part of your routine, which means habits, and how much did you actively decide to do?

7. HE SURROUNDED HIMSELF WITH
THE WRONG PEOPLE

Then who are the right people?

They're the ones who encourage you, who lift you up, who might have opinions and criticism about your ideas but share their concerns because they want you to succeed.

The right people are those people who support you when you have a goal, who understand that you want to grow as a person. They're the ones who don't feel threatened by the fact that you are fully engaged in growing and developing.

The right people are the ones who make you smile when you think about them.

The right people are the ones who accept and embrace change—even when it feels uncomfortable.

The right people are the ones who can admit that they were wrong.

The right people are the ones who have the mental flexibility to change their opinion when they hear a persuasive argument.

Harry didn't really have any support when he started on his health journey. His wife wanted him to watch TV and drink wine. His co-workers thought that he should have a few beers and be one of the guys. Nobody encouraged him. Even if nobody directly persuaded him to continue to live in an unhealthy way, he didn't have any real supporters.

It would have been so helpful if his wife had simply said she was pleased he was getting in better shape because she wanted them to have many more years together. She might even have considered her own less-healthy habits. I don't mean that she needed to suddenly follow Harry's exact health plan, but sometimes it's easier to create change if we help one another.

A gym buddy would have helped as well. Perhaps a coworker who was also looking to lose a few pounds. If there are two of you, your friend can encourage you when you get discouraged.

Everything Is Impossible

For certain people, just about everything is impossible. The first thing they do when they hear an idea is to start looking for faults. Soon enough, they'll have found no fewer than five reasons why it isn't going to work (which is a bit of overkill because one would be enough).

These are the kind of people who would criticize you if you walked on water: they'd just claim that you only did it because you can't swim.

Stop listening to that kind of talk. When people say something is impossible, it means that it's impossible for *them*. Not for you.

If you want to start a business, then you shouldn't listen to your brother who works as a nurse. Or to your friend who has never run a business. The person you should listen to is somebody who has already started several enterprises of his or her own. And preferably has hit a few roadblocks along the way. That's the person with the right experience.

You shouldn't take advice about the world from college professors. They have no idea how the world really works. They can explain theories, not practical reality. And you shouldn't take exercise advice from a couch potato.

Negative people can be exhausting in the long term. Especially the pessimists who claim that they aren't negative, just realistic. But most of what you worry about is never going to happen. That means the optimists are the true realists. Being surrounded by negative people is like breathing poisoned air. You can only inhale so much before it starts affecting you. Negative people affect you mentally. They break your spirit, your desire to move ahead. They point out faults and shortcomings in everything, and when you ask them to stop, they tell you that they're only telling it like it is.

Surround yourself with the right people. Full stop.

What Should You Do with Your Relationships?

Let's say that you have the fantastic goal of starting your own business. Your friends are going to helpfully explain that you don't know anything about the field. Your brothers and sisters are going to call you a reckless risk-taker who doesn't understand that the well-paid, secure job you currently have is much better. Even your own mother is going to tell you to sit down and take it easy instead of working on a Sunday.

I understand that you love your mother, and she certainly loves you, too. She believes in what she is saying and she wishes you well. But her advice won't help you reach your goal.

This is why close relationships are so hard. If you don't have the same vision for the future, you'll end up getting in each other's way.

So What Do You Do?

The short answer is that you thoroughly consider the relationships that don't work.

The first time I heard about a man who cut off contact with his parents, I was shocked. I'd never heard anything so extreme. But when he explained why, I was less judgmental.

His parents were critical of everything he did. They were negative about his education. They questioned his choice of profession. They talked disparagingly of his wife. They didn't like the area where he lived. His mother complained about the way he dressed; his father complained that he drove the wrong type of car. At family dinners, all he heard was that the food wasn't perfect, that there was a base-board missing in the kitchen, and that the children weren't polite enough.

After every encounter with either of them, he had a stomachache for a week. The anxiety, worry, and endless criticism were just too much. Finally, he informed them that he didn't want to have contact with them because all they did was criticize.

That's a really hard choice, and I'm not telling you to break off your relationships. But if a person in your life does nothing but in-troduce negativity and create problems . . . something needs to be done. Act. Discuss the problem with the person concerned. Reduce the amount of time you spend with him or her. Set clearer boundar-ies. But do *something*.

Lena Surrounded Herself with the Right People

Just like having a dedicated gym buddy, it helps if your partner is on board. Lena avoided that potential pitfall. Lena's partner was with her all the way. In terms of other supportive voices, Lena faced dif-ferent challenges. Her own mother was the greatest problem. When she saw that Lena had lost more than fifteen pounds and had actually started running again like she had in school, her mother said in her own way that Lena didn't look healthy. She was looking too thin and pale. Lena said that she'd never felt better in her adult life, but that didn't make any difference. Her mother suggested time after time that she should go to the doctor because of this "sudden" weight loss.

Lena Got Rid of People Who Were Holding Her Back

It wasn't just verbal criticism, Lena's mother brought cakes and sweets every time she visited. She literally filled Lena and Catherine's pantry with unhealthy things. At first, Lena didn't say anything, but after a few months of the silent battle, they finally confronted the issue. Her mother had come by and made dinner for Lena's teenage daughters. The girls had embraced Lena and Catherine's new healthy lifestyle. And what their granny served them, and also expected Lena to eat, was a total catastrophe from a nutritional point of view. Lena and her mother had a terrible fight, and, to be honest, their relationship hasn't been too good since that.

When I met Lena, I asked her how overweight her own mother really was. She thought it was somewhere between forty and sixty pounds. That, of course, was the problem. Lena's mother compared herself to her daughter and didn't like what she saw.

This was Lena's greatest challenge. To be able to live the way she wanted, she was forced to become more distant from her own mother. Lena made her choice and stood by it. They're still in contact today, but it isn't as warm as before. Her mother still can't accept seeing her daughter in good shape and enjoying a brilliant career. She herself had no education and worked in an administrative position her whole life. On the few occasions she still drops by at Lena and Catherine's new, very nice house, she often complains about something. She comments on the fact that Lena sometimes works from home, that she takes classes in the evenings when she should be at home with her daughters. *Can't you just sit down for once?* is one of her mother's favorite comments.

Lena told me that this was her greatest sadness. Her mother couldn't accept that she had grown as a person and had a new perspective on life. But Lena doesn't regret anything. *It's my life and I need to live it the way I want,* she reminds herself.

When I listened to Lena, I realized that this exhausting process also helped motivate her to keep working toward her goals. It helped keep her on track.

8. HE DRIFTED . . .

The last point is perhaps the hardest to see. Harry didn't keep his eyes on the ball. When the results are slow in coming or there are simply no results for a long time, you may not be able put your finger on what's wrong. When other things come into your life and steal your focus, then you begin to drift away from your goal.

Incidentally, often to Laterville.

One Degree Off Course Creates Big Problems

If you don't clearly see the effects of your actions, then the goal you imagined becomes a little hazier every day that passes. It takes so little for everything to go wrong.

If you are going to fly from Miami in the south to New York in the north, and the pilot sets his instruments slightly wrong, let's say just one degree, then you won't end up in New York, but somewhere in the North Atlantic Ocean. Just one degree wrong. That's not much, is it? But the result? Plonk.

In Laterville, things are comfortable. Everything just goes along smoothly. And you don't even notice that all ambitions and goals have simply . . . vanished from the radar. That's when self-awareness and introspection come into the picture.

How did I end up in such bad shape? How could I be totally broke? Why am I facing a divorce? How could Elin get the job instead of me?

You haven't done anything terribly wrong. You simply haven't paid enough attention. It might just have been one tiny degree wrong, and after twenty years you end up in the sea. That's how it happens.

An airplane that is flown manually is actually off course more than it's on course, but it nevertheless usually lands where it should because the pilot is correcting the course all the time. If the plane slips off course by a single degree, the pilot needs to steer back one degree. If the plane goes three degrees off course, the pilot needs to correct the course by three degrees. The pilot has a system for keeping the plane on course.

Your path to long-term success is to acquire a similar system. You need a system to warn you when you're off course and help you with a plan to get you back on track again.

The Magic of the Red X—How to Keep Track of the Tiny Details

Many years ago, I worked at a place where we had a couple of smokers. One day, one of these colleagues—we can call her Lisa—went in to see the boss and said that she wanted to stop smoking and that she wanted to let him know that her mood might be a bit up and down in the next few weeks.

Her boss, of the more hands-on type and always eager to help, immediately took things into his own hands. He gathered all the staff together and announced that Lisa was now going to be much healthier. To really show his support, he hung up a monthly calendar outside her office door where he marked the date with a big, red X.

This X, he solemnly proclaimed to us, *is Lisa's first day as a nonsmoker.*

Then, in front of the group, he got her to promise to put a new X on the calendar outside her door for every day she hadn't smoked.

This approach turned out to be smarter that anyone involved first realized.

Lisa struggled with her nicotine addiction just like anybody else who has tried to quit smoking. But adding a new X to that calendar every day gave her motivation to keep going. The other smoker in the firm did everything he could to get back his smoking buddy, but she persisted. Week after week, month after month, X after X—until going back to her old habit would have been a terrible defeat.

She simply didn't want to break the chain.

We Would Rather Keep What We Have Than Gain Something New

The psychological effect of this is twofold. On one side, it feels good to put an X on a list. It's the same feeling as when you cross out an item on your to-do list after you've done it. It feels good, and that's because of the dopamine kick you get when you give yourself this feedback.

The second effect is described in Nobel laureate Daniel Kahneman's research. He calls it "loss aversion," which refers to the unwillingness to lose something. Changes that make things worse—losing something—have more mental impact that improvements or gains. It's worse to lose than not to win.

The practical effect is interesting. We dislike losing twenty dollars more than we love winning twenty dollars.

If Lisa had gone back to her smoking, she would have lost her struggle and would have wasted months of red Xs. I remember in the break room she said things like, *I've done this for sixty days, so I can't give up now!*

None of us really understood what was happening, but she didn't want to lose the effort she had invested. And she hasn't smoked since that day.

We simply hate losing things, and apparently we've always felt that way. Once upon a time, when we lived on the savanna, loss could mean a direct threat to your life. Not having anything to eat led to death, while having a surfeit of food really made life only a bit more comfortable.

The same applies to marking an X on a calendar. If you've filled a whole month with red X after red X, then you want to keep them. You've worked hard for them, you've earned them. You're going to keep them, goddammit!

How You Can Use the Magic of the Red X

How can you make use of this extremely simple method to keep yourself on course, and not end up in a nice house in Laterville?

Hang up a calendar of your own on the wall. An old-fashioned paper one. Hang it up with the month fully visible so the whole house can see it.

Every time you do the right thing—take a step toward your goal, keep up a good habit, or take steps to break a bad one—put a big red X on that day. Every day you stick to your plan, check it off.

If you're working on breaking a bad habit, then put an X on the calendar when you didn't smoke / drink beer / buy chips / lounge in front of the TV instead of reading a book / put off making that important phone call / or talk over your partner. Or put an X for every positive choice you make—every time you tell your partner you love him or her / stay focused at work / go for a run / get home early enough to tuck the kids into bed.

Because it works both ways.

How long do you need to keep it up? Until the temptation to stop has gone away.

This differs from individual to individual, and naturally it varies depending on what habits you want to create or break. The median is normally around 66 days, so you should stick it out at least that long. But the fact is it can be anywhere between 18 and 254 days . . . so don't be discouraged if it takes a bit of time.

This very simple approach is equivalent to how pilots use a gyroscope to keep a plane on the right course.

Perhaps you have a vague feeling that *it can't be that simple.* That's okay. Sometimes the simple can be difficult. And how do you know that it won't work before you've even tried it?

Regardless of whether your focus is health, relationships, finances, career, education, or something else—tracking your progress will help you stay on course.

What Activities Do You Need to Track?

What habits do you want to establish? This can be just about anything. Go back to the section about breaking bad habits and consider what prevents you from following through on your good intentions.

I'd even go so far as to suggest that you tell your family / friends / work colleagues / boss / neighbors what you're doing. And ask them for active support. Hang up the calendar. Show it to everybody who wants to have a look.

No, it isn't embarrassing. Yes, it's going to be a bit weird at first. But how eager are you to really change? If your family sees that you've put a red X on the calendar every day for two months, they'll help you get back on track if you miss a day. The right people are going to say, *Hang on—shouldn't you be crossing off another day?*

Think of it like a sort of savings. If you set aside $5 a day for sixty-five days, then you won't want to throw $325 into the trash just because you don't want to put in another $5. No, no. You want to keep going. And *you are going to keep going* once you have started this simple system.

When you succeed—give yourself a reward. An appropriate reward—*not* something that is the exact opposite of what you're trying to achieve. For example, if you are trying a six-month period without any alcohol and made it through the first three months, then you should *not* celebrate with a night on the town. But you could buy yourself something really nice.

Lena Didn't Allow Herself to Drift

In Lena's case, her mother (without realizing it) inspired her to continue. The more her mother told her to take things easy, the more committed Lena became. And this worked for Lena. But she also kept a record of what she was doing. She had a notebook, and in it she wrote down:

- the number of sales calls she made every day (thirteen);
- how many stairs she'd climbed every day (the minimum requirement was one thousand);
- how many calories she saved every breakfast (the sandwich and coffee had 265 more calories than the morning egg, so she added 265 calories every day in her notebook);
- how many pages she read every day (the minimum requirement was ten).

It wasn't any harder than that.

And What Were the Results of All of Lena's Activities?

Did Lena's efforts bear fruit? Was it worth all the effort? We only need to look at her results. Because the results never lie.

Last year she was named Leader of the Year at her company. She has twelve colleagues who report directly to her, and she's responsible for a division that consists of more than three hundred people.

Her salary has increased by 600 percent since the day of that seminar.

She's been able to set aside enough savings that her daughters won't need to take out student loans for college.

She and Catherine don't have a mortgage despite the fact that they live at an address many would kill for.

Lena lectures a few times a year (that's how I got to know her) about her transformation from being a member of a team to becoming a respected and successful leader. She inspires thousands of men and women every year.

She and Catherine celebrated their tenth anniversary the same day that Lena had her fiftieth birthday.

She can still wear the same dresses she wore in grad school, which amuses her daughters (but not her mother).

However, the father of her daughters has harassed her family, forcing them to move out of Sweden. So, despite all this success, she still struggles with her own setbacks. As I said in the beginning of this book, nobody is immune to difficulties and adversity (which is why Lena is not her real name).

Lena's Advice to Others

Lena's parents taught her to work hard and not boast. That made her modest and means that she might not be the first person you notice when you walk into a room. Her self-confidence is so strong that she rarely opens her mouth to assert herself.

When I asked her what advice she gives to people who want to change their lives, she had two things to say:

The first is that if she can do it, then anyone can. If she can drink water throughout the day, then anyone can. If she can make time to read a book, then everyone can find time to read a book. If she can make three extra sales calls, then so can you. She's not the slightest bit unique.

She quickly learned that she was just as capable as the majority of the people she met. It took her a while to get over her inferiority complex about people who were in higher positions and had fancier educations. Once she had succeeded in liberating herself from her mother's negativity, she experienced new freedom in every part of her life, including her career. Of course, she wishes that her mother had been able to see how good all these changes were, but since her mother refused to see it, Lena made an active choice and created distance between them. She hopes that in the future their relationship will return to what it used to be.

Her second piece of advice is to always *adapt to the circumstances*. For example, she started reading books about marketing, but as her own sales went through the roof, she aimed higher and started to think about the alternatives. She began to think about leadership. When she was offered her first management position, she was already well equipped to lead a team.

When the company offered her a top position in another country, she didn't say, *But I live in Sweden*. She discussed the matter with her family and decided to take the chance and move abroad. She knows that it isn't forever. She can come back. But since her daughters are studying abroad and Catherine works internationally, it really doesn't make any difference.

Lena's final words during our last conversation were as follows:

My greatest asset was that I found it easy to step outside my comfort zone. It was never really a problem once I had realized that life could be so very much more. Nowadays, I actively search for things that I've never done before. And I'm excited about what I'll find. I'm never going to stop. I'm never going to go back to the person I was ten years ago.

SUMMARY

The eight points we've just gone through are crucial in determining whether you will meet your goals. Following them is not a 100 percent guarantee of success or security, though. They don't promise that you'll end up king of the castle if you follow them to the letter.

But if you follow them long enough, your chances of success will be far, far higher.

You won't know for sure until you have tried them, right?

Now it's time for more good news.

Attitude

A transformational journey like this will not happen by itself. It requires long-term effort to create lasting change. And your attitude to that change can be what decides whether or not you will succeed.

Your view of yourself and your own potential has a huge impact on the outcome of your efforts. Attitude, it's often said, is the key factor. Your attitude toward everything you see and experience. Your attitude toward what you do, your attitude toward others, your attitude toward yourself, your attitude toward the world around you.

If your attitude toward reading this book is open and you're willing to take in the content, you'll have a good tool to help you move forward in your life. Your chance of achieving true change increases.

But if your attitude is just to look for things to criticize, then you won't learn anything at all. You'll stay exactly where you were.

If your attitude toward your coworkers is that they're lazy idiots, they're not going to be keen to help you when you need them. But if your attitude is that they're brilliant and helpful, there's a much higher likelihood that you'll work well together.

If your attitude toward your partner is that he or she is the person you want to live with until you die, then you're going to find energy to stick with him or her even when things are rough. But if your attitude is that your partner doesn't have a clue, then you're not going to make it very long.

CHANGING YOUR ATTITUDE CAN BE COMPLICATED AND TRICKY

Attitudes are often based on things we've heard, seen, or experienced. We often embrace our parents' attitudes. Sometimes that's good; sometimes it's bad.

A close relative of mine, for example, is a person who casually states that everyone living on a particular street is a villain and a thief. Why? Because the houses in that part of town are so expensive that the owners must be involved in all sorts of shady dealings. When another relative, neither a villain nor a thief, moved to that neighborhood, the relationship essentially ended. The first relative stuck firmly to his attitude that if you lived on that street, you were an underhanded Scrooge. For years the unfortunate relative who had simply bought a nice house dealt with lies and idiotic comments.

If you're going to reach your most important goal and live the life you want to live, then you need to be aware of your attitude. It isn't about standing on a stage and shouting *Yes, I can!* Sure, do that if you want to. Maybe you'll make some new friends that way.

No. What I mean is that you need to listen to what you say to *yourself.*

You need to make the active choice to believe that you absolutely can follow Harry and Lena's eight points and reach your goals. You need to choose to believe that you have what it takes. You simply need to trust in yourself and your own ability.

As I've shown, there are no secret magic formulas to achieve success. There's no magic here at all. You don't need to meditate or visualize. You don't have to have a personal coach who costs the world. You don't need to write down your goals in a book every night and put them under your pillow. The methods I've described here are extremely simple. They're well tested and they are available for anyone to use.

Anyone who puts in the right combination will be able to open the lock. Even you. If you use the code, that is. You don't need a coach, a special education, or a ton of money. What you need is the right attitude and the conviction that you can manage it just as well as anyone else.

Regardless of whether you choose to call it self-awareness, self-confidence, self-assurance, or whatever, it means a deeply anchored belief that you have what is necessary.

CHANGING YOUR ATTITUDE IS A CHOICE

Believing in yourself is a choice you make. It's an attitude you develop over time. You need to choose to ignore what your past looks like. Forget how it was before. That's just history at this point. What's done is done, and there's no point crying over spilled milk.

Blaming a sad childhood—or a low salary or not having any money or not knowing the right people or a lack of time—is a choice to have a particular attitude. You're the one who chooses your own attitude. But that attitude has nothing to do with reality.

An old classmate from school, a pleasant and clever boy, got good grades and went off to college. He studied two years at Stockholm's prestigious business school, and then spent two years studying law simultaneously at Stockholm University. He completed the last two years of his legal studies in just one year. Five years later he had two very good degrees. Absolutely brilliant. You'd think that a guy like that would end up at the top of any organization, wouldn't you?

The truth is sadly different. He finds it hard to keep a job, regardless of how good it is. And the reason is his attitude. He believes that he isn't good at anything at all. He persuades himself that he's about to be exposed as totally incompetent. He thinks he was lucky to get through those five years as a student and that he lacks ambition, that his health isn't going to hold up, plus a whole lot of other completely irrelevant excuses.

The last time I bumped into him, we were both past fifty. He didn't feel well, didn't like his job as an administrator in a small firm that didn't pay what it should. He was waiting to be fired.

This guy's IQ is probably higher than that of 99 percent of the whole world. And I really do like him. There's nothing wrong with him. But there is something wrong with his attitude.

WHAT ABOUT YOUR OWN ATTITUDE?

When you look at the eight points I listed earlier in the book, do you genuinely feel that you can handle each and every one of them? Or do you think that it's fine for everyone else but that it won't work for you? If you don't know for sure that something is going to work, then you aren't going to do anything. You wouldn't be alone in thinking that. But it is a problematic attitude. The only way to know if something works for you is to try it yourself. Nobody else can do it for you.

Give it a fair try!

You can go from the top of the list right down to the bottom. Take the points one at a time. Can you find a *why* of your own? Do you know what your goal in life is? And so on. You can think whatever you like.

It makes no difference to me. But the attitude you choose is your own responsibility. And the very same moment you choose to believe that these steps aren't going to work for you, you've also accepted 100 percent of the responsibility for where you're going to be in the future.

Your attitude toward yourself is your own responsibility.

I'm not fond of jumping up and down and cheering that *everything is possible*. No, no. Not everything is possible. But a great deal more than we think is possible. We just need to believe.

UGH, I'M TOO OLD!

Before I started my own business, I was an employee for sixteen years. For a long time it was a secure job, and then it suddenly wasn't. As a former bank employee, I've seen firsthand how a team shrinks when cuts have to be made. So eventually I got out. For a period I ran a company with some business partners, before (after another seven or eight years) starting a business of my own.

We can discuss the pros and cons of all those stages, but sometimes I'm bothered by the feeling of having wasted parts of my life on the wrong things. But even though in retrospect I think the years were wasted, I gained important knowledge and insights that I still carry with me.

Many people have started new enterprises late in life. There are many examples.

Have you heard of Dagny Carlsson? At the age of 99 she took a computer course, and when she was 100 she started a blog that received a lot of attention in the Swedish media. She was immediately designated the oldest blogger in the world. After that, she wrote books, hosted a radio program, and at the age of 104 made her film debut. So don't say that it's too late. As I write this, she's 107 years old and is evidently thinking about getting a boyfriend.

BUT I DON'T HAVE A PROPER EDUCATION!

That's just an excuse. Educational qualifications can be of great help, but only if what you study gives you the tools to reach your goal. You don't need a four-year degree from a university to start your own business. You don't need five years studying psychology to work with people. You don't need to learn five languages to travel all over the world. You don't need a university degree in nutritional physiology to eat sensibly.

Besides, the statistics are clear: lots of the world's most successful people have hardly any education at all. It doesn't seem to have prevented them from being successful.

And if you do lack important knowledge—then go out and acquire it! Take an evening class, search the internet. Realize that it isn't the *diploma* you need. It's the *knowledge*. If you want to take a class just to have something to hang on your wall, then you've got it completely wrong. The classes are so that you can do a better job—nothing else.

BUT I'M AFRAID THAT I'M GOING TO FAIL!

We all are. All of us have fears of various types within us. It doesn't help to hide away. Fear only disappears when you act *despite* it.

I don't know how many salespeople I've met who have been afraid of being turned down by clients they need to call. And even though I understand that fear, the problem is not going to be solved by avoiding your job. On the contrary, it only gets worse by delaying the inevitable. A salesperson has no order before he calls. If he calls and is told no, he still has no order. What has he lost? Nothing!

Not long ago, my son found himself in a situation people call "between jobs." But he didn't apply for new jobs because he was afraid of being turned down, or that he would be laughed at, or that somebody would criticize his experience.

In the end, he plucked up his courage and went around to nine different employers in one afternoon. One of them got in touch seven minutes after he left and offered him a job for a trial period. What do you think happened to his mood? His attitude toward looking for a job was suddenly totally different. Not that it mattered, because after the trial period he was offered a permanent job.

I'M JUST NEGATIVE, OKAY?

There's a funny story about a guy who thinks he has won millions in the lottery. He seems to be the only winner, and the future looks bright. He jumps in the air, shouting with joy. When his girlfriend comes home and points out that he had some numbers in the wrong order, he deflates like a popped balloon. But, she says, *Wasn't it nice that you felt so wonderful, even for a little while?* He had the capability to be happy. Now it was a question of doing something with it.

It's the same with anger, being grumpy, or just looking for faults everywhere. They are all attitudes you choose yourself.

If you want to, you can choose to look at your options with positivity. I'm not suggesting you lose your foothold on reality and jump into the void in the hope that somebody will throw out a net in time. But my proposed plan doesn't involve leaping over tigers, or ideas for world domination. It's just based on ordinary common sense, one step at a time. I would even claim that it is fundamentally without risk.

BUT EVERYONE ELSE SAYS THAT . . . !

No, no. You're listening to the wrong people again.

You've heard the following saying: When you're twenty, you worry about what others think of you. When you are forty, you stop caring about what others think about you. But at sixty, you realize that they didn't think about you at all. They, like everybody else, were focused on themselves.

Most of the time, people are far too busy worrying about themselves and their own lives to notice yours. And the ones who do actually think about you are probably wondering what you think about them. So forget about all of that.

Let that insight be your guiding start. You don't need to wait until you're sixty to use it. You can start today. Leave Laterville and start living life.

SUMMARY

Work on your attitude. If your attitude doesn't fit with your plan, then it's going to be an obstacle. You need to take a good look at what your attitude is toward the things that matter.

First, write down your complete plan for success in a list like the following:

- Reexamine your *why* very carefully and write it down clearly.
- Write down your chosen goals, again using as few words as possible.
- Have another look at your list of the three most important activities that will help you reach your goals. If anything is vague, make it more concrete.

- Look at your bad habits and write those down, too. Remember that bad habits include any habit that hinders your progress toward your goal.
- Decide how much time every day, week, or month you'll devote toward your goal. And remember that changes take time.
- If possible, set up a schedule for when you'll do what.
- Make sure you have at least two people close to you who will support you and help you to make progress. Write down the names of the unsupportive people you don't want to talk to about the project.
- Decide on a method of tracking your progress.

Now look at this simple plan. Take a pen and paper and write down all the reasons you can think of for why you should *not* follow the plan you've created to reach your goals and feel successful.

Can you honestly find any problems with it? Are there any obstacles you haven't addressed? Which ones? What can you do to clear them away? Good; go do it.

But how do you feel? Do you feel genuinely positive about starting, or are you still thinking up excuses and waffling, so that nothing will get done? If that's the case . . . then you still don't have the right attitude. Until you have the right attitude you won't be able to make this plan work.

So How Do You Work Smarter?

In the first part of this book, we talked about how easy it is to waste your time on silly things. So how should we use our time? Are there ways to be smarter in how we use our time? Yes, actually there are. And most of them are about your own attitude to the concept of time.

The most common rationalization I hear, both from myself and from others, is: I am absolutely going to do all of that—when I have time.

And one of the big problems we have today is that there is never enough time.

On the other hand . . . there's never been more time than there is now. The question is only what you choose to do with it.

PANIC AS A SYSTEM

One of my former colleagues had a rather entertaining homemade priority system. Carina had seven letter baskets on her desk neatly stacked on top of one another with a handwritten label on each one.

Starting from the bottom they read: UNIMPORTANT, NOT VERY IM-
PORTANT, FAIRLY IMPORTANT, IMPORTANT, URGENT, ACUTE, and *PANIC*.
The interesting thing was that the exact moment she put a piece of
paper in one of the baskets—she forgot about it. Most likely, not even
she understood the system.

We called her the Bermuda Triangle. Everything that came within
her orbit disappeared without a trace.

THE RIGHT TASK, RIGHT MATRIX

Willpower isn't enough. I'm sure you want to use your time in some
sort of orderly fashion. Even if you're reasonably effective with your
time, you'll want to become even more efficient if you can. The problem with all models on the theme of time management is that they're
based on logical thinking. Give priority to this, delegate that. Sure.
That's all great. But we're not logical and rational creatures. We're
emotional. If you had set aside a Tuesday evening so that you could
catch up on some work at home, but your two-year-old toddles in
and wants to play, then your entire system breaks down, because
you're an emotional being and want to spend time with your child instead of your work. I'm not going to say anything about that, except
that the work won't get done.

The most common way of handling time is based on making priorities. People talk about ranking various tasks based on how urgent they are and how important they are. But while there's nothing
wrong with prioritizing, there is an obvious limitation to that approach: priorities don't *create* more time.

All they do is push the tasks around on your to-do list, so that
number 7 becomes number 1. Priority methods borrow time from one
task and give it to another. You still have the same amount of work.

Apart from the fact that you've wasted some of your time on—yes, exactly—setting priorities.

If you rank how *important* something is, then you know how *much* the task is worth.

If you rank how *urgent* it is, then you know how *soon* it needs to be done.

What is lacking is the more long-term viewpoint of considering how *important* the task is to achieve a certain goal. Because it does take time. So the question is: *Is the task valuable enough to merit that time?*

The question you want to ask yourself isn't: *What is the best and most important thing I can do today?*

The right question is: *What is the best thing I can do today that will make things better tomorrow?*

The whole term "time management" is a little suspect. Time passes, as I've said, regardless of what we do. What we need is perhaps a bit of *self-management*.

Now I'll give you a simplified model that is designed to help you establish priorities without actually taking things off your radar. Get rid of anything that doesn't belong on the list at all.

On the left side, we have wrong tasks. The activities you really

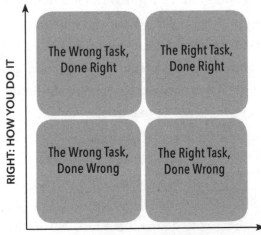

never need to do. Never ever. These aren't just given a *lower* priority. They should simply be *deleted forever.* That is why they're called the "wrong" tasks. But if you do choose to do wrong tasks, you can (as you can see in the matrix) also carry them out either the right way or the wrong way.

On the right-hand side, we have right tasks. These are tasks you should do. You can either do them in the right way or in the wrong way. Four fields, and everything is clear for you. It's really quite simple, isn't it? It doesn't need to be any more complicated than this.

Naturally this is a simplification. To all the management consultants I'd also add: there are other models, many of them very complex with various levels of priorities, but this one is perfectly adequate to illustrate the problem. We tend to complicate things unnecessarily, and often it's the consultants who get everything in a tangle. We invent systems that are so complex that we will be needed forever to interpret them.

THE RIGHT TASK RIGHT

Always do the right task in the right way. (You don't need to be Einstein to understand that.) If you do the right thing in the right way, you'll find yourself among the top 3 percent of salespersons, healthcare assistants, bosses, consultants, plumbers, self-employed people, driving-school instructors, authors, psychologists, brain researchers, or whatever you want. It works like magic.

THE RIGHT TASK WRONG

The second best thing is to do the right task but in the wrong way. Why? Well, the *right* task done *wrong* is still the right *task*. Since it's not particularly likely that you'll be the world champion at everything right away, it's a good idea to perform the right task as often as you can so that you start to get better at it. If you don't know how to do it the best way, ask somebody who has mastered it. Then do the same.

THE WRONG TASK WRONG

Spending time on tasks that don't lead anywhere, and doing them sloppily, too—no thank you. Throwing yourself into something you don't have the slightest knowledge about, and then doing it badly on top of that? Undeniably millions of hours are spent doing exactly that in the corporate world.

Wasting time on the wrong tasks that might create more problems than if you'd never done them in the first place? Drop those things in somebody else's lap. There's always somebody who likes to do, and who can do, stuff that you neither like nor are good at.

THE WRONG TASK . . . RIGHT

This is potentially the greatest problem. This is a really insidious trap and the greatest time thief: doing the *wrong* task *right*.

One out of two might not sound too bad. But the wrong task done right is undoubtedly the worst of all four categories since it makes the situation look deceitfully good. It's extremely easy to be tempted to do something you feel you're very good at. This is where you feel safe, doing things you know how to do.

But think again. Being clever at something that doesn't even make any difference? Can you imagine a worse waste of time and resources? Becoming really excellent at something that doesn't have the slightest connection with the job needing to be done is pure madness. What could be more inefficient than doing something perfectly that didn't need to be done at all?

TIME THIEVES

The two fields on the left in the figure in this section are time thieves.

Sometimes you can't avoid time thieves. If you work in an office and the printer gets jammed, you have to pull out all the different drawers and push them back in again searching for that one irritating sheet of paper. But does that mean you should study to become a printer technician when you have the time? Hardly. You ask somebody who knows. You do not, I repeat, *do not* become an expert on repairing printers. That's the kind of thing you should actively prioritize away. Delete those things from your consciousness and your to-do list.

But how do you know what's a time thief? What if there was a way to know what the wrong way to spend your time would be . . . in advance?

In fact, there is!

WHAT DETERMINES HOW YOU SHOULD SPEND YOUR TIME?

A good question that doesn't have a single answer, but the right thing to spend your time on is usually *What takes you toward your goal?*

If you want to visit Kiruna in the far north of Sweden, you take the train going north. The right thing, done right. If you take the train going south, you won't get to Kiruna. But the train is the right method, so the southbound train would be the wrong thing right.

What would be the wrong thing wrong in this case? A bicycle going south might be your answer, but this isn't completely black and white. Theoretically, you might make your way to Kiruna by cycling southward. After many miles and a lot of swallowing of cold water you might arrive at Kiruna's impressive gates.

THE MISSING LINK

To be really certain about the right thing to do, we need to add the tricky factor of time. If, for example, you need to be in Kiruna tomorrow morning, then your possible choices are suddenly limited. In that case, you can't even answer "by train," because you might not get there in time. You might have to fly there.

The correct definition of the right thing to do would be: whatever helps you reach your goal at the time *you need to arrive there.*

So the correct diagram should look like this:

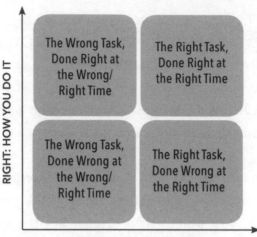

THE RIGHT THING AT THE RIGHT TIME IS DETERMINED BY YOUR GOAL

Your goal determines what you should do with any free time you have.

What's the right thing to do right now?

What's sometimes wrong is also sometimes right. What's wrong for you might be right for somebody else. What's wrong for you right now might be right for you some other time. Confusing—I know. That's precisely why the timing is important.

This is not an exact science, either. And you can do whatever you want whenever you want to. You don't need to follow this approach at all. But if you want to accomplish what you've made up your mind to do, then it might be a good idea to consider:

What is the right thing to do just now?

Put a yellow sticky note on your computer screen. On the bathroom mirror. On the kitchen fan. On the steering wheel. On the inside of your sunglasses.

Set the alarm on your mobile phone so that it vibrates once an hour during work hours, and whenever it rings ask, *What is the right thing to do in this moment?*

But stop wasting time as if you have unlimited amounts of it. Regardless of how old you are, you don't. It's time to take time—your time—seriously.

Besides, you already know what the right steps are. They're the three tasks that you gave the highest priority to on your list of activities that will help you reach your goal. Do them. If you can manage to do other things, too—go for it! But not otherwise.

SUMMARY

Time is your most important resource. Nothing is as valuable as your time. It's a resource that you'll never get any more of and that can't be re-created once it's past. You can't store it, and you can't get any more by swapping with somebody else or buying it.

Twenty-four hours a day. That's what you get.

You can get more of everything else, but time is limited.

How good you are at handling your time depends a lot on how you choose to look at it. Your attitude is key here as well. When you're young, it's easy to think that there is so much time that there's nothing to worry about. But the older you get, the more often you'll find yourself reflecting on the fact that time is far from endless.

Sit down and seriously consider how you think about the time you have. Does it feel like you use it for important things? Do you feel that you use it on worthwhile activities? Do you do anything positive with the time you have?

If the answer is yes, then congratulations! If the answer is uhmm . . . then you simply need to reconsider.

But, again, everything begins with you knowing where you are going—and why. It's not until you have both a goal and a reason that you'll know the right things to do and when to do them.

There is, perhaps, no right or wrong way to look at this issue of time. Per usual, people work differently. Which leads us to the finale.

Self-Awareness Will Lead You Down the Right Path

Before we summarize everything, we need to look at what's perhaps one of the most important insights you can have about yourself. By now, you know exactly what your colors are according to the DISC model. But let's take a quick look at what you could face in the form of risks and more specific pitfalls. Naturally, not all of this is connected to your communication profile, but there are definitely clues as to how you could avoid unnecessarily sleepless nights.

A central theme is that few people succeed entirely on their own. Often they need the support of others.

HOW RED BEHAVIOR CREATES PROBLEMS

You Reds have never found it hard to set goals. It's in your nature to be goal-oriented and focused on results. That's definitely a strength. The challenge is your tendency to set goals that are so demanding and seemingly so unachievable that it can be hard to get others to go along with you. Some people aren't even going to see the point of trying.

There's something you need to realize. I know that you understand, intellectually, that nobody can manage everything entirely by themselves. But the Red temperament also involves a permanent feeling of "I can do this myself." You're likely to rush ahead and then see who follows along.

This is a mistake. Without a team around you—coworkers, employees, colleagues, neighbors, relatives, friends, and not least, your partner—you'll probably never reach your goal. You might explain this away by saying it was the wrong goal, but no people, not even you Reds, manage on their own without support from those around them. The world has become more and more dependent on our ability to cooperate.

If you are primarily Red, then you're facing a challenge here.

Everyone else.

But have you ever heard of a successful hermit?

You need to train yourself to handle and work with the people around you. If your self-awareness is good, you'll already have learned this. But be aware that nobody is an island.

Your Path to Success

Your method of meeting others can be the key to how you reach your goals and become ridiculously successful. Memorize the following:

Most people take more time to come to a decision or give an answer than you do. You'll often be the fastest in the room. Sometimes you won't have any choice but to calm down and adapt your pace. If they can't keep up, then you don't need a team. . . .

Besides, people around you can misunderstand your very direct approach. Getting straight to the point at a meeting is effective, but the majority of the people you meet prefer a somewhat less direct method. They like to have a cup of coffee and mention something about the weather, about the economy, about the reason that you're having this meeting at all.

Yes, yes, you're right and they're wrong. But we're talking about simple solutions.

You can start by asking how people feel. And then listen to the answers. You won't believe how much valuable information you can obtain that will affect the project.

Don't just talk about how something will benefit you. Emphasize that you are not the only one who will gain from what you're doing.

Your way of looking directly at people and maybe raising your voice a little when you're feeling passionate can make people think that you're angry. I know, you haven't been angry in God-knows-how-long, but not everyone is like you, that's for sure. If people are afraid of you, then you're already heading toward trouble. If that's your goal, fine. If not—take it easy. If you're concerned or actually irritated, say, *Don't take this personally, but I'm starting to get worried about our deadline.* Try it. It's going to work a lot better.

Another thing: once we finally reach harbor, realize that a little break might be necessary. We know that you aren't satisfied even when you've reached your goal. That's okay, but let people relax a little. Then you can get back to work again.

And that's your strength. Setting new goals, always striving to move onward and up. Just use it in the right way.

You don't have to be satisfied. But it's good if you can stop for a moment and congratulate yourself on your victory. Then . . . back to the battle.

WHO SUFFERS AS A RESULT OF
YOUR YELLOW BEHAVIOR?

You're a really nice chap, you know that? If you're mainly Yellow, then you have lots of fans. In fact, you're one of those popular people everyone else would like to be. Which means that you find it easy to attract people to your vision and your ideas. Or to you. With your excellent vocabulary and your natural talent for communicating effectively, you don't have any problems drawing others in to your projects, regardless of what they are.

But . . . that brings with it a variety of challenges.

People are going to want to join in, which is good. The risk is that they're going to say exactly what you want to hear. They know that you can be easily offended. You take things personally. Which means that your gang might try to protect you from bad news.

Besides, you aren't one of the world's best listeners. And people know that. They are actually very aware of the fact that you don't listen to what others say. And even if you hear the words, inside your head you're going to rewrite the conversation so that you hear what you want. It's only your ideas that count.

This is something you share with the red profile. If you have both red and yellow in your profile, you're definitely in trouble in this area. Both colors have no problem convincing or persuading others about ideas. But even though you're a creative person, you don't know everything. And when you share your best ideas, some people are going to think that your feet have floated off the ground—again.

How to Retain Your Popularity

One way of avoiding this pitfall is to make a few plans on paper. Take a step back and consider things. *Would this actually work?*

And now we come to perhaps the most important topic I want to talk to you about: your ability to follow plans. Many of you Yellows are excellent when it comes to creating plans for others, but you can't manage to follow the plan yourselves. If you even manage to get something down on paper—you aren't a world champion at documentation, either—then the question becomes whether you'll be able to find the paper an hour later.

I don't mean to be a naysayer, but you're not extremely structured. I'm rather convinced that if you've gotten this far in the book, then you've got lots of wonderful ideas based on what you've read. You'll certainly think that some of these exercises are great.

But have you stopped a single time and actually done any of them? Or have you thought, *That is so obvious that I'm just going to remember it?* Nope, that isn't good enough.

You need to surround yourself with the right people. And who are they? Perhaps folks with some blue in their profiles. Don't freak out, but some blue is a good complement to your visionary, creative, and inspiring self. Together, you could accomplish great things. All you need to do is talk through how you both like to work and how you could cooperate on area X.

In general, you need to pay a little less attention to your gut feeling, and focus a bit more on what the facts say. Do some strategic thinking about your amazing new project—whether it be personal or professional. There's nothing wrong with being fairly concrete now and then.

You might run into some speed bumps on your way. That's okay. You are a realist, aren't you? You know that you'll meet with setbacks, but don't let that intimidate you. You keep going on, since you have your plan. The advantage of your plan is that you don't need to have it in your head. You only need to write it down and then read what it says. It couldn't be simpler.

So mark off some time in your calendar today and make your plan. Follow the eight points in the book; that's enough to get you started.

HOW GREENS CAN GET WHAT THEY WANT WITHOUT WORKING UNTIL THEY DROP

As a Green, you're essentially a relationship person. You like people, but not too many at once, and preferably ones whom you already know.

Also, you don't like dealing with change. Sure, you realize that it's not ideal to just tread water all your life. Even if you're a secure, stable person, you still need a few new things in your life.

I'm not sure how you would personally describe success. It depends a lot on what your driving forces are. But your behavior doesn't often illustrate a desire to break old patterns and establish new ones. Even though there are some Green people who accept change, there are not many who actively search for ways to create these changes.

And this is one of your major problems. You might have read lots of good ideas in this book, but there is a risk that you'll put them aside and just "think it over."

Of course, it's good to change one's attitude, and there are positives to establishing new habits. But those old habits just feel so good! Or, they might not necessarily feel good, but at least they feel secure. And should you really go around trying to change everything?

The good news for you, my friend, is that there isn't very much you need to do differently. You only need to take on one little thing at a time, work at it, and then move on. No giant leaps necessary. Just ordinary, simple things.

Working with others is what you do best, but you should be aware of the fact that others might think that you're a bit slow at the start. Even when you have the facts and evidence laid out in front of you, you do tend to . . . wait and see. Only you know what you're actually waiting for.

How to Move at a Reasonable Pace

Regardless of what you would like to change and regardless of how you define success, you need to surround yourself with the right people. You're good at handling relationships, but sometimes you're a bit too kind. You need to dare to be more direct with others.

The people around you are going to think that you are nice and kind, but it's possible that they're also going to think that you don't really ever kick into gear. They might see your hesitation as a negative. Even if they want to help you, you might not have the same kind of drive as the Reds and the Yellows. On the other hand . . .

The Reds would really complement you. I know, that feels far-fetched, but think about it. Somebody who's good at getting things to happen would combine well with your slightly milder approach. That could be a really excellent combination.

Working together and cooperating well could lead to some great successes for you. You could share the work between you. The Red can help push you a little, and stretch your goal, while you have the patience necessary to wait for the result.

And a Red partner, when it comes to exercise, or marketing, or doing DIY projects at home, or anything at all, will make you be specific about what you really want. Sometimes you're a bit too vague, even for yourself. A Red person could, with your approval, of course, really get you to reflect and become aware of what you'd like to change. When everything feels right. And they're good at grabbing your hand and simply pulling you along. They don't listen too much to objections. If you have a good relationship, this person can just nudge you along in front of them at an acceptable pace.

And you'll thank him or her afterward.

THE REASON WHY YOUR BLUE BEHAVIOR IS NOT THE PERFECT SOLUTION

So you have mainly blue in your profile.

You are good at drawing up plans, and I'd be surprised if you haven't taken sheets of notes already. You probably haven't written directly on the book, though.

You've listened, absorbed, and can see a lot of the logic in my suggestions. You definitely like the idea that success comes only if you take the time to let it grow. And you're the most patient of everybody here. You realize that speed is not the goal. It is quality that counts, right?

Fine. We agree on that.

Uhmm. Did you also see my comments in exactly nine places in the book that it doesn't make a difference how much you know or how much you're capable of doing if you don't actually do anything?

We've both heard the expression, "If you fail to plan, then you are planning to fail." But what does that mean? It means you need to go from thought to action. You don't need to talk with anybody, but you do need to act. Your time at the drawing board is over. You need to trust me on this. Now, off you go and act. If you do nothing besides rephrase and polish up your plans, then nothing will ever happen. And that would be a problem, right?

Since you, like the Red folks, are more interested in substantive issues than in relationship issues, there's a risk that you, too, will decide to do everything yourself. That would be most unfortunate. The idea that you're best at everything is incorrect. You aren't. Not even if you've taken the class. There is always someone better. Bring them into the process. Accept their help.

Your tendency to strive for perfection will prevent you from moving forward. Take this as a serious piece of advice from one per-fectionist to another. Perfection is the ultimate threat to progress. Waiting for the perfect opportunity—just tweaking the plans a little more, looking for even better alternatives—that doesn't go anywhere. There is no perfect moment. The time has come to act.

The people you surround yourself with see your lovely plans and elegant presentations. What they're waiting for is something to hap-pen. When they look at your documents, they also see goals that don't look too challenging. That's because you are a cautious general. Listen to others and see if you can challenge yourself a bit more.

Appoint somebody you really rely on to have a look at your plans and help you to evaluate everything you've laid out.

Your Method to Achieve Acceptable Quality

You need to start to trust other people. They know an awful lot of things that you don't have a clue about. You can start by trusting me when I say that the methods in this book really work.

You need to drop the idea that you don't really have any proof of that. Since you haven't followed somebody around for seven years, you don't have concrete evidence that this plan was what led to his success.

That's true. But look at your own method. Consider the place you are right now. You are there thanks to, or perhaps because of, your "homemade" method. If you're 100 percent satisfied with the result, then don't change anything. If you want more out of life, then you need to change things up.

If you want to experience the best quality life in terms of your health, your career, your financial position, your immediate family, and your long-term plans for the future, then it's time now to accept that all the answers don't exist.

Perhaps you're thinking that it doesn't feel right to invest five years of your life in something that might not work perfectly. I understand that, but I have one question for you: How long does it take to wait for five years and not do anything at all?

I know that you aren't afraid and that you don't feel hesitant because of low self-confidence. Rather you're waiting because you are wondering where you can get more concrete evidence. Okay, send me an email and I'll give you the details.

SUMMARY

Regardless of what your dominant colors are, or your primary driving forces, you have qualities that will definitely help you on your way forward. But, unfortunately, you also have qualities that could throw a wrench in the works. That's what I've tried to address here.

You could choose to ignore them. Or you could really understand them and do something about them. As usual, it's your choice and your responsibility.

I took note of the feedback that life gave me. It wasn't something that came completely naturally. I was an underachiever, performing far below my potential. Then, I got tired of feeling mediocre.

Over the years, I've changed my opinion of myself. Nowadays, for example, I control my red streak very well. It often made itself known in the presence of the wrong people when I opened my mouth and fired off some less-pleasant comments. I still don't have complete control over it. You only have to ask people in my inner circle. Or maybe don't do that.

The yellow column, which is also fairly high in my profile, was probably what people around me noticed most when I was younger. When I was young, I was a lot more sensitive about what people thought about me than I am today, so I made an effort to be popular. It's debatable whether that worked. My approach was to be the prankster who joked and kept people in a good mood and tried to be funny. I can still be funny, but that's more of a tool than a need these days.

I don't have any green to speak of. My apologies to all those I have forgotten to get in touch with.

And my blue factor, that's very high. I actually like it, because it gives me an annoyingly good memory for what people say to me, and I'm good at making plans. Now that I've learned to take those fancy plans and transform them into concrete action, I'm much better off.

29

Maintaining Your Success

Now you have the answers to 95 percent of all questions. If you follow the ideas I've presented, you'll come a long way no matter what your goal is. And I want to congratulate you on your desire to make new dreams for yourself. You won't regret it. Just remember one thing: it's easy to start new things, but not as easy to carry them out. Some laws of nature are hard to avoid. But there are solutions to that, too.

What does a rocket need in order to leave Earth? An awful lot of power and huge amounts of fuel. Breaking through the atmosphere and leaving Earth's orbit uses up almost all the fuel in the tanks.

But what's interesting is that this isn't a problem at all, even if the journey is going to be very long. Because once the rocket has left Earth's orbit, it needs hardly any power to maintain its speed.

The same principle applies when you're going to start a new direction in life. If you want to go from setback to success, you need to kick up the speed for a while. Work harder on your goal descriptions, your habits, keep a better check on your own ideas and the people around you.

But you also need to keep things in hand. Maintain your momentum.

Don't ease up until you have a head of steam and start seeing results. The risk is that you'll relax far too soon and start drifting off course.

If you've gone around with a few extra pounds for a few years and are now living a healthier lifestyle, you're going to see results after a while. You're going to notice that your pants are a bit looser around the waist and you'll have more energy.

Congratulations!

THIS IS A SERIOUSLY DANGEROUS PLACE

This is when you'll start thinking you've earned a reward.

The reward can be anything at all, from a tiny piece of chocolate to a fancy dinner out on a Saturday evening with your sweetheart. Or a month's vacation in some pleasant, sunny place.

It's not wrong to give yourself a reward for your progress, but this is where there's a risk that it will all go south. If you break your new good habits by celebrating with chocolate, you might sabotage the whole project. Because if you munched on chocolate all your life up until six months ago, it's going to take much longer than that to break the habit.

One little piece of chocolate leads to . . . what?

Exactly. Another piece of chocolate.

Who knows where it will end. The risk is that it ends in a stomachache and regret.

Reward yourself, by all means, but not with something that goes against your original goal. Buy yourself a sharp new shirt, or go for a day at the spa. Avoid rewarding yourself with something that caused your problem from the very beginning.

You need to stick to your new, healthy lifestyle—or whatever change you've made—until you've left Earth's gravity. And when you've reached your goal, then perhaps—and I repeat, perhaps—you can allow yourself a piece of chocolate. But you know what? The chances are that such a long time will have passed that you won't even want it. For real.

BUT HERE'S THE GOOD NEWS

Once you've gotten up to speed, it's going to be much simpler to keep your pace. Sticking to your plan will, after a while, feel like a quiet walk in a forest. You're going to wonder what you struggled with six months ago.

The same thing applies when you're saving money. If you've decided to set aside $100 every month until you have reached $5,000, then you can't stop at $2,000. That would be letting yourself down. You need to remind yourself why you need that $5,000. To start using some of the money to buy something meaningless would be stupid, really stupid. But it's very tempting.

Just like when you want to get into better physical shape, you need to hold on a little longer and make sure that you really do reach your goal of $5,000 in the bank. And you know what? Even though it might sound a bit sad: The more money you have in the bank, the more you'll want. When you have reached $5,000, you might very well want to aim for $10,000. This means you're going to be very careful about spending money when you're out shopping, and only buy things you actually need.

How do you reward yourself when it comes to saving money? Really, you shouldn't go shopping at all. But I can understand why you do. Perhaps you've written something down on your calendar for a year from now. If you've saved X amount, then you can go buy product Y. Or something like that. You need rewards, as I said. But remember—do the job first, then you get the reward.

If, before you've reached your goal, you fall for the sales trick—

"Save $50 if you buy this weekend"—then you're going to fall straight into the trap. Remember the simple math: If you pay $200 for something that really costs $250, you haven't saved $50. You've just consumed $200.

Stick to your tight budget until you've achieved momentum.

Once you've reached supersonic speed, it's easy to maintain that speed, but you need to accept that it might take some time to get there.

Don't let go too early.

Remember why you created your goal. Stick to the plan.

FORGET THE MIRACLE METHODS

Throughout this book, I've tried to impress upon you that you will have to have a degree of patience. You need to be content with the fact that there are no quick fixes. They don't exist.

There aren't any miracle methods. You can't get abs with the help of an electric thingamajig ten minutes every day in front of the TV. You can't count on becoming financially independent by investing in Bitcoins. Your relationship with your partner is not going to flourish after just one visit to a therapist.

It almost makes me feel sad every time I hear somebody exclaim, *If only it were simpler!*

Of course, I've also sighed in a similar way, but long ago I accepted the fact that the world doesn't work like that. In some cases, it's a hard and unjust society we live in. But when I sober up from my own self-pity, I realize that despite extremely difficult circumstances, an enormous number of people do succeed in what they take on. Why shouldn't I?

We're so impatient, so demanding, and we want such quick results that it's hard to achieve anything at all.

Bad habits are easy to build, but they can be very hard to live with.

Good habits take time and are hard to build, yes, that's true. But they're extremely easy to live with. So give them the time they need.

So stick to it. Once you're up to speed, you don't need to do much to maintain your pace. You're going to smile at your former self and wonder what you complained about.

Keep at it until you have some momentum. Then you're home free.

THE STRANGE AND UNTRUE IDEA OF LINEAR SUCCESS

Look at the figure on this page. It shows examples of things to focus on when you want to achieve success. It doesn't matter in what area. You do these things, work hard, and so on. Then you achieve success. You're at the top of your career, you have acquired honor and fame, you have money in the bank, or you have a body worthy of an Olympic athlete.

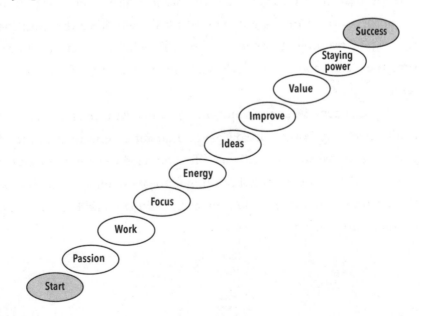

Great. Well done.

But what next?

The question about momentum still applies. Your effort and energy mean that you'll arrive where you want to be. But . . . what happens if you stop doing the right things? If you stop keeping track of your time, of your waistline, of what you put into your mouth, of how you talk to your partner? If you start getting up later in the morning and don't keep arriving early at work, the way you did when you were building your success? If you suddenly start wasting your new money instead of saving for retirement? What happens if you simply revert to your former, less-focused self? If you start to drift away . . . toward Laterville?

There are lots of examples of people who made their way to the top. But for one reason or another, they stopped focusing on growth or development. And soon they found they were no longer at the top. When you stop doing the things that took you there, then—first slowly, but soon much faster—you tend to return to a place that is often worse than where you started.

Imagine an athlete, a sprinter, who has just been declared the fastest in the world. How long do you think she will keep that position if she stops training? Her competitors will be licking their lips every time they read about the world champion's late nights out on the town.

You can't achieve success and then just expect it to stay there. As if it's something you own. You have to do something to retain it. If you want to live an extraordinary life, you need to do extraordinary things. And you are, regrettably, obliged to go on doing those things. Once you've gotten where you want to be—don't relax. Keep pushing forward with your new lifestyle.

WHAT SUCCESS *REALLY* LOOKS LIKE

Now look at this image. This is what success really looks like—when achieved in a nonlinear way. It's an ongoing cycle, not a straight line. Success demands that you keep your eye on the ball all the time.

If you want to achieve success, you must demand it of yourself through hard work and sharp focus—every day, for the rest of your life. In the world we live in, stopping is the same as starting to roll backward.

But the world doesn't care. It's up to you to decide what you want to do about this.

The world won't demand that you keep yourself in good shape and eat healthily so that you don't have a heart attack. You do, however, need to demand that of yourself if you want to live to be a hundred.

The world won't demand that you read books or develop yourself in some other way to increase your knowledge and make yourself more employable; you need to do that yourself if you want to build a career.

The world won't demand that you build up an immense emergency fund for your family, but if you want to do that, then you have to demand it of yourself. Otherwise you'll continue to go on living with just three months of rent in the bank.

You can choose to define success for yourself. That's what is so great about it. You, and only you, decide what is important for you. But you should be aware of the fact that success is something you are renting rather than something you own.

And that is one of the reasons why it's sometimes rather lonely at the top. Only a few people manage to get there—and stay there.

WRITING YOUR WAY TO MOMENTUM

Imagine an author like John Grisham. His first book was published more than thirty years ago. It took him five years to write while he was working as a lawyer in a little, unimportant firm in the South. Hardly anybody bought the book. Even fewer read it. Five thousand copies were sold, and he bought half of those himself and pressed them on people he knew. Do you know what that book is called? You would have to be a true Grisham fan to answer. The book is called *A Time to Kill*.

But while he knew how badly his first book was doing, he wrote *The Firm* as a gamble. That sold immediately, was made into a film starring Tom Cruise, and, in a flash, everyone knew who John Grisham was. His success was a fact. He wrote a book a year for ten years, and I think virtually every one ended up as a major movie. He must have earned buckets of money. He could leave his ordinary job and do what he wanted. John Grisham could have retired at the age of forty-five.

But he kept on publishing books. There's a new one almost every year, and has been for more than thirty years. Now, John Grisham certainly likes writing, but far fewer people would remember him if he'd stopped after ten books.

Besides, I happen to know (as an author, I'm curious about how the top writers do their work) that he has *not changed the writing process that took him to the top.* He still has other people do all the research so that the facts are correct. He still lets certain specific people read the first version. And he still pays attention to their feedback and makes changes as a result. And his books continue to sell. The reviews are fantastic. You don't need to love books by Grisham, you don't even need to like thrillers—but it's hard to ignore the fact that he's still doing it right, even though he, objectively, doesn't need to. Now he does it without any great effort. Because he's achieved momentum.

THE KEY INSIGHT

This is one of the most important lessons I myself have learned. You can't stop once you've started. Starting a journey toward the goal of your dreams—be it to see all the countries of the world before you die, or to be financially independent, or to have your own business and be able to work with your family, or to win an Olympic medal—is an active choice to live a different sort of life.

My task is not to judge somebody for how they've chosen to live their life. But for those of us who choose the path to success, it is an ongoing cycle.

I feel that I'm fairly successful, even though I, of course, can't compare with John Grisham. But I've been published in forty languages, and readers seem to like my books: they get in touch with me and tell me their stories. I lecture in many different places and meet fantastic people all year-round.

But the day I start being careless about my commitment, the day I can't be bothered to read other authors' books anymore, the day I convince myself that I already know everything, the day I stop pushing myself in my lectures and no longer test new things regardless of what my critics might say . . . that's the day I stop growing. And then it will all be downhill.

Like when you throw a ball up into the air. If you watch as it reaches its highest point, for a moment you might think it's hovering there. But it isn't. It turns in the air and then gravity pulls it down to earth again. Faster and faster.

YOU CAN'T CHANGE SOMEBODY ELSE, BUT YOU CAN CHANGE YOURSELF

When you think about that, it's fantastic news, isn't it? To have power over yourself and your own future. Now you just need to remind yourself that you have this power.

You can always decide what is most important for you and start there. You know how to break patterns, end old bad habits, start a new routine, begin new and better habits. A bright future awaits you.

And so my advice, once again: Start with something small that you'll succeed at. Gain a little self-confidence. Then try something bigger.

Make sure you keep working in the same direction until you've achieved momentum.

And then never let up.

POSTSCRIPT

In New York in 1934, the unemployed alcoholic William Griffith Wilson was admitted into a hospital to detox. In the hospital he had a spiritual awakening and started to convert other alcoholics. He worked hard but didn't succeed in converting many. When he complained to his wife that he didn't think that his method worked— nobody is sober!—she answered, "Oh, yes, *you* are sober."

Perhaps you've heard that story before. But it illustrates something I want you to take with you: By helping others to move ahead, you will also make yourself stronger. By trying to make others successful, showing them what you did, encouraging them, supporting them, saying that you believe in them, you yourself will benefit more than they do. There's no better way of building up yourself than by building up others. And besides, it feels good when you do something for others. So my request is this: if there is something in this book that works for you, tell others about it. Spread the word; show them what you did. By all means, give a copy of the book to everyone you meet. I've nothing against that, of course. But most of all, explain to those around you what you found useful.

So go back to the beginning of the book and read it again. This time have a pen and a sheet of paper next to you.

And one last thing. Let me know how it went. Because I collect success stories.

Further Reading

Brown, Brené. *Rising Strong*. Random House, 2015.

Burnett, Dean. *Idiot Brain: What Your Head Is Really Up To*. W. W. Norton, 2017.

Canfield, Jack. *Mastering the Art of Success*. Celebrity Press, 2017.

Carnegie, Dale. *How to Win Friends and Influence People*. Vermilion, 2009.

Cialdini, Robert B. *Yes! 50 Scientifically Proven Ways to Be Persuasive*. Free Press, 2008.

Covey, Stephen. *The 7 Habits of Highly Effective People*. Simon & Schuster, 1989.

———. *The 8th Habit: From Effectiveness to Greatness*. Simon & Schuster, 2006.

DeLuca, Fred. *Start Small, Finish Big: Fifteen Key Lessons to Start—and Run—Your Own Successful Business*. Mandevilla Press, 2012.

Duckworth, Angela. *Grit: The Power of Passion and Perseverance*. Scribner, 2016.

Duhigg, Charles. *The Power of Habit: Why We Do What We Do and How to Change*. Random House, 2014.

————. *Smarter, Faster, Better: The Secrets of Being Productive.* Random House, 2017.

Fabritius, Friederike, and Hans W. Hagemann. *The Leading Brain: Powerful Science-Based Strategies for Achieving Peak Performance.* TarcherPerigee, 2017.

Hill, Napoleon. *Success Habits.* Macmillan, 2019.

Jeffers, Susan. *Feel the Fear and Do It Anyway.* Ebury, 2017.

Jiang, Jia. *Rejection Proof: How I Beat Fear and Became Invincible Through 100 Days of Rejection.* Harmony Books, 2015.

Kenner, Soren, and Imran Rashid. *Offline: Free Your Mind from Smartphone and Social Media Stress.* Capstone, 2019.

Kishima, Ichiro, and Fumitake Koga. *The Courage to Be Disliked: How to Free Yourself, Change Your Life and Achieve Real Happiness.* Allen & Unwin, 2019.

Levinson, Steve, and Chris Cooper. *The Power to Get Things Done (Whether You Feel Like It or Not).* TarcherPerigee, 2015.

Levitin, Daniel. *The Organized Mind: Thinking Straight in the Age of Information Overload.* Penguin Books, 2015.

Levy, Ariel. *The Rules Do Not Apply.* Little, Brown, 2018.

Robbins, Anthony. *Awaken the Giant Within: How to Take Immediate Control of Your Mental, Emotional, Physical and Financial Destiny!* Free Press, 2003.

Robinson, Ken, and Lou Aronica. *Finding Your Element: How to Discover Your Talents and Passions and Transform Your Life.* Penguin Books, 2014.

Schwartz, David J. *The Magic of Thinking Big.* Touchstone, 2015.

White, Jennifer. *Work Less, Make More: Stop Working So Hard and Create the Life You Really Want!* John Wiley & Sons, 1999.

Index

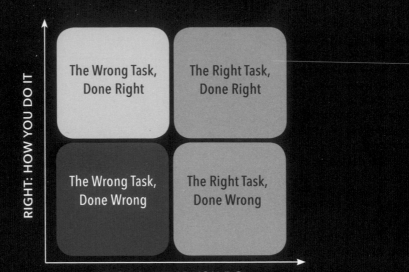

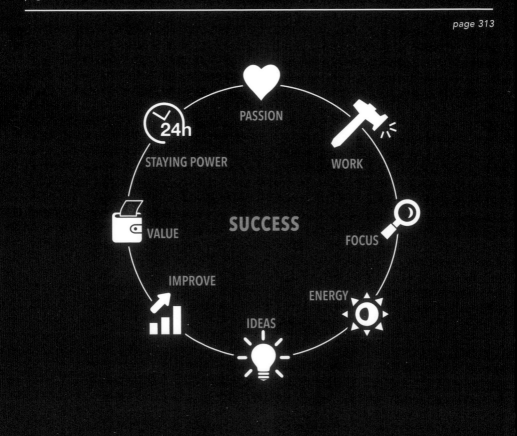